MW00467227

SHADOWS
&
VINES

C.D. Britt

C.D. BRITT

www.authorcdbritt.com

Cover Artwork and Map by GermanCreative
Editing by Rain Brennan

ISBN (ebook): **978-1-7372652-0-7**
ISBN (paperback): **978-1-7372652-1-4**

TO MY FAMILY FOR HELPING ME FIND MY VOICE.
IT'S BEEN A HELL OF RIDE AND IT ISN'T EVEN CLOSE TO
OVER.

Contents

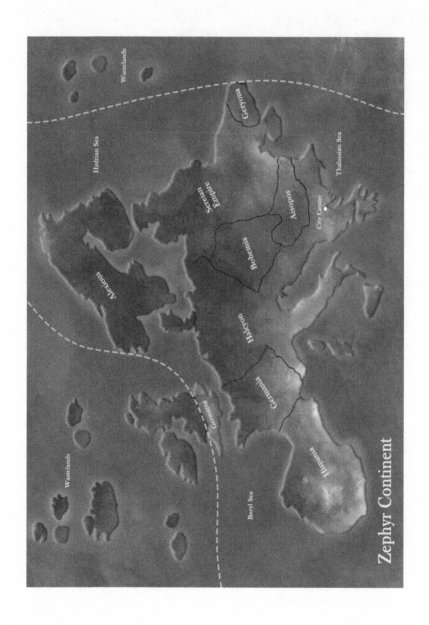

Zephyr Continent

PROLOGUE

840 A.D., SOMEWHERE IN SCANDINAVIA

Persephone watched from atop the hill that overlooked the battleground. The mortal warrior, his leather armor creaking as he walked, had yet to notice her. Blood, not all of it his own, mixed with sweat, tears, and war paint across his face and down the long braids that tangled at his temples. He checked for survivors among the dead, hoping to see that some of his men had lived. If he could not bring them home alive, he would fulfill his promise to honor their bodies with a proper burial.

Persephone knew this soul. This soul, throughout his lives, had always chosen war. Something that conflicted with his true nature, the one Persephone saw when she guided his soul to the afterlife.

She rarely guided the dead to her realm, preferring to take care of them once they arrived, but this soul only ever called to her and not Thanatos, her Reaper.

And she answered, escorting him herself to Elysium.

There was very little Persephone did not understand about death, but the warrior soul's ability to summon her to the deaths of his men and his own was one of them.

When the life the soul had lived was assessed, it proved to be deeply caring and affectionate, regardless of its mortal coil. It never mattered what body he was born into; his spirit was always that of a warrior. He was always standing between the innocent and certain doom. He did not bring his army to war for power or land, but for justice and freedom.

His face was solemn as he prayed to the old Gods, ones she knew were not real, for his fallen brethren. At that moment, he allowed his emotions free. Losing his comrades was a hell he would live in for the rest of his mortal days.

The Viking finally looked up at Persephone, somehow sensing her presence as he always did when she came to take his soldiers to their final resting place, and Persephone delighted in the eye contact that no mortal should be able to make.

He placed his fist over his heart and lowered his head. She wondered as she watched him if he held a latent power, but she saw no unbound abilities when his soul crossed her gates. Just the lovely soul she felt more and more affection for over the millennia.

Though the man bowing his head before her did not know her, his mortal mind thinking her a Valkyrie, his soul always remembered her. As if she were home to him as he was home to her.

After returning his gesture, Persephone called his slain brothers to her. The perished warriors heeded her call to avoid trapping themselves in the mortal plane as a soul without a vessel. They used her as a gateway to the Underworld, a world attached to this one that only the dead could find—a veil between this world and hers where she cherished and guarded her souls.

Before they passed through her ethereal form, each soul stopped and placed a fist over their heart as they nodded to their general in respect. And although her warrior watched on, he only ever saw her, not his men, and she always wondered why.

She felt the souls as they passed through her and was overwhelmed by the love they felt for him. When so many other leaders received anger and betrayal from the souls of the soldiers lost to their mortal world, their deaths a fault on the part of their leader, this one did not. This warrior's men died knowing that their leader fought beside them and for them, and they loved him as they did their own kin.

Persephone was fascinated, awed by such respect.

After the last soul passed through her, Persephone looked at the warrior again, knowing she would not look upon his face until it was his time. Until the countless wars finally punished his psyche too much for him to continue the fight.

The mortal man that the soul currently inhabited smiled at her, always a handsome smile, then turned from her and began the funeral rites to ensure the mortal bodies were given their proper respect.

"Until I see you again…" Persephone whispered to him, the wind carrying her voice. "My warrior."

CHAPTER 1

2164 A.D., CITY OF HALCYON

Persephone sat anxiously in the back of the car as she stared out the window at what remained of the human world. The Moirai, the three deities older than time itself, had summoned her to their headquarters at the Fates Consulting Group.

She was hesitant to heed the summons, knowing that what was waiting for her was nothing she would care to hear. She was already well behind schedule for the day, and her Chief Financial Officer at Cerberus Financial was breathing down her neck. But she knew that to ignore the call of the Moirai would just invite even more inconvenience in the future.

Lost in her thoughts, she watched the city of Halcyon move past her through the car window. Halcyon was one of the few urban centers to survive humanity's Great War, the cataclysmic conflict that had brought an end to the human era nearly a hundred years ago.

Beyond its advantageous position between a mountain and the Thalassian sea, Halcyon had benefited from inhabiting the old lands of Mount Olympus. The city was now considered the world's capital, though the world was a much smaller place. Zephyr, the remaining land of what was once been called Europe, was the only continent with life thriving upon it.

The large, curving building that was Fate's Consulting Group came into view through the car window. The spiral metal building reaching up so high in the sky, it looked as if it could touch the heavens above. In it was the Moirai, who never left their private little retreat, high above the middle of the bustling city of Halcyon.

Although Persephone didn't like to leave her realm much, much less if it was to visit the Moirai, she did enjoy Halcyon and its magnificent beauty. Perhaps its proximity to Olympus gave her a sense of nostalgia, even though it had been many centuries since she and her sisters ruled from Greece. The names changed, titles were forgotten, lives were lost, but the land held the memories of millennia.

And it was all as well since humanity never seemed to capture the truth of the Gods in their beliefs. The Gods, who were not quite what the humans thought they were.

Persephone and her sisters had lived among the humans at various points throughout history, fighting alongside major armies or dancing with lords at fancy balls. Overall, they allowed the humans to govern themselves and, for a time, had chosen to let the humans live as they willed.

It did not take long for them to see what came of the humans without the interference of the Goddesses; the greed and blood lust. Humanity found themselves lost to their baser urges of conquering and killing. They brought the world to a standstill with their Great War, using horrible weapons until there was barely any humanity left. Only barren wasteland now surrounded Zephyr, some of the landmasses lost to the seas.

They now lived alongside the ruins of what once was and a reminder of what could have been.

Enough was enough.

After the Great War left civilization in shambles, Persephone and her sisters determined that a new level of godly intervention was needed. Since the sister Goddesses held no true universal power to hold the humans accountable, as that was up to Chaos, they decided to direct their rule as the humans had, through institutions that gave structure to the post-war world.

The three sisters stepped into roles that controlled the human's accessibility to such disastrous methods of harming their fellow man.

One of Persephone's sisters, Hera, became the Archon, the ruler of Zephyr. She oversaw the Senate, the central governing body comprised of representatives from across the continent.

Amphitrite, her other sister, held power over trade routes as the

11

leading government official in charge of the Zephyr Maritime Administration.

Persephone led Cerberus Financial, the umbrella organization of all financial institutions in the post-war world. She held power over the economy, and any weapons of war could not be bought without her knowledge.

The sisters used Halcyon as their central location in the human world and were able to maintain relative peace in the great city. The Goddesses could only do so much to rule the human realm without an all-out dictatorship, but they held enough power over government, transport, and the financial system to keep humans in line.

It wasn't the world peace the human's ancestors had dreamed of, but it had gone from a forest fire — both literally and metaphorically — to small manageable fires here and there.

Persephone was unsure of how much the human populace knew of the Goddesses. Sure, their identities were still unknown among man, especially Persephone's. She was the sister who did not spend much time among mortals outside of work.

She was to guard the dead, and that was something she did well.

Closing her eyes to the world outside her window, she wondered what the Moirai had in store for her. She was not summoned to their domain as often as her sisters were, and so she couldn't formulate a good guess as to their antics. Hera, with all the time she spent in Halcyon, would have probably known the Moirai's intention before they had called for her.

The town car turned onto the main road that ran through the city and they finally neared the large spiral building. They had made better time to the central tower than she had expected, and so she didn't have much opportunity to stop and mentally prepare herself as best she could to handle walking into a situation blind.

Her sisters happily reminded her almost every time they crossed paths that Persephone was a bit of a control freak, and this impromptu meeting was pushing her controlling tendencies to the edge.

She worked to remain a paragon of calm to keep as much to her mortal form as possible. However, she found it easy to slip into her Goddess form when she was stressed or around smaller deities who triggered her magic's dominant instincts.

Still, she did not want the humans to see her other form. She could only imagine their fear when she had black eyes, blue flames, and shadows swirling around her, not to mention the horns and black claws.

Those *really* did not help with public relations.

Persephone opened her eyes as the car came to a stop in front of Fates Consulting. The sun glinting off its metallic surface was almost blindingly bright. Hearing her driver cut the engine, she took another moment to prepare herself. She had enough experience and had heard plenty of stories from her very dramatic sister to know walking in and out without some fanfare was not possible.

Her driver, Charon, opened her door a couple of minutes later, probably sensing that she needed a moment. Charon had served faithfully by her side since she took up her mantle as Goddess of the Underworld. Deceptively frail and dressed in the finest driver's suit, Charon bowed slightly as Persephone stepped out onto the sidewalk.

"Charon," she growled in warning once she exited the car, straightening her black pantsuit and rolling her shoulders back. It aggravated her to no end when her people did this, the bowing, and they damn well knew it. Only Charon and Thanatos had the audacity to tease her this way.

"Forgive me. I am old and forget easily," he said, smiling coyly. Persephone tilted her head to look at him and arched a brow.

"I allow you and Thanatos far too much leniency. I need to start demanding more respect. Perhaps a century in the Torture Fields will suffice? Thanatos could use a good disemboweling."

Charon let out a loud, rusty laugh. "You'd give him too much joy to know he got to you. He'd consider it foreplay, the cheeky bastard," he stated with a wink.

Rolling her eyes, she conceded that the man she had trusted to bring her souls and coffee would indeed still be an ass in any form. Maybe she could let Cerberus, her loyal hound the financial institution was named after, romp around in Thanatos' room later. Persephone knew that was the only true way she could infuriate the man.

As she walked into the Fate's Consulting firm, she felt all she had planned for the day go straight out the window. She knew that whatever the Moirai had in store for her was going to make her life so much more difficult than she needed it to be right now.

Hopefully, it wouldn't take more than a day to handle, but she prepared for the worst.

***

Persephone had found the Moirai to be consistent in one thing and one thing only—their dramatic natures. The room where they worked the strings of fate changed with their moods.

Today, her seat in front of the Moirai was a crushed black velvet armchair that shimmered with an impression of Persephone's shadowy magic. Hera had warned her of this. They were reminding her of her position and status as the Goddess of the Underworld by placing such a chair for her to sit in.

She allowed herself an internal groan as she lowered herself into the seat.

Wearing white robes, the Moirai were in their three-sister form that some had once called the Fates. One sister appeared old, one middle-aged, and one young, but their minds were ancient and blended among each other. When they moved together to form one being, the Moirai, their faces shifted between the ages, a very off-putting sight to behold. This had driven many mortals mad in the ancient years when they had dared to look upon them.

"Percy!" Clothos called out, her head tilted like a playful puppy. "You heeded our summons!"

Clothos was the most outgoing of the sisters, the most likely to be friendly to the Goddesses.

Persephone remained sitting stiffly in the chair, but she bristled at the childish name Clothos had used for her. Persephone's face was cold and stoic, the most natural expression, or non-expression, for her.

"I wasn't aware I could deny," Persephone stated blandly.

A broad smile crossed Clothos' face and Persephone was sure it belied the trouble she was about to release onto her.

The Moirai toyed with the Goddesses as they did all things, and that smile was just another twist of the string. Although Persephone thought being sequestered to the top of the tower was enough hardship for the Moirai, she couldn't stop herself from wanting to dole out some torment

14

of her own from time to time. Her sisters surely did, and she assumed it was usually in frenzies of emotion.

Persephone, however, never fell to her emotions. They did nothing to move her forward or help her do her job.

"I spun the most beautiful string so very long ago…" Clothos stated fondly, her voice now soft, the childish quality almost a whisper, as if she were sharing a secret. "Then it turned black. No light escaped my beautiful string. The weave absorbed the darkness. So incredibly sad…"

Waiting patiently with her hands folded in her lap, Persephone kept her face completely indifferent.

They could go on like this for a while.

Patience, she thought and reminded herself that sometimes they were lucid enough to give her more than tiny fragments of their visions. *Sometimes.*

"Lachesis measured it five times before we summoned you. It was so exceptionally long, but now my beautiful string must be cut!" Clothos cried, a single tear falling down her cheek.

Persephone refrained from letting out a long, irritated sigh. She did, however, roll her eyes mentally. Clothos weeping was just a normal day at the Fates. Knowing she needed to say something before the full dramatics began, she took a breath. "Clothos, your string is a mortal's life, and life must be cut for the mortals to remain *mortal*. Why am I…?"

She hadn't finished before Atropos took her scissors, ones that seemed to be made from pure starlight, and cut the string.

A blinding light flashed for a moment, turning the entire room white as Persephone felt the tug on her soul. A tug harder than she had ever felt.

She immediately shot up from the chair and swayed. Her body felt all the signs of a shadow portal opening and pulling at her. Panic filled her at this new sensation, as she had always controlled her shadows and the portals they held. Her eyes widened and moved to the Moirai, who stood next to the cut string. The string itself had begun to fade away as the sisters turned as one to look at Persephone. With their heads tilted in thought, they watched as Persephone's shadows swirled around her, preparing to claim her.

"Life and death must balance!" Clothos yelled out in a sing-song voice as she did a giddy dance.

15

Persephone reached her hand out to hold on to the chair just as everything turned black around her.

CHAPTER 2

Persephone had never in her existence been forced against her will through a portal before, much less one crafted from her own power. It was extremely disorienting. Violating. Her nerves were raw, and her bones felt like they were coming out of her skin.

She watched the darkness bleed away into the dim, yellow light of the run-down hallway as the shadows dissipated around her.

Persephone's wicked temper lowered the temperature as she took in her new surroundings. She was in what appeared to be a dilapidated motel hall.

Completely empty.

The wallpaper crumbled, exposing drywall, which in some places was water stained. The smell of mold and decay would have been overwhelming to a mortal's sense, and she wondered if anyone actually paid to stay in a hellhole like this without some sort of nefarious purpose.

Before she could curb it, she let out a low, angry, predatory growl. In that moment, she felt mildly homicidal.

Fortunately, there weren't any humans in the hall to hear the growl.

Unfortunately, the Moirai weren't here either. She could really do with taking out some unholy anger on the presumptuous beings.

Taking a deep breath, Persephone moved to push her hair out of her face but stopped when she noticed something causing resistance in her hand.

The string that had been cut.

She was holding Clothos' string in her right hand, her grip tight like it was a lifeline. It was pulled taut, as if attached to something nearby.

Walking in the direction the string led her to, Persephone turned a corner and saw where it disappeared through a door.

Since the string was not of this world, it did not have to heed the barriers of the mortal realm.

Only she, as an otherworldly being herself, could see the string or even hold it in her hand.

As she neared the room, Thanatos suddenly stepped out through the wooden door and into the hall. In his spectral form, his Reaper's body flickered with power.

"The soul is not calling to me, but I sensed your presence," he said without greeting.

"It's good you're here," she told him. Her tone darkened when she added, "The Moirai sent me here. And let's just say it lacked finesse."

Thanatos shook his head and muttered something about ancient, meddlesome biddies. Although he was in his unearthly form, Thanatos was not in his full Reaper regalia. No dusty robes to be found. Instead, he wore jeans and a t-shirt with a cartoon reaper holding up his skeletal middle fingers.

He and Hecate seemed to shop together for annoying shirts that half the time made no sense to Persephone. She was not typically concerned with the cultural fashions of the current era, and sadly, the fabric monstrosities had been darkening her door for a year now.

"Dress for the job you want, I suppose," she mumbled, and Thanatos looked down at his t-shirt as if he had forgotten what he wore.

"Levity in the Underworld is the only role Hecate and I take seriously," he stated, bowing like a gallant knight of old. He'd never been a knight, even when the metal-armored men had lived and rattled across the mortal realm.

Persephone closed her eyes, sighing and pinching the bridge of her nose.

"Robes," she growled. She opened her eyes just as his robes settled over his shoulders, as if sentient themselves.

His true form was what mortals always referred to as the Grim Reaper, a skeletal and foreboding wraith, but humans in the past had been confused on who Thanatos exactly was. Yes, he was the Reaper, but he was also known as Hermes when in his mortal form. Both

Hermes and Thanatos had been worshiped as Psychopomps, but humans had over time separated the trickster God from death incarnate.

Truly, Thanatos was a mixture. He embodied the lightness that could be found in death, as well as its cruel unpredictability.

Even now, his human form flickered across his Reaper form, as if the familiar icy blue eyes and olive skin were transposed onto the bones of the Reaper. His black wings tucked firmly against his back, but she noticed a shake of irritation in the feathers.

At least she wasn't the only one perturbed by the Moirai's antics. That raised her spirits a little bit.

Thanatos caught sight of the string Persephone held and frowned.

"They bound you to this mortal." His voice was not the smooth bass she was used to, but something gravelly and as ancient as he was. As much as Thanatos joked with her, he was quick to find his serious persona when the situation called for it.

Especially if it could cause an issue for his friends, Hecate and Persephone, or his realm, the Underworld.

"Apparently so. Why, I do not know. Clothos made a nice string," she stated the last few words in a mocking tone as she held up the almost transparent string. "Which means I get to play tour guide to the Underworld today."

Thanatos simply made a *hmm* noise from his throat.

"He is full of death," he muttered absently, speaking as much to the surrounding hallway as he was to her.

"Most dead people are," she deadpanned, her eyebrow arching at her friend's skeletal form.

He snorted at her comment, which sounded like wind through a tunnel without his physical nose.

"His soul is stained with the blood of others. He is one who has kept me very busy."

Now Persephone found herself intrigued. If Thanatos felt that, then this soul had spent a lifetime killing. She thought maybe that was why the Moirai had sent her. She could always use another reaper in case of a catastrophic event. It would help move the souls through quicker, leading to fewer lost souls haunting the riverbanks. Even one lost soul was too much for Persephone.

She started towards the door, but Thanatos stopped her.

19

"It's messy, Persephone," he stated, the concern deepening in his voice. "The mortal has several gunshot wounds, but I read intentions along his soul line."

Persephone felt an itch at the back of her mind of other souls who had come to her realm after committing such an act. People who died of suicide usually passed into her realm not knowing someone loved them. Once they met the judges and felt the pain of the loved ones left behind, they begged to go back. Persephone could not restore their lifeline, which tore at her even if no one ever knew it. Sometimes a soul was so close to the living realm and could be sent back for a second chance.

Something that never happened as much as she preferred.

She wished there were ways she could intervene, but even the Goddess of the Underworld was limited to the rules of the universe. She couldn't heal the souls while they lived, but she was their caretaker in death. Their guardian.

Death could not create life, no matter how much she wished she could.

The mortal in the room before her had intended to end their life. Perhaps they were murdered before they had the chance to complete the act, but it did not matter. His intentions to end his own life would color his judgment in the Underworld.

The most worrisome part of all this was that she had a strong suspicion she knew who was behind that door.

Pushing past her nerves, she pulled the door open with her free hand and stepped into a room that smelled strongly of blood.

She continued inside to see the body laid across an old plaid couch. *Him.*

It was obvious someone had been working desperately to save him. Discarded bloody cloths and gauze were scattered around the room. Some still rested on his bloody torso, where his shirt had been torn open. He didn't receive his killing blow here, she knew, but this was where he was brought by someone to administer first aid. On a rickety wooden coffee table, a handbook laid open to a page on wound care. A military pack lay forgotten in the corner, contents strewn across the floor. Then she caught sight of the gun lying next to the pack.

A weapon he would have used to take his life had someone else not done it for him, she surmised.

Looking around the almost pitch-black room, Persephone had no issue seeing the soul pacing on the other side of it. Souls had an internal light. Their life energy hung around them even after they passed the gates. They faded away with time if they were not escorted to the other realm. The stress and agitation she often saw with the newly dead surrounded the soul as well.

Turning to Thanatos, Persephone tried to ignore the soul in the shadows. To gather herself before she went to him and looked into his eyes once again after so many years. She felt the soul deep pain emanating from him.

"Please tell Charon I am bringing this soul to him myself," Persephone whispered to Thanatos.

As she steeled herself to face the soul, she felt Thanatos' power leave the mortal realm. She was alone now with the one who had called to her for so very long.

"Stop," she ordered. Her Goddess voice sent the word as a deep echo, her power rippling across the space between them to disrupt his frantic pacing. The soul looked up, and she found herself struck mute by the nothingness she saw.

There was no missed future within his eyes. All his previous mortal shells had held missed opportunities and futures.

This was a new and troubling development.

Persephone took in the rest of him as he ran his transparent hands through his dark blonde hair. A scar ran through his left eyebrow and extended to his temple. His nose looked to have been broken once or twice, but it hardly detracted from his handsome face, slightly oval but with a defined jaw. He had a bit of cleft chin, which made his face even more attractive.

She could see through his torn shirt scars that crossed over his abdomen, like roads running between and around his bullet wounds. Wounds still dripping with blood. He must've held on for a while after obtaining his mortal blow since the body had not been dead as long as Persephone had assumed. No one who was working to help revive him was in the room, but she heard a soft whimper from somewhere down the hall.

He was silent as she walked towards him. Reaching out her hand, she used her Goddess voice again to tell him to halt. His body finally stopped, but without his control. He stared at her hand, which she kept human as not to scare him with her claws. She needed him to look at her again, look her in the eyes one more time, but instead he stared at the glimmering string between them.

Looking at her right hand, the one she held out to him, it seemed as if he was trying to piece together an impossible puzzle. Their eyes finally met again, and she caught the most beautiful, piercing green eyes she had ever seen on a human. They appeared almost back lit. Were they this green just a moment ago? She could have sworn they were brown, or maybe hazel?

Persephone blinked. Establishing a psychic connection with a soul did not involve being distracted by a striking pair of eyes. She focused again, reaching into the deepest part of his soul until she was immersed in his feelings and memories of his mortal life.

She trembled at the energy that pulsated from him as she unraveled the soul's immortality. Their connection flared and she got what she needed. Not his future, but his past. His life until now played out before her in brief glimpses, nothing to tell her the full nature of him, but she already knew this soul was him.

Her mortal warrior.

Persephone watched the moments that made up the genuine goodness of a person. Mortals always underestimated these moments that caused a ripple effect much larger than they could ever know. Still, she noted, no future. As if he was never meant to have one.

Then it hit her all at once and took her breath away. This was the soul's end. No reincarnation.

He had no more lives left, and her heart broke at that revelation.

There would be no more poignant meetings on battlefields, no more powerful stares across the axis of death. The one mortal who ever saw her, called only for her, would be gone.

Persephone pulled herself together. She could mourn for her strange companion, who had kept her company throughout time, later in the privacy of her own room. There was no room for sadness in reaping.

Every moment of his most recent life ran through her. She felt every ounce of pain and joy. How he hunted and killed as a mercenary, the guilt catching up to him when he came back home. The things he saw

22

when watching a potential target. Rape. Murder. Abuse. Things that made his soul sick and pushed him to nearly drink himself to death.

She felt the intense loathing and disdain he harbored for the world around him. Worse was the burning hatred he aimed at himself.

Now that he accepted his death, she felt his solace that the world was free of one less monster, and his regret that he hadn't taken more with him.

Persephone felt the fear when he realized his death would not mean he could slip peacefully into the ether. The knowledge that there would be no peace for him. She wanted to scream and tear the world apart. This world that had been too cruel to him, the man who had stood before her for centuries.

Immersed in his soul, she felt its call stronger than ever. The call so compellingly warm with a deep sense of familiarity.

Now that she could explore the contours of his soul, Persephone recognized a bright core of power within him. It was free, she realized, with the death of its mortal shell. She wondered if this was how he was able to see her as a mortal throughout his lives. How he was able to call the Goddess of the Underworld as no mortal had before.

"Devon Aideonous, I am here to offer you immortal life."

The words sprung from her mouth without thought and she realized the tickling trace of the Moirai's magic had taken hold of her voice. Was this why the Moirai had sent her through the portal? A mortal turned immortal? The Moirai had known about this soul's latent power and had laid this out well before his death. Persephone was just another one of their puppets, strung to do their bidding.

Oh, the irony, she thought, tightening her hand around the lifeline.

"A life where your power means never raising a weapon again. To make right when so much in the world is wrong. I am giving you a chance to correct the many injustices you have witnessed." She made her hand into a fist before unfurling her fingers to reveal six small, red pomegranate seeds. "Eat these seeds and leave this place between worlds. You need not fear life nor death."

It was a relief to Persephone in that moment to realize that he would not be leaving earth and returning to Chaos. No, he would be bound to the Underworld by the will of the Moirai working through her.

As the man before her—Devon—stared at the seeds in her palm, his soul's glow started to lose its color. He was being pulled to the Underworld without a coin or Reaper. She did not want him lost to Styx, wandering the shore of the river for a hundred years. She gave a push of mental persuasion. Just a small one, and even then, she wondered if that was something she should do.

He took a huge breath and gazed back at his body, what was left of him, before looking down at the floor. Finally, after the string was almost completely lost to the ether itself, he stepped forward nearly toe to toe with her. Not an ounce of fear showed in his beautiful green eyes.

Confusion and anger, but not fear.

Persephone was unsettled by the directness of his gaze. Her eye contact with mortal souls was reserved for exercises of her power. The dead rarely met their queen's stare of their own volition.

Keeping his eyes firmly on hers, he took the seeds, placed them in his mouth, and bit down.

In the next moment, his soul was gone. The room was silent aside from the first-aid book's pages fluttering lightly in the sudden vacuum.

Persephone released her breath, knowing she had bound the soul to her in the Underworld.

Not as a man, but as something more.

CHAPTER 3

A groan slipped through Devon's lips as he woke up, unaware of even having fallen asleep. Blinking, he realized he was not in his bed or even the motel room he had previously used as a base of operations.

Confused and his mind hazy on the previous day's details, he attempted to push himself up into a sitting position, only to find his arms as weak as a newborn colt. He fell back against a wooden bench seat, barely moving his head in time so he did not slam his temple against it.

Wood? His mind scattered, unable to hold a train of thought for any decent length of time. A strong sulfuric smell burned his nostrils as he tried to steady his breathing.

Focusing his eyes, he found he was lying on wood, surrounded by darkness. The wind whistled in the unending shadow around him, blowing through what sounded like a cavern. He felt a chill, the temperature lower than he remembered it being before he had passed out. His body rocked gently as he heard water lapping at the wood beside him.

He was on a boat, he realized. He couldn't remember getting drunk last night, and he knew he never did that while on a job.

Sometimes, after particularly heinous jobs, he felt like he needed the alcohol to numb the pain. Though he could not remember doing the job at all, much less finishing it. A black hole sat in his memories and not one clue as to how he ended up passed out on a boat in a dark cave.

Another attempt to lift himself only caused a wave of dizziness to wash over him. His brain felt foggy, as if he hadn't slept in days. His vision doubled for a moment as he reset his equilibrium and struggled into a sitting position. His arms and legs felt like lead, but the longer he sat up, the more he felt some sort of strength wash over him.

An unfamiliar sensation ran over his entire body as if something as soft as feathers was moving along his skin. He shuddered at the light touch before a humming noise grew loud in his ears. A sudden pop sounded in his mind and he jolted forward, grabbing the wooden seat of the boat in a white-knuckle grip.

What the hell was that? he thought as his vision cleared and he scrambled back. Ahead of him, a cloaked man perched at the front of the boat, steering with a long pole dipped into the water. Devon glanced into the water—a river. He was not the greatest swimmer, having come from the old country where it was all farmland and small ponds, but he could make a decent go of it in a life-or-death situation.

Keeping the cloaked man in his peripheral vision, he craned his neck to determine the best exit from the boat. He caught sight of the riverbank. People ambled along the river, seeming to move without any real direction. The hair on Devon's arms stood on end. This was not right.

His mind tried once again to play over his previous day and how he might have gotten here, but he only saw glimpses—of a street, blood, and black eyes. Flashes of memories that he could not be sure were all his.

Definitely had one hell of a drinking binge, he thought to himself.

He rubbed his eyes a moment before looking back out. He knew he had been nowhere near a body of water this morning. In fact, he was sure the city his job was in was completely landlocked, with no rivers to speak of nearby.

Escape. He had to escape. To jump out of this boat before he got even farther from his base of operations.

Peering over the edge of the boat, he could see that the water was pure black, but looked relatively calm. Large white fish swam right underneath the surface. When he reached out to touch the water, a rough voice broke the quiet.

"I wouldn't do that if I were you," the cloaked man warned. "They have no coin, so they stay there. Your soul is allowed admittance, but if you end up in the river, I cannot help you. Those souls will pull you right in," the rusty voice murmured, just loud enough for Devon to hear him.

As if summoned, a skeletal hand breached the water and reached for Devon, barely making contact. He fell back against the bottom of the vessel as the boat tilted dangerously to the side before straightening out again.

The ferryman let out a harsh, ragged laugh as he moved them further along the river with that long pole that never seemed to leave the water. Slowly, hesitant if he really wanted to know, he looked back at the people milling about the shore. He realized the people seemed to have an almost eerie blue haze of light around them. There was no source for the light aside from the people themselves. They looked like... ghosts.

As he watched the shore, more of them appeared, seeming to materialize from the darkness in their blueish, eerie forms. More and more filled up the shoreline, moving with purpose now. They crowded the river's edge and kept pace with the boat. A few even mindlessly stepped into the river and immediately disappeared beneath the surface, caught in skeletal clutches. One, less mindless than the others, flailed as they tried to return to the shore to no avail.

Devon swallowed and tasted bile.

"They can sense your soul, so they want nothing more than to pull you down to wallow with them. Stay in the boat, and you will be fine. It takes a hundred years of wandering before they can cross the gate without coin, and you do not want to join them."

"Coin?" Devon asked, watching as another phantom stumbled into the river. Her gown looked ripped and torn, the style from hundreds of years before the Great War.

The ferryman plucked a coin from a bag tied around his waist. "A coin means your soul debt is paid and you can pass through the gates."

The ferryman's hand holding the coin looked almost as skeletal as the hands passing underneath the boat. Devon shivered, but the skeletal ferryman either did not notice his reaction or did not care.

"You've no need of coin since you took the seeds. No one has been offered the seeds before," the ferryman explained as he put the coin back into the bag.

Devon suddenly felt a deep sense of dread wash over him. This was not the result of a drinking binge. He was not dreaming at all.

"I'm dead," the statement rolled off Devon's tongue as he thought the words. His entire body stiff with shock and disbelief.

"Not truly, but the Goddess will fill you in on the details. I am simply to deliver you to the gates. Thanatos will meet you there and will take you to the Goddess' domicile. Should you get distracted and wander off, well, it's eternity down here, and the wrong place means you cannot regain what you've lost." The ferryman finished his cryptic message right as the river opened up into a giant cavern.

"Goddess?"

***

Persephone paced the length of her office. Thanatos and Hecate eyed her from where they sat by the fireplace, the wood banked with blue flame.

"A new immortal," Persephone muttered. "Made with my magic." It was enough of a violation to have her own shadow portal used against her, but the core of her godly magic materialized against her will. Persephone shuddered, thinking of the innocuous looking seeds. "Why would the Moirai foist a newly made immortal upon me?"

Hecate leaned her chin on her steepled fingers, her silver hair swaying around her cheeks. "An immortal has not been made in millennia." She pinned her gaze on Persephone. "This all stinks of fate."

"Meddling hags." Persephone grumbled.

Thanatos stood and moved to stop Persephone's pacing, grasping her shoulders in his sure grip.

"It can only be one thing," he said. "The man was surrounded by death, even in life." His Reaper form flickered for the briefest of moments. "He's a new Reaper."

Persephone shook her head. "It can't be." She thought of the words that rang out of her when she gave him the seeds, a script she hadn't written. Had it all pointed to an eternity of reaping?

"Yes, it can," Thanatos insisted. "The Moirai spin the future. The human world has been fragile since the Great War. Two reapers would

28

cement your realm's ability to handle any chaos in the coming decades."

Stepping out of Thanatos' hold, Persephone resumed pacing.

"That would be charitable," she said skeptically.

"Nothing else makes sense," Thanatos argued.

"In the days of old," Hecate interrupted, "only heroes or favored mortals were gifted immortality."

"He's certainly no hero," Thanatos scoffed. "Death clings to him almost as much as it does me."

Persephone whirled. "He's no favored mortal, either."

Hecate raised her brows and Persephone avoided her gaze.

"Regardless of what he did in his mortal days, he's immortal now," Thanatos said, "and bound to this realm with your magic." His head turned towards the far-off gates, as if sensing movement in the river at the realm's entrance. "And now, he's here."

When she calmed her racing thoughts for a moment, she could feel the activity too, like a light tapping on her realm's doors.

"I'll fetch him and bring him to the sitting room," Thanatos announced. He nodded at Persephone and vanished in a shadow jump.

In the silence of Thanatos' absence, Persephone's anxiety increased. Hecate's keen stare burned, as if her eyes were twin torches.

"You know him," Hecate stated calmly.

Persephone dropped into a nearby seat and sighed.

"Yes," she admitted.

"He's your warrior."

"He's not my anything," Persephone said. "But he is the mortal who has called me through the ages."

"As he called you today?"

"It was different this time," Persephone told her. "But the soul couldn't have had much time to send the call with how quickly the Moirai shuttled me to him."

"You two are connected," Hecate said. "Have been for ages. It's not a coincidence your warrior is the only human to receive immortal life from your seeds."

"That's what I fear."

***

Devon was still reeling when the cloaked man guided the narrow boat toward the cavern's shore. A large gate appeared on the cavern's far wall, stone inlaid into the rock. Devon could recognize security measures when he saw them. This was an entrance into a fortress.

Another wave of dread sizzled in his veins, his heart pumping faster, which was a slight relief.

If he had a heartbeat, that was good.

Two colossal statues stood sentinel on either side of the gates, looking like soldiers from an ancient era. Alert, spears at their side and swords sheathed on their belts. Had they not been a hundred-foot-tall towers of stone, he would have thought them alive. The details of the carved statues were impeccable.

Devon watched the statues as the boat moved closer, the river's current aiming them right to the heart of what he knew was his final destination.

As the boat hit the shore, scraping across the rocks as it settled, an enormous cloud of smoke materialized in front of them. It moved to take the form of a person the moment the ferry came to a complete halt.

A large man with pitch-black feathery wings appeared in front of them as the last of the smoke dissipated. The sight caused a jolt of memory to sear into Devon's brain before it was lost again. His most recent memories were too slippery to hold on to. His mind was circling and finding no purchase on any thought that could make sense of all this.

"Thanatos, this is Devon Aideonous, his soul debt paid—"

"I know, Charon," the man introduced as Thanatos said as his wings unfurled and flexed behind him. The black feathers seemed to absorb the surrounding light.

Devon noticed the man had a black sleeveless cloak and tattoos that seemed alive on his arms. Devon felt another memory simmer under his consciousness' surface before it was gone just as suddenly. Devon lingered on the wings.

Skeletons, ghosts, magic, and death.

He wondered if he was stuck in a bad dream. His work made him familiar with nightmares, but this was far different than the terrors that had him sweating in his sleep. Much more real.

"Come," the man, Thanatos, demanded as he turned to enter the gates creaking open in front of them. The ferryman, Charon, offered Devon a hand to help him out of the boat, looking a bit perplexed at the words Thanatos had spoken.

Even with the ferryman's help, Devon still landed ungracefully on the shore, falling to his hands and knees. A skeletal hand from the river grabbed his ankle and began pulling him with remarkable strength. Devon attempted to kick off the hand at the same moment Charon hit it with his pole as he cackled like a mad man. The hand released its grip and Devon fell back on his butt. Gasping, he scrambled backwards, away from the water.

"Better get a move on then," Charon stated cheerfully, using the pole to push the boat off the bank and back into the black, inky river.

Devon watched, dumbfounded, before he pushed himself up and dusted his hands off on his pants. He put a sizeable amount of space between him and the shore. As he righted himself, the noise of tapping against stone reached him.

Slowly, he turned toward the gates to see a massive, three-headed dog standing beside Thanatos at the opening.

Holy hell, Devon thought, it is the size of a grizzly bear!

With pure black fur like Thanatos' feathered wings, the monstrous thing had three heads beset with eyes like simmering coals. Flames writhed in its eyes and fanged mouth.

Thanatos patted its flank and the beast rumbled so loud and deep it made the hair stand-up all-over Devon's body. As Thanatos whispered something in a strange, guttural language, the animal turned its heads to Devon. They watched him suspiciously as Thanatos continued whispering, rubbing his hand over the animal's back before giving another liberal pat to the dog's flank.

At what he assumed was a command, the animal walked up to Devon, its nails clacking on the ground as he moved. After all his time as a mercenary, he could honestly say nothing intimidated him as this hell hound did.

He managed not to shake in fear as each of the gigantic heads sniffed him. All three heads huffed out a breath, which came out sounding like one huge, loud one. Devon took in the animal as it watched him, both of them sizing each other up.

Before Devon could do anything else but blink, the large animal turned and walked through the gates, passing the colossal statues.

"What was that?" Devon asked Thanatos.

"He has your scent now," Thanatos explained as he himself headed toward the gate at the far wall and gestured for Devon to follow. "As long as you are behind the gates, you are safe. Cerberus will guard and protect you."

Ahead, the beast let out a huff but did nothing more than that as it continued its walk. That sound did not inspire confidence.

"Keep me safe from what?" he asked. "Those things back there?"

Devon had always assumed everything went dark when you died, and the earth took you back, which may have been wishful thinking on his part. He had never thought for a moment that the afterlife would need their own kind of security.

"The indebted souls, yes," Thanatos replied. "Cerberus and the gates protect the Goddess' realm from anyone and anything that tries to enter, or leave, without permission." Devon wanted to ask for more elaboration, especially on the leaving part, but Thanatos continued. "Let's get you past the gates so they leave you alone."

When they reached the gate threshold, Devon paused. The air was tense and thick. He put his hand out in front of him and felt some kind of thick liquid between him and the other side of the gate.

"Keep going. It keeps them out but not you. You just have to push through," Thanatos ordered, giving Devon a little shove.

Devon was sure that if Cerberus could roll all six of his eyes he would have as he watched Devon continue his struggle through the wall of gelatinous air.

After a moment, and another annoyed shove from Thanatos, Devon fell out to the other side.

His ears popped as if there was a dramatic change in altitude.

The world around him was bathed in a warm light emanating from what looked like a bright red sun, though it seemed abnormally close to wherever they were. It was freezing for having such a closeness to... Earth?

He found himself atop a hill, several roads trailing from his place near the gates. Out in the distance, he could see tiny villages, fields with people moving around, and an enormous castle at the far edge.

Rivers were there, too, though they were flowing at a more sedate pace than the one he had just been on. Not to mention there did not seem to be any dead people wailing along the shoreline.

It seemed like Earth except for the bizarre sun and a feeling of lightness to his body he didn't feel when home.

"This is unreal," he mumbled and Thanatos let out a loud guffaw, making Devon's head snap back to look at him.

"You've no idea." Thanatos slapped his hand on Devon's back and gripped his shoulder. As Devon lifted his foot to take another step, the world—the Underworld — went black.

CHAPTER 4

Devon stumbled into an entirely different place. When the darkness disappeared, he realized he was now in what looked like an ancient castle's parlor. He caught himself on the edge of a winged back chair and spun around to face Thanatos. "How in the--"

The man's dark eyes glittered with amusement. "Take a seat," he said. "She'll be with you shortly."

Devon lowered himself into the chair he'd leaned on. "Who?"

Thanatos sat in a matching seat across from him. "The lady of the house." He pressed his fingers to his mouth and unleashed a shrill whistle. Devon flinched as the three-headed beast appeared at his side in a burst of shadow, now the size of a normal dog. Thanatos nodded his head toward Cerberus. "His mom... well, adopted mom."

Cerberus released a low growl in confirmation.

Dread curdled in Devon's abdomen. He turned his hands over again and again. The three-headed dog stared at him with fire in his eyes, literally.

He noticed his hands looked remarkably different. The skin once tanned from working in the sun now a pale beige and no more scars from handling blades or burns from explosives.

Before he could check his scars anywhere else, he heard the doors to the room open.

A petite woman with honey skin and silver hair walked in. She wore jeans and a sweater that stated in large letters, 'Resting Witch Face'. She sauntered into the room with a swagger Devon would have thought someone the size of a pixie would be unable to pull off. As she came closer, he noticed her eyes looked to be the color of liquid mercury.

"I admit, you've piqued my interest," she said, surprising him again. Her appearance indicated that she'd have a sweet, lofty voice, not the sultry one that came out. She looked barely over the age of twenty, but something deep in his bones told him she was older. Much older.

"Is this heaven or hell?" Devon asked.

Thanatos chuckled but silenced the moment the woman's silvery gaze cut to him. The hound in the corner growled a little but didn't bother stirring, its three heads still on the floor, lazily taking in everything.

"This is the Underworld. There is no heaven nor hell. The moon is purple. The sun is red. Yet, regardless of such things, you are most certainly surrounded by the dead," she hummed a little after her statement.

He stared at her for a long moment.

"Does anyone ever laugh at that?" he asked, watching her, and wondering if they would torture him with horrible rhymes for all of eternity.

The woman looked a bit affronted at this.

"I've used it for well over 200 years," she snapped, her hands going to her hips, her many bracelets jangling.

They stared at each other for a moment in silence.

"And of those 200 years…?" he let the statement trail off as her eyes narrowed.

She threw her head back, letting out a boisterous laugh.

"Oh, I am going to like you, aren't I?" she looked him up and down. "Well, it will be interesting to see how this all plays out." She waved her hands in the air as if she was showing some grand prize to a game show winner.

"But for now, I must attend to my duties. Be good, mortal man." She glanced to Thanatos. "And you too, Reaper." She winked as a silver circle of light swirled around her, and she blinked out of existence.

Devon was so alarmed by the stranger's visit, and exit, he barely heard the door open again.

This time, a guard on either side of it held it ajar.

A woman, one that stirred his fragmented memory, strode in and Devon was sure his heart stopped.

He put his palm over his heart, finding a heartbeat again.

Holding his hand to his chest a moment longer just for reassurance, Devon watched the woman closely. She was darkness to the light of the woman who had stood before him only moments ago.

She was tall, lithe, her walk graceful like that of a dancer. Long, straight black hair was brushed back from her face. A face that would have been the beauty of aristocratic nobility in ancient times with her thin nose, sculpted cheekbones, and a thin oval face with alabaster skin. She wore a black silk dress with a long v down from her collar bones to mid stomach, her breasts slightly peeking from the sides, and her sleeves flared out.

Though she looked like a lady of some great noble family, Devon could feel she was something more than human as she moved to stand in front of him. He could almost see some color around her, like an aura, for a moment before it faded away.

Her eyes moved over his face and she nodded subtly before taking a seat next to Thanatos. The hound moved from Thanatos' side to hers. Its tail thumped restlessly as it gazed up at the woman with its normal canine brown eyes. Eyes that held an intelligence that told anyone that this was no mere dog.

The woman scratched behind the beast's ear as if it were the family golden retriever.

She then turned her lightning blue gaze on him and looked him over, her intense focus so laser-sharp, Devon began to feel awkward.

He was an anomaly, he knew that, and he was way out of his depth here. It was obvious from everyone's reactions so far that this was a first.

"Devon Aideonous, mercenary of the mortal world," she greeted solemnly, her hand on the back of the dog's neck.

He squinted at her opening statement of his identity and the fact that she did not introduce herself.

No, hi, hello, I am the devil, and you are in hell, he thought as they stared at each other in silence for long moments. Devon, unsure of what to say to her, wondered again how in the hell any of this was real–this beautiful woman in black with glowing blue eyes scratching behind the ears of what was only moments ago a three headed monstrous hell hound with eyes of fire.

36

Sitting there with his jaw on the floor would not lend him any help in dealing with the woman he knew had to be the Goddess. Devon rose to his feet and her eyes narrowed at his attempt to even the playing field between them.

Thanatos shifted subtly in his seat. The hound moved itself to its full height as well beside his mistress, back to being wary of Devon. He was sentry again, with intelligent eyes, ready to take on any threat to the Goddess. To tear said threat apart. Piece by bloody piece.

Slowly, she finally stood and stepped towards him until they were only a foot apart. This close, he realized he was only an inch or two taller than her.

Her blue eyes pierced his gaze. The way she stared made him feel like she was peeling back layers of his soul. Just as she had done when he was only a soul without a shell.

He felt suddenly caught off guard by that thought and wondered where it had come from. The tiny hairs on his skin stood on end again, his fight-or-flight instinct so ramped up that he was tempted to bolt for the door.

"You've been tormented by demons for so very long," she whispered. "I guess it doesn't really matter, though, does it? Still ended up in the same place."

His eyebrows arched in confusion, but he stayed quiet through her assessment.

"You realize you are not dead. You are very much alive," she said, finally addressing him instead of her whispered statements.

This information sent a wave of shock through him and memories flooded his mind. Nothing about how he died, but ones of him looking down at his own body, lying on the floor of some horrible motel room as the Goddess and a winged skeletal man stood over him.

"How? I saw my body. I saw what had happened. The blood was everywhere," Devon muttered, feeling a cold, creeping numbness at even saying it out loud.

As much as he tried not to let the memory take hold of his mind, it horrified him to see himself with glassy dead eyes and his chest not rising and falling with breath as his skin turned blue.

Devon remembered he had been in such a dark place recently, feeling as if no one cared if he lived or died, and wondered if he had

37

done this to himself. The thought he could end his own life nauseated him.

He spent his entire life fighting for other people but forgot to fight for himself, forgetting he also deserved a chance. He knew that if he had survived, he might have still ended everything, and that made him sick.

Devon was unsure if he necessarily wanted to remember how he died, but he knew deep down he needed to.

Reality brings little comfort.

"Something larger than you, or me, stepped in and kept you from true death. I may be a Goddess, but even I cannot see the future or decipher the reasoning behind the Moirai's deeds."

"A Goddess? Moirai?" he echoed, his voice low and unsure, still stuck on the words he had learned in history lessons so long ago. Ones that were obviously much more real than he had ever thought.

Devon knew she was not of this world but hearing her say the words outright made it even more surreal. She was an actual Goddess, a higher power that came to his death to guide his soul from the mortal realm.

"I never... the history books..." he was fumbling his words, but she nodded patiently in understanding.

"Yes, history has had plenty of ideas on who and what their gods were. We even acquiesced to this, to a certain extent. You see, history has not been kind to female rulers. The gods you read about - Zeus, Poseidon, and Hades, the brothers who ruled sky, sea, and the Underworld, were just our alter egos. Created to appease and help us work alongside humans."

"They do not exist," he whispered.

Her only response was a simple shake of her head.

"The only powerful beings watching over you were Goddesses, which were my sisters and I. Kind of changes your perspective on the fairer sex, does it not?" she asked with only a tilt of her head to show it was an actual question and not rhetorical.

"The other Olympians..."

"The senate in Halcyon is made up of demigods, children born of Titans and humans. They have powers in relation to the ones you know of as the Olympians. But, no, there are none that are Olympians in the way you think of."

"So… am I a demigod?" he asked, unsure of everything at that moment.

"No. That would imply that you have power and cannot be killed in the traditional sense."

His eyes widened a fraction at this. *Killed in the traditional sense?* As if he had spoken aloud, she answered his question.

"Mortals are easily killed. A demigod would not have fallen from a gunshot wound, which, taking in your body after death, was how you died. To kill a demigod, you must use hydra's blood or sever their head from their body and burn them in a sacrificial fire."

"And a Goddess?" he asked and immediately wished he hadn't as her eyes narrowed on him. Suddenly, Devon felt her in his head again, her gaze holding him frozen as she flipped through his memories like a photo album. From his first memory of helping his father plant a tree, through all the guilt, pain, and depression until the moment a bullet ended everything.

He now had the memory of his death, and he felt relief that he had not been the one to end his life.

However, he never saw his killer, he realized as his mind played out his last moments. The bullets that struck him had not been from anyone in the room with him. The only logical explanation was a sniper, but he wasn't sure. It didn't matter though. He would hunt them down and end that person as they had ended him.

His mind whirled at viewing it from an outside point of view. He didn't recognize this cold and calculating mercenary as himself. He had always known deep down that he wasn't built for that lifestyle, both physically and emotionally.

He remembered his father begging him not to join the government forces, and the memory brought back that horrible feeling of betrayal. He had not honored his father through his choices. His memories were now running slower through his mind as if coming to a stopping point as he closed in on the moment he ceased to exist—the moment he decided that he would take this chance at a second life offered to him with the seeds.

The Goddess broke her powerful, searching gaze and Devon returned to his body in the present moment. He tried to cover his immense discomfort at his deepest self being on display for her.

39

The tension of her presence released inside his head as she left his mind. The memories of his life that the deity had stirred fell back into the recesses of his subconscious, but he felt fuller, less lost with the recovered knowledge of his death.

The Goddess nodded and stepped away from him, her facial expression showing nothing of what she was thinking. Her emotions did not move over her face like the women he had met before. She either had one hell of a poker face or was cold blooded to the core.

"You will be no threat to me, Devon," she intoned. "This will be your new home. You may call me Persephone."

New home? "If I'm not a demigod, why am I here? How am I alive? What am I?"

The Goddess looked away, glancing for the first time to Thanatos, who sat quietly in his seat.

He nodded.

"You, Devon, seem to be a Reaper."

CHAPTER 5

She watched Devon as he took in her words. Wordlessly repeating them as if committing them to memory.

His stare became fixed on the fire in the corner of the room, blue just as all the fire in the Underworld was. He seemed lost for a moment before he said, "A reaper? What the hell is a reaper? Why me?"

An admirable question. One that Persephone herself had. *Why him?*

"Your rescue from eternal death was mandated by the Moirai, but your life is now linked to my powers and the powers of the Underworld. The seeds," she explained, "tied you to my realm."

The seeds had been fragments of her essence, the same energy that coursed through her realm. She hadn't consciously known she could give such a gift until the Moirai deemed it so. Persephone chafed at the intimacy of it. Although she had known the soul for millennia, he might as well have inhaled the shadow smoke of her innermost power.

"An immortal denizen of the Underworld," she continued, careful to not reveal her uncertainty, "serves the realm. A Reaper serves by transporting the souls of the dead from the human realm to the river, where you arrived at my gates."

Devon's brows furrowed and he flinched away from her. Closing himself off completely felt wrong to her, but she would not push him. She had to choose her battles wisely with him.

"The dead? When I took those fucking seeds, you said I'd never have to kill again. Was this some kind of fucking trap? I didn't have the choice in life to be anything other than a monster, yet here you are making me a monster for all eternity!" His calm facade crumbled, replaced by a lethal anger that snapped into place in the blink of an eye. She took a moment before responding, wanting him to hear her words and not be so engrossed in his own anger.

Thanatos appeared next to her, shadows licking at his sides. Persephone sent him a quelling look. She understood Devon might be confused since he had been disoriented from the separation of body and soul when they last spoke. Damn the Moirai for not giving her more to go on and leaving them confused and wandering the realms for clues.

"I said you'd never have to raise a weapon again. Reapers do not kill. They guide the souls home."

Devon glared. "I tried to escape killing in my mortal life, and now I have to be surrounded by death for eternity?" he snarled through his clenched teeth, his nostrils flaring, looking every inch the dangerous predator that he was trained to be.

Thanatos tensed. "Death is not murder, mercenary," he warned, his voice deepening and verging into his Reaper form. "You will do well to censor your words when you speak harshly of death in this realm. Especially with the Goddess."

As quick as the anger appeared, a look of utter defeat wiped it away as he turned away from her. That was so much worse than the anger. She knew the depression that had been a cloud over him as a human was trying to claw its way back in. She knew she had to be patient. He was going to need time to accept this new reality.

He had a life before he was plunged into all of this, she reminded herself. It would take Devon time to adjust, and she would make sure she was beside him every step of the way.

"I'll never escape it," Devon whispered more to himself than her. "All of eternity will be me watching people die."

She could visualize the disheartened look on his face as he looked towards the wall, taking in the sconces as they flickered with blue fire. He was trying to rebuild his wall of nonchalance, but it turned into a losing battle.

"Let me go back to the mortal world and live my life." He said, turning to face her. "I promise to be peaceful and not raise a hand to another person. I will not kill. I will do something better with my life. I will help people, I swear," he implored, his voice choking a bit on the last word. His green eyes full of an emotional upheaval that was far too much for one person to endure.

Persephone closed her eyes, truly feeling for this man. She could only imagine how overwhelming this must be for him. Opening her eyes, she looked at him and surprised them both by placing her hand on his cheek as she whispered, "I can't. I am so sorry, Devon."

She watched as he finally won the fight to rebuild the wall between them. His face went back to the cold indifference he wore so well, though his hands shook a bit as he folded his arms across his chest. Devon's mask was how she would forever think of the look he now wore.

He stared for a moment at her before stepping out of her reach.

"Don't be sorry." Taking a deep breath, he continued, "My choices are obviously the sole reason I am here, and I need to own that." he clenched his jaw, his Adam's apple moving as he swallowed before starting again, "So, tell me what I need to do. Might as well get started."

Persephone glanced at Thanatos.

"You'll train. With me. We'll hone your immortal powers for the work of reaping."

"But, first," Persephone interjected. "We'll acclimate you to life here in the palace."

Devon glanced around the parlor. "I'm going to live here, then?" he asked.

Her castle was large, which in truth was ridiculous since it was just her, Cerberus, and the shadows. Thanatos and Hecate had their own places to retire to at the end of the day.

She was curious how he saw her home. Hecate mentioned on more than one occasion that wandering souls could mistake the halls for dungeons, that they may look around for heads on pikes in such a place.

Which was a silly thing to say since anything like that happened in the Fields of Punishment and she knew it.

Although the castle was made of stone, Persephone had made it comfortable over the centuries with relaxing furniture, unobstructed windows, and a library full of books written by mortals over the course of history.

"I am assuming since you are bound to the Underworld as I am, that you would spend a large majority of your time here," she explained, watching his face take on a look she couldn't quite decipher.

"What about my old apartment?"

"Perhaps with time, we can find a way to allow you to inhabit your mortal domicile again."

He raised his eyebrows at her.

"What did I say?" she asked, confused at the look he was giving her.

"Nothing, just the way you speak." He chuckled dryly. "Sorry, it's not anything I'm used to. 'Inhabit your mortal domicile'. I'm not sure why I find that so funny right now." He huffed out one last laugh as he looked around some more, putting his hands back into his pockets—a nervous gesture much like when he ran his hands through his hair.

She stayed quiet. This was something she did too when she was nervous, forgetting the current slang of the times. Hecate would pester her about it before meetings, that if she broke into her formal tongue, people wouldn't be able to focus on her overall point.

"So," he sighed, rocking back on his heels. "This is it? This is my life now? Forever?"

Persephone was almost afraid to speak, to lock him into a fate with her words. But that was silly. That was the Moirai's job, not hers. "Yes," she told him.

"Being a Reaper is not so dull," Thanatos told him. "You will have power. You will help deliver justice where needed, relief where deserved."

The emotions—the awkward discomfort, the confusion, the anger—bled from his face. He became cold, just as he appeared in her visions of his past. "But that relief will elude me."

"The darkness of your mortal life will fade," she told him softly. Hers had.

As she watched him process her words, she realized she could not tolerate the distance his cold demeanor wedged between them. Persephone was not sure why, but it mattered that he was open and kept nothing from her. Long ago, before she even came into her powers, dishonesty was something she could not forgive.

"We will get you acquainted with your new powers as an immortal, but I must ask that we are always honest with each other. That you never lie to me. I need your oath that you will be truthful." Her eyes lit up brighter, ready to seal the pact between them. She knew most oaths

44

were done over water from the River Styx between gods, but perhaps one Goddess and a bonded immortal was enough for it to take.

"Yeah, sure." He was not looking at her again, which would not do. She needed his eyes, she needed this sealed between their souls if it was possible.

"Devon," she demanded in a voice only a Goddess could use. "Look me in the eye and swear this oath to me. Do you promise me honesty in all forms?"

He finally looked up, and his eyes were so cold that she had to force herself to stay still. To not demand he cease this charade.

Finally, she saw a flicker of something in his gaze only to realize it was another round of building anger.

"Yes, Persephone. Honesty always with you. But only you," Devon stated matter of fact, not even glancing at Thanatos. "And right now, I really hate everything about this place, even you. I both want and need to hate you." She could see the truth of that statement and the anger at the unknown causing such turmoil. She watched as Devon struggled to keep control of his emotional state.

She noticed the moment Devon felt the oath move through him, like it was forging a new pathway in his mind and carving itself into his soul. She was used to the feeling of a sworn oath, but he wasn't.

The oath flashed over his eyes.

A small growl left his lips, but he said no words. Instead, Devon just Watched her with such an intensity that Persephone wondered if the oath was a good idea after all. His face eventually settled on the unemotional stony mask he wore moments ago.

They looked at each other in complete silence. Yet, this time, she was the first to look away.

This soul, the man standing in front of her, she had watched for years. Generations.

She understood his hatred, logically. She hardly paid attention to her emotional state, so the fact that his words hurt baffled her. But they hurt. A lot. He had meant so much to her. It surprised her to find that the thought of him hating her felt like a knife between the ribs. Straight into her heart.

It made sense as she represented the entire upheaval of his world. She wondered for a moment if he felt the bond that had formed between them when he took the seeds. She reached for it, having shut herself off to get through this moment but needing to know his true feelings. To her relief, she found that his hate for her was not real. It was a reaction to the potent emotions he felt.

She closed the bond. His end felt strong, but murky and unsteady. The reason for their bond was something only the Moirai knew, but he had not accepted it yet.

So, she would keep the bond closed until he did. She knew for a man like she was realizing Devon was, having no control over his life and emotions was a form of torture. This bond would cause more issues in his coming to terms with everything, so she kept that information to herself for now, and made sure the bond was closed tight.

Giving him a firm nod before turning, she beckoned him to follow her. She knew enough about people to realize she should have been more of a host to him before demanding he swore oaths to her. It would take some getting used to, having someone from the mortal realm in her domain when she was used to being alone and doing everything her way.

This was going to be quite a change for both of them.

***

Persephone hoped he did not reject the strange and beautiful place she called home.

Living among the dead was not for the faint of heart.

He needed to know the whole of the Underworld, even the truly hellish places. Even the places she dreaded acknowledging the most, the secrets there worse than any punishment.

As they wound through the hallways of her too-large home, Persephone pointed out the rooms open to his use, such as the library and various sitting rooms. She hoped the quotidian reality of the castle would settle his mind from the magic he'd experienced thus far and prepare him for the magic he'd see outside.

"How many people live here?" he asked.

"You are the only..." she searched for the word, "guest here."

"Where do the... dead people live then?

"The souls," she corrected, "live in different regions of the Underworld depending on the life they lived. Other immortals reside in this realm as well, not all because this is their afterlife, but because this is where they can truly be themselves. Some work for me."

"Like Thanatos?" he asked. "And the silver-haired woman?"

Persephone smiled at the mention of her friends. "Yes. They have homes near the castle."

"And," Persephone continued as she guided him through the halls, "they help me run the realm. The Underworld is the only place for souls to rest and not all of them are guilty of a sinful life."

"Respectfully, Goddess," Devon said, "that is not my experience."

Persephone nodded.

"A true, pure soul that has committed no wrong doing is rare," she conceded. "But I've seen the lives and deaths of billions of mortals, and it is even more rare to find one wholly unworthy of forgiveness and fair judgement."

Devon was quiet at that.

She took him to one of her favorite places in her home, a secluded balcony that overlooked one of the highest points in the realm. Persephone stepped out onto the narrow ledge and beckoned Devon to follow. "Come see for yourself."

When Devon joined her, Persephone splayed out her arms at the land below. The crimson sky cast a warm light over the landscape. From this vantage point, they could see rolling hills and rockier, darker mountains.

"We have different areas for different souls," she told him, "Immortals and lower Gods ensure that, had the souls committed a crime in life, their punishment fits the crime."

She pointed towards the mountains. "Beyond those peaks, there are the Fields of Punishment, where souls with the darkest stains face consequence."

She watched him as she spoke, his eyes narrowed and his head tilted as he took in the words that must have differed from the stories and fables of his childhood.

"If a soul has led a good life," she continued, "Then they are not met with any trials here in the afterlife. They will be judged worthy of living in the blessed land, the Elysian Fields. They will not remember their human lives. For some, that is the only true peace they have. In order for that to happen, they drink from the River Lethe. The only way to restore their memories is to drink from the counterpart, the Pool of

Memories, but the Titan who watches over it calls for a debt. Those debts are never worth it," she stated matter-of-factly, her hands clasped in front of her. Her body language saying nothing of what she felt or thought.

He watched her, and she was sure he would ask about a loved one, as they always did. People never seemed to truly understand that the person they lost to death would not remember the person they were in life.

Mortals always thought no matter what power was at work, their loved one would overcome it and remember them. The hurt when they realized that person no longer held memories of them, the ones they made and the life they lived, was incredibly sad to watch.

Devon took a deep breath. Persephone had taken him to the balcony to assuage the shock of being in a place so different from what he knew, but she could see the light of a thousand thoughts flashing through his eyes.

"Forgetting," he murmured. "That does sound like a reward."

Persephone remained still. "Immortals cannot drink from the River Lethe," she warned stiffly. "It is forbidden for anyone who is not bestowed the final gift."

He hummed thoughtfully. "And so, no heaven? No hell? Just fields and rivers? Remembering and forgetting?" He looked away from the landscape and drilled his gaze into hers. "Just you, Goddess?"

She nodded. "Just me." And wasn't that the lonely truth?

CHAPTER 6

Devon followed Persephone as they worked their way through the gothic, winding hallways. Sconces that held fire as blue as the crown the Goddess wore were lit along their way. The hellhound plodded loudly behind them as they walked, taking inventory by sniffing every nook and cranny like a typical dog would in the mortal realm.

She halted abruptly in front of a door. Had he not been aware of his surroundings instinctively, he might have run right into her. He watched as she put her hand to the door's center instead of on the knob to turn it.

"What is your favorite memory from your childhood? One untouched by the pain you felt in the mortal realm," Persephone quietly asked as she peered over her shoulder to him. The question took him completely off guard.

Devon was so busy taking in the details of the castle as they walked, trying to remember the way should he need an escape plan, that her question made him reroute his train of thought.

However, the memory he tried to keep untouched by the darkness popped up into his head unbidden. When he had the fortitude to push past all the gloom and find that inner light, the memory was as alive and colorful as it had been when he lived it. Devon hesitated to give too much of himself. Right now, she represented everything he was fighting against and what he needed to escape from.

Unfortunately for him, she seemed to have unlimited patience and hardly seemed irritated at his delayed response.

Finally giving in to their little stare-off, he sighed and ran a hand through his hair. She probably did know everything after her time in his mind earlier, so there was no point withholding that precious memory.

Everything and everyone from the memory had perished, so it was not like she could use it against him. He had no one in the mortal world anymore she could use to hurt him.

He was being ridiculous, and he knew it. Only his pride kept him from making the logical decision in this moment.

"The forest next to my house growing up. My father." Devon felt himself get a little choked up at the thought of his father. He wished he could see his childhood cabin just one last time; it would be worth everything he had to deal with.

"My father and I used to go out there and build things," he said, remembering the feeling of sore muscles, sweaty skin, and accomplishment. "It was how we would spend time together when he was not working with the forest conservation groups. Camp and things like that. We lived in a cabin, right at the western border of the Great Forest. It had always been my safe place."

He looked at her now, the Goddess. The way she was looking at him, he knew she was seeing it all play out across his face, no matter how much he attempted to control his emotional response outwardly.

He could feel her eyes study him a moment longer before she turned to face the door, pressing her hand harder against the center of the wood. Her palm lit up bright blue and light pulsed out from under her hand. The blue light moved across the door and underneath it into the room on the other side.

After the last of the light disappeared, Persephone moved her hand down to the knob and opened the door.

She turned and waited for Devon to enter the room. As he stepped past her, he could feel her trailing closely behind.

Once Devon saw the room though, he no longer cared she was there.

The visual was overwhelming. A punch to the gut followed by a warm hug. His emotions were all over the place. His heart pounded loudly in his ears and his knees felt weak. He attempted to take a deep breath into his lungs, only to find he could barely get in any air.

Almost scared to touch anything and find out it wasn't real, he stood in the doorway as he took it all in. His mind was zapping and short-circuiting, unable to make sense of what he was seeing. He felt her place her hand on his shoulder, and though his instinct was to pull away, he didn't. His entire body was locked into a battle of anxiety, shock, and nostalgia.

It was his old cabin, the exact room of the cabin that he and his father had worked to make perfect for him. The log fireplace in the corner was lit and spread a comforting warmth throughout the room. His bed covered in the same plaid green comforter that he knew without touching was comfy and warm. His mind was able to remember the exact texture of the fabric and the walls made of logs.

Turning, Devon noticed a window in the room. The window did not open to the same Underworld he had seen upon first arriving, but a wooded area remarkably similar to his forest.

Something to explore later, he thought.

Meandering around the room, he waited for something to be amiss, to reveal itself as the illusion it was. He picked up a framed photo next to the bed. It was old, the colors tarnished a bit beneath the glass, but he recognized it instantly. A photo of the old cabin that existed in a world that felt far from this one.

He hadn't noticed a tear had fallen onto his cheek until Persephone stepped towards him and carefully wiped it away with her finger. She held it out in front of her to look at it as if it was something alien to her. He laughed, feeling a little embarrassed.

"Do you not cry, Goddess?" his voice was rough with emotion he could no longer contain. He may not trust her, but his gut instinct told him he was not going to be able to hate her for much longer. As much as he both wanted and needed to.

No, she would not be a threat in the way he thought, but it scared him she might be in other ways he could not contemplate.

She had done more for him in a few hours than anyone had since his father had died.

Life. A home. Comfort.

She looked up at him, perplexed. "I haven't. Not that I can remember."

He could see the truth in her eyes, but he knew she could not be without emotion, having seen it several times on her face since they first spoke.

He shook the thoughts away, needing to focus on one overwhelming dilemma at a time.

Breaking eye contact, he looked down as he watched her wipe the rogue tear onto her gown He smiled a little at the simple yet human gesture. However, he lost his smile just as quickly, knowing that way led to trouble.

The woman already fascinated him, had him wanting to know more about her when only moments ago he was desperate to hate her. He needed to step back and create some distance. He would learn his purpose, do the best he could to honor his promises, then find a way out of here.

As nice as her gesture was, she was not a priority to him. He was here to take the second chance offered to him and make his life worth something. Even if it was only accomplished in his afterlife.

"Thank you," Devon finally said, his voice cracking a little as he warred with his emotional state, trying to allow the cold numbness to take back over. He wasn't used to people concerning themselves with how he felt and what he might need, so it was difficult.

"I was always happiest at my cabin, surrounded by nature." He coughed to clear his throat, regaining a bit of control. "This means a lot."

Looking out of the window, the dark forest beckoned him like a mother calling her child home. He leaned against the window frame and marveled at just how much it looked like the view from his childhood window.

"This is a window to the forest near where you grew up. It is the best I could do," Persephone whispered, coming to stand beside him. "If I could give you the actual forest, the cabin, I would."

He whirled to face her.

"Why?" he demanded with more force than he meant, his voice a crack of thunder in the near-silent room.

Devon felt his chaotic emotions threatening his control again.

She simply tilted her head, taking him in, the loud demand doing nothing to disturb her calm. Devon genuinely wanted to know why she, a stranger, and a Goddess, would concern herself with someone like him. Did she do this for every poor human in the afterlife? Or did she take pity on him after throwing him into the eternal unknown? She must have ulterior motives. He couldn't trust her, even if he didn't really hate

52

her. He'd never trusted anyone, and he wouldn't start now.

Especially not with someone who spent their time among the dead.

"Why are you doing this for me? Anything for me?" He pressed.

Her brow furrowed with a look of pure confusion, as if he had just asked her the secrets of theuniverse.

"Because you deserve to feel some happiness, Devon. Humans either deny themselves simple happiness or overindulge. So rare to find someone who is balanced." She grimaced as she said that last word, as if it left a foul taste on her tongue. She gestured toward the woods. "I can only hope you can find some peace here."

Peace. He turned the word over in his mind.

He did not explain how after he left for the government service, his dad had died, and the land foreclosed on, gone forever from his family. The place he'd returned to after his hellish missions was a mirage.

It hurt again, the loss of his home, even as he stood in its replicant. He had planned to move back after his enlistment was up to marry and raise his children.

The loss had led down the road to mercenary work. His dream had been ripped out from under him, along with the only person who really cared about him. Yet, he felt like this woman, this Goddess, gave him a small piece of his dream back.

Had she been human, he would never accept the gift she had given him. He could feel some part of himself that was lost and drifting come back to him. Something in his mind was moving into place, something long lost to the darkness and sins of his thoughts and deeds.

Something that felt a lot like salvation for his soul.

CHAPTER 7

Devon paced his new bedroom, thinking through everything the Goddess had told him. His anxiety was a real and tangible thing as it moved alongside him as if part of his own shadow.

He needed to know what he was up against as far as the Goddess and his new powers. Yet, despite his best efforts, his overwhelming thoughts held no resolution to his problems. The only logical thing to do in his current state was to regroup after a hot shower. He couldn't think straight covered in his grimy clothes stiff from his own dried blood.

Looking around the room again as he pulled off what was left of his tattered shirt, he had to admit that he felt a bit more grounded here in this replica of his childhood room.

Like he could breathe again, even if the room was a ruse to trick him into compliance.

Outside of the window, he caught sight of a doe running through the woods. The lithe grace almost reminded him of the Goddess, bringing him an instant overwhelming feeling of joy. Memories of watching the forest creatures as a youth while he sat out on the front porch speaking with his father, learning his letters, and reading.

Years, so many years since he had seen this view. He allowed himself a moment to think of how much he needed this after years of darkness and self-hatred. Finally, he could go back in his mind and visit the man he was before the mercenary. Maybe the Goddess had created this illusion on purpose to give him a false sense of calm, but he could finally breathe.

Devon had died, and instead of going to a dark place for eternity, he was here. Looking through a window to his childhood forest, reliving his past, and realizing this was a fresh start.

He could either rail against everything just to make himself miserable, or he could find out what he was capable of and move forward. He had never been one to act out in a situation just because it did not work for him at the moment. He was a problem-solver, and right now, he could make this situation work for him.

This was his chance to, maybe not undo his sins, but move forward with a moral and just purpose.

Something inside his soul called out for that. The darkness had been stifling and caging some part of him. No longer. He would work with the Goddess, and once he knew what he could do, he would plan out a road to a new future.

He wished death had not been the catalyst for his life change, that he had been alive to have this revelation, but dwelling on the past would do him no good.

Devon snapped back to reality when he caught a shadow move in his peripheral. He turned to see what had cast it but found nothing and no one in the room with him. He closed his eyes, recognizing a lot had happened today, and his mind was tired, creating literal shadows where there were not any.

He needed to stop thinking and take a shower. Check out his new home, grab a drink, and then sleep until someone came to check his pulse.

After all, dying and coming back to life was exhausting.

Once inside his private bathroom, he noted that the room looked nothing like the tiny bathroom he'd shared with his dad in the cabin, but it was decorated similarly with wooden logs. Instead of the old buckets and poor plumbing, he'd been given what could only be described as an upgrade.

A walk-in shower that was large enough for him to share with more people than he would find enjoyable to be around. Beside it was a clawfoot tub that looked very much like it belonged in the Gothic castle.

Throwing his shredded shirt to the floor, his smooth flesh caught his eye in the mirror. No more scars. The scars his body had carried for a lifetime, constantly punishing him with a map of his sins, were gone. The scars that reminded him of how close to death he'd been, and the monster his survival had created, had simply vanished as if they'd never been there.

Only unblemished and pale flesh moved over his muscles.

For a moment, it was difficult to breathe—a common theme today. Those scars were not something he had ever wanted to keep, but he had grown used to them. He had used them to punish himself with memories that were better forgotten. Refusing to let himself forget, lest he go down darker paths.

Devon continued undressing but paused when his hands moved over his tactical pants. The combat knife still strapped to his right thigh, next to his holster that should have held his pistol had he not dropped it after losing consciousness.

He'd only arrived in the Underworld with what had been on his person, on his... corpse.

He began to unstrap his weapons, pulling his unused tactical gloves from his pocket. He hadn't had time to get his chest rig into place and wondered if that would have changed the outcome for him.

Devon could remember the burning of a bullet that had torn through his shoulder. The immediate shock of it, yet the pain hadn't entirely overwhelmed him thanks to the adrenaline that had raced through his veins. He'd moved on instinct in the direction the bullet had come from.

Nothing. The room was empty.

His eyes cut to the windows. No bullet holes.

Devon had spent years evading assassins paid enormous sums to end his life, and one had finally managed to succeed. He had always been the prey as much as the predator in his line of work.

He'd caught the flash of the gun firing from the vacant dark corner before he felt the pain of another bullet searing through his chest.

Everything disappeared after that, his entire consciousness ripped away from him. His next memory was of those beautiful, glowing blue eyes.

Jolting back to where he stood in his new bathroom, Devon grabbed the counter's edge and took a deep breath. His lungs felt tight, on the verge of hyperventilating from a memory that still seemed so hazy and unclear. The enemy was invisible in his mind. While he could not fathom how his adversary could have been invisible, he was perhaps blocking the face of his murderer from his mind in some form of self-preservation.

Devon undressed completely, kicking aside his pants stiff with blood, and turned the shower handle to the hottest setting.

Looking back at the rags of what had been his daily uniform, piled unceremoniously in the corner, he wondered when he last wore anything but black. Not since before he joined the government service, after he'd stripped himself of his military uniform for the last time. A person could not see blood on black clothing.

He stepped under the steaming showerhead and let the water burn away his mortal life. He couldn't drink from the River Lethe, but he could do this.

How had he ever thought his life was normal? He had become so immersed in his role as a mercenary, a harbinger of death and destruction, that killing was easier than breathing. Seeing evidence of that life against the backdrop of this peaceful place troubled him. He'd been a truly horrible person. He'd never enjoyed the killing, not like some, but that hardly excused him.

He looked through the glass shower door at his pile of clothing on the floor. The sum of his sins; a lump of dirty rags, weapons, blood-covered military I.D. tags, and painful memories. His memorial.

He turned away, scrubbing himself clean until his skin was raw and stinging.

***

Devon stepped out of the shower, a gush of steam following him into the bathroom. He wrapped a towel around his waist but paused when he noticed from the corner of his vision that his discarded items were missing. Even the dirt and flakes of dried blood from his things had vanished from the floor, cleaned away as if they'd never been there. He didn't care what happened with the ruined clothes, but he hadn't heard any noises nor saw anyone enter while he'd been in the shower.

He had lost his touch if people were able to sneak up on him. He needed to focus on keeping his guard up. Complacency in his world led to death, but he never thought about what happened when a person was already dead. He thought on this as he secured his towel and opened the bathroom door.

He was suddenly immersed in his past.

Walking through the front door of the cabin, he went to the kitchen for his after-school snack as he did every day.

Before he made it too far into the cabin, he caught sight of his father sitting at the kitchen table. Usually, if the sun was up his father was outside, having no patience for remaining indoors when the beauty of the outdoors called to him.

"Hey, Dad," Devon greeted, curious about his father being inside when the weather was perfect.

"Ah, Devon! Good, good. You're home. Come with me." His father moved around the table, grabbing onto Devon's arm as he walked past him. At fifteen years of age, he was almost as tall as his father. It wouldn't be long before he surpassed him in height.

His father moved through their small cabin before coming to a stop in front of Devon's door. Grabbing both of his son's hands in his, his father smiled. Something he did not do often, the man was very serious most of the time, so Devon took great joy in these moments.

"You are a man now and a man needs a space of his own."

"I have my room, Dad," Devon interrupted.

"Yes, yes. You do, but it is not truly yours. You haven't made it your own yet. Not as a man. Just as a child."

Before Devon could argue, his father threw open the door to his room.

Devon slowly walked in, dropping his school bag on the floor as he took in what his father had done. He had created a whole new sanctuary for Devon.

A bed and desk made of oak, a plaid comforter Devon had eyed in the market, and a new shelf that boasted several mementos from their adventures together.

A smile crossed Devon's face before he turned and threw his arms around his father in a rib crushing hug.

"Thanks, Dad," Devon whispered to his father, knowing he had built this all by hand. It explained some of the missed dinners, the hours his father spent holed up in his workshop.

His father cleared his throat, rubbing Devon's back a moment before he broke away. His father was not one for overt affection but did his best when it came to his son.

"I do expect good grades and good choices to be made here."

Devon resisted rolling his eyes.

"Don't worry, Dad. Study only, no girls. Got it." Devon couldn't help the laugh that bubbled out. His father stood with his hands on his hips, shaking his head.

"Get used to your room. It is your turn, but I'll make dinner." His stoic father left the room, closing the door gently as he left.

Devon looked around his room in awe before throwing his arms out to the side and letting himself fall backwards onto his new bed.

Heavenly.

CHAPTER 8

When Persephone shadow jumped into Devon's chambers the next morning, she stumbled backwards against a sudden force. Devon seethed above her, his forearm pressing her chest. Their eyes clashed and the panic vanished from his green irises.

Devon took a sharp step back. "What the fuck was that? You just magically appear without knocking?"

Persephone straightened and smoothed a hand over her chest. Those green eyes had been so… close, sparking with anger. "Usually, yes," she said.

Devon frowned. "Well, for future reference, don't do that with me."

Persephone nodded. She had to remember that humans now had attachments to their privacy. It was only a few millennia ago that her sister Hera had a habit of light jumping into mortals' homes in the form of animals. Messy business, that was.

"What I did, it's calling up a portal to move between spaces in the same time frame. Creatures of shadows, like myself and Thanatos, call it a shadow jump," she explained. "My sisters are creatures of power from earth and life, so they call theirs light jumps. You will learn how to do this in time, but you will first need to know how not to end up in random places. If it is a soul that is ready to depart, you will naturally feel the pull. However, when you are not dealing with a soul, it is more difficult. You will need to know the place you are going, as detailed as possible, or have some form of a connection to the person if shadow jumping to find someone."

"So, that's how I'll move around as a Reaper?" he asked. "Teleportation."

"Essentially," Persephone agreed. "Although, there's some more flair and finesse to it. There's jumping for your own purposes of movement, and then jumping to answer a soul's call. There is a difference."

She watched him mull this over. The man had dedicated his life to his work, his mission, and now he had a new one. For the briefest of moments, Persephone recalled him as he was when he lived as the Viking Chief.

Bloody.

Determined.

Steadfast.

The glimpsed memory faded almost instantly.

"Would you like to try a shadow jump with me?" Her words surprised him. It took Devon a second to realize what she asked before he gave her a quick nod.

The shadows swirled up around him, moving over them and between them, her hold on his shoulder never letting go. The shadows took over her vision, for the barest of moments, and in that instant, they were in a whole different place.

Persephone had shadow jumped to the prominent hill not far from the castle that overlooked the Underworld's entrance. Devon wobbled a bit, trying to get his footing on the loamy knoll. She pretended not to notice how embarrassed he always became when he was not in complete command of himself.

"That was," he murmured, "... unpleasant." He blinked, as if clearing his vision from the disorientation of the shadows.

"You'll adapt to it," she said. "If you are indeed to live in service to the Underworld, you will learn to shadow jump in order to heed the call of the souls, preventing them from becoming rogues."

She looked over at him when he said nothing in response, only to find that he was barely listening. He looked over the realm, his eyes wide in fascination.

"Holy shit," Devon muttered, mindlessly stepping forward.

She followed his line of sight to the gates, the two monumental stone structures that stood between the living and the dead, standing sentry to the Underworld. A long stone wall, that looked well over twenty feet tall, framed the gates and fenced in the Underworld.

"We are not of the mortal realm or Earth, really, but I suppose the most mortal understanding would be that we are a pocket of the human world. One with an infinite amount of space to hold the dead of thousands of generations.

"The veil you crossed is what holds our world from the living, so there are no dead escaping here. History may have led you to believe that we are underground, but that is only because you must follow the river beneath the surface to access the portal to our world."

His eyes followed her description, taking in each area she pointed out.

"There are two large openings where the river flows from above, creating access points to the underground from the mortal realm. We call it the River Styx, and as you know, it takes you to the main gate."

As she finished speaking, she watched his eyes move over the river, as it curved around a rocky corner to the gates. From where they stood, the gates sat atop a hill, the long stone wall reaching out as far as one could see on either side of the gates. From the gates, paths made of cobble stone led down into the Underworld. There were two points in the wall that allowed the Styx to branch off into various rivers beneath it. The water flowing more sedately as the rivers and paths crawled through the Underworld.

"Should a very much alive person follow the river, they may only find caverns. If they were to die there, this place would show itself."

"The sun... the moon... It seems like a whole other planet. How are they different if we are only in a pocket of Earth?" Devon asked, seeming to understand, and moving the conversation forward.

"Not a true planet, but a rift opened by Tartarus to create a pocket for the dead to still be able to access from Earth. That is the true sun, but it as you see it through the veil," she explained.

"As Goddesses," she started, changing the subject to continue with the tour. "We make our oaths on the River Styx, so it does have another purpose aside from transporting souls. Cerberus is behind the gate and keeps souls from escaping the Underworld. No one can leave without my say." Persephone pointed to a building, or pavilion, right inside of the gates. It looked like a Parthenon from ancient Greece. "The judgment hall. They determine where you end up in the Underworld.

There are three judges, almost worse than the Moirai, with their nonsense. Blind and prone to ramble," she muttered. "They choose from the three parts of the kingdom as to where a soul spends eternity. An area for people who are not necessarily good, but not truly evil, that we call the Asphodel Meadows."

Devon looked at where she pointed to see several fields where people worked the land. They seemed just to be existing but not completely unhappy.

"The Fields of Punishment that my Furies, whom I will introduce you to in time, especially enjoy working." She pointed to the fields that were north of the Asphodel Meadows. The fields were filled with gore, torture, and bloody chaos. What looked like the human's idea of demons tortured the souls, the screams not audible from where they were standing, but yet another veil covered it so that it did not disturb those living around the Fields of Punishment.

"They each conduct a punishment fit for the crimes the person committed in life. A person murders people in the mortal realm, then the murderer is to have the same done to him for eternity by one of the Furies. They each have their own sins they've divided between them to punish. No mercy on the souls whose crimes overlap between two of the Furies."

She could see from his face that the Fields of Punishment turned his stomach, his knuckles turning white as he clenched his hands into fists.

Sometimes she had to reassure herself that the people there were being punished according to the crimes they committed in life. The Furies could be a little too enthusiastic when a new soul came in.

Still, it was a lot to take in even for her sometimes, even as someone who spent eras seeing it. Devon might've been a seasoned mercenary, but he had only been here less than a day.

"That's where I belong," he said, so quietly she barely heard him. Devon stared hard at the fields, his fist turning white from clenching his hands into fists.

Persephone watched his eyes flicker a bright green for a moment, the glow dying down just as fast as it had appeared.

She turned back to the fields, away from his morose stare. Unsure of how to approach this with him, she found that the truth was all that she could offer him.

"Only the judges know what would have been," Persephone whispered. "But I do not believe you deserve such a fate."

She watched his profile out of the corner of her eye and waited to see if he accepted her words as truth.

"So," Devon said, clearing his throat. "That's where the seriously evil ones go. What mortals think of as their hell?"

"No," she said as her voice iced over.

Devon turned to look at her, taking in her tone and its abrupt change.

"Those truly evil go to Tartarus." She sighed without making eye contact with him, taking in what looked like a hill of rocks in the middle of a vast desert. The barren fields around it with bones sticking up from the sand.

Knowing what he would ask next, she pulled him into a shadow jump before the words could leave his lips. Moments later, they stood not on a gentle hill, but on an outcropping of boulders.

She didn't really see the rocks, their dark and forbidding edges. Instead, she saw the memories of what had led to her father being trapped below. Trapped in a world that was exactly what Devon would think of as hell.

The pain, the blood, the fear, all more for her sisters than herself. Screaming for them to run as her father, her own flesh and blood, cut her down. The man she trusted to care for them, for her mother and her sisters, turned on them when he knew they held nothing but love and loyalty towards him.

She could still hear Hera's screams as she yelled to the heavens for someone to stop her father.

Persephone blinked and cleared her mind. Devon took in their new location from beside her, distracted from noticing her silence. Now was not the time to conjure the memories and spirits that belonged to another, older world.

Beneath where they stood was a hellish pit of flames and evil. The only entrance was through the gate that was buried under the boulders. A gate that required the blood of the guardian to open.

The River of Phlegethon ran alongside them, the dividing line between what was Tartarus and the rest of the Underworld. The Phlegethon was quite literally a river surrounded by flames, the black sand of the shore a never ceasing fire to welcome the newest members to Tartarus.

Between them and the river of fire was the boneyard. Never named, just simply referred to what it was: a boneyard. Chained souls rummaged through the bones, cast-off from the Fields of Punishment. Those chalk-white fragments had belonged to the mortal bodies of souls whose crimes warranted more than just evisceration in the Fields of Punishment. They were damned to walk past their decaying mortal flesh as they entered Tartarus, as it was the ultimate offense to have the mortal body kept in the Underworld and not buried above by loved ones.

Cast-offs to the boneyard were rare, as it took someone doing something so vile and evil that Tartarus was not enough.

She watched two souls, chains clanking as they stumbled about, looking for something that only they could see. These souls were at their search, day and night, never ceasing, and only ever found old bones for their effort.

"This is Tartarus," she stated, attempting to keep her voice steady, but folded her arms around herself to ward off the feeling of doom coming from the solitary gate.

Devon shuffled hesitantly. "And it's like hell?" he asked. "Where the evil is really punished? With eternal fire and everything?"

Persephone almost laughed, but it would have been an empty one. How humans craved the idea of eternal damnation. What comfort it gave them.

"It's not punishment as much as it is a prison," she told him. "The inhabitants of Tartarus can never be free, never released. It is the only place in any realm that can contain forces so evil that, if released, their reign over the world would be an unending apocalypse."

Like her father.

***

Persephone shook her head, seeming to dislodge a dark thought. Her expression had changed when they'd arrived at Tartarus. She became more serious and troubled. Devon could swear he even picked up a hint of fragility, but he didn't think it could be possible for this Goddess to feel even an ounce of mortal weakness.

She turned away from Tartarus and held out her hand. "I have one last thing to show you."

He took her hand quickly, more than ready to leave the awful place. No matter how much Persephone said the place wasn't hell as he knew it, his instincts told him nothing but fiery perdition waited for any being in that pit.

They landed in a bustling village full of life, which was not something Devon had expected to see here in the Underworld. There were small buildings made of stone, cobble streets that were lit with gas lamps, and storefronts that reminded him of the older villages in Germania. An open-air market lined the alleyway near them, between two buildings.

People, dressed in clothing that seemed to be centuries of fashion and culture merged together. They socialized and moved about as they laughed and caught up with their neighbors. They all radiated a happiness Devon had not felt in so long, and their blissful state was catching. He felt his shoulders relax at the joyful atmosphere around him.

"This is Elysium, where the people who have led noble lives go. They can choose to be reborn or stay here. Should each one of their reincarnated lives be noble, they would go on to the Isles of the Blessed." Persephone touched his shoulder as the shadows moved them to another part of the realm. To an island that looked to have been pulled straight from a dream. A literal paradise.

Waterfalls, lush forest, and though Devon could see no one, he knew they must live a life that their mortal souls would've never even had the capacity to dream of.

"Do they also not remember their lives? Like the ones from the Asphodel Fields?" he asked as he stepped forward to get a better look. Devon was in awe of the beauty of the island, which could've been easily mistaken with the mythical garden of Eden from the Christian religion.

"No, none of the souls do. They all take a sip of water from the River Lethe, and all their mortal memories are gone," Persephone explained.

They remained quiet as they took in the magical place.

"I won't be here, live here," he surmised.

"Correct."

He looked to her. "Why did you take me here?" he asked. To bring him here to show him beauty that he would be denied.

A wistful expression lightened her features, and instead of stunningly beautiful, she became heartbreaking.

"Because I wanted to show you that there is more to this place than sadness and cruelty."

CHAPTER 9

Devon knelt in the sand and his hands clenched into fists, the grains of sand falling through his fingers.

Failed.

He had failed. He had failed all of them.

Why was he always the one left standing? Why was he not killed in battle with his brothers in arms? His survival must mean a slight against his Gods. How had he angered them to not let him die in battle, die honorably?

He opened his eyes at the sound of a sword being unsheathed. Looking up, he saw a large figure blotting out the sun, the surrounding light so bright that he couldn't make out the features of the person's face.

Devon could only close his eyes, not wanting to see what happened next, and felt weak. He had only moments ago lamented over his failure to die on the battlefield yet could not look death in the eyes.

"Open your eyes," the man growled, his voice not human at all. "You will face me."

Devon swallowed, gathering his wits before he opened his eyes. The figure held the tip of his sword to Devon's neck. He could see nothing but eyes glowing gold against the shadowy planes of the person's hidden face.

"You've nowhere to run any longer. I am older than time itself and I will find you. Every. Single. Time." The faceless warrior ran his sword through Devon's neck, the death immediate. Devon never felt the blade, it was far too fast.

A quick death; more than he deserved.

His eyes were open, his body unmoving, but he could see his soul leaving his corpse.

Could see his killer stepped forward, where the essence of Devon stood over his mortal flesh.

The warrior threw his sword to the side, an afterthought, before grabbing the shoulders of Devon's soul, as if he were still alive.

As sudden as his death, he was the essence of himself. Looking out from his soul's eyes as he watched his mortal body scatter in the wind.

He turned to face the warrior, only to find him still faceless with glowing eyes. Eyes that screamed at Devon that he was far more powerful than anyone could ever fathom.

The man's hands clamped down on Devon and he felt himself being pulled into the man. He knew, somehow, what was happening to him.

"No!" Devon yelled, struggling to free himself as the shadows that made up the man dissipated and began to wrap around him. He could feel the tug of his soul, himself, as he was pulled. He knew he was heading to the Underworld now.

He was being reaped by his murderer.

CHAPTER 10

Devon shot up in his bed, taking in the room around him.

The replicant of his old cabin.

Shutting his eyes in relief, he ran his hands over his face.

Unable to stay in bed a moment longer, the adrenaline from his dream still running high, he threw on his clothes. He had to get out of his room and out of the castle. He needed some air, and he needed to be alone in this new place without someone looking over his shoulder. He needed a moment to himself to think.

Moving down the stairs at a clipped pace, the shadowy servants he had heard referred to as "Reevkas" began to manifest at the bottom of the stairs.

Before they could take their human forms, he ran through them, dispersing them back to the shadows. He grabbed the large, gothic handles to the doors that stood between him and the Underworld and pulled.

Not bothering to shut the doors behind him, he started running. He needed space, having not had a moment truly to himself since he came to the Underworld.

As he ran, he notice how he didn't seem to tire and he hadn't really started to sweat. He knew he was in shape, always working to keep his body in top form since that could mean life or death, but this wasn't even human.

He stopped and turned back to look at the castle, to gauge the distance he had run. It looked like he had gone at least 5 miles, and he wasn't even slightly out of breath.

Putting his hands on his hips, he turned and looked at the surrounding space. He was on a cobblestone road between two pieces of farmland. It looked like an old country road in his native Germania.

Feeling something heavy land on his psyche, he fell to the side of the road. Sitting, he put his elbows on his knees, his head in his hands.

This was forever. He couldn't even fathom that. That he could exist for more than a hundred years, but forever? Never ending. Knowing he would never die. That he would see the rise and fall of empires, watch the world destroy and rebuild itself time and time again, and he would be exactly as he was now.

He wouldn't grow old if the state of Persephone and Thanatos was any indication. He would always be... this.

He felt a scream bubble up his throat before it poured out of him. He rolled to his hands and knees, punching the ground as he yelled again and again before collapsing.

Nothing changed.

Even his knuckles only bled for a moment before they healed, and in his anger he busted the flesh open again.

This was it. This was immortality.

Rolling onto his back, he looked up at the sky. The purplish moon hung above him, taunting him with the memory of the moon he had gazed up at when he was unable to sleep as a mortal.

A tear slipped down his cheek and rolled back into his hairline. He felt fear. Fear at the unknown, fear at not understanding what eternal life could truly mean. In theory, he understood what it meant, but to really live for eternity?

He closed his eyes and let the tears fall for the Devon who died in that horrible motel room and the Devon who was raised from the dead. He mourned himself.

Most of all, he feared what he would become.

CHAPTER 11

Persephone stood at the window of her office, looking out over Halcyon. The city was asleep, but some lights twinkled against the backdrop of the nighttime sky.

She had come to finish up some leftover contracts but found she could not focus on anything but Devon.

Looking away from the sleeping city, she turned back to her desk. It was simple, a large desk, organized and with few items, as she hated clutter. Two black chairs for guests, and an executive bathroom with all the modern amenities.

Nothing but black and white. Clean and organized. Plain.

She was certainly lacking in the creative decorating department. She needed color. She needed life in this tired and sterile place.

Unable to stand staring at the four walls of her office any longer, Persephone called her shadows. As they heeded her call, she thought of the one place she could go outside of the mortal realm where there was always color and life.

Before she could blink, she was standing in front of the little cottage lost to the imposing Castle behind it. The cottage was very... *quaint*. Persephone would describe it as that at least. Yellow and blue, different herbs growing in containers around it, and a pack of barking dogs standing there to greet Persephone.

"Back!" Hecate yelled as she opened her cottage door, her eyes wide at seeing Persephone there at her doorstep. "Well, come on in. Ignore my furry army."

She moved from the door as the dogs parted to let Persephone through. A few nudging her as she passed, earning a tiny pat on the head as she walked through them to her friend's domicile.

Shutting the door behind them, Hecate looked out at her pack through the tiny window in the door. The dogs were her family as much as Persephone and Thanatos were. They were loyal, loving, and would protect Hecate in any and all situations. Much like Cerberus. Although, Cerberus held a more human like intelligence than animal.

"What brings you to my humble home?" Hecate asked as she moved from the door to the kitchen, making tea for Persephone before she even asked. The woman loved to mess with herbs, whether for tea or witchcraft.

"I am unable to grasp what is happening," Persephone started. "Try as I might, everything the Moirai has done so far is absolutely baffling. Could they not have graced the Underworld with another Reaper without using me? Why even send me another Reaper? Why this particular soul?"

Persephone pulled a kitchen chair out and fell into it, mentally exhausted from all the questions in her mind.

Hecate turned from where she had put the kettle on the stove and leaned back against the counter. Her sweater proclaimed that she was a 'winey witch'.

"Your shirt is misspelled," Persephone informed her friend. Hecate only smirked.

"No, it's not."

Persephone rolled her eyes before she looked out the cottage window.

Herbs grew outside, aligned in rows, potted and flourishing. Nothing could truly grow anywhere in the Underworld except Elysium.

She envied her friend's little garden. The life that Hecate cultivated with her hands, even if it was not in the ground. She'd found a way to bring it forth.

"Let me see what I can find out," Hecate broke Persephone's thoughts with the offer.

"I'm sorry?"

"Devon. Let me look into what the Moirai have up their sleeve. It may lead to nothing since they hold their cards close to their chest, but it is worth a shot."

The kettle whistled and Hecate turned back to the stove to prepare the teacups. Persephone could think of no reason not to let Hecate look into why the Moirai would create an immortal from a mortal soul.

Hecate sat the cup of tea in front of Persephone before she settled herself in the seat across from her.

"You think you can ascertain the Moirai, of all deities, and their schemes?" Persephone let out a little laugh before blowing on the hot liquid in her cup.

Hecate returned her smile and arched an eyebrow.

"You question my sleuth skills, my Goddess? I'll have you know that Thanatos and I keep a very, very close eye on anything Underworld related. As I mentioned when Devon first ate the seeds, I knew his soul was the one that called to yours."

"Touché." Persephone clinked her teacup against Hecate's. Hecate was in fact able to bring information to Persephone that seemed impossible to know otherwise.

"Yes." Persephone placed her teacup down on the lemon-yellow tablecloth. "Let's figure out exactly what their little game is."

Hecate paused for a moment, obviously reworking her thoughts on how to tell Persephone something she most likely did not want to hear.

"From what I can sense, and what I can see with my eyes, you two were meant for a path that ends with you together. A soul does not call to another for the simple pleasure of hearing it speak. It calls because the soul sings to it, calls to them, and finds a home in their embrace."

Shadows swirled around the room, covering them in darkness before Thanatos appeared in front of them, blocking the heat of the fire.

"Yet another girls' night where you failed to invite me," he stated with his hands on his hips.

"Your invitation was lost in the mail," Hecate replied with a saccharine smile.

"Yes, just like all the other invitations over the past hundred years. You two are starting to give a guy a complex," he asserted before moving to sit in one of the empty chairs at the table.

"I was eavesdropping at the door just now," Thanatos started.

"Of course, you were." Hecate interrupted, rolling her eyes.

"And I can keep an ear to the ground, too. Help out moonlight over here." He moved his hand in reference to Hecate. "Gotta say though, the man, regardless of why he is here, is tossing all your hormones around like glitter. You're busy trying to figure out how to deal with him and the feelings he's giving you in your nether regions. Not something I saw coming."

Both Hecate and Persephone stared at him, their eyes wide. Throwing his arm around the back of Persephone's chair, Thanatos crossed his ankle at his knee, the picture of male masculinity.

"You wonder why the invites are consistently lost, huh?" Hecate murmured, taking a sip of her tea.

"Yes, we will address that later." He played with the ends of Persephone's hair. "My point is, you've never been bound to anyone in such a way as this, and you are in new territory. I've yet to connect with a soul in such a way, and I imagine I'd be scared out of my mind. But I wouldn't walk away. This is something precious, and I think a nice chat between you two will help illuminate how incredibly astute I am on this subject."

"For one second there, I considered apologizing for never inviting you, but the end of your inspirational speech reminded me of why." Hecate let out a little sigh.

"I knew it." Thanatos shook his head, his hands going over his heart. "Well, ladies, a soul calls to me." He stood and turned his back to them as the black robe moved over his shirt and jeans and his body went skeletal. "Should you need further assistance and wisdom, I am but a shadow jump away." His shadows moved around him quickly before he disappeared.

"He was surprisingly more obnoxious before you came around." Hecate squeezed Persephone's arm. "And not in the cute and lovable way he is now. Whether you like it or not, my friend, you bring out the good in people. This you will do for Devon as well. Mark my words."

CHAPTER 12

Devon found himself summoned to Thanatos residence for training. By summoned, he meant that Thanatos shadow jumped him as he was taking his first bite of breakfast.

He landed in a heap on the floor of what looked like a dojo and jumped back up, still holding his fork full of eggs.

"Welcome to Apparition Station! Reaper Manor! Death…"

"Damn it, Thanatos! I was eating!" Devon yelled at the showboat of a Reaper as he threw his fork at him.

Thanatos only laughed as the fork disappeared into shadows before it could reach him.

"I've let you play around the castle and cry in the road enough." Devon raised his eyebrows at Thanatos when the specter of Death admitted to watching him.

"But," Thanatos continued, "now it is time to work. I want to see what the new Reaper is made of!"

The smirking Thanatos rubbed his hands together.

"Man, you're an asshole," Devon muttered under his breath.

Thanatos started to bounce on the balls of his feet like a boxer readying himself for a fight.

"Not the first to tell me that, not the last. Now, if you're done crying, we can figure out how to train you to be the second-best Reaper who ever lived."

Shaking his head, Devon knew it was useless to argue with the deranged man.

"Fine." Devon threw up his hands. "Let's start. You've already ruined my day and it's only begun."

"That's the spirit!" Thanatos stopped moving around like a boxer and stepped forward to where he was face to face with Devon, a few inches apart. "What do you feel?"

"Awkward and homicidal. Back up a step, would you?"

"Perfect. You are uncomfortable with my closeness. Do you fear me?"

Devon kept an eye on him as Thanatos walked around him, sizing him up. "Not anymore. I did, but now I just find you incredibly annoying."

Before Devon could see Thanatos move, he felt the pain of Thanatos' fist hitting his jaw. It was hard enough to knock Devon back several steps, and he was only just able to keep himself from falling.

"Change." Thanatos demanded, his voice no longer joking.

"You psychopath! Why would you do that? Change what?" Devon asked, bewildered and angry. He held his jaw as Thanatos squinted his eyes. Devon felt some kind of force pulling at him, like Thanatos was inside his chest and moving his organs around. If Thanatos wasn't standingright across from him with his arms crossed, Devon might have thought the Reaper was trying to rip his heart out.

"I am trying to pull at your Reaper powers, to help you take on your Reaper persona. You need to be in Reaper form in the beginning to feel the souls before you acclimate and are able to sensethem in any form."

Devon felt the pull again, stronger, almost painful now. It was beginning to overshadow the pain in his jaw.

"Stop…" Devon muttered through clenched teeth, closing his eyes as he tried to focus on something else.

"No, your magic is stubborn like you. I have no idea why…"

The pain was intense and now he was sure Thanatos was trying to kill him.

"I can hit you again if that will provoke you to change or I can continue pulling your magic with mine. It gets a lot worse, believe me…"

Devon felt something in him snap, like a rubber band breaking and the tension was gone.

His eyes flew open and he looked to see Thanatos, standing back up from being knocked down, and dusting himself off.

"Ah, there you go," Thanatos replied, his smile that of a shark scenting blood.

***

After a day of training with Thanatos, Devon was in need of a strong drink.

He raised his hand to grab the attention of a nearby Reevka, who appeared in solid form as an older, gentlemanly butler.

He realized he didn't know if it was actually appropriate to call them Reevka or not. If there even was a politically correct way to address them.

Lowering his hand, he watched as the Reevka caught the movement and made his way to Devon, thankfully not turning into a moving shadow.

"What can I do for you, my Lord?" the Reevka asked in a polite and proper accent.

"It's Devon," he stressed, a bit firmer than he had meant to be. The Reevka raised his eyebrow in question. "My name is Devon. I am not a Lord. Sorry, that was probably rude. I just really need a drink and absolutely no additional information or weird things to happen as I walk to my room."

Devon was blabbering like an idiot, his mouth running away as his brain was far too tired and overwhelmed to rally his systems back under his control.

"Any preference, sir?" the Reevka asked, his lips upturning slightly before he settled his face back into a stoic expression.

"Whatever you have that gets me in a state of not giving a shit who, what, or where I am."

The Reevka only blinked but seemed completely unruffled as he nodded his head in agreement.

"Very good, sir." The older gentleman bowed and became a cloud of shadows and smoke. The Reevka blending into the hallway's shadows and disappearing.

Devon sighed. He wondered if this would ever feel normal to him. If he would find his footing here in the Underworld. Running his hands through his hair, his habit created out of frustration through the years, he summoned the strength to walk up the stairs.

He ran through the mental map he created earlier in the day so he did not end up wandering the castle for the next five hundred years. He managed to find the room a lot easier than he thought.

He also found an almost imperceptible pull to the room. Perhaps the memories that he had pushed way down deep, seeing the only home he truly felt belonged to him again, had created a mental tether to the room. Or maybe it was more of Persephone's magic.

Right now though, he didn't care about new mysteries. He pushed into his room, thinking only of being alone. Shutting the door with his foot, he pulled off his shirt to ready himself for bed. As his hands went to the zipper of his pants, a flash of light caught his attention. It disappeared and left behind a decanter of alcohol and glass on a table between two chairs.

Like a hound on the scent, he moved to the table. Not bothering with the glass, he grabbed the decanter and took a swig as he sat down in one of the seats.

Enjoying the familiar fire of whiskey burning its way down his throat, he heard a soft knock at the door.

"Come in." He closed his eyes and leaned his head back against his chair. He knew who it was before she even said a word. Thankful that she had knocked and not just shadow jumped into his room, he opened his eyes and raised an eyebrow at her in question.

Persephone stood there plainly, not a flicker of her Goddess form appearing. Even without the crown, she managed to cast a glow. She glided to the table and lowered herself into the chair beside him. The Goddess glanced at the generous drink in his hand but didn't say a word.

"Would you like a drink, Goddess?" he asked, leaning forward to reach the glass. When she nodded, he poured her a dram and passed it over. Her pale, slim fingers grasped the glass carefully below his hand.

"I gather from the nightcap that training was educational," she said wryly.

Devon released a dry laugh, so course it could be mistaken for one of Cerberus' barks. "You can say that." He sunk deeper into the chair. "I don't know how you all do it."

"The work will get easier with time," she told him. "And don't worry if your powers aren't coming to you- "

"No," he interrupted, "I don't mean the… magic, as much as it still blows my mind that the word now applies to me." He caught her gaze, the blue eyes that had seen civilizations rise and fall. "It's the time. I don't know how you do this work, forever." He shook his head. "How am I supposed to wrap my head around immortality when I spent my entire adulthood expecting to die every day?" He laughed again. "I did die."

Persephone took a sip of her drink. "When I was young, time passed slowly," she murmured thoughtfully. "As I grew older, time compounded, and the years went by like days." Another sip. "Before I knew it, the empires I recognized had fallen, only to be replaced by others. Humans changed, but only marginally. You'll find that, in the Underworld at least, humanity seems ironically consistent." Her eyes drifted to her glass. "They always die."

"What do you do?" he asked, bristling a bit at her mental painting of humans. "While the humans die and Thanatos reaps them?"

The Goddess lifted her stare to his. "I oversee the demigods in the Underworld, hold court, arbitrate problems. My magic supports the realm," she explained, then paused. "I also govern some aspects of the human world."

Devon raised his eyebrows. "I thought you were the Queen of the Underworld."

She straightened. "I am," she agreed. "After the Great War, my sisters and I stepped in to take a more active role in the recovery of humanity, putting in place structures to prevent conflict reaching that level again." She paused. "You have heard of Cerberus Financial, yes?"

"Yes," he finally replied, stretching out the word.

"I am the head of the company," she stated.

Studying her, Devon tilted his head. She was the head of the largest financial company in the world. This seemed almost too much, and without thinking, he shook his head as if to disagree. He tried to think back to who was always mentioned in the news, though he rarely paid enough attention to the photographs in the social papers.

"I thought Korinna Porter was acting head of the company."

Persephone simply smiled.

"She is. Korinna Porter is the third generation to run Cerberus Financial since it would be odd to the world if the same person who founded it were still running it, correct?"

"Another alter ego," he murmured, shaking his head in disbelief.

"Yes."

"You trust your employees with your identity? I cannot imagine showing up looking exactly the same as your 'Great Aunt' who just died." Devon asked, shocked she would have that much faith in mortals.

She let out a laugh that caught him off guard. How fair was it that the Goddess of Death should have a sexy laugh?

Devon slumped in his chair. "Goddess, C.E.O., what else? Do you rid the city of crime at night and visit orphanages?"

"I do not actually do as much as I have in the past," she said.

"In the beginning," she continued. "It was easier for me as Persephone to be the C.E.O. and founder. However, with time humans would obviously become weary of seeing the same face and it was natural to allow the company to move on as it would if the real founder had passed on without direct heirs. Korinna is my great niece in the eyes of the human world." She swirled her drink and took another sip.

"Cerberus Financial allows me to monitor and curtail the economic extremes that allowed for the Great War to happen." She leaned back in her chair, mirroring his posture. "Even Goddesses learn from our mistakes."

"Your sisters do this, too?" He was surprised by Persephone's active role, but he was much more deeply troubled by the idea of these faceless Goddesses having such a direct hand in society.

She nodded. "Amphitrite oversees the waterways and transportation. Hera handles the government aspects."

Devon waited for her to elaborate, but she left it at that.

He took another drink. When he offered to fill her glass with a gesture of the decanter, she shook her head.

She eyed him with a thoughtful glint. "You should shadow me," she said definitively.

Devon canted his head. "Literally or figuratively?"

Her lips quirked with amusement, but she pressed them down into seriousness. "Come with me tomorrow. To Cerberus Financial. You can see how it works, the business of being an immortal." She glanced briefly at the decanter of alcohol. "Perhaps it will soothe some of your worries."

His lips twitched into a smile. Two worlds to rule, and she was concerned about him.

"That would be good." His smile stretched further. "I suppose I will call you Korinna, then, not Goddess?"

"Call me Persephone," she said, "At least when we are here. Tomorrow, you'll call me Miss. Porter." Her blue eyes danced with amusement. "We need a reason for you to come with me into meetings, follow me all day." She considered him for a moment.

"I think with your background and demeanor, security detail would make the most sense. Some upcoming mergers are not all around accepted, so people would believe I might be in need of some protection."

Devon only raised an eyebrow at her.

"Yes, that should work out just fine. I will notify my secretary tomorrow about getting you into the system with my access level." Persephone did not wait for a response and was nearly out the door before he called out to her.

"Goodnight, then, and thank you." He cleared his throat, which had gone hoarse. "Persephone."

The Goddess paused, stiffening at the doorway.

"Goodnight, Devon."

CHAPTER 13

The next morning, Devon looked over himself in the mirror at his black button-up shirt and black slacks, realizing that maybe it was time to stop looking so dark and dreary all the time. Before he could change into something less gloomy, a knock at the door stole his focus.

Before he even reached the door, he realized he could sense Persephone on the other side. That small tingle that went down his spine when she was near had become pretty damn familiar.

She was an enigma, and it angered him that she intrigued him so much.

Thoughts of her and his new life, an unending one if the Goddess' estimations were correct, had kept him up last night, tossing and turning. Part of him felt helpless that his entire existence and world view had been upended, but the other part accepted the changes. Really, his mortal life had not been great, but he had been a man in charge of his days. Now, his days yawned ahead of him and he was entirely dependent on the good will of the Goddess of the Underworld.

He needed to regain his composure, but it felt like there was some part of him he couldn't control. Like a stranger looked out through his eyes, something far more powerful than him, and that stranger recognized the Goddess.

Wanted her.

The wall he always had between himself and others was crumbling faster than he could try to rebuild it. He worried it would be a pile of dust by the end of the week.

Before he opened the door, Devon closed his eyes and focused on the feel of her power. It was pulling a sense of nostalgia from him, one that he couldn't put his finger on. As if it was some childhood memory that anchored his soul, yet the memory itself eluded him. He wondered if they might've met before because a piece of him felt she was connected to him.

Another soft knock pulled him back from his thoughts, and Devon shook his head to clear it. As he opened the door, he caught sight of blue and black smoke around her, which disappeared as he focused his eyes on trying to find her in it. He finally saw her, her appearance making him struggle for words.

She was standing there in black slacks as well, with a white button-down tucked in, the top two buttons open, showing a necklace that looked like a pomegranate and matched her earrings. Her bluish-black hair pulled back into a low, sleek ponytail and those damn heels that gave mortal men heart palpitations.

"You look nice," she commented, taking in his appearance. "Are you ready to leave?"

It was slightly intimidating that the woman before him ran the financial world, but also arousing. That was the only word he could think of when he looked at her in her business attire, standing tall, ready to make people bend to her will. She was most definitely a force of nature in her own right, Goddess or not.

A squeak of affirmation left his lips before he could stop it. Her eyebrows arched as if asking if he was okay, but he nodded before she could speak.

He forced himself to calm down. He could be around her and not have scandalous thoughts. He was a grown man, not a pre-pubescent teenager.

"Lead the way, boss." He put his hand out towards the hallway, his face stoic and unlined. He would keep his errant thoughts at bay the best he could. Remember who offered him the seeds that bound him to the Underworld for eternity.

She smiled but did not walk out the door. Instead, she held out her hand for him to grab. He took a moment to steady his mind, remember his anger and why holding her hand meant nothing.

He finally reached out and wrapped his fingers around hers. He was never an affectionate person, and his lifestyle had taught him not to trust anyone touching him unless he controlled it. Someone could always have a knife or bullet with his name on it.

But Persephone's hand, her soft and dry palm, warmed him to his soul. If he even had one of those anymore.

"We will shadow jump from here. I want you to really focus this time on the sensation at each moment of the jump, starting with when you feel the pull. I can show you things like this throughout our day when the opportunities arise. You've already shown an ability to do your own jump, so it should not take long for you to do this independently," she directed. He began to feel the pull, a slight tugging on his thoughts.

"I feel it," he told her.

She nodded. "Now, I will command the jump by visualizing the place I want to be. Shadow jumps require great detail, so create as much detail as possible in your mind of where you want to land. I will lead this time since I know where we need to go."

He saw the lightest whisper of smoke rise from the floor, moving upward over his legs.

More smoke came, increasing and becoming denser, moving higher up their bodies as if to swallow them both. He held out his free hand and watched the shadows follow the movement, wrapping around his skin and rubbing against him like a cat begging for affection. When the shadows covered them both from head to toe, the dark cloud swirled like a black tornado.

"Ready?" she asked, the smoky shadows swirling at a faster pace, picking up momentum. Staring at the smoke in fascination, he nodded. The smoke moved closer to his body and laid against his skin right before a sensation of losing balance struck him.

Before he could jerk his hand free to try to stabilize himself, the feeling vanished. The smoke faded and Devon blinked at the sudden light burning his eyes. He realized he and Persephone were standing on the sidewalk of a busy downtown metropolis. His limbs were once again heavy as if gravity were stronger here than in the Underworld.

The mortal realm.

"Welcome to Halcyon." She waved a hand around her, encompassing the city that towered above them like a behemoth. The skyscrapers dwarfed even the mountains behind it, whose peaks he could only glimpse in the empty space between the towers.

Looking around, he realized he had never been to this city before, which was interesting since he was sure he had been to every corner of the world. Or what was left of it.

It was so different from the village he had grown up in. He had to be in the city center, standing beneath a huge tower that looked like it was spiraling into the clouds. Halcyon was by far the most modern city he had ever seen in his life. A city that seemed untouched by the Great War.

He thought of the dirty, harsh cities he'd frequented as a mercenary and wondered how Halcyon could be so different–yet the same. Like all other cities, Halcyon struck him with a feeling of being smothered. Maybe it was the crowds and the metal towers. Devon found himself whirling his gaze around, looking at all the detail and life pushing through the city's metal skeleton.

Looking at everyone going about their mundane lives, Devon felt even more disconnected from them than when he lived as a mercenary. Having seen and been to the Underworld, knowing that there was, in fact, more, made everything here feel foreign. The Underworld was hardly home to him yet, but it had opened a gate to something more inside of him.

"Amazing, isn't it?" Persephone asked, watching him as he glanced around.

He wondered if he could tell her the truth. That Halcyon was beautiful, but he was more drawn to the forest behind it. The one he knew was at the bottom of the mountains he'd caught glimpses of while looking around.

"It is," he told her, hoping she would mistake his dazed tone for awe.

A childhood memory of planting crops with his father came to mind. He'd watched them grow large and healthy despite the poor season the other resettled families had experienced. Whatever his father planted always seemed to flourish in the bleakest environment, save one thing–Devon.

He wondered what his father would say if he could see him now, standing beside a Goddess in a metropolis. He wondered if his father knew anything about the power lurking in his son's mortal body.

Devon cleared his throat, as if that would clear his thoughts.

Persephone extended her hand, nearly touching his shoulder, and he fought his natural inclination to step out from her reach.

"Devon…?" Her hand dropped to her side.

He needed to focus. On Persephone. On the task at hand.

He pointed to the tower across from them. "Is this Cerberus Financial?"

A small frown flickered over her expression and she shook her head.

"No, if you don't mind a slight walk, Cerberus Financial is right around the corner."

Without another word, she turned and started to walk, not looking back to see if he would follow.

***

As they started up the steps to the front door of Cerberus Financial, Thanatos walked out with his long, almost leisurely strides. He was in his mortal form, wearing a sharp dark blue suit, his black hair cropped at the sides in the current style. His olive skin and piercing blue eyes have had mortal women falling over themselves for him for millennia.

After so many centuries together, this man had become one of Persephone's closest friends. The relationship that of a brother and sister. She trusted both him and Hecate more than most anyone else, which was why they were on the board of directors at Cerberus Financial.

The smile that crossed Thanatos' handsome face warned her that he was setting a trap for Devon, which brought her out of her musings.

Oh no, she thought.

He loved to bait and prank people.

Seeing Devon had returned to his deceptively calm demeanor, the same he had worn with perfection before, she held onto hope that Devon could handle whatever Thanatos threw in his direction.

Right before he moved in front of her, Thanatos threw her a smile, the dazzling one he'd used through the eras to woo and seduce women, and she knew right then what Thanatos had planned. She was unsure of Devon's feelings for her, good or bad, but if Thanatos had his way, they would find out in the next few minutes.

It surprised her to see Devon rise to the bait so quickly, moving closer to her, putting his hand against her lower back. Persephone tried not to show how shocked she was at him initiating contact. She looked over to him and caught the surprise on his face, too.

He had not meant to do that, she thought.

Carefully looking over to catch Thanatos' eyes, she watched the knowing smile cross his face.

It was only going to get worse from here.

Persephone raised an eyebrow that promised torture if he kept this up, only to be met with an even more sinister smile from Thanatos. Oh, he was begging for her to give him a reaction he could latch onto for the rest of the day. He would be unbearable to deal with if she did, so she kept her face neutral.

"Good morning, Dove. Devon." He nodded from her to him.

Dove.

Yup, playing his hand right off the bat. He was begging for the Fields of Punishment today.

She watched Devon narrow his eyes at the endearment, but thankfully he held his tongue. Thanatos simply winked at them both, which made her close her eyes and attempt to stifle the urge to banish him right here in public.

"You work here?" Devon asked, pulling his hand all the way back to cross his arms over his chest. The feel of uncertainty she had just felt from him disappeared as if sucked into a vacuum. He was no longer giving away any emotion for Thanatos to grab hold of and use. The two of them were like a cat and a mouse, only she wasn't sure who was the cat and who was the mouse.

"Yes, when I am not as fleshy and a bit more feathered," Thanatos replied with a huge grin.

Devon was quick. "Ah, yes," he stated blandly. "Busy guiding souls, grabbing coffee, and torturing me with your presence. I bet your days are packed to the brim." His voice was cold and formal. She had to admit, she was a little impressed by Devon's handling of Thanatos. It usually took people a few decades to navigate the Reaper's mercurial personality.

Thanatos laughed, then walked over to clap Devon on the back, promptly ignoring Devon's slight flinch.

"What has our Dove gotten you into today?" Thanatos asked.

Devon stepped back and Persephone stiffened, surprised by the pang of emptiness she felt almost immediately

The Moirai said that he would balance her… was her reaction to the distance between her and Devon also the old biddies pushing them together? She couldn't deny how she's been drawn to her warrior over the centuries, but this iteration, Devon, had only stopped looking at her with resentment that morning.

"Persephone," he growled to Thanatos, catching both of them off guard. "Her name is Persephone."

She wasn't sure why she didn't tell Devon that Thanatos only used that term to get under her skin, but she found herself intrigued by his reaction. She guessed she wanted to know how Devon was feeling too, and though she knew it was wrong, she hoped Thanatos' little game gave her something to work with in terms of his odd behavior. She'd seen billions of mortal souls, but the humans still fascinated and puzzled her. Especially this one.

"And she chose me to be her personal security," he added, edging closer to her.

An interested gleam shone in the Reaper's eyes.

Oh, he was enjoying this way too much.

"Ah, you're the new bodyguard to keep our Goddess healthy and hale. Good. You and I both will be with her all day long so I can go over both your mortal job and your Underworld job while we are here." He looked at Persephone to confirm, but she shook her head. Thanatos' head tilted in silent question.

Should she even try sending him out with Thanatos to collect a soul just so he understood the process? Would they find out what exactly his powers were by doing so? Or would that be too dangerous?

She remembered Devon's negative reaction the first time she indicated he may become a Reaper, and her stomach sank.

"Actually," Persephone replied. "I need to speak with you about that, Thanatos."

Thanatos nodded, a question mark still stamped over his features, and stepped towards Cerberus Financials' entrance. With that, the games were over and the business of the day was back on. Thanatos opened the front door for her and Devon trailed in her wake, keeping a close eye on the Reaper.

Sighing, Persephone feared she might suffocate with these two-flinging testosterone at each other all day.

CHAPTER 14

Devon stood to the side of the conference room beside the door, arms folded as he watched Persephone speak to a group of clients. He'd nicknamed them in boredom.

Grumpy, Lumpy, Dumpy, and Pervy. Not the most creative names but fitting in his observations. All of them older and graying, but Grumpy distinguished himself by communicating only through grunts and eye rolls. Lumpy was extremely overweight, his flesh attempting to escape the tight, untailored clothes. Dumpy, sitting insignificantly in the corner taking notes, looked like he hadn't met a shower or washing machine in months.

Pervy was the one that Devon kept his eyes on. The one holding his attention most, as his behavior agitated that strange place deep inside of Devon that saw Persephone as his.

The part of him he was trying his best to ignore these days.

Pervy seemed not to notice Devon watching him as he stared at Persephone. Pervy's beady eyes tracked her chest as she leaned forward to jot something down or her ass as she walked over to present something. He knew Pervy was visualizing her completely naked, and Devon found himself holding back growls he didn't even know he could make.

However, he had managed to rid Pervy of some self-confidence when he caught Devon's eye and shrank back from Devon's glare.

Persephone was amazing, in that she radiated power and authority, and loathe as he was to admit it, he could understand a tiny bit of Pervy's fascination. He just hoped he was a lot more discreet about it.

He wasn't sure how Thanatos tolerated these meetings. Thanatos just sat quietly at the other end of the table. His focus mostly trained on Persephone. Occasionally, the Reaper's dark stare would settle on Devon.

Curious.

Probing.

The playful man gone.

Devon knew plenty of men, brothers in arms, whose disposition switched between lively and deadly serious. The change usually happened when the gunfire started.

When the room emptied, he watched her take a seat at the head of the table. She didn't bother with goodbyes to Grumpy, Dumpy, Lumpy, and Pervy.

An assistant, a plain young woman, guided them through the door. As Pervy passed by Devon, he tripped over his feet and stumbled into the hall.

From the corner of his eye, Devon caught sight of a forest green haze following Pervy from the room. He blinked, and it didn't disappear.

Devon looked around to see if anyone else could see the flicker of color. No one watched Pervy, the potential hallucination trailing him, but Devon caught Thanatos' eyes. The Reaper was watching him. Did he see Devon's interaction with the perv?

He took a deep breath. As he calmed, the green blur dissipated. Was he hallucinating?

"Devon," Persephone hissed. Her pale, slender hand suddenly grasped his wrist, and he jerked his gaze to her.

Her eyebrows lifted, and she canted her head toward an incoming group of people. The next meeting.

"Careful around the humans." She warned.

Careful?

Devon's head snapped to look at her, but Persephone was already accepting the next meeting's attendants. It was his power. The deep green mist around him had been his power, the very thing that made him immortal.

He glanced at Thanatos, who leaned back in his seat as his eyes flicked between Devon and Persephone.

Devon sighed and made himself comfortable against the wall again. He allowed himself to be distracted by watching her work. He was fascinated by her body language, the steepling of her fingers or a tilt of her head, and the power she wielded over the room with any slight movement or glance. Here was the woman who had ruled the Underworld, and apparently parts of the human world, for thousands of years in her natural element.

Some of the men tried to posture and act like they were the ones in charge, but they only met her cool disregard. When one of them spoke out of turn, she easily put them in their place with a simple raise of her eyebrow. How was this the person, this predator, the same woman who sat and sipped whiskey with him? And even more, how was she the same Goddess who plucked his childhood home from his mind and showed him a new world?

As interested as he was in detangling Persephone's personas, he lost attention as the meeting droned on. Devon imagined Thanatos was similarly distracted.

He could still feel Thanatos' thoughtful stare on him throughout the meeting. Perhaps he was figuring out ways to make Devon uncomfortable, as he had the entire day so far.

The leaning into her during lunch (Devon tried not to stab him with a knife), and the secret looks when a client said something that had obviously brought some internal joke to the surface (flipping a table during a business meeting was most likely prohibited, but he came close to doing it). Devon came the closest to losing his cool when Thanatos had leaned in dangerously close to whisper something in her ear and pulled back to give her a too-big smile. He could not kill Death, but he could probably give him a world of pain. He knew if Thanatos kept this up, it would happen very soon. Very, very soon.

Devon was mad at Thanatos for his behavior. Mad at himself for not controlling whatever it was inside him that begged to fight anyone who even glanced at Persephone.

While lost in his thoughts, Persephone finished the meeting. The group mindlessly nodded and agreed to whatever was said. Shaking hands, making after-work plans, all happy with the conclusion.

The woman introduced to him that morning as an assistant to

"Korinna" looked thrilled by the closing of the meeting. As the last member left, the young woman praised Persephone and promised to ready the contracts by the next morning.

The assistant headed to the door with an armful of papers. As she passed Devon, she moved close enough to brush his arm, and he caught her eye.

He returned a little smirk of his own. As he watched her leave and disappear down the hallway, he glimpsed back at Persephone's face from the corner of his eye.

He wondered if she even realized she had narrowed her eyes at the assistant.

When he faced her again, Persephone quickly angled her face away from him, leaving him to wonder what all was going through her head. Was it the same territorial feeling he had felt when Pervy watched her like she was his next meal?

She silently finished putting her notes away. Her back jerked as she shoved the papers into her case and shouldered the bag a bit too aggressively.

Thanatos stood, drawing Devon and Persephone's attention. "Do you have anything else planned at Cerberus today?" he asked Persephone, his tone serious.

Persephone looked slightly bewildered before answering, "No."

"Good." Thanatos nodded. "We're going to train."

Persephone started towards the door. "Excellent. I'll finalize some things while you-"

"You'll be joining us," Thanatos interrupted.

Persephone halted.

"If you don't mind," Thanatos added with a smile.

"Why?" Devon interjected. His instincts stirred. The Reaper was up to something.

"Our Goddess here can help facilitate your magic," Thanatos answered. "And it was her seeds that gave you power and immortality to begin with," he added, "so it stands to reason that your magic will respond to her presence.

"He's right," Persephone agreed. "It's worth a try."

Devon couldn't tell her no, say that he didn't want Persephone there to see him struggle.

"Alright then," he agreed.

Persephone nodded and raised her eyebrows at Thanatos. "The basement?"Devon straightened. "What's in the basement?"

"There's a warded floor below ground, known only to the immortals who pass through the tower," Thanatos said. "We can train there without causing any disruptions."

Decision made then. Persephone led them out of the room. As they turned into the bank of elevators, Devon put his hand to Persephone's back. He guided her through the elevator doors, telling himself he only did it to get them the hell out of there.

Devon's back burned from the force of Thanatos' stare. He wondered how honest he was being with himself regarding the Goddess.

It seemed as if Thanatos already knew that answer.

CHAPTER 15

Using her access card, Persephone pushed the button for the basement, the men at her back. She could feel the tension rolling off Devon, and the smugness saturating the air from Thanatos.

What was Thanatos up to now?

The ding of the elevator and the doors opening up to the basement pushed her out of her thoughts and into the cement room. It held just that, cement walls and floors, some fluorescent lighting. Nothing else.

It was a place to put people having issues containing their power… or those who refused to even try in the first place. It was the perfect place to try out Devon's powers. Thanatos was correct in that regard.

She stepped aside for the men to pass. She was unsure of what she would be doing, having never trained a Reaper herself. Thanatos was around before she took over the Underworld.

Devon moved to the center of the room and Thanatos moved next to her, running his arm across her back and around her waist. Surprised at Thanatos' action, she looked up at the man, who simply winked at her.

She cut her eyes to Devon, who watched Thanatos like a hawk. His eyes were locked on the hand at Persephone's side. She tried to not roll her eyes. Thanatos had unusual methods for training.

"What? No punch for me today?" Devon asked, his eyes now narrowed at Thanatos. She could feel the anger radiating from Devon and hoped Thanatos knew what he was doing.

"Punch?" she asked, but the only answer she received was Thanatos pulling her closer to his side and whispering into her ear, "Just roll with it."

Even if she was not attracted to Thanatos in that way, the feel of his breath across the shell of her ear made her shiver. When she turned to look at Thanatos, his face was abruptly close, barely an inch away from hers.

She yanked away from Thanatos as a green light flashed in the room. One moment Devon was six feet away- and the next, the green light appeared between her and Thanatos as Devon shoved him away from Persephone.

Her hand flew to her mouth as she looked at Devon's back heaving with anger. He hadn't noticed yet what he had done. He was running off of his anger... his jealously... and couldn't see past it.

"Green, huh?" Thanatos laughed as he dusted himself off and moved to Persephone's line of sight, but not between her and Devon. She saw Devon's shoulders stiffen once he realized he had moved.

That he had shadow jumped.

Devon turned to look at her, his eyes wide and panicked as she took his hands in hers.

"It's okay. That was a shadow jump, although the green light is new, but it's normal. All of this is normal," she soothed. Devon's power was leaking now that the dam had cracked.

She needed to calm him before it burst.

She didn't get the chance before Thanatos hit her with a blast of power, knocking her back a few feet. Her head snapped up and her vision darkened as her eyes went black. In her Goddess form, she could see Thanatos and Devon's souls as she righted herself. Thanatos stood like nothing happened, staring at Devon. As if he hadn't just blasted Persephone back.

Devon looked between Thanatos and Persephone, confusion marring his brow.

Thanatos shook his head, and in a split second, shadow jumped to Persephone as he put his hands around her throat. She seethed and called her shadows to fight against Thanatos' own darkness. In this place, she couldn't call her other powers, just what she held inside of her. She couldn't call to the dead to do her bidding; they wouldn't hear her through the ward.

Her nails sharpened and turned black as they dug into Thanatos' wrists, his hold loosening as she began to burn him with her flames.

He smiled apologetically, but her eyes still blackened with magical rage.

Suddenly, Thanatos was gone, replaced by a pure green fire that blinded her. She shook her head and waited for her vision to clear.

When her sight returned from the blinding white, Thanatos was on the ground, a good ten feet away and unconscious. Turning, she caught sight of Devon, or at least he looked like Devon.

The man before her was covered in deep emerald flames, his eyes glowing the brightest green. He — it — *Devon* turned slowly, looking from Thanatos to her.

She couldn't move to him, her shock holding her still.

"It's been too long, Goddess," was all Devon said in a voice that wasn't his own before he collapsed to a heap on the floor, as unconscious as the Reaper himself.

***

"What in the fates did Devon hit him with?" Hecate asked as she attended to the unconscious Reaper laying across one of the couches in the castle study. It had been a job to shadow jump two unconscious men to the Underworld after calling Hecate to help heal Thanatos with her magic. She couldn't have her Reaper out for too long. Souls would still call. Still need to be guided. Persephone sat beside Devon, brushing the hair away from his brow and willing him to wake.

Glancing up at Hecate's question, she opened her mouth to answer, but was interrupted by Thanatos letting out a low growl.

"What in the fates did that asshole do to me?" he grumbled, attempting to sit up, but Hecate pushed him back down.

"He kicked your ass and I wasn't there to see it. It would've made my day, but alas, here I sit to help heal your head and ego." Hecate let a sickly sweet smile cross her face as Thanatos scowled at her. Thanatos pushed her hands away and sat up, wincing.

His eyes cut to Persephone's and widened.

"Did he really call Godfire?" he asked, going still. Hecate gasped and jumped up from Thanatos' side. Her hand went over her mouth as she crept closer to Devon, staring at him like he was a new, unknown creature.

"Are you certain?" Hecate whispered behind her hand. "There is no way in fates that is possible—"

Devon shot up from the couch with a hoarse shout, his chest heaving with exertion and his face sweaty as if he had just run a marathon. Something that was not the reaction an immortal would have when running. No, this was different.

"What happened?" he yelled. His panicked eyes flew to each person in the room until he settled on Persephone. She knelt next to him and carefully grasped his hands in hers.

"Good news, I do not believe you are a Reaper after all," she murmured. She attempted to smile, but it felt stiff. Devon's expression dropped from panic to confusion. She ran her hands over his, trying to think of what to say, of how to explain it all.

Thunder rolled in the Underworld and Persephone stilled.

"Oh, no," Thanatos groaned from across the room.

Persephone looked up and clashed gazes with Hecate. Her silver eyes rounded.

Devon squirmed beside her. "What's wrong?"

Another peal of thunder rumbled through the realm. Thunder in the Underworld only meant one thing.

"My sisters are here."

CHAPTER 16

Devon stood from the couch with everyone else in the room. He was unsure what was happening, but reading the room told him it was most likely not going to be a fun treat for surviving Thanatos' training.

A Reevka opened the double doors to the study and a beautiful woman with golden blonde hair walked in wearing a white pantsuit and gold jewelry. She was followed by a no less beautiful woman with long auburn hair and turquoise eyes, wearing a flowery sun dress and sandals.

The air shifted, tensed.

Electricity moved violently over the blonde woman's clenched fist. Both of the women stared at Devon, one with anger and one with curiosity.

"Hera. Amphitrite." Persephone stepped between her sisters and Devon. This only made the blonde woman's eyes narrow further. Devon was pretty sure Persephone had just painted an even bigger target on him with that action.

He sidled closer to Persephone. Catching Thanatos' eyes, he caught a look of respect on the Reaper's face.

That did nothing to help ease Devon's anxiety.

"This is Devon, we were just finishing Reaper training—"

"He is no Reaper," the blonde woman stated, cutting off Persephone as she strode even closer, stopping just a step away from him. She assessed him keenly, her eyes glowing pure gold.

"We were under the impression he *was*, Hera," Persephone growled at her sister. Wisps of her shadows flicked around her in warning.

"Well," Hera looked from Persephone to him. "What impression do you have now? Would you like me to tell you what I felt, dear sister?"

Hera's head tilted, her eyes taking in every inch of his face. Uncertainty twisted in Devon's chest. All he knew was that he needed to keep Persephone safe, even from her own sisters as Hera paced around them with slow, predatory steps, looking them up and down. She paused in front of Persephone, hovering close to her shoulder.

A look of discomfort crossed Persephone's face.

"Get out of my head, Hera," Persephone demanded roughly, rounding on her sister.

Hera stopped her examination and, from the relief on Persephone's face, delving into Persephone's head as well.

Everyone stood with bated breath, silently waiting on what this powerful woman in front of them would do. What she knew.

"I felt," Hera stated slowly, opening her electrified hands. Persephone tensed next to him. "A God awakening."

Before anyone could respond, Hera clapped her hands together, and the room went white.

***

Another forced jump. Persephone was ready to murder her sister. Righting herself, she realized they were no longer in the study — they were standing before the Moirai.

A very pleased looking Moirai.

A very angry looking Hera stood in front of the Moirai, facing off with them while her, Devon, and Amphitrite got their bearings.

"Oh, Hera! How sweet of you to visit us little old biddies!" Clothos gleefully greeted as the other Moirai sisters chittered enthusiastically.

Persephone knew her sister was not truly Hera right now, but the Goddess. She *also* knew her power could level the building if the Moirai wards hadn't dampened it. Previous errors in judgment had shown her to be powerful enough to bring down entire cities should she become enraged enough. Even still, diminished power sparked around Hera.

"What have you post-menopausal hags done now?" Hera demanded through clenched teeth.

Her presence seemed to swallow everything around her, making the air go static.

The Moirai chittered, which only managed to enrage Hera further. Upon seeing her sister losing herself to her rage, Persephone stepped forward.

"How? Why?" Persephone asked the Moirai. She did not demand as a Goddess might have but looked to them for actual guidance. She had held onto her calm demeanor while caring for Devon, but now that they stood before the Moirai, Persephone was desperate for answers. The man she'd madeimmortal was undeniably more.

Devon stepped up to her side, catching Clothos' attention.

"You were one of my favorite strings!" she gushed, beaming at him with the wide eyes of an adoring fan.

"Uh, thanks?" he muttered, staring at the Moirai in confusion.

"Not now, Clothos," Persephone snapped and tightened her hands into fists. "Answer me."

Devon put his hand over one of her fists, giving it a squeeze, and the Moirai collectively purred at his gesture. At the sound, he immediately released her hand and stepped back a little.

Clothos stood from her throne and walked calmly to Persephone, blithely ignoring the fierce anger emanating from Hera. Putting her hand to Persephone's cheek, Clothos looked deeply into her eyes. Persephone felt human in this moment, unsure of her path, more now than she ever had—lost to her fate just as the mortals who roamed the earth along their minuscule timelines.

"Balance, my sweet," Clothos said in her lilting voice. "This is needed to succeed in the battle ahead. Time will tell you all you need to know, for this cannot be forced along any faster than fate itself. Difficulties that can no longer be moved by you alone are building in size and strength. You, and your sisters, must overcome but are not alone in this anymore. The balance, it will help to put everything right again when everything has gone terribly wrong. This, your fates, will correct the wrongs done to this world."

Clothos glanced between Persephone's eyes searchingly and released a breath. Smiling, she stepped away and returned to her throne, releasing Persephone from her gaze's hold.

Seated, the Moirai looked closely at the three sister Goddesses, as if sizing them up for a fast-approaching challenge.

"What does that mean?" Devon asked, his hands in his pockets.

"It means they have no fucking idea," Hera seethed.

"It *means* that this is all meant to balance," Clothos reiterated.

"How?" Amphitrite stepped forward finally, moving between Hera and Persephone. "How does awakening a new God balance us? Does it not throw us into chaos if we are splitting our powers into fourths?"

The Moirai looked at each other, their eyes wide, before they looked back at the Goddesses.

"There was never just three of you, my darling Amphitrite," the Moirai responded in unison. Devon muttered under his breath, something that sounded like "creepy."

The theatrics only agitated Hera more. Persephone almost felt bad for the Moirai in that moment. Almost.

"Who are the others? How were we unaware there were others?"

"Time will tell… time will tell…" the Moirai began to chant.

"Oh, for the love of…" Hera growled. "Here they go. That's all we are getting," she said, her voice only loud enough for the sisters to hear her over the Moirai's chanting.

Persephone looked to Devon. He looked as lost as she did in that moment.

"We will figure this out," she whispered as she reached out and squeezed his upper arm. He gave her a small smile.

"Well, thanks for that nonsense, you old crones. A fortune cookie would've been more helpful," Hera shouted and left the room in a flash of light. A flicker of a dying spark was all that was left in the space she had occupied.

***

Persephone hesitated outside of Devon's room, her fist held up to knock. She knew everything was in a tailspin, but she needed to speak with him. She needed to reassure him, maybe even herself. She also could not stop thinking about his words, his look, when he was lit with Godfire in the basement of Cerberus Financial.

As if he finally recognized her. Recognized her in the way she needed him to. To see all his past lives and the affection she knew he had to feel for her as she felt for him.

Without allowing her thoughts to stray any longer, she knocked on the door.

"Was wondering how long you would stand out there. Come on in," Devon called through the door.

She stepped in to see him sitting on his bed, his elbows on his knees and his head hanging between them. He didn't look up as she shut the door and leaned against it.

"I know it's a lot," she started and his low chuckle followed her words.

"Understatement," he muttered.

Sighing, she pushed from the door and went to sit next to him on his bed. Crossing her legs, she folded her hands over her knees and looked out his window to the forest of his home. She hoped it brought him a small amount of comfort in the chaos surrounding them.

Looking back at him, she watched him worry his hands, his eyes locked on the ground. She moved her hand to rub his back, hesitating a moment before pushing forward. She ran it over his shoulders, feeling that was a safe place to give him comfort. He stilled for a moment, his breath caught, before he released his tension and allowed her to continue.

She wondered if telling him the truth of their past, their passing timelines in his mortal lives, was the appropriate thing to do now after all the stress and shock of the day. Her hand halted a moment, her conscience pushing her towards disclosure, when he looked up at the window across from them.

"I was jealous," he stated.

"What?" she responded, her thoughts trying to catch up.

"At Cerberus, when Thanatos was all over you, it drove something inside me mad. As if the fact that he was unaware that you were…" his voice trailed off as she removed her hand from his back and placed it back in her lap. "I don't know why I reacted that way."

She froze, unsure if she should tell him now. It was a perfect opening.

Why yes, Devon, your attraction has been there over the past eras and it is mutual. Kiss?

Shaking his head, he looked up at her.

"There is something inside me, something that I can't understand or

104

control. If... if I let this thing out, if I am a God... what happens? How do I get control?"

She smiled a little, taking his hand in hers and interlacing their fingers. Why she felt the urge to do this, why he allowed it, she did not know but she was grateful.

"You will control your powers. You will wield them as well as I do, with time. It is not the matter of controlling your powers as much as how you use them." She glanced away.

"That's reassuring," he stated, his hand squeezing hers. "Seems like you and your sisters managed to get it together and the world is no worse for it."

She looked right at Devon. She knew what she needed to say, to do. It wasn't something she wanted... but he needed to know.

He was a God now, and it was much more than lights and Godfire.

She called the shadows and pulled him with their clasped hands to stand up with her. His eyes looked to hers right as the shadows encased them.

***

Persephone shadow jumped them to the bone-littered desert outside Tartarus. Devon stumbled on the rocky surface before steadying himself.

"Why are we here, Persephone?"

Persephone couldn't look at him, look at the face she'd grown fond of as she revealed her most loathsome secret.

"The day I told you about Tartarus, I said that it was meant to contain evil immortals," she started softly, "Do you remember?"

"Yes," Devon murmured.

She took a deep breath. "I left something out," she sighed. "I neglected to tell you that Tartarus was designed to hold my father."

Silence.

Devon spoke carefully. "Why is he in there?" he asked. And though she did not want to answer, she knew it was best he understood why her father needed to stay contained.

She would tell him the truth, their oath of honesty went both ways, but she worried about how he might look at her after she told him.

105

Would he associate the evil that was her father with her?

Swallowing, she took a moment to figure out how exactly to explain it to him. Her hands were shaking a bit and her throat felt dry, the words not coming forth for her to speak. This was a subject she hardly ever allowed herself to think about, much less talk about. Her sisters rarely even spoke of it with her, preferring to look forward and not back.

"My father had it in his mind that any children born to him and my mother were a threat to his power. He was a powerful Titan, who married another powerful Titan, my mother. He never wanted children, but if he had to have them, he wanted them weak and not a true threat to the power he had usurped from his own father."

She felt Devon's attention on her, on the distress that must be painted clearly across her face.

Closing her eyes for a moment, she continued the story she never spoke of.

"That my father would lose his power and be cast off as his father had been before him was his deepest fear. My grandmother and uncles helped my father in overthrowing my grandfather, but no one knew that until my father himself was cast into Tartarus.

"My mother knew my father was not willing to allow anyone to overthrow him the way he had. She knew he would always see us as a potential threat, so she begged another Titan to find a way to keep any offspring from being born Titans. My mother bore my father all girls, all mortals.

"Thankfully, the Titan who helped our mother had bound our powers beneath mortal shells. The Titan did not, however, inform my mother that should we die, we would be as powerful as the Primordial Gods. The Gods before the Titans."

Devon crossed his arms, his face pensive as she told him of her origins. She wasn't sure how to take his lack of reaction, so she continued.

"My father, being paranoid, didn't care that we were mortal children. He still feared us, thinking we'd somehow become powerful, and he would be no more able to stop his downfall than his own father had been.

"He waited until my mother left one day to watch over a woman stuck in the long hours of labor," Persephone hesitated a moment, her

106

mind going back to that day.

"He killed all but one of my sisters using a knife covered in hydra's blood, just to make sure we died. I remember my vision going black as I yelled for my sisters, my father standing over me holding the knife dripping with my blood." Persephone faltered, her voice hitching.

"My sister, Hera, was able to escape and find mother. All while my father hunted her down like an animal."

"Holy shit," Devon muttered as he ran a hand through his hair.

Such an understatement, she thought.

"When my mother followed Hera back home, she found us all dead, our mortal bodies lying exactly where our father struck us down. She took Hera and hid her, making deals with Titans and Gods alike. My sisters and I had been released from our mortal forms, our souls merged with the power deep inside each of us, and we became Goddesses in our own right. More powerful than we ever would have been had we lived and died naturally as mortals. My mother's deal bound our souls to our power. We lived but no longer under the constraints of the mortal form. As souls.

"Hera survived in her mortal form, hidden away in the mountains we had been born in. When she came of age, we found her, those of us who could still hold on to the mortal realm and withstand the pull of the Underworld."

Taking a deep breath, she continued, "We had no way of killing our father ourselves since we hadn't understood our powers and our abilities to manipulate the mortal realm, so Hera offered to be our vessel. Together we banished our father, but the power we funneled through Hera, who held her own latent power inside her, was more than her mortal body could withstand. She died and became a Goddess just as the rest of us had.

"The Titans had no leader in my father anymore, so they split up. Some fell into the long sleep and others disappeared, perhaps to walk among mortals.

"That left the realms unguarded and the power unbalanced. In the void of my father's banishment and the Titans' abandonment, there was us. New Goddesses. Our raw power transformed to fill the vacuum. We were bestowed mantles, rule over the realms, and all the responsibilities that came with them. By then, only three of us had been able to bond to our latent powers and endured the half-life of souls on the mortal plane to become titled, empowered deities." She paused, struck with grief again for her long-lost sisters, Demeter and Hestia. "Amphitrite became the Goddess of the seas. Hera, Goddess of the skies and Queen of Olympus. And me," she spread her arms wide and let them fall to her sides, "Goddess of the dead and Queen of the Underworld."

She then turned to fully face Devon. "He cannot be freed. If he were to walk the mortal realm again, he would bring what you call Hell on Earth. Pulling all of his Titans into a battle I am not sure we would win this time. He is dangerous, and my sisters and I have to keep him here at all costs."

"Where is your mother?" He waved to the rocks with true confusion in his eyes. She was thankfully prepared for that question.

She looked up with the sadness she felt every time she glimpsed Tartarus from her palace. Watched Devon's eyes go from confused to sympathetic, for which she was grateful. It was reassuring that he seemed to understand without her having to say it out-right, but she would tell him, nonetheless.

"The deals my mother made to protect us... we never knew the consequences of them. One of her bargains was that she would become mortal and remain as such until she died a mortal death." She watched the questions roll across his face and answered before he could ask them.

"I am thankful to her every day for doing what she could to help us, and my only relief is that she is in Elysium. Her death is as much at his hands as ours was." Her tone grew cold, as it always did when she spoke directly about her father and his deeds. Even millennia later, she held darkness in her heart where her father's love should have been. Her mother, Hestia, and Demeter all died mortal deaths, when they should have all lived through eternity alongside her. Persephone wondered again what her immortal life would have been like had sweet Demeter and steadfast Hestia been able to bond their souls with the godly powers their mother fettered upon their birth.

Turning away from Devon and Tartarus, she looked out to where the river of fire was active and alive, a perfect representation of her ire towards her father.

Silence fell over them again for too many heartbeats.

108

"Why did you tell me this?" Devon asked. "Why take me here?"

"You are a God, Devon," she said, voice rasping as she turned to face him again. "A mortal- born God. On one hand, I don't want you to feel... alone... even though my transformation was long ago." She took a deep breath and nodded toward the entrance Tartarus. "On the other..." she considered her words, "I wanted to make sure you really understand now that you are a God."

"Understand what?" Devon prompted.

"What the hunger for power can do to a God. And how the paths of Gods can end."

CHAPTER 17

Sitting on a chair next to the window in his room, Devon looked out over the trees and the animals flitting in and out of the shadows. His mind was a whirl of information, none of it hitting home.

He was a God.

A God.

How does one respond to finding out they are not only immortal, but have some kind of power that can manipulate the actual world around them?

He was a God, but not only that, he was a God of the Underworld.

He laughed at the irony of him being a mercenary turned Underworld deity. It was unbelievable and he could only laugh at himself.

His laughter died when he thought back to Persephone's revelation of her past. He could see her fear in speaking about it, not the fear of speaking of something he knew was difficult, but he could see she worried he would look at her differently. He supposed he did, but not in the way she most likely thought.

She was amazing. She had lived through something he wasn't sure he could without his entire psyche fracturing. His heart hurt for her and her sisters, that someone who they loved and trusted to protect them did something so vile. He couldn't help but imagine looking up into the eyes of your protector and feeling such betrayal.

A tear slipped down his cheek before he rubbed it away with the back of his hand. He may be having a difficult time understanding his new role and coming to terms with his own immortality, but he had

Persephone beside him. She was helping him through this incredibly difficult transition.

Who helped her? Who held her hand when she lost her mortal body and became a powerful deity? One with an overwhelming amount of responsibility that she had to step into immediately at that. Looking out his window, he wondered at how she hadn't lost her compassion. She gave him so much more than he deserved because she felt for him.

She may not show it outwardly, but he knew deep down she was a woman who cared. A lot. She would do anything for her sisters, her friends, her souls... for him.

That thought deflated any and all animosity he had as his head fell back against the chair. He had been somewhat cruel in his struggle to adapt when she only wanted to help.

This was his life now. He was saved, maybe not in the way he had hoped, but it was better than the alternative. He needed to look at it as that. If she could survive the worst, he could survive this.

***

Persephone stared into the dancing flames as she sat in her chamber's chair by the hearth, her legs pulled underneath her.

Her thoughts were abstract and overwhelming. She held a glass of wine to her lips as she tried to calm herself. Her nerves caused her hands to shake a little as she took a drink.

She'd told him. She told someone.

Even alone in her bedroom, she felt raw and exposed.

Sharing your darkest secret is exhausting, she thought sardonically.

And Devon. Devon had looked at her with understanding. Persephone's heart twisted, thinking of the horrors he'd experienced in his few short decades in his mortal life that he could empathize with thousands of years-old trauma.

He'd always been somewhat sad in all his lives, she realized dully. Although she'd never spoken to him, lived beside him as she did now in this life. She'd only caught glimpses and flashes of his lives when she accepted his death call. Spending time with him, conversing with him, felt surreal after sharing largely one-sided encounters with his reincarnations.

She'd been honest with him at Tartarus, but she still had secrets.

Guilt pounded through her. It felt like too much change, too many revelations to settle on him in such a short amount of time. He'd just learned of his godly status. To compound that discovery with the news that their souls, such as they were, had bonded through the centuries of a thousand violent lives seemed cruel.

Yes, that is what she would tell herself.

A light tap at the door pulled her out of her thoughts. She sat a moment longer, debating on whether she was wanted to deal with anyone. She was already in her sleep clothes, ready to slip into bed, and most likely not get a wink of sleep thanks to her runaway thoughts.

She sighed as she put her glass of wine aside and stood, rubbing her palms on her thighs as she walked towards the door.

Both terrified and hopeful that Devon was on the other side.

She knew they needed to talk. She needed to explain his soul calling to hers, but she was unsure what purpose the information could hold since she did not know why herself. Why had he called to her, over and over again, throughout the entirety of her time as Goddess of the Underworld?

Opening the door, she was stunned to see Hecate standing there. Usually, after a long day, Hecate was at her cottage near the Asphodel Fields, doing some gardening for her spell work.

It relieved her though, as she could really use a friend right now.

She waved Hecate inside to join her as a second wineglass appeared by way of one of the Reevkas.

"I sensed your presence outside of Tartarus," Hecate said, stepping into the room. "I am guessing that had to do with Devon?"

Persephone sighed and poured Hecate a glass of wine, topping her own glass off, too. She passed the glass to Hecate, and they both settled into the chaise, sipping quietly. Throughout the centuries, Hecate was always the one to know Persephone's moods before even Persephone herself did.

"Mm, Dionysus Vineyards. Good stuff," Hecate murmured.

When Persephone still said nothing, Hecate prodded. "Now tell me why you took our newly minted God-boy to the worst place in all the realms?"

Persephone tried to wrangle her thoughts into making sense.

"I told him about my father." She was expecting some shock, but Hecate only nodded as if she knew this would happen. Persephone felt a sense of relief at Hecate's non-reaction. After her sisters had attempted to crawl through her mind for answers, it was nice to have someone who would just sit and listen.

"How did he respond?" she asked softly as she spun the wine glass between her hands by the stem.

"I think he understands, Hecate," Persephone murmured.

Letting out an indelicate snort was not what Persephone had expected from this news, but Hecate was not one to give a person what they would expect. Only her truth, which was why Persephone adored her so.

"Of course he does, Persephone." She shook her head tiredly. "It probably has something to do with how his eyes go all intense and twinkly when you're in the room."

Persephone reeled backward. "You cannot be serious, Hecate."

Hecate arched a brow in response.

"You haven't seen anything about our bond in your inquest, have you?" Persephone asked warily.

Hecate's expression grew serious. "There's a connection there," she said. The witch frowned. "And it's deep. Fundamental. It could be because it was your magic that technically woke his."

"Or?"

"Or," Hecate trailed. "It could be something more. I need more time to analyze the magic. Research a few spells I haven't used since the Roman Empire was in England."

Persephone sighed and took a long pull of her wine.

"The Moirai do not fuck around when they decide to stir shit up, do they?" Hecate joked dryly, her bracelets clinking as she raised her glass in a mock cheer.

Persephone looked at the fire, her thoughts becoming increasingly frantic and unfettered.

"How do I explain any of this to him when I do not truly understand it myself?" she asked her friend, knowing Hecate knew exactly what she meant. "I do not know how to do all this. How to speak to him, much less how to explain how deep this all goes... how far back it all goes. He already has dealt with so much in just a small timeframe. How do I add

113

to that? How do I... how do I become what he needs me to be?"

Persephone clenched her fist, feeling something bubble up inside her. Something strong and hot like fire. *Angry flames*, she thought. It felt like flames in her chest and throat.

Hecate immediately put her glass down before she moved to kneel before Persephone, taking her hands in hers. Squeezing them tight, Hecate leaned her head against their knotted fingers.

"I feel so weak," Persephone murmured, her eyes burning. The feeling was so foreign, it held her attention for a moment before Hecate spoke again.

"I've never seen you act stronger." Persephone's attention jerked to her friend before her, gazing up at her with pure sincerity.

"You've always been in control, handled everything because being the Goddess was easy for you," Hecate continued as she lifted her hand to brush the tear from Persephone's cheek.

Persephone blinked in surprise at the drop of liquid on Hecate's finger. "Now you are dealing with something so out of your comfort zone, you feel for the first time. You are allowing your emotions to surface. You are allowing them to release so they will not hold any control over you."

Moving back to sit next to Persephone, Hecate pulled Persephone's head to her shoulder, running her hand up and down Persephone's arm.

Just like she did when Persephone herself was new to this world and grieving for her sisters and her mortality.

In this very room, many moons ago, she had helped Persephone adapt to no longer being human, and here she was helping Persephone find that humanity once again. That balance.

"This brings back memories," Persephone said with a watery laugh as she wiped away the tears from her eyes.

"Yes, and you were just as stubborn and strong-willed then as you are now. Look how far you've come from where you were," Hecate sang the words a little, swaying them both with her arm wrapped around Persephone.

"How old are you?" Persephone asked, just as she had that first night when she was new to her domain. Scared and unsure of her next step.

"I will not answer that. Perhaps at your next millennial life crisis," Hecate stated, chuckling softly before growing serious again. "It is normal to be scared when the emotional stakes are this high. You've never let yourself feel this much the entire time I've known you, but I believe if anyone can handle this, it is you."

"I cannot do what I need to do emotionally for him, Hecate." She looked up at her friend's face, desperation crawling under her skin. To make the feelings stop. "I only know how to guard souls. Emotions are complicated, and they are beyond me; I was killed before I knew adulthood. When I was brought back, I mentally had to grow into a body far more mature than my own. I never knew adolescence, true youth." Persephone was losing herself in her thoughts, losing herself in her past.

"You have everything you need," Hecate soothed. "Remember what I said? A soul calls to another to find its home."

There was so much unknown in the situation with Devon, and it frightened her. But this, a chance for a home, scared her most of all.

CHAPTER 18

"It's been hours," Devon grumbled, his irritation overriding any good mood he had. "We still have no idea what my power is or what it does except blast people across the room when I'm mad."

Which he was on the verge of doing now.

Persephone simply stood in front of him with her arms crossed, looking at him but not really seeing him.

How could he train for a job he had no clue about and with no parameters?

"You say you feel something inside of you, something you do not understood nor have the ability to control. What happens when you tap into that willingly?" she asked, her eyes now on his.

His head rolled back on his neck, looking at the basement ceiling of Cerberus in exhaustion. He really did not want to summon whatever he felt deep down; it felt dangerous and his prey instinct screamed to avoid it. Repress it.

Looking back at Persephone, he caught the irritation in her face before she smoothed it out.

Yeah, he understood that. He was living that.

"I don't know how to poke the beast. Perhaps if Thanatos was here, I'd feel more comfortable letting it loose to throw him around a bit."

"I can take some hits," Persephone growled.

He felt something rise up in response. Something telling him that if he hurt her, it was game over. Whatever voice or feeling that was, it was enough to scare Devon into inaction.

"I know you can, but the scary beastie inside me is not having that."

She raised an eyebrow. "Scary beastie?"

He only nodded. Not in the mood for her to poke fun at his term for whatever parasite was currently running amok in his brain. He was not in the mood for much these days.

He rubbed his hands over his face before dropping them to his sides, shaking them out. "Let's try again."

He spent another hour calling, and failing, to raise the beast inside.

Whatever was inside of him was dormant, stubborn, or torturous.

***

Persephone watched Devon closely. She could never tell what he was thinking. The man seemed to have lived a life completely emotionally shut off from the rest of the world. His thoughts barricaded where no one, probably not even himself, could access them. He was closed up so tight, his powers were being stifled, which was not a good thing. She had decided the bestway to pull his powers to the surface was to teach him some of the simpler ways of control.

She would simply start with him doing his own shadow jumps and work with him from there.

"Close your eyes and think of your room at the castle," Persephone started, using a soothing voice to coax him into relaxing.

"Think of the colors of the room, the placement of the furniture, the window, and the forest beyond. Now, think of a specific spot in the room and visualize standing there in your mind."

He closed his eyes, and she took a chance, taking his hand in hers.

There was still the initial hesitation at her touch, but he seemed to be more accepting of it and didn't jerk as if to pull away like he once did.

Running her thumbs over the top of his hands, she watched his eyelids twitch a little. He was obviously trying to focus on his task, but she wondered if she distracted him at all like he did her.

Such a small thing it was to hold a person's hand. Something that could be overwhelming for someone who was not used to such a touch.

She knew the connection needed to be forged between them somehow. Something more than the Moirai and their string. She refocused on Devon, knowing her mind was beginning to wander.

"Now that you have that visual in your mind, imagine you are connected to that spot by something. Perhaps a rope, and all you have to do is give it a little mental tug. Don't fight the sensation when it pulls back at you."

With his eyes closed, she watched as he jumped a little, indicating he felt the tug. She was a bit surprised when instead of dropping her hand, he tightened his around hers.

She began feeling the disorienting hit of the jump, and felt as he adjusted himself closer to her, holding her tight against his body with one of his hands wrapped around her waist. His other hand holding hers between them.

Closing her eyes, she allowed him to pull her into the jump with him. Something hit the back of her knees and she fell back with Devon on top of her.

Cracking one eye open, she realized they had landed on his bed and his body was almost flush with hers. She never realized how muscular he was until his body was completely pressed against hers, hard and heavy. The thoughts swirling in her head were hardly decent.

They were silent for a moment, looking around at both the room and situation they had found themselves in before looking at each other.

Suddenly he broke into a burst of laughter. The sound was contagious, and she found herself chuckling, too.

He no longer wore the cold expression he had perfected, but a smile that spoke of relief and pride.

Devon had done it.

Her laugh turned a little strained as her thoughts went from borderline sexual to completely indecent. Their laughter pressed their torsos even closer together. If he settled an inch or so more, he'd be flush against her.

Thankfully, he lifted off of her before she embarrassed herself.

When he started pacing, she wondered if she already had.

Persephone pulled herself up into a sitting position. The lightness and joy of the last moment had shifted to something else, something edgier. Devon abruptly halted his pacing and sat beside her.

A breath gushed out of him and he went incredibly still.

"That was insane," he whispered, stunned.

She could tell his body was humming with electricity, both from adrenaline and... she wasn't sure what else. Something in his eyes

118

lingered from when he was on top of her.

Lust?

Was that not a normal human feeling when two people found themselves attracted to each other?

Before she could dwell on that thought, she noticed a soft green light emitting from him.

The green light gradually covered his body, starting from his eyes and hands. It crawled right over the surface of his skin, not really touching him, but close enough to where she knew the light was most definitely coming from him.

She stood and moved to him. Entranced by the illumination, she found herself reaching out to touch his arm where the green light moved in an almost affectionate manner. As her fingers traced the light along his forearm, it gave her the lightest zap. Not a painful zap, but an acknowledgment of her.

Power recognizing power.

Persephone was in awe. She touched him again lightly with her fingers, this time prepared for the tingling shock. Gooseflesh rose along his skin where she touched.

"Holy shit," he muttered, closing his eyes as Persephone ran her fingers up his arm. She moved over his shirt, up to his neck and jaw. An almost white light followed her fingers before it reverted back to green.

She glanced up at his face to find his eyes open and looking at hers.

They were lit with Godfire. The glow, verdantly green, was so bright that it rendered her speechless.

Almost as if in response to his Godfire, her own blue light flickered around her. Her hand against his stubbly cheek was caught between their two lights, bathed in blue and green.

Her thumb stroked the tender skin under his eye before she smoothed her hand down his cheekbone and back to his jaw. His breathing had started to become a bit unsteady, and his eyes became brighter.

She yanked her hand back and stepped away. His eyes tracked her every movement. Persephone blinked and felt her cheeks warm. *Was she... blushing?*

She spun on her heel and rushed from his room, not glancing back once. She'd recognized what had taken over those glowing eyes. It was the God looking back at her, the immortal soul that had spoken to her at that first training session, and not the man. And she refused to do anything without Devon's consent or knowledge.

It was necessary she left to keep from altering their relationship forever. To keep herself from making him completely hers.

***

After Persephone's hasty escape, Devon stared at the door as it slammed shut. He was looking out through his own eyes, he knew that, but he didn't feel in control of his body.

His arms and legs were under the control of whatever had taken over and lit him up green.

Devon flexed his fingers, checking to see if he had control again before turning and sitting on his bed.

He fell back and stared at the ceiling, his mind in complete disarray at this point. He moved his arm up and looked at it. The green light had been moving across his skin, yet it was now perfectly normal and completely unblemished.

Nothing was out of the realm of possibility anymore, Devon thought. But to light up green was definitely not something he thought would come with his new powers.

The feeling he'd had right before the thing inside him took over, it was like he was plugging into something larger than himself. His entire system was buzzing, and he felt an immense power thrumming along his spine.

When Persephone had touched him, the power reached for her as if using her as an anchor of some sort. Like she was keeping him from floating away or keeping the power from overloading his system.

Staring at his hands, he looked them over, wondering if the light was from her proximity or if that was something he could call back himself.

A sudden thought slammed into his mind before he even realized it was forming.

He truly wasn't Devon anymore. He wore his physical self, held his memories, but he was something else. Something that had been inside him all along, even as he trekked through the mortal life of Devon.

Nothing about this creature inside him was foreign, but something

120

that had always been there.

As a mortal, he was better at ignoring it he supposed.

When Persephone had told him about how her death had unleashed her power, her true form, that had to have been what happened to him.

Somehow, he had the power of a God, one that was latent underneath his human form. Now that God was free. That God was him.

That God wanted control.

Slowly, his hands fell back to his sides.

"Persephone," he whispered out loud into the room.

This being inside him, the God, knew her. *He* knew her. They called to each other.

He pushed himself up to a sitting position, his breathing coming out a bit louder than he wanted. This had to be all part of some larger cosmic plan.

If he wanted to know his powers, who he was, he had a feeling the Goddess had to have more information than she was sharing. She may not know she had the answers, but she did, and he would find them.

Tomorrow, he would get them from her.

***

Sand.

Again.

Crap.

Devon pushed up to sitting, the sand everywhere again, but this time there was not any blood or an ancient, faceless warrior killing him and stealing his soul.

Leaning forward, Devon put his elbows on his knees and his face in his hands. His mind was exhausted. He dealt with enough questions, thoughts, new revelations during the day, he wanted a break at night.

Looking back up, he took in the surrounding sand.

So empty.

The nothingness was disorienting, and he felt a strong level of anxiety bubbling up inside him.

It was too open, too... dead.

Suddenly feeling like he needed to escape, he started running. There was nowhere to run to, but his body moved anyway. It wouldn't stop. His mind told him it was fruitless, but his body moved of its own volition.

The sand kicked up behind him, his feet trying to push forward, his steps sinking in before he pulled them free again.

He closed his eyes and pushed harder, faster, more determined. He finally allowed his mind to clear and just run.

Suddenly, he wasn't running on sand.

He opened his eyes to see he was running on packed dirt. His steps moved faster, stronger.

As he ran, trees and vegetation shot up from the ground, covering him, and protecting him from the unnatural state he was escaping.

His relief was palpable, and he looked back over his shoulder, the desert no more, lost to the forest.

His head whipped around right as he slammed into the ancient warrior, knocking himself back as everything went black.

Devon jolted up in bed, the dreams leaving him feeling unsettled. He looked out the window, wondering what that had meant.

Had he gone to his forest? Was it for comfort?

Exhausted, he fell back on his bed, as he prayed no more nightmares bothered him that night.

***

Tapping her nails on the throne, Persephone listened to a villager from one of the nearby towns populating the Underworld speak on some potential advancements. Things the mortal world had, but these souls did not remember them. It was interesting how human culture, human curiosity, was so ingrained in the souls.

"I approve and thank you for bringing this before me. Please, show kindness to your neighbors and offer them the same opportunity."

The villager thanked her profusely and bowed. She felt a tiny smile creep on her face at the happiness she saw before her.

That was before the doors opened and Thanatos walked in. He looked way too serious for anything good to be happening. She noticed her guards, who lined the wall and guarded the door, stiffen at his presence. He was one of her generals when the army was called to act, and they deferred to him.

She wondered if Devon would take that role in the future.

"Goddess," Thanatos stopped before her throne, bowing.

Oh, this was not going to be good.

"I apologize for the interruption"

"Forgiven. Speak," she ordered, sitting up straighter.

Standing, he held the presence of a soldier.

"I've been summoned to collect a larger than normal amount of souls. Not in one general area either. They are spread out across Zephyr."

"Plague?" she asked, having not heard anything from her sisters in that regard.

"No, these are all seemingly natural deaths. It is not an astronomical increase, but something I wanted to make you aware of. This could cause issues at the gates if the trend continues."

She nodded. It wasn't unheard of to have a larger number come through or have very little at all. The humans went through waves of change and it was common for the numbers to vary.

Still, she would acknowledge his concern.

"Thank you, Thanatos. Please keep an eye on the situation at hand and let me know if anything else catches your eye."

He bowed before turning abruptly and walking out the doors the guards had moved to open for him.

She tapped her nails on the armrest.

"Any other concerns?" she asked her audience, hoping this was it for the day. She was tired and determined to take a mental break from everything pressing down on her.

The remaining villagers only shook their heads as the guards opened the throne room doors. She stood up, her legs tingling from sitting for so long, and made her way gratefully out the door before anyone could stop her. She was in desperate need of a break, mentally and physically, and she was going to take it before any more problems found its way to her.

***

Closing her eyes, Persephone sipped her wine, allowing herself a moment of reprieve. She sat in the conversation chairs in one of the sitting rooms, enjoying the warmth of the flames.

Too much was changing. Too many unknowns.

She was so lost in thought, when she opened her eyes again, she jolted a bit at noticing Devon seated in the chair next to her, looking at the flames as well.

"Wine?" she asked, moving a glass to him.

He shook his head, not saying anything as he stared at the fire, obviously as lost in the dark as she was these days. She wondered at his thoughts, he was so quiet as they sat.

"Why would I be made a God?" he asked, his voice low.

She turned to look at him, her eyes taking him in.

"Why would I?" she asked him in return.

He looked at her. "Your parents were Titans. Mine were... not anything powerful."

He turned away again, leaning forward with his elbows on his knees.

"Are you completely sure your parents were normal mortals?" she asked.

He laughed, shaking his head.

"They were nothing special. To me, my dad was my hero, but he lived and died as all humans do."

They sat in silence for a while longer. Him, lost in some far away thoughts. Her, lost in him. His posture, his pensiveness. The whole of him before her.

"I am nothing special. I've done nothing to deserve this second chance, or this power, whatever it may be."

"You are certain of this?" she asked, placing her glass on the table between them. He turned his head, looking at her, and simply nodded.

"Tell me of Devon. The Devon who lived, the life you remember." She sat back in her seat and watched him as he looked back at the fire.

His Adam's apple bobbed as he swallowed and lost himself in thought. He was going back to somewhere in his mind, a place he hadn't been in years.

She wondered if he would say anything, he was silent for so long, before the words started to flow.

"I was raised in Germania at the foothills of the Brücke Forest along with other refugees from the old Russian territories after the Sereian Empire gained a foothold prior to the Great War. It is interesting now that I think about it. The forest my family chose to settle in earned its

124

name for the bridge that souls crossed over when they died on the battlefield."

He laughed a little at the irony of that before he went on. She continued to watch him as he moved through his past, lining it up for her to hear.

"We lived in a small village that had been used as a military stronghold during the Great War, so of course, as a boy, I explored those ruins while my dad worked to keep the forest alive and thriving. As I am sure you know, the foothills are all farming communities. None of the luxuries of the old world like in the more populated parts of Germania. You know I never rode in a car until I joined the government forces, and they picked us up in this old truck that was in no way legal by Zephyr standards, smoke came from the back of it, and it stunk like one of the local farmer's hen houses.

"After training, we had our first mission in Sereia, and it baffled me that the people there looked nothing like me, yet they lived in villages like where I was from. Members of my unit looked down on them, were rude, and snubbed them since many guys had never seen a village before."

Devon stopped talking, lost in a moment and working to find his words.

"One night, I snuck out and went into the village during one of their festivals. Their culture was beautiful and amazing. They had these crazy dragon-looking puppets that several people would wear and walk through the streets. There was this old woman who made me dinner, and I ate with her family. Her daughter and grandsons told me stories of their ancestors and the reason behind the celebration. These people were so open and welcoming to me when they faced such hostility from my unit."

"It's okay if you don't want to talk about it," she whispered when she felt his hesitancy, not wanting to add to his stress.

He shook his head, and she was unsure if that was for her or him. "The third time we went back, we had a new Captain, a guy barely older than me by a few years, and I wondered how he had risen so quickly up the ranks. He was proud of the history of Germania, even the darker parts, and hoped it would rise again as it did when the continents were whole. Honestly, I knew there was something too dark about him, but I

125

was young and didn't know what to do about it. I worried saying something might cause issues with the promotion I was up for, which seems so dumb, butI was naïve.

"We went into another small village, similar to the one I remembered the first time we visited Sereia, and he just told them it was now under Germania control like that was all it took to conquer a city. Those of us in my unit were unsure of what to do until the Captain walked up to a man who was standing at the front of the people of their little village.

"The Captain just walked up, put a bullet between the village leader's eyes, right in front of his young son and daughter."

Persephone closed her eyes. As Devon spoke, she noticed his accent becoming more prominent, lost to his childhood.

"The guys around me, whom I trained with, joked with…" He swallowed, his emotions bubbling to the surface. "They all started fighting the villagers. Killing them, and I just froze. That was when one villager hit me with something — I'm not sure what. Maybe a tool for digging? Anyway, that was where my scar here came from." He moved his hand to where the scar above his eyebrow had been. "Must have used the sharp end, but it knocked me back and pulled me out of my shock. I didn't think right then, just reacted. I ran until I found where their houses were lined up at the edge of a wooded area and yelled at the people to go into their homes and lock the doors. Several put their children in, but they refused to stay themselves, choosing to fight instead."

"Fates…" she whispered into the darkness.

"Yeah. I was scared and unsure, but I refused to harm these innocent people. I couldn't harm my unit either, not the young men like me who were fighting out of panic and the fear of not obeying orders. I was stuck in the middle of an impossible situation, so I ran back, the fighting having slowed since more of them were dead than alive on either side of the battle. I couldn't find the Captain, so I searched. I had my service weapon ready, no idea what I would do with it, when I heard crying. I ran around to see a small shed, the door propped slightly open and guarded by two guys in my unit I never really cared for. I watched as the Captain came out, zipping up his pants. I watched as one of the guards walked in and heard the screaming start again. The Captain came to me and asked me if I wanted a turn as if he was asking if I would like a drink of water. That was when I heard a man screaming at them to stop, that his wife was pregnant. The Captain just raised his gun and ended the man while his pregnant wife was violated by the same men I had stood beside since my service had begun. Something cracked in my mind, my vision distorted, and I raised my gun…"

Silence permeated the air. Persephone put her hand out and was thankful when he placed his hand in hers, entwining their fingers.

"I shot the Captain just as he did those two men. The guard outside started for me, yelling, and… and vines I didn't see moments before had tripped him. I hit him with my gun, and as the other guard came out, his pants around his ankles, I shot him, too. Then… I ran. I knew they would hang me. I knew I committed treason and could never go home. So, I took jobs for money using the skills I learned throughout my service. I couldn't stay in one place and earn a living since I was being hunted by my own government. I was staying off the grid in my safe house in Alexious when the jobs were sparse, the heavy snowfall of that country good for keeping me undercover."

Devon stopped for a moment before starting again. "That was when I realized I had a chance to hunt my old unit, which I did, and ended up meeting my friend, West, during that time. He was on a suicide mission to end a few of the same men's lives. I offered him my services, and he paid well. I had no idea who he was before I met him. Two men who kept their secrets close and only allowed a shallow friendship. Truthfully, the only friendship I ever really had."

"I took those souls, the ones from Germania that caused so much harm and hurt. They may still be in the Torture Fields. Their deaths on earth were nothing compared to what happened to them here," Persephone offered as a small penance for the pain and anguish he felt.

He gave a slight nod as they lapsed into silence, both of them digesting the dark memory.

"I'd love to go back to Germania, see the Great Forest, but I am not sure I could handle it if everything I knew was destroyed. At times, those memories are all that get me through the dark nights, and I need to keep them as they were. I just… the one thing I regret is not seeing my father again before he passed away. To tell him I was sorry for not coming home, for leaving in the first place."

She squeezed his hand, watching him. He wouldn't look at her, but she could see the tears glisten as they fell down his cheeks. She stood, still holding his hand, pulling him up. Before she realized what she was doing, she had pulled him into a hug.

He lost himself, crying on her shoulder.

She closed her eyes, running her hands up and down his back in soothing motions. She could see it clearly now. His darkness. His past. The power he held inside himself. She loved it. All of it.

She loved him.

And wasn't that another dilemma?

CHAPTER 19

Devon made a decision.

He would shadow jump. Alone. He had yet to do it without Persephone present at this point and had no idea how the shadows would take to him, or if they would even heed his call.

It was the middle of the night in the mortal realm, or at least he believed it to be. So, he thought his best option would be to jump to Cerberus Financial.

It was after hours, so no one should be there to witness his humiliation should he turn up in a less than refined manner in a less than desired place.

Closing his eyes, Devon attempted to pull the shadows to him as he did with Persephone. After several attempts, the shadows hardly even stirred.

Taking a deep breath, he closed his eyes again and thought of where he needed to be, visualizing the office he had spent many boring afternoons. The mahogany desk, the floor to ceiling windows... Persephone.

Persephone, standing looking out those windows, her long black hair falling down her back like silk. Her lithe form silhouetted against the city lights. The feel and taste of her power, its strength cocooning him.

"Devon?"

He heard her voice. Persephone. He was in his room, and he could hear her. Taking a deep breath, he allowed himself to settle into the visual, take her in.

Taking a step back to sit on the bed, he slammed his foot into something hard.

"Fuck," he grumbled, opening his eyes, and finding himself not in his room but Persephone's. The woman that had been the whole of his thoughts moments ago stood before him, covered in a lace nightgown.

Green light lit up the room. His eyes glowing.

Looking up at her eyes, he could feel raw power ripple through him. His thoughts starting to haze as he took her in.

Persephone. His Persephone.

Before he was aware of his thoughts, or actions, he was in front of her. His hands moved to her jaw and pulled her face to his, stopping inches from putting his lips to her own.

"How did I forget how beautiful you are?" he whispered, only catching her eyes widen before his lips took hers.

He kissed her like a man possessed and, after a momentary pause, she finally came out of her shock to return the kiss. Her hands moved around his neck, pulling him against her. Their bodies aligned perfectly as their tongues danced and teeth clashed.

Her hands fisted his shirt while he pushed the kiss deeper, losing himself completely in her. The sudden explosion of glass halted their kiss, both of them jumping back from each other. The room was pure green light and broken glass from the window. He caught sight of Persephone staring at him, her hand to her mouth, her eyes wide in shock.

He was hit with a sudden wave of dizziness before everything went white.

***

"I'm impressed." Thanatos walked around the bed, tossing an apple up in the air, and catching it before taking a bite. "I've never kissed someone unconscious before."

"Thanatos, not the time," Hecate grumbled as she checked over Devon.

Persephone paced in the corner of the room, out of the way of them both, biting her fingernails in worry.

She did not know what had happened, but she very much doubted that it was from kissing her.

Had his power finally been too much? Did the God take over and push Devon

130

out? Would it even still be Devon when he woke up?

Thanatos simply ignored her as he sat on the bed beside Devon while Hecate worked her magic on Devon.

Thanatos took another bite out of his apple, looking at Persephone.

"Dressed for the occasion or was this a surprise dalliance?" he asked, adjusting his plaid pajama pants, and dripping a bit of apple juice on his cartoon reaper shirt. One stating something about a next intended victim with yet another middle finger.

"Who says dalliance anymore? Also, please shut up, Thanatos," Hecate stated firmly, her eyes closed and her hands moving over Devon's head.

"I was getting ready for bed, and he just appeared," Persephone whispered. This could not be good for her heart, immortal or not.

"Shadow jump?" Thanatos asked around his mouth full of apple. Hecate shot him a disapproving look.

"Animal," she murmured and continued working.

"No, not shadows. Wind and leaves." She thought back to that moment, so absorbed by the shock of him showing up, she hardly noticed any details.

Now, she realized how much she missed.

"Wind and leaves?" Thanatos barked out, almost choking on his apple. Even Hecate turned to face her with a shocked look on her face.

"Yes. Nature. His power is in nature."

"Well, the Underworld sounds like the perfect place to put a Nature God, don't ya think, Hellcat?" Thanatos turned to look at Hecate only to receive an eye roll at his pet name for her.

"Even with his inferior intellect, I do have to agree with Thanatos. That seems very odd that a God of nature would be here." Hecate looked down at Devon.

"Yet here he is, bound to death when all he represents is life," Persephone whispered, her voice holding a deep sadness.

Before she could speak further, she was wrapped in Thanatos' arms.

"Don't fret. Perhaps he will bring life to the Underworld. Change is not always bad, just scary. The good thing is you've got me and Hellcat to help you, just as we have done and always will," he finished, pressing a kiss to Persephone's forehead as he held her tightly in his arms.

Persephone felt a knot loosen in her chest at Thanatos' words. They

131

had always been there for her, just as she was for them. They may not be of her blood, but they stood by her just as her sisters did.

"Thank you," she whispered so faintly she wasn't sure they could hear her.

Thanatos replied with a tight squeeze and put his chin on her head.

He gave her the comfort she desperately needed.

***

Devon came to consciousness with a panic he hadn't felt since his days working for the government. Unaware of his surroundings for a moment, he tensed up and opened his eyes to assess his environment before he recognized his bedspread.

"Oh good, you lived." He heard a familiar male voice from the corner of his room.

Thanatos.

Why was Thanatos sitting in his room?

"What happened? Why are you here?" Devon croaked, his throat dry.

"I am here because Persephone had an issue at Cerberus Financial and was not able to continue watching what easily could've been your corpse. I'm also here, of my own volition I assure you, to make sure if you do stop breathing, I rid the castle of your body, try to find a human that looks like you, and hope Persephone doesn't notice. Persephone didn't ask me to do that for her, but I felt like it was a thing a good friend would do in this situation."

"Ignoring that statement, let's circle back to why I would need to be watched while I sleep?"

"Yes, about that." Thanatos slapped his palms down on his thighs before pushing to stand up.

"You created a portal and showed up in Persephone's room, went all God on her, kissed her, destroyed the window, and passed out. I'm assuming this was your first time being intimate with a woman, and it was too much for you. It is okay. If you have questions, I am here."

Devon ignored Thanatos, replaying what he had just said in his mind. He remembered creating the portal and then waking up here.

He kissed Persephone.

Covering his face with his hands, Devon let out a loud sigh, wondering how messed up everything was now.

His face shot back up to where Thanatos stood, looking out the window with his hands in his jeans' pockets as if waiting patiently for Devon to catch up.

"Is she okay?" he asked, suddenly worried he might have done something to hurt Persephone.

Thanatos turned back to look at him, raising an eyebrow. For once, Thanatos didn't have his trademark smirk on his face. "Luckily for you, yes," he answered and Devon released a breath in relief. He wasn't sure what he would do if he somehow hurt her.

"Why would it do that?" he asked, troubled.

Thanatos frowned. "It?" He shook his head. "The God... it's you, Devon."

He stepped away from the window and toward the bed.

"You'll do well to remember that. You are ignoring it, and your heart, for some idiotic human reason I cannot fathom. Accept who you are and stop with all the martyr bullshit."

In a swirl of shadows, Thanatos disappeared, leaving Devon with the feeling that he had spoken a truth. A truth that Devon needed to hear.

Even if it was nothing he wanted to admit.

***

Persephone had just closed her eyes, exhausted from her tears and finally comfortable in her bed, when a bright flash lit up her room.

"Great..." she murmured, opening her eyes to Hera standing over her bed, hands on hips.

"Great? So, this means we now have everyone's powers under control?" Hera asked, sarcasm lacing her voice.

Persephone rolled onto her back, putting her hands over her face.

"I'm working on it, Hera," she grumbled through her fingers.

She felt Hera's hands on hers before she pulled them away from Persephone's face.

"Do you not understand what a God with uncontrolled powers could do to the world? You are here in the Underworld, but chaos ensues above. The instability is felt around the realm."

Hera sat next to Persephone on her bed, her face creased with worry.

Her wonderfully short-tempered, sarcastic younger sister was worried. That was not something Persephone had seen in a long time.

Pushing up to her elbows, she looked at Hera squarely, face to face.

"I understand. I do. We just… are having issues getting his powers to even surface, much less gain control of them."

Hera pushed some hair out of Persephone's face. "Then you know what needs to be done, sister."

Persephone threw her arms over her face with a grunt. "I do have a business to run during the day, Hera…"

"This takes precedence and you know it. The woman who is always ready to do what must be done is stalling. Have something to confess, darling?" Hera asked, a twinkle coming to her eye that made Persephone freeze for a moment.

Did Thanatos or Hecate tell her of what happened with Devon? No, they wouldn't… would they?

"Fine. Tomorrow." Persephone reluctantly agreed.

"Good," Hera's dazzling smile of victory crossed her face. "I look forward to seeing it."

Oh, she bet Hera would.

***

"What is this place?" Devon asked, moving through the forest. Persephone had woken that morning with a sense of determination and gone directly to Devon's chambers to commence training again. He hadn't mentioned the kiss, and the subsequent incident, so she didn't either.

She could hardly look him in the eyes as she'd shadow jumped to the familiar woods.

"The forest below Olympus. Sometimes, when we have issues pulling our power… or controlling them, this is where my sisters go to get everything put back to rights."

When she finally entered the large clearing, the same one she'd used to meditate on her powers through the centuries, she turned to look upon Devon for the first time since their kiss.

Well, the kiss between her and his God persona.

Oh, this was awkward.

He was staring at her, lost in thought, before he cleared his throat and looked away. Great. He knew.

Damn, Thanatos.

She sighed, pinching the bridge of her nose between her thumb and forefinger before she looked back to him.

Hera was right. They needed to resolve his issues pulling his power forward. Leaving it like this would cause a serious imbalance, and the last time there was an unbalanced power structure, there was a war. A mistake they could not afford to repeat.

"The area around Mount Olympus holds the power of all the Gods that ever were. It restores us when we are weakened. It gives us a boost when we are lacking. It gives comfort when we struggle. It will give you the confidence to pull your power forth."

Devon simply watched as she spoke, his eyes on her lips.

She looked away from him, turning to the lush forest around them. The mountain the Gods had called home since the beginning of time itself.

"Look," Devon started. Her shoulders tensed, knowing what was coming. "I know... I kissed you... or part of me did..."

She whirled, unable to handle this moment. The embarrassment of this situation was too much.

"It is fine, Devon. It was nothing. Sometimes our powers cause strange things to happen when they are out of control," she reassured. She smiled at him, but it stiffened as his face seemed to fall at her words.

What had he expected her to say?

She shook herself and turned away again, feeling awkward and uncertain.

Focus on what we are here for, she told herself. *We do not have time for this.*

"The most important part of this is that you connect with the ancients who rest here. The ones who fell to the long sleep, they can guide those of us who are in power."

Stepping forward, Persephone put her hands to the ground, letting the power of her ancestors run through her.

Hello, child, she heard in her mind. A smile crossed her face. As a young Goddess, she had always wondered who spoke to her and her

135

sisters here. Hecate told them it was the Primordial Gods, most likely. Could be Chaos itself. Either way, it was someone who cared for them in their own way.

"I've brought a new God, just awakened. I ask that you help him find his balance. To find relief from his powers and guide him into them in the way you did me and mine so long ago."

The ancients did not respond verbally but sent a pulse of power down the mountain and through her and Devon. The pulse causing the leaves to ruffle and the branches to sway.

Persephone took that as a blessing to proceed.

"I don't want to interrupt your moment here... but who are you talking to?" Devon asked.

"My ancestors. The ancients. Whoever resides in this mountain. They helped me as a young Goddess, so I am asking for them to help you. Put your hand to the ground and listen closely."

Devon stood with his hands in his pockets, looking at her incredulously. He glanced over to the mountain as he let out a chuckle, moving to run his hand over his mouth.

"Okay," he finally said, shrugging. "I am sure Thanatos is around somewhere getting a good chuckle."

"Thanatos does not have a connection to the mountain."

Devon was on his knees now, his hands on his jean clad thighs as he looked up at her.

"Sure..." he laughed, putting his hands to soil.

She stayed quiet, listening to the wind whisper through the trees. Even if her true place was the Underworld itself, she felt safe here. Home. As if she had grown and moved away but came back to the first place she had ever known. An adult returning to their childhood home.

The green light caught her attention. She looked down to where Devon knelt. He illuminated rays of emerald magic over the ground in front of him. He looked up at her, his eyes normal, no Godfire.

Their eyes held a brief moment before he suddenly jumped up and back.

"No!" he yelled, his chest heaving.

"What?" she was in front of him before he moved again.

His eyes were wild, looking around, every direction as if perceiving a threat.

"Devon!" she grabbed him by his shoulders, trying to pull his focus to her. He seemed disconnected right now, as if he had been disengaged from his surroundings by connecting to the powers of the mountain.

His eyes finally locked on hers.

"It wants too much control. Whatever this thing is, it's more than just me. It's a whole other person!" he yelled, pulling away and his hands going to his hair. "I am not going to willingly give into something possessing me. Hell no."

"Stop, Devon. Calm yourself," she whispered, trying to soothe him. "That is part of you. That is the God inside of you. If you can learn to control your powers, you can find a balance where he is not the one always in control. He will help you when you need guidance on your powers, but he is to be at your side, not at the front."

Devon finally settled at that, looking at her with such hope in his eyes.

Hope and wariness.

She nodded, hoping he believed what she said was true.

"Then I guess let's get to work," he whispered back, his hands still shaking.

Giving him a smile of reassurance, she nodded.

"Fantastic. Now, hit me with your power."

***

Persephone pushed her hair back from her face and took a deep breath. Mount Olympus was as good for her as it was for Devon's training. She gathered strength from the remnants of old magic in the air.

When she opened her eyes, she found Devon watching her from the other side of the clearing.

He could now call up his Godfire and push out surges of power without being controlled by the inner God.

Progress.

"I will be attending a function this evening," she told him as she walked over to him. "The staff will be notified, and you are welcome to do as you please around the castle in my absence."

She stopped in front of him. "I should be back before sunup in the human world, but the Reevkas will be there if you need anything."

He said nothing as he watched her.

He finally exhaled, as if reaching a decision.

"No need for that, Persephone," he said. "I'll go with you. I am sure a Reevka can find me a fancy suit that will fit."

She blinked and reeled back a bit, examining his expression. He was serious, he actually wanted to go with her. She went between shock that he invited himself to her event and relief that he made the choice to attend. He had taken back control and made his own decision.

Persephone found she was pleased he wanted to come.

Pleased and anxious. She wouldn't have the ability to control the situation as she did when they were in the Underworld or at Cerberus Financial. They would be directly exposed to anyone there that had power.

Considering it was an event run by demi-gods, and even the minor ones could hold an incredible amount of power, he would be exposed to a lot of it in one small area. And for a considerable length of time.

"I can hear you thinking and mulling over all the ways this is a bad idea, but I am going," he decided. "I can't be locked away for fear of my powers. If you are with me, you can help keep them under control." He raised an eyebrow, almost daring her to argue.

With a weary mind, all she could do was nod.

Waking up this morning she had managed to tell herself she was unaffected by him, that she could control her thoughts and impulses, but his proximity had made a liar out of her.

She was used to people obeying her word and letting that be the end of it. She had a feeling that would never be an issue with Devon in her life.

"I have a few more things to do before we leave," she said. "I advise you stay here to practice and meditate." She began to gather her shadows around her.

Devon nodded. "What's the dress?"

A smile twitched at her lips. "Black tie," she told him.

This man was dangerous. Maybe not yet in power, but he was learning quickly how to unsteady her. When he had full use of his power — and a tuxedo–who knew if she would be left standing.

***

After Persephone departed in a swirl of shadow, Devon pressed his back against a tree and closed his eyes. The forest around him thrummed with energy.

All except one spot.

Devon's eyes snapped open at the sound of breaking twigs.

Thanatos stood in the clearing with his arms crossed.

"Here to help practice?" Devon called out, forcing himself to step from the wide tree at his back.

Thanatos scoffed. "Not quite." He stepped closer. "I had to watch over you, make sure the baby God didn't make a mess."

More of this?

Devon squared his shoulders. "I handled myself fine, didn't I? Nothing happened."

"And maybe that's the problem."

"What?" Devon frowned. "You want me to go 'God' on her?"

"I want you to accept yourself." Thanatos was grim.

"I am," Devon balked. "I do. I'm trying to preserve myself."

"You are the God. The God is you. It's a part of your soul. The part that held your power through reincarnation. The part that remembers your lives."

"Lives?" Devon interrupted, his voice going higher than he cared for. "Reincarnation?" He held his arms wide. "You're telling me that the consciousness that takes over my body when my powers go out of control is...?" Devon faltered, unable to find a word fittingly bizarre enough.

"Your immortal self?" Thanatos supplied. "Yes."

Devon's arms dropped to his sides. "So, more me than I am," he muttered. He felt like there was something missing, something more that he should be talking about.

Suddenly, he straightened at a thought that crossed his mind. "The kiss. Why did he... I... do that?"

Thanatos nodded, as if this was the question he wanted him to ask. "Something in you recognizes something in her," he said. "But it's not my job to tell you what that is."

The Reaper started to conjure a portal. Shadows swirled in the tall

139

grass. "Next time your God-self pops up...try having a conversation."

And with that, Thanatos shadow jumped, leaving Devon to contemplate what it meant to know oneself. Especially when oneself came with two versions.

CHAPTER 20

Persephone had kept herself busy with Underworld demands all day.

Now she looked herself over in her full-length mirror, happy with the final results — smokey eye makeup, slicked back hair that fell down her back like a waterfall, and a tailored floor-length gown.

Her dress was made of deep black silk that shone with a blue hue when it caught the light at certain angles, just like her hair did. The dress was figure hugging with an exposed shoulder and a slit running up her left thigh, which made it a lot easier to walk around in. Blue sapphire studs sat in her ears and her neck glittered with a necklace that matched.

Though the earrings looked beautiful, they were a gift from the Cyclops, and they had more than the purpose of just looking pretty.

She and her remaining sisters were each gifted something after they released the Cyclops from the Underworld when they banished their father, who had kept the Cyclops imprisoned without any real cause.

They gifted Hera a necklace that could create the most destructive lightning bolt; Amphitrite was given a ring that could both calm and anger the seas; for Persephone, she could turn invisible when she rubbed her fingers over the earrings.

She rarely used this, instead preferring her shadows to shield her, but when going to events like this she found it useful. In the mortal world, pulling shadows around oneself caused a stir, and sometimes these events had politically powerful mortals in attendance.

These events also had the type of people who would not hesitate to cut someone's throat, metaphorically and literally. It never hurt to have everything in her arsenal ready to go, especially the ability to disappear without fanfare.

Something Devon would learn soon enough was that one of these minor deities could turn into an enemy in a blink of an eye. Just another reason Persephone trusted so few people.

They may not like to rub elbows with the Goddess of the Underworld, but they would not hesitate to take her power for themselves if she were in a weakened state.

Naturally, with her being a Goddess, they could only lessen her power and self, not abolish her completely, but Persephone refused to take even that chance. Losing her power may very well kill her mind, if not her body. It was a crucial part of herself and she would not take a chance that there could be a coup, especially not at an event Devon was attending, so she made sure she had her earrings.

A final look in the mirror had her wondering what Devon saw when he looked at her. When he first met her, he had told her he hated her, despised her for what she represented.

That was nothing new to her. People were angry when vulnerable.

She was not loved by the humans or other deities as her sisters were, people were naturally afraid of death. But that didn't mean it hurt less at the rejection. When people knew and worshipped the Gods so very long ago, they worshipped all except the God of Death.

The name of Hades, her alter ego, was never to cross the lips of a mortal for fear of bringing death upon themselves or their house. Therefore, her persona became that of an ice queen over time, withdrawing from the people who rejected her so readily.

She couldn't do that with Devon, and that was something she feared, his rejection.

She knew she cared for him in a way she had never felt before and the idea of his dismissal chilled her bones.

Enough, she thought. *She would not allow anyone to cause her to question her self-worth.*

Even him.

She heard Devon as he moved down the hallway towards her room. She looked at the old grandfather clock in the corner of her room and realized it was time to go. She grabbed her clutch as she moved to the door, her hand hovering on the knob.

In the back of her mind, she felt a slight tingle, an itch almost that she had never felt before. It baffled her, and as much as she tried to access whatever it was, it seemed out of reach. Turning, she tried to take in the room with a Goddess' eyes, seeing if there were someone here human eyes could not see.

Nothing but a sense of something being off. The knock at the door brought her out of her thoughts.

She opened it to Devon on the other side looking absolutely dashing in a black tuxedo, with a black button-down shirt, and black tie. His hair was slicked back, showing more of the face that was usually hidden beneath his messy dark blonde hair. Dark eyebrows, his piercing green eyes, nose a little broader than all the nobles she had been around in the past. She noticed he was clean shaven for the first time since he became an Underworld resident.

He looked amazing like this, but she found herself wishing he was back to his normal self — hair mussed up from him running his hands through it constantly and the shadow of a beard.

Regardless, when she saw him, her heart missed one of its beats. She stopped herself before she could do something out of irrational lust, like drag him into her room, and pulled herself together with a smile.

"Ready?" she asked, trying to keep an unfazed look on her face. Devon, looking somewhat dumbfounded in that moment, simply nodded.

She realized he had not said a word since she opened the door and that helped to cement the smile she was struggling to keep up. Perhaps he was speechless because of her? She dared to hope.

After a little shake of his head, he put his arm out for her to hold.

"You look amazing, Persephone," he whispered as she took his arm.

Returning an appreciative smile to him, and maybe a blush, they left her room to move to the stairs. As they began their descent down them, she pulled them into a shadow jump.

They ended up across the road from a venue where doors were being opened as guests milled about.

Attendants for the evening greeted the arriving guests at the large doors built to look like her gates in a way. The building had the look of a large Greek pavilion on the outside, but Persephone knew this place had a grand ballroom and plenty of rooms to meet in secret. Something she knew her sisters were probably meaning to take advantage of tonight.

143

Though she loved her sisters dearly, she did on more than one occasion feel jealous of their ability to do as they pleased in regard to having trysts.

Something she never felt comfortable doing.

It would take months for her to commit to taking a lover and even then, it was kept completely without attachment or strings. She would only allow attraction but not passion. It was easier for her to not have to focus on controlling herself, releasing her powers in a moment of desire that could cause problems in the future. Something she knew all too well could happen with consequences that could not be undone. A soul could detach from their body, leaving a shade, or her fire could cause a mortal's death.

"Stay near me for the evening, no matter what. I can act as an anchor for your powers if you are in close proximity." She didn't look at him while she said this, instead watching the guests move out of their way as they walked towards the entrance. The instrumental music from inside the building carried to them as they approached.

"Of course," Devon replied with absolutely zero inflection. She kept from glancing at him to see if his expression matched.

She felt a lot better having him next to her and not across the room where anyone could sense he was not mortal. She had worried that something could trigger a response from him that she could not intercept fast enough.

Liar, she thought to herself.

She would keep repeating this half-truth that it was the only reason she wanted him near her until she believed it. She was sure by this point they both knew the real reason, or at least part of the real reason.

She pulled on the cool exterior she had perfected as they approached the mass of people milling about in the foyer.

Show time.

***

"Tell me about this event," he asked as they walked up the stairs to where an attendant was waiting to take their items.

"This is one of the charities that my sisters and I are financial backers for." She nodded to the attendant who took her purse and jacket before showing them the way to the ball room.

Devon's hand moved to her lower back as his other hand took the return ticket for their items, tucking it into the inside pocket of his jacket.

"It is run by a woman I met many years ago through Amphitrite. She was recovering from an extensive amount of trauma. We worked with her to create this foundation for victims of all forms of abuse. There are counseling services, shelters, job programs, and educational funding. We have lawyers who help to tell their stories and fight with them for their independence from the abuser and any who helped, or stood by, while the abuse happened."

Devon looked at several photographs placed along the walls with stories written and framed next to them. Success stories.

"That's amazing," he whispered, truth ringing clear in his words. He had seen enough of the dark side of man to know how hard it could be to escape an abuser. Much less make a life that couldn't be pulled out from under them.

"Korinna." A woman walked up bringing Devon out of his thoughts. He had to remember what Persephone's name was among the mortals.

The woman was shorter than Persephone, both her eyes and skin like honey. Her dark hair hung in ringlets, a snake necklace wrapped around her neck, with snake bracelets dangling from her wrists. A long silver dress with a green shimmer to it was wrapped around her athletic form. Stunning fell short on describing this woman. She could have been a Goddess in her own right.

She moved with the grace of a ballerina as she took Persephone's hand in hers. "I am so grateful you could come!"

Persephone smiled at the woman's enthusiastic welcome and before either of them could blink, she pulled Persephone into a friendly hug. Devon felt something as he watched Persephone navigate the affectionate touch.

Warmth? Tenderness?

Persephone pulled back a bit stiffly, but her eyes softened as she looked at the woman with an affection that spoke of a long friendship.

"Of course. You know I would never miss one of your events." She turned to Devon to introduce him. "Devon, this is Medusa Perrin, the founder I was speaking to you about. Medusa, this is my friend, Devon

145

Aideonous."

The woman turned to him and put her hand out to shake, the snake bracelets jangling on her wrist.

As they shook hands, he caught an unbelievable strength in the woman's eyes that reminded him of an immovable stone. He felt a kinship with her without even really knowing her.

It was almost like he read her soul and could see the character of it. She was a formidable ally and, most likely, a terrifying enemy.

He was glad in that moment that Persephone had a friend to match her in strength.

"It's very nice to meet anyone Korinna calls a friend," she said, a smile on her lips. "That would make you a friend of mine as well," she told him, putting her other hand to her chest to cover her heart as if making an oath.

"I'm honored," he replied in total honesty. Her smile and nod as they released hands told him she both knew he spoke the truth and approved.

"Please, go and enjoy yourselves. I have to make more introductions." Medusa bowed slightly before turning to another couple walking through the doors.

Persephone touched the woman's shoulder before she could walk off, and something passed between the two women. It spoke of old friends using their own language.

"I'm doing fine," Medusa assured Persephone before she winked at her and made her exit.

Devon returned his hand to Persephone's back, which he noticed was becoming a habit for him. As if his hand did not know where to go or what to do unless it was touching her somehow.

He leaned in to whisper in her ear, "It was good to meet a friend of yours, especially one who is not annoying. Like Thanatos."

She chuckled. "I do not have many. As you will see tonight, I am not exactly a welcome presence among many mortals or deities."

That stopped him, with his hand going from her back to her elbow to stop her, "What do you mean?" his tone a little harsher than he intended as a protective instinct took over for a moment. She had brought something out in him that had been repressed for years. Something that felt a lot like peace.

He realized how much of a hypocrite he had been to even judge people for thinking that.

Had he not just acted the same way toward her since he became an Underworld citizen? She smiled, but it did not reach her eyes. She knew what he was thinking.

"Devon, I am what people fear. I represent an unknown to them and people do not handle the unknown well. Hera can create a storm and though there may be damage, people have lived through storms before. People do not live through death. They do not come back to tell what waits for them on the other side. People fear me. That is the burden I carry. But it is one that I do so knowing when they reach my realm, I will care for their souls. They fear me in life but need me in death. I am okay with that, but it does lend itself to a lonely existence."

In that moment, he truly saw the two sides of this Goddess. This woman.

She may act cold and calculated in the presence of people she did not know well outside of her very small circle. But, in the Underworld, he saw the warm, intelligent, beautiful soul that hid beneath the coldness of her gorgeous exterior.

Devon could see how a person with a weaker constitution would shy away from someone with her power. He also saw that behind all her confidence and control was a woman who felt those slights bone deep. She was not as unaffected as he had thought.

"People do fear the unknown, this is true, and something I can personally understand. But you radiate strength and intelligence, and if they could look past their own fears, they would see someone well worth knowing. Something I plan to keep in mind from now on. I am honored to stand beside you, even if I haven't acted like it."

He put his elbow out again after releasing hers, patting the hand of her arm as she wrapped it through his.

"You and your pretty words," she teased. He caught a glimpse of the true Persephone before she returned to her Goddess persona. Her armor.

He chuckled. "Not something I was well known for when I was mortal. Guess I am evolving after all."

"That man was always in there. Never forget that," she told him as she tightened her hand on his arm for a brief moment and gave him a

147

dazzling smile.

They crossed the double doors to enter the ballroom, him feeling lighter on his feet for the first time since returning to the mortal world.

Hecate and Thanatos walked in, arm in arm from another entrance, and he wondered if this was something more than just a date between friends. Thanatos wore a dark tuxedo, looking every bit the young model straight from Hispania.

Hecate looked gorgeous in a black gown; her silver hair pulled up in a detailed hair style with black beading. They nodded to him before a couple moved over to speak to them.

There were so many people, mingling, laughing, sitting, and having a drink. His eyes caught flashes of color here and there, and he realized he could differentiate who was mortal and who was not.

A new sense of his power, he thought, and wondered why he had never seen these flashes of color in the Underworld or at Cerberus Financial.

It was overwhelming, the stimuli, and he had to push the instinct down to snarl at people as he passed. It felt almost like he needed to assert some dominance. An almost territorial need to keep people away from him… and, he slowly realized, Persephone.

"You may feel different among these people," Persephone explained almost as if she could read his mind, "since our building dampens powers in order to protect from an attack within. Here you are unbound and will sense more and be able to do more. If you feel off in the slightest, we need to excuse ourselves and find a way outside to calm you."

He nodded and swallowed down the urge to go on a rampage and build a wall of bodies around them. He did not want to ruin her evening, but this was an intense feeling. He would need to do his best to control himself.

As much as he hated to be a burden, he knew if it became too much, he would have to alert her. He had to keep his wits about him, he thought, as a man passed by him and barely touched Persephone's shoulder. Devon had to take a deep breath not to follow the man and rip off his arm in his anger that the man had dared to touch the Goddess.

"Devon?" Persephone asked, moving in front of him to get a good look at his eyes.

He took a huge breath in and shook his head.

"Sorry. I'm fine," he said as he grabbed her hand and squeezed in reassurance.

He felt her power going through his hand and into him, calming him, anchoring him. He felt a huge wave of relief wash through him at having physical contact with her.

"Thank you," he whispered as he squeezed her hand one more time.

A woman holding a tray of glasses filled with champagne walked up, offering them each a flute. He grabbed two, handing Persephone one and taking a sip from his.

He was able to get himself back under control now that Persephone had blunted the power radiating off the crowd.

A few people greeted Persephone and Devon with him being introduced as her date for the evening. He found he enjoyed the idea of being her date, of letting himself relax into that role, even if it was all a ruse.

A woman with golden curls framing her face and a purple dress that might have been a bit too tight for a formal occasion caught sight of them and headed in their direction.

Persephone leaned in close to whisper in his ear, causing some surprisingly heated thoughts to enter his mind. He was thankful for the woman's approach right then. A distraction was sorely needed.

"Mind your words with her, she can turn them into weapons," she warned before turning to the woman as she entered into hearing range.

"Glad to see you could attend, Pandora," Persephone greeted. Her tone not matching her words.

Pandora nodded but her eyes were locked onto Devon.

"Who do we have here?" Pandora asked, making an unsuccessful attempt at bedroom eyes. She looked him up and down and he was thankful when Persephone stepped closer to him, placing her hand on his arm as she introduced him.

"Let me introduce you to my date for the evening. This is Devon Aideonous. Devon, this is Pandora Deidamia. She is one of the world's leading virologists. As hard as that can be to believe sometimes."

Pandora laughed. One that sounded incredibly fake and insincere.

"Oh, Korinna, your words wound me. I swear, you act as if I have some hidden box of viruses to unleash upon the world." Her smile reminding him of a viper ready to strike.

Persephone returned the smile. One that was predatory and cold. One that said she found Pandora lacking and unworthy of a battle.

"Oddly specific, Pandora," Persephone returned the words in a deceptively mild tone. Obviously, something happened in the past between them involving biological warfare.

He knew better than to ask. Ignorance is bliss and all that.

"Though if only words could wound, then perhaps these trite conversations would be moot," Persephone continued as she ignored the aghast look on Pandora's face. "As for a box of viruses, I am unsure if the last few plagues haven't been entirely your fault," Persephone confirmed what Devon had just been thinking as she took a sip of champagne.

Persephone's eyes continued to watch Pandora lazily as the woman in front of them took in her words.

Pandora let her smile slip as her stare grew malicious. "How is hell these days?" A caustic tone colored her words. "Lonely, I bet. Have you managed to find someone to look past your bed full of blood and bones?"

She looked at Devon on the last remark with a smirk of victory in her eyes. Persephone smiled as if Pandora were simply asking about the weather and not trying to weave malice into her words. Attempting to cut at Persephone's identity and lack of companionship.

"Darling," Persephone started, her voice sweet yet cold somehow. "You try so ridiculously hard to use words to cut, hurt, and deceive because that is all you know. Imagine your world should you pull people up instead of trying to bury them beneath your off-brand heels. Perhaps you might find that the gossip you spread like disease will eventually come back to haunt you. And, when I see your soul come through my gates, the damage you have done will stain your soul so black even a Goddess cannot find redemption in you. Now then, please enjoy the rest of your evening. I hear they have canapes coming out soon."

Persephone ended this by turning her back to the woman. The ultimate insult among the social elite he supposed. Persephone was telling her she was inconsequential and feared nothing from her.

Pandora stared for a moment longer before she turned on her heels to skulk off.

CHAPTER 21

"Wow." Devon laughed under his breath.

"Nothing but an annoying fly on a perfectly enjoyable summer evening," she muttered and took a generous sip of champagne.

He caught sight of Hera walking towards them with a faint trail of gold behind her.

"Oh, thanks. You ran her off to her hovel before I could get my hooks into her? Honestly, Persephone, you cannot let me enjoy myself at all can you?" Pouting, Hera summoned over a server to grab a glass of champagne.

"Oh my," she murmured, eyeing the server walking toward them as she licked her lips.

"Darling, I think we should enjoy ourselves tonight in a carnal fashion. Find me after the speeches." She winked at the young man and ran her fingers along his cheek. The man jolted a bit, as if given a little shock, before giving an overly enthusiastic nod. Hera gave him a light little pat on his cheek before her hand went to the bust of her gown to remove a room key. She slipped it into the server's jacket pocket with a pat. The man smiled and returned to his rotation around the ballroom.

Hera turned back and spoke to Persephone and Devon in a quieter voice. "The only true joy I get from these events is a wild evening with some beautiful lovers. We all go home blissed out after. It is a wonderful experience. Persephone never enjoys herself such as Amphitrite and I do. Honestly, I would think Persephone would be the one who could find herself with a harem should she wish."

Persephone rolled her eyes, but Devon felt his muscles tighten. He tried to relax before Hera noticed his urge for violence rising in his chest again.

He put his hand to Persephone's back casually and immediately felt the urge lessen. Thankfully, Hera was too busy talking about harems to notice his momentary lack of control.

"Though, now that I think about it..." Hera tapped her lips with her pointer finger as she trailed off. A feminine growl left Persephone's lips as if she already knew what Hera was about to say. "Oh, come now sister, Devon is probably aware by now you are no virgin. In fact, Tristan is here tonight." She winked at Persephone, an indulgent smile on her face. Before either of them could respond to her, she simply turned and walked off without another word.

Hera waved to a group of people in the corner and passed by the waiter she had chosen for the evening. Devon watched her run her hand across his chest, causing the man to take in a startled breath as his cheeks flushed with arousal.

"Tristan?" Devon growled as he turned to look at Persephone. Persephone placed her hand on his chest to send calming power over him.

He felt the same out-of-control feeling like he did the first night in the Underworld. Emotions too close to the surface for him to manage or contain.

"Yes, a lover. I did have them. I haven't been with any in a while though. So, no one has been roaming the castle at night on their way from my bed." She used a soothing voice as if to calm a wild animal.

What must she think of him? He couldn't even understand himself at the moment.

Devon felt the tightening of his jaw, the clenching of his fists. He knew he could not, would not, guarantee any man's safety should he catch them leaving her room at night.

He would happily add to the incoming souls that day.

His urge to keep anything and everything away from the Goddess was unlike him. He knew it wasn't him in control right now, and that only added fuel to the growing inferno inside Devon.

This place was triggering the power inside of him. The God was far too powerful for Devon to fight. He was trying to remain in control, regardless of its futility.

"Korinna, so good to see you again," an older gentleman greeted and

Devon lost focus on his internal struggle for a moment. The stately man approached with an elegant middle-aged woman at his side. He took Persephone's hand and bent to kiss it.

Devon could feel pulses of power coming from the older man, ones that actually had Devon's power retreating almost as much as Persephone's power had.

"I have been excited about discussing an upcoming investment with Cerberus Financial, but I have been unable to contact you as of late," he said as he let go of Persephone's hand and stepped back to his partner's side.

The two of them reeked of old money, the kind that couldn't imagine the grime and darkness Devon had seen.

"Mr. Murphy," Persephone started, before nodding to the woman. "Dr. Murphy, so good to see you both. I apologize, I have been out of the office more than usual recently. I will speak with my assistant bright and early Monday morning about setting up a meeting." Turning to Devon, she placed her hand on his shoulder.

"Let me introduce you to my date this evening," she started but halted when a younger man walked up to stand next to Mr. Murphy and his wife.

Dark hair, golden skin, dark brown eyes all in a dark blue suit with a white button up, the young man exuded a laissez-faire attitude, but Devon froze as they locked eyes. His entire body went rigid, and he was sure Persephone picked up on it.

Before she could finish her introduction, the young man stepped around the older man and stood squarely in front of Devon.

"A pleasure to make your acquaintance," he said. The man greeted Devon as if this was the first time they had met. He showed no inclination that he knew Devon. Had been his closest friend for years. He put his hand out in a friendly greeting, but his clenched jaw told another story as he stared Devon down.

He had not seen West since his death. He remembered the tears in West's eyes as he worked to stop the bleeding. When he checked Devon's pulse for the last time to feel the fading heartbeat as Devon was lost to the darkness. West screaming at him to hold on. That he couldn't leave him, to just hold on.

Devon finally pulled his hand from his pocket and shook the hand

153

West offered.

West used a crushing grip that promised there would be a discussion to come. And Devon better have a damn good explanation.

"Ah, let me introduce you both to my son," Mr. Murphy stated, shocking Devon out of the stare down with his old friend.

"He just came home from a jaunt out of the country, and I am looking to finally bring him into the family business. Korinna, let me present to you the heir of the shipping and transportation empire that is Oceanus industries, Weston Murphy. I am hoping he can make some business connections tonight for when he is ready to step into my shoes."

West let go of Devon's hand and turned to shake Persephone's as he gave her a smile that did not meet his eyes.

"You can call me West."

She released his hand as he shot another look at Devon. Anger and hurt flashed before being replaced by his signature look of boredom he had worked hard to perfect.

"If you will excuse me, I see someone I've been needing to speak with." West nodded goodbye to them and walked away. His shoulders tense as he grabbed a drink from a tray and disappeared into the crowd.

"I apologize for his behavior. He has not really been himself the past few days since he returned from overseas. A friend of his died recently, and it has been incredibly difficult for him. They seemed to have been close," Dr. Murphy explained as she watched her son walk away, a look of concern in her eyes.

Mr. Murphy placed a hand on her shoulder, but his eyes were not on his son's exit.

They were focused squarely on Devon.

Had he not known better, he would have thought the man had somehow put the puzzle pieces together, but there was no way he could truly know what happened, or who Devon was now.

Persephone put two and two together herself and slid a quick look to Devon. He gave her an almost imperceptible shake of the head.

"I am so very sorry to hear that, Dr. Murphy. You will let us know if there is anything we can do to help your family through this time of healing?" Persephone asked as West's mother turned back to look at them, her smile saddened.

Mr. Murphy grabbed and kissed Persephone's hand one more time.

"Of course, and please always know that no matter what, we at Oceanus Industries are here for you, too. Tides are changing, my friend. Take care not to get swept away." A concerned smile crossed his face as he used his other hand to pat the top of hers.

Persephone gave him a smile of confusion, as if the words carried a heavier meaning than either of them could decipher at this point in time.

"And Devon, so very nice to meet you."

Something transpired between Persephone and Mr. Murphy right then. He watched two shades of blue smoke create a haze around the two people and realized Mr. Murphy was more than he seemed.

Mr. Murphy nodded in goodbye and turned him and his wife to another couple that had been waiting for their turn to speak.

It turned out he didn't know his friend, the heir of an empire, quite as well as he thought.

Devon went back over their conversation only to realize that Persephone never gave Mr. Murphy his name and yet the man had called him Devon.

"We will find Weston after the event," she whispered, only to receive a distracted nod from Devon. His mind whirled and tried to put together any clues about West's identity that he could have missed.

Something to reconcile the man who had just stood in front of him as the one he had fought alongside, been deployed with to every dangerous place left in Zephyr.

His mind was consumed by this new information and he had no idea what Persephone had said or with whom she conversed. Everything was a fog around him.

Persephone touched his arm and the world filtered back in. He heard Medusa instructing everyone to have a seat for the speeches as he blinked back into his new reality.

They found their tables where their names were adorned in a gold script on dark green place cards. He took in the formal tableware and really wished he had some idea what to do with all the forks.

It was like a novel where the poor boy goes to dinner with the fancy family. He sits there with his thumb up his ass as he eats stuff that is probably a garnish and slurps his soup much to the embarrassment of everyone at the table.

This entire evening was well outside of his comfort zone.

He watched other people, copying them in the hopes he didn't make a bigger fool of himself. Not something that had bothered him before, but he didn't want his actions to have repercussions for Persephone in the mortal world.

A man with dark brown hair and eyes sat next to Persephone. He was obviously one of those guys who looked like he spent his entire youth breaking girls' hearts. The man oozed the type of confidence that said he knew he could score with minimal effort.

Devon was immediately annoyed by him. He didn't miss the way Persephone's posture went rigid as the man sat next to her and Devon's eyes moved to the place card where the man had seated himself.

Tristan Wade. Of course, it was her ex-lover because tonight was not already a nightmare. His eyes swung to where Hera was seated next to what he assumed was her date, with Amphitrite and her date next to her. She winked at his scowl, and he narrowed his eyes in suspicion.

He had hoped she'd not caught on to his embarrassing internal jealous rampage earlier, but of course she had. She would no doubt enjoy making him incredibly uncomfortable. He was learning Hera was adept at making any situation a battle of wills.

"Tristan," Persephone said in way of greeting. His smile in return made Devon want to knock all of his teeth out. When Tristan leaned forward to kiss her cheek, Devon almost broke his water glass.

This reaction only widened Hera's smirk, a smirk that immediately raised his blood pressure.

Him and Hera were going to have words later.

He tried to keep his heart rate under control and come off as unaffected as he took a drink of his somehow unbroken glass of water. He tried not to listen, but still caught every word.

Persephone's sisters were also eavesdropping. Though they were hardly being discreet about it.

He watched as Amphitrite hid her smile behind her glass while Hera's face outright glowed at the awkwardness of the situation. They were entertaining themselves at his and Persephone's expense.

"I really enjoyed our time together the last time I saw you. I am staying here tonight, so I thought perhaps…" Devon caught sight of the

156

man's hand moving to her thigh under the table as he whispered his invitation into her ear.

The only thing that allowed him to keep that hand was Persephone's response, as she took his hand and moved it away from her. She placed it back on the table without an ounce of tenderness.

Even at her shunning of the man's affections, Devon felt his muscles go rigid and a burst of energy passed through his veins that he had never felt before.

It moved from his head, down the entire length of his body, and seemed to move into the floor at his feet. He did not see any green light, so he assumed he had not physically lit up, but he couldn't help wondering where that surge of power went.

Persephone moved her other hand to Devon's in an attempt to send calming energy. This move was not missed at all by Tristan as his eyes narrowed on her hand covering Devon's.

She ignored Tristan as her fingers wrapped around his, and in a moment of boldness, he turned his hand and entwined their fingers. Persephone raised her eyebrows but said nothing.

"Oh wow!" A woman bellowed from the balcony, but Devon was watching Tristan's reaction and calculating how quick he could stab the man with the steak knife.

Everyone else was too busy watching the drama unfold between the two men to notice what had made the woman shout out with such enthusiasm.

"Tristan, let me introduce you to my date, Devon. Devon, this is Tristan, an old acquaintance."

Tristan looked unhappy about the introduction but raised his hand for Devon to shake, the snarl on Tristan's face became an unfriendly smirk.

A small rumble made the room tremble, which captured everyone's concerned attention.

Everyone but Devon, who focused singularly on Tristan.

Persephone touched Devon's shoulder as she shot more calming energy into him. He caught her looking over at Hera with a warning scowl.

Was Hera somehow adding to this influx of his power? Was that what the warning scowl had been for?

157

He didn't dare look away from Tristan, determined to be the one to maintain eye contact. He'd deal with Hera later.

A middle-aged woman came over to get Persephone to meet a benefactor. She started to decline, but Devon shook his head.

"Go, I am fine," he whispered.

She simply stared at him a moment and glanced to her sisters before she nodded in agreement. Standing, she put her hand on his shoulder and left it there. She wasn't leaving, instead making the other benefactor come to her. All because of him. He felt like a burden right then.

Because of him, she couldn't rub elbows with the elite. She had to babysit him and make sure he didn't accidentally burn the building down.

He angled away from Persephone and took Tristan's outstretched hand, trying not to break all the bones.

"Hello Devon, how do you know our Persephone?"

Our Persephone?

He was definitely going to kill this man if he said anything like that again. Devon tightened his hand to the point that Tristan blanched in pain.

"Fate threw us together. I can't say she has said anything about you to me, Mr. Wade." He let the words carry over to Tristan who looked angered by that before an ugly scowl took over his face. "Guess she is not quite your anything anymore, huh?"

"One would assume," Tristan responded as Devon finally released his hand.

He was only slightly gratified to see Tristan shake it out a bit before placing it back in his lap.

Thankfully, they were quiet enough not to be heard, since Tristan was not quite the gentlemen he appeared to be. Devon was going to end this night covered in the man's blood.

Tristan edged closer to whisper over the sound of the crowd. "I understand you staking your claim, and I get it, she is an interesting creature. Though, I've never seen her continue to hold a plaything for longer than a few weeks. So just remember. Once your time is up, I'll be waiting." Tristan grinned wickedly before straightening back up in his seat.

Another small rumble, like thunder, from the open door that led out

158

to the gardens caused several people to gasp and move back inside.

Devon was only thinking of how much blood splatter might get on his clothes once he stabbed Tristan to notice what was happening outside.

"Watch yourself, Tristan," Amphitrite growled. "You speak of my sister."

He was about to choke the man to death with his own necktie, his hands moving of their own volition from his lap when Persephone returned to her seat, pulling her chair in.

Her demeanor was irritated and aggressive as she put her napkin back in her lap. Everyone went still. The tension thick as bulletproof glass.

"Tristan, please remember our last tryst ended with me expressing my interest had waned. Please do not misinterpret the fact that it was a disappointing match for us both. In trying to spare your feelings, I think I mislead you. My apologies. Thank you for bringing my misleading words to my attention. I do not think I will have further need of your affections of any kind."

Hera choked a bit, covering her mouth, but her eyes were full of laughter. Amphitrite's eyebrows were up, her lips pulled into a devilish smirk.

"Are you really going to act like that just because this week's side dish is throwing a tantrum?" he demanded, throwing his napkin on the table.

"Oh Tristan, go tend to your ego elsewhere. I am trying to eat, and the thought of your dick is putting off my appetite." Hera waved her hand in dismissal.

Tristan shot the Goddess a withering glare. "I do not need to hear anything from the woman who defines daddy issues."

"Oh darling, we don't have the time, nor you the credentials, to even begin to understand my issues."

"Bitch," Tristan whispered under his breath as he shot up from his seat.

Hera tapped her nose and winked at Devon as she took a sip of wine.

"Wait until you're cast off, too," Tristan snarled the words at Devon. As if using them to strike Devon would mean anything at this point. Tristan had been put in his place. Any moves he made now were defensive.

159

Devon moved to stand, and though not as tall as Tristan, he could hold his own. Devon had always been a formidable figure against anyone of any stature.

"Mr. Wade," he started. "I think maybe you should find somewhere else to lick your wounds. Staying here and yelling about your lack of sexual prowess will only embarrass you further." Devon watched the man blather a bit before he shot a glare at Devon and went to find another seat across the room. Devon sat back down and looked at Hera. He just knew she had set up this little confrontation.

She nodded as if in approval of what had just transpired, as if Devon didn't feel his heart pounding loudly in his ears. The confrontation still boiling his already far too heated blood.

"Did you enjoy that, Hera?" Persephone asked, her eyes flashing with blue Godfire for just a moment before the embers in them dulled. Gone as quick as it came.

"Oh, sister, I truly did." Hera let loose an amused smile towards the pair of them as she lifted her glass in toast to the nightmare she just helped to create.

CHAPTER 22

Devon tried to calm himself, but the more he tried, the tighter his skin felt.

His nerves tingled along the surface as if he had bugs crawling underneath his flesh. The sudden movement of people around him made the sensation worse.

The floor beneath him shook.

What are they yelling at?

Overloaded, he felt like his eyes were going to pop out of his skull from the pressure building there.

His hearing was suddenly a loud roar, and he, vaguely, heard his name. A hand wrapped around his arm, pulling at him. He couldn't even focus, his vision blurry.

When his vision did clear for a moment, he found himself on a balcony.

How did I get here?

His brain felt like it was melting in his skull.

Persephone's face came into view. It almost seemed like she was under water. Or maybe that was him? His vision was rippling, his hearing roaring, his heart thundering.

His head suddenly jerked to the side as if someone slapped him, but he felt nothing. The din inside him dulled enough for him to recognize Persephone attempting to neutralize his power, but it wasn't working.

It. Wasn't. Working.

Panic truly set in.

Persephone had never mentioned how Gods could die — could an explosion do it? Like the one building up inside him?

A man suddenly appeared behind Persephone. He could see that, and abruptly the feeling of internal combustion lessened inside him. Almost as if transferred to someone other than him.

The man. The man was too close to Persephone. No one should be that close to her but him.

Only ever me.

Anyone else was a danger to her. To them.

That was all he could think as his mind recognized the man, Tristan, behind Persephone. He was saying something to her, Devon's ears still not hearing anything but a loud roar.

It was Tristan, then it was his old Captain. The one Devon knew was dead, yet he stood before him. One moment Tristan, the next, his greatest nemesis in his life.

It was when Tristan/The Captain touched her arm as if to pull her away, something in him snapped.

No.

He will not touch her!

Before he knew it, Persephone was behind him as he faced the man. An ear-splitting cacophony rattled the windows. The sound of glass breaking as shards pelted them like rain. And as suddenly as the man who wore both Tristan and the Captain's faces had appeared, he was gone.

***

Persephone heard people scrambling to see what had happened, but thankfully Hera got there first.

As Archon, she had calmed the crowd and moved them from that part of the building. Amphitrite looked over to her from where she helped guard the doors with a question in her eyes. She seemed to notice Persephone wrapped tightly in Devon's arms, unable to move an inch.

Persephone shook her head that no, she did not need help. Amphitrite nodded before she turned to help their Archon guide the people to safer ground.

162

She blinked at what had transpired in mere seconds.

Devon had covered her body with his own as he took down half of the building. The glass and debris hitting him instead of her.

His power.

His power had just demolished the west side of the building and gardens and he was not at all aware of it yet, she could tell.

Devon was breathing heavily in her ear and she could almost sense that he was scared to look and face what he had just done.

"Is he dead? Are we dead?" Devon asked, and the question almost made her laugh before she settled her hands against his chest to push him back. She felt his hesitation to let her go, and to her surprise, he crushed her to him for a moment longer. When he did finally release her, he held her at arm's length with his eyes still closed.

"I don't want to look," he muttered, dropping his hands before he moved them to his head and grabbed fists full of hair.

She was about to reassure him when he took a deep breath and released it on a sigh, his eyes opening as he turned to take it all in.

The stone that was once the wall and part of the balcony was now reduced to rubble. The fountain was broken, sputtering water over what was now overgrown gardens.

Vines had crawled up the walls and pierced through the stone to bring it down, some vines still holding in place pieces of the wall and part of the balcony.

Green fire had blasted out like a backflash and broke windows.

It looked like a war zone.

She noticed his vines had moved to keep them safe, their side of the balcony held up by vines alone.

Concerned he might lose control of them, she pulled at his arm to move them onto a stable surface.

"Why… why did I react like that?" he asked more to himself than her.

"Your emotions were heightened for some reason, most likely Tristan agitating you." She watched his hands glow green for a split second when she said his name and decided to try to avoid speaking of him while Devon was in such a volatile state of mind. "Your power is tied to your emotional state, so when they became too much for you, you did not know how to focus and control them. This is something we have to work on."

He turned his head to the side to look at her, his eyes lit with green Godfire. He said nothing.

Just watched her.

She held his gaze, standing confidently in an attempt to inspire confidence in him as well. A nonverbal statement that everything would be alright.

Turning to fully face her, he stalked closer, invading her personal space. She didn't dare move an inch, unsure of what his intentions were and her curiosity driving her to find out.

As he moved even closer to where they were almost touching, she could feel his body heat as they stood face to face. Toe to toe.

He stared into her eyes, his lit so brightly one would hardly be able to decipher the emotion in them, but she saw his confusion and something more. His face moved closer to hers and she knew in that moment he intended to kiss her. Lay claim to her.

She wondered if she should back away and break the moment. He was still emotionally vulnerable, even someone as detached as her knew that. Could see that.

She had the desire to kiss him, and that was more than she had felt in a long time, but she did not want him to do it because his God form was making him.

Yet, she did not step away.

His breath moved across her lips as she watched his eyes begin to close, hers closing as well in anticipation of the moment her lips met his. She felt his nose bump over hers as he moved his lips softly to hers.

A scream of pain rent the air, bringing them back to the moment. Devon took a step back, his face horrified again.

They both turned to where the scream came from, moving into the hall right after finding several injured people.

"I did this..." Devon said, horrified and pale with shock.

Persephone moved and knelt down to help one woman who was trapped under a pillar, which thankfully was not too heavy. At least not for a Goddess.

A groan from nearby had Devon moving that direction, where a man with a bleeding head wound was wobbling, trying to stay upright as he made his way to the exit. Devon was quick to grab cloth napkins from a nearby bussing station to staunch the bleeding while Persephone helped the fallen woman up.

Devon had gotten the man to an onsite medic before Persephone had calmed the woman enough to stand after removing the pillar.

Persephone looked up to see Devon approach her, perhaps to help, when someone in the corner of her vision halted him in his tracks.

"Devon," someone, a woman, said as she moved up next to Persephone. The woman's attention completely on Devon.

Persephone looked between both Devon and the woman, her mind throwing out question after question, when the woman she was helping to stand groaned.

"Apologies. Let's get you some help," Persephone told her as she walked past Devon. In the chaos of the last few minutes, emergency responders had arrived. When one approached her, Persephone encouraged them to see to the woman in her arms.

Persephone looked over her shoulder at the woman in the blue dress with Devon. Her gown rippled around her in shimmering waves and her long red hair flowed past her bare shoulders. The light caught on what looked to be a nose ring and where she had thought the woman's red hair was pulled back on one side, it was actually shaved.

"I thought that was you." A soft smile coming to her pretty face.

"Sasha," he whispered back, his voice soft. Persephone knew what this was, she was not so adept at emotions that she failed to notice when two people held a certain level of intimacy.

They were lovers in his mortal days.

Persephone took a step away from Devon as the woman — *Sasha* — took a step closer to him. Sasha kept her shining eyes on Devon.

"You... they said you were dead." A tear dropped down her cheek and that was more than Persephone could take. To see someone from his mortal life that he cared for.

Why had she not thought about a loved one left behind? The people he had been taken from.

She was being selfish, thinking only of her desire to have Devon as hers. She turned to leave as she felt a throbbing pressure in her chest.

It was the answer to a question she asked herself daily since meeting him. Could they ever be more?

No.

She needed to see him as a friend and only a friend. Persephone could not let her heart lead her any further astray. She closed her eyes and let the cold-hearted Goddess flow through her veins, pulling her mental shield back into place. She squeezed her bond to Devon so tightly closed, she wondered if it would ever open again.

"Persephone," Devon finally seemed to notice her as she moved to step around this woman, his lover, and back out to the hall. She turned her head to look over her shoulder and shook her head. As she left the balcony, a feeling of power radiated off of Sasha.

Interesting that he had not chosen a mortal to love.

It didn't matter. She would not stand in the way of him and his lover, or his past. That was for him to navigate and decide on what should remain. She could feel something between him and the woman, and if it were love, she would not begrudge him this. He would stand beside Persephone as nothing more than a friend and she would accept that. All she wanted for him in this second life was happiness. With or without her.

So why did the thought of him not being hers feel so horrid?

Persephone moved out of the way of several guests as they filed out of the ballroom and were instructed to leave the area of the damage. The distraction was enough that she went unnoticed until she came upon her sisters.

Amphitrite looked bewildered, and Hera leaned against a column with her eyes on Persephone.

"Everything alright, sister?" Hera asked, her tone bland but her eyes intense.

Persephone nodded her head, unsure of how to discuss what all had transpired.

Hera was her usual self and managed to gain all the details she needed without a word spoken between them.

"His power was a bit out of hand, but as we all remember when we first rose from the dead, our emotional baggage did its own damage." Hera smirked, "Though, he seemed a bit territorial."

"Hera, let it go," Amphitrite warned as her attention moved to Hera. "Not here."

Hera only waved Amphitrite off.

"It seemed like he wasn't even aware of why. Like a dog pissing to show ownership, but unaware of why he hiked his leg."

"Enough." Persephone only used that one word but put full force behind it.

Hera pushed off the column and moved gracefully to stand in front of Persephone.

"Is there more to your relationship with him than we thought?" This time Hera's voice held none of the teasing tone. Her face completely serious.

Persephone closed her eyes as she shook her head, but she felt hollow inside at her answer.

As she opened her eyes again, she caught Hera's gaze assessing her.

"Perhaps he needs some stress relief." Hera smirked, but Persephone was not going to be baited. She knew what Hera was doing, something she always did to manipulate Persephone into admitting her feelings. Hera seemed callous, but her actions had proven in the past to have a rhyme and reason.

She wanted the truth so she could wield her sword in any battle that helped to protect her sisters, and she'd get the truth however she needed to.

"Perhaps a quick tumble with that saucy thing will help take the edge off of his uncontrollable powers…"

Persephone stopped herself before she bit out a scathing retort. That was what Hera wanted.

Ever since their youth, Hera knew how to make Persephone think and admit to feelings she would otherwise push deep down. Hera always using herself as the bad guy in these situations.

Persephone stepped past them but stopped to look over her shoulder at her sisters. She caught concern in Hera's eyes before she let her face slip back into a devious mask.

Persephone simply whispered, "*Perhaps,*" before she walked away.

CHAPTER 23

Devon lowered the hand he had put out to stop Persephone as he watched her vanish into the crowd.

A creeping numbness came over him.

Something deep inside him rebelled and told him to follow her. To finish that moment. To kiss and claim her as his.

Instead, he turned to Sasha.

One problem at a time.

It stunned him that his entire past was coming down on his head in one night. West, and now her.

On top of Sasha's surprise disruption, he noticed a sea green haze around her. Sasha was not all she seemed to be.

He could feel power, though not as strong as his and Persephone's, radiating from her. He realized the colors he saw around the people were physical manifestations of their power.

"You're not human." He stared at her aura, tilting his head at the flash of shock in her eyes.

Had everything he knew from his old life been a lie? What was real and how did Sasha work into all this? Had she seen West? Was West human?

The room had been too crowded for Devon to feel anything from him.

He pinched the bridge of his nose with his thumb and forefinger to ward off the headache from the growing questions.

"I was picking up something powerful, but I thought it was just her. What happened to you, Devon?" she asked as she moved to him.

Petite but deadly, that was always how he had seen Sasha. They had an on-again, off-again fling while he stayed at one of his safe houses between missions. It was never more than that.

Merely two people who found comfort in each other for a brief period of time. He had, at one point, thought she was a friend. Obviously, he really didn't know what a friend was since every person he had ever known aside from his father had lied to him.

"What are you, Sasha?" he asked, not ready to delve into his own death and explain how he had no idea what was happening to him. That was a vulnerability he was not going to share.

Especially not with someone who did not trust him enough to share her own secrets.

"I'm sorry, Devon. I never meant to mislead you. Please know it was not something I kept from you for any other reason than I wanted to know what it was to feel human," she whispered, her eyes pleading with him to understand. "After my father went to the deep sleep, and my brother took over, I saw an opportunity to live among the humans. I went to a remote place and got a job, lived among humans who did not know who I was or what I could do. It was… nice."

He could only stare at her and wonder what she was even doing here. He was sure she read it all in his eyes because she sighed and looked out over the demolished grounds.

"Wow. You did all that?" She laughed a little, but the humor seemed artificial and forced.

She shook her head and sighed as she turned to face him.

She ran her hands up and down her arms in a nervous gesture he had never seen before. When they met, she had a confidence that drew him in, a way about her that told the world they had to accept who she was because she would never apologize for it.

Standing in front of him was a totally different woman. A stranger to him now.

"My name is not Sasha. That is a name I used because it sounded more human. My real name is Minthe." He could see how much she needed him to accept what she was saying. To forgive her for her lie.

"I am a Naiad, or River Nymph. My brother, the one you ran off, is Tristan the demigod of the River Cocytus."

Devon stared at her a moment as pieces fell into place.

"In the Underworld? That river Cocytus?" he asked, his voice barely above a whisper.

She only nodded in reply, looking out into the garden at the damage he had caused to avoid his gaze.

What were the odds that his ex-lover would be the sister to Persephone's ex-lover?

The man who had pushed him to the point of destroying the building he was currently in.

He would laugh if he wasn't about to pass out from emotional and physical overload.

"Wow. Okay," he muttered as he ran his hand through his hair. This was apparently his new daily routine, being confused and out of sorts.

"Are you..." Sasha, or Minthe now he supposed, watched him a moment before she continued. "Are you and the Goddess in a relationship?"

He widened his eyes in shock at her question.

She just confessed to lying to him and now had the audacity to question him?

Her eyes held hope, that maybe he wasn't and perhaps Minthe could have another chance at him. Have him back as they had once been. Lovers who took comfort in each other's bodies when the nights were long and lonely.

He shook his head at her.

"Not really seeing how that is any of your business, Minthe." He couldn't help the sneer that came with her name. He was tired of the lies.

Her eyes widened a moment, but she finally gave a sad and solemn nod.

Biting her lower lip, she looked up at him beneath her lashes. "Are you bound to the Underworld?"

He was unsure how much information he should give her, but it would hardly be anything more than what everyone else knew in the Underworld.

"Yes. When I died, she offered some seeds to me. Somehow, in this weird acid trip of a life I live now, that bound me to the Underworld." He knew his face and tone were angry, aggressive. He wasn't sure how not to be angry right now if he was honest.

Now that he was face to face with his past, he was questioning everything.

Should he have let himself move on to true death? Why did he take the seeds in the first place?

It seemed so clear in that moment.

He was forever bound to the world of death, full of some destructive power that could collapse entire buildings and would never be allowed the bliss of forgetting his past and his actions.

Stuck in his thoughts and heading down a dark rabbit hole, he didn't notice Minthe moving closer until she took hold of his hands.

"I shouldn't admit this, but I came here for you. I thought I saw you in the Underworld, jumping across the realm with Persephone. I knew I needed a moment to talk to you and this was it. I had to convince my brother to bring me." She squeezed his hand in hers. His large and calloused to her small and smooth. "We were great together Devon, and this is our chance to do it right. Do it in a way that we hold no secrets from each other."

He stared at their hands but didn't truly see them.

Looking back up into her eyes, he wondered if he could allow himself to slip back into the role of her lover. To take back some semblance of control in his life.

As he squeezed her hands back, he watched her smile grow as hope lit her eyes once more.

***

Persephone shadow jumped to the riverbank of Cocytus, wondering why she would even care enough to check on Tristan after his childish behavior in the mortal realm. But alas, he was part of her domain and therefore her responsibility.

To an extent.

Her instinct was also telling her that something was off with the river near Tartarus and the boneyard, so it was a good excuse to check on the area since Cocytus ran alongside it.

She looked out at the boneyard, seeing nothing amiss, waiting for Tristan to sense her there and find her himself.

Usually when she stepped onto the shore, he would immediately come to her, but this time he stalled. Or perhaps he was busy licking his wounds in silence, not wanting to face her after he disgraced himself. She was grateful for the spare moments to look around without distraction.

"Goddess," she heard his low baritone from behind her. She turned to face him and took in his changed appearance. In his domain of the river, he radiated charisma.

On the darker, lonelier nights down here by herself, he had appealed to her as a way to satiate the need that all creatures have.

She was not an idiot. She knew she felt nothing more for him than she promised. She had made that clear on every occasion that they spoke.

She finally put a stop to it when she noticed he was searching for more than sexual companionship.

"I am tired and would like to go to bed soon, Persephone. Can you just say what you need to say so we can finish this?" He rubbed at his temples, such a mortal thing to do.

"I was simply checking to see if you were alright," she inquired, her eyes narrowed as she watched him. He was not acting like himself. His normal swagger gone. But a dressing down in public could do that to a man's ego, she supposed.

He put his hands out to the side as if to show her his unblemished self as he turned a full circle before looking back at her with an eyebrow raised.

"Hearty and whole. Anything else?" he asked, his tone brisk even for him.

She only nodded.

"Not at this time. Take care, Tristan," she said, her tone even and clinical. Their situation, his behavior, was causing them both to act out of character.

Thankful he didn't want to discuss the evening any more deeply, she began to conjure her shadows. She could be back at the castle before Devon returned, and he was the only one she wanted to speak with tonight.

He was the one who needed her, wasn't he? An image of him locked in an embrace with a red-haired woman flashed in her mind's eye. Well, his *powers* needed her, at the very least. And she was afraid she'd left him alone too long after his eruption. She had left Hecate and Thanatos there to watch over him from afar, but she felt like it should have been her instead.

"Wait..." Tristan called, and she had to stop herself from grinding her teeth.

She attempted to school her expression so he didn't see her irritation as she turned to him. She may have checked on him, but she was still angry and had nothing further to discuss.

"I am sorry for my behavior at the gala. To be honest, I was jealous. Extremely jealous actually. I know it has been a long time since we were together but seeing you with him made me feel barbaric and possessive," he said, his face chagrin as her jaw dropped. "I am truly sorry for my actions."

She heard the words he said, but something inside her told her to tread with caution. The situation was only going to cause unwanted confusion and discomfort in her soul.

He was on her in a millisecond, and she stumbled back in shock as his arm wrapped around her waist to catch her. His hand moved to her face, hesitant at first, but only a moment before he cupped her jaw.

"I've been in love with you for ages." He was serious, she realized, and she panicked at the sincerity in his expression. Her eyes widened. "I've taken what you were willing to give, but it was never enough," he continued. "I wanted to have you in other ways. Like enjoying each other's company over dinner or you coming to me after a long day and we converse before falling into bed."

"Tristan," she growled, pushing at his chest but his arm was a steel band around her.

"I never said anything because I thought with time, you'd feel the same way. But that man, he seemed to have a connection with you that I never had. Whether you know it or not, he would never help you run this realm as I would. Where you are the queen, I would be your perfect king."

Her heart was pounding, and she didn't know if it was from Tristan's proximity or the urge to escape. She put her hand to Tristan's wrist to move his hand away from her face.

When he saw that he was about to be dismissed, he took his chance and had his lips on hers before she could blink.

He had moved with a stealth she had never known him to have. His tongue pushing into her mouth to assert claim before she was able to have a cohesive thought.

Once her brain was back in fighting shape, she shoved him back and swiped the back of her hand across her mouth.

"Enough, Tristan," she growled, angry that he had managed to take it that far. And even angrier she hadn't had the foresight to stop it.

She noticed someone standing near them in the shadows from the corner of her eye.

Turning her head, she saw Devon leaning against one of the dead trees near the banks, his arms folded over his chest and a blank expression on his face.

Not one of jealousy, which bothered her after that moment on the balcony, but perhaps his power had been more of an influence on his behavior than she had originally thought.

"Does he always follow you around like a stray dog?" Tristan asked, his teeth sharpening as he started to change forms.

"You need to watch your tone," she ordered. "He is no longer a mere mortal and is capable of power greater than even yours. You would be wise to heed my warning on this before you end up ripped apart by vines." Her hands fisted at her sides. "I believe Devon left you with a significant warning of what could happen earlier this evening," she muttered before turning to move toward Devon.

Tristan growled and grabbed her elbow, twisting her back around to him.

Green flashed and leaves fluttered as Persephone felt herself pushed behind someone. As the light faded, she saw that Devon had opened a portal and was facing off with Tristan.

"You were warned," Devon's voice was harder and lower than she had ever heard from him.

"You've been here for all of a week and you think you've earned a place at her side?" Tristan laughed.

"Gentlemen," Persephone cut in, stepping between the men facing off. "Enough."

She used her magic to calm Devon, thankful they were in her domain where her powers were stronger.

Devon looked at her and she froze before any other words could leave her mouth. His eyes were not lit up. The God was not at the forefront of his consciousness.

174

Tristan took advantage of her distraction and made his escape, turning into water and splashing back into his river.

Devon's head swung around in time to watch the last of the water that was Tristan escape.

"Coward," Devon hissed.

He was still irate. She could tell by the clenched jaw and fists but kept her observation to herself.

"I was unaware Sasha was Tristan's sister," he growled, his voice still as gruff as it was during his stand-off with Tristan.

"Yes," she conceded to his change of subject, "Little Minthe has been gone so long, I didn't realize that was her." With her face fresh in her mind, she could remember the tiny nymph from long ago.

"Minthe. I thought her name was Sasha, but nope, just her way of fitting in the mortal world and pretending," he muttered, the anger in his voice evident.

"You knew her from your days as a mercenary?" she asked, unsure of why she would want clarification on something she was sure she already knew.

Devon nodded once, quite stiffly she noted.

"It surprised me to see her here. She worked as a bartender near my hideout in the northern country."

"Kept each other warm on the many long winter nights?" She smiled sardonically. She chastised herself for allowing jealousy to get the better of her. It was burning through her, and she found she was not as envious of human emotions as she had previously thought.

It was downright annoying not to have control of one's emotional state.

He looked at her, then glanced back to the path in front of him. His hands moved into his pockets as he flexed his jaw back and forth.

"Just ask what you want to know," he said. "Yes. We slept together. I would go, we would do our thing, and I'd bolt. I never stuck around. Not with any of my lovers and especially not her. That was then and it will never happen again," he stated with finality.

She stopped him with her hand to his elbow to make him turn to her. She was never one not to speak her truth.

"I am sorry. I shouldn't have pried into your past. My apologies. You've had an unbelievably overwhelming night."

He only nodded as he stared past her.

"It's fine. We both have a past," he told her. "I get it. All I ask is that if you stand on a balcony and almost kiss me, or this God that keeps possessing me, at least wait a good week before you let some other guy stick his tongue down your throat. Makes a man feel a little cheap."

His eyes lit up before he disappeared in a flash of green light. A gust of wind swirled the leaves that had fallen where he had just been.

CHAPTER 24

Persephone shadow jumped back to the castle to find Hecate waiting for her in the foyer.

Hecate stood at Persephone's abrupt appearance. She grabbed the Goddess by the arm and pulled her into one of the receiving rooms off to the side of the entryway.

Persephone nodded to the guards who stood sentry by the door, their blue and black uniforms crisp with boots polished to a perfect shine. Swords sheathed at their sides, greaves, and pauldrons black and shiny with skulls on them, which indicated whose army they served.

The Underworld's army was full of souls that had need of a life in service to be truly happy. Even if they could never remember the soldiers they had been, or the battles they had fought.

Their pitch-black eyes watched her vigilantly, and they bowed as they pushed the doors open for her and Hecate.

She wondered for a moment if this would have been Devon's fate. If the judges would have put him here as a guard, to serve the army of the Underworld.

She followed Hecate in the lamplit room. Shadows flickered across the walls, simply the absence of light and not the souls serving the castle.

They were completely alone.

Hecate whirled to face her right as the guards closed the door behind them. She threw her hands out and the walls grew silver in color, rippling as if water streamed down them.

Persephone shot Hecate a look of concern.

"What is going on that you need to put a spell of silence around us?" Persephone asked, tracking Hecate's every move.

"The river. Why did you visit it?" Hecate simply looked at her. Her eyes were mercurial, the witch pulling the strings and Hecate the puppet.

"To check on Tristan—"

"The real reason? That was not the *whole* reason, was it? You felt something there, didn't you?" she asked. That Hecate might have felt it too told her it wasn't all in her head.

"No, I felt something on the side of the river near the boneyard of Tartarus," she replied as she took a seat.

Hecate mirrored her and did the same.

"There was an amplifier at the gala," Hecate divulged quickly as if she was full of information and was trying to get it out to relieve the tension inside of her.

"A what?" Persephone jolted from her seat and started pacing, "Why would an *amplifier* be there?"

"Not just at the gala." Hecate stood, her eyes following Persephone as she paced back and forth across the room. "It was targeting Devon."

"What?" Persephone stopped abruptly and moved to Hecate. "How do you know this?" She grabbed her friend's shoulders, but quickly dropped them and moved to the nearby window. She crossed her arms across her chest as she waited for Hecate's response.

She shocked herself at the show of emotion but curbed her thoughts as she watched Hecate's eyes return to normal, the pupils and whites coming back.

"Someone there knew about Devon and was trying to test his powers," Hecate stated carefully. She paused, waiting for Persephone to grasp what this all meant, even though the statement was clear enough. She explained, "I felt a surge of his power building while at the table before it blew the top off outside, but there was residue of someone else there. I felt someone else's power swirling with his. It didn't feel like normal power, but like a spell. A booster spell someone put out with an intentional target. That target was Devon."

"We've been careful on who all knows the situation…" Looking at the silver silence spell, she looked to Hecate. "You think someone here in the Underworld is the reason why?"

"I do not know, but I am not ruling it out. We both felt something at

178

the river, something I recognize as the same signature as the amplifier at the gala. I have no idea if it's just the whole power structure finding its new place with Devon, or if someone is working against us."

"Well, that is just great. Not only are we at the mercy of the Moirai and their ominous predictions, but we have someone here working against us." Persephone felt like screaming. She was in danger of losing control of her emotional state for the first time in centuries.

They both looked at each other. She knew what Hecate was about to say.

"Tristan, was he acting out of character?" Hecate asked, already knowing the answer.

Persephone turned from Hecate and threw the doors open with her powers, breaking the silence spell Hecate had cast.

The guards outside of the doors turned to her, she knew her eyes bled black as her soldiers readied themselves to carry out her orders.

"Bring me Tristan of Cocytus right now," she growled. The guards did not hesitate as they shifted into their shadow forms to retrieve the river deity.

She noticed a Reevka stood near the front doors, waiting to open it for whoever was on the other side.

She knew who the Reevka waited for.

Persephone made her way to the door for another much-needed talk.

***

He heard the clicking of heels before she sat next to him.

His heart finally found a steady rate at the scent of her and the feel of her power as it wrapped around him. She must be able to do that without knowing because after his behavior he doubted she would intentionally do anything nice for him.

"I can leave if you want, I just wanted to make sure you were okay first," Persephone explained as she sat next to him on the front steps of the castle. She stretched her legs out in front of her and smoothed her long dress over her thighs.

Devon pulled his face away from his hands and looked at her. Her expression held none of the manipulation that Minthe's had. As far as he could tell, Persephone was always up front with him.

They promised each other honesty in the beginning, and he was incredibly thankful for that now.

"I did not handle that well back there and I am sorry for it," he began to explain, but she cut him off.

"No need." She didn't look at him, but instead stared at the Asphodel Fields laid out to the right of them. The souls milling about in their daily routines.

"Hecate discovered someone had trained an amplifier on you tonight. I thought you should know your powers going out of control like that was not your fault."

Devon's eyes narrowed. He was not exactly sure what all that entailed yet he still felt aggrieved enough about what transpired to allow that vindication.

"I also think," she started again, "we can agree your powers are tied to nature."

He laughed. "What gave it away? The vines? The deadly flowers someone found later in the corner of the garden? Thankfully no one else was hurt... or killed."

"Everyone who attended that evening is fine and resting. Hera made sure of it. They also have no idea any of that happened, thinking they had a wonderful evening and went home to bed. Do not place anymore blame at your own feet. It does nothing but trip you up should you decide to move forward."

He leaned forward to place his elbows on his knees and clasped his hands together in front of him. The silence permeated the air again. His thoughts were racing. He wanted to let the mishap at the gala go. Let himself have some grace.

"Seeing Tristan and Minthe, it threw me off..." he started only for her to hold her hands up for him to halt.

"I understand, Devon. You owe me no explanation."

"No, stop," he said, facing her fully. "I get some asshole found a way to amplify everything, but those feelings were already there. I was overwhelmed by seeing people I thought were my friends, that I trusted, only to find out they lied about everything. Then that Tristan guy comes in and starts..." Devon stopped and hung his head.

"I don't get any of it. The feeling, it was powerful, but it was something I must have felt before this." He leaned his body back to

180

where he balanced on his forearms as his head dropped back to look at the starless sky.

"I think at this point, I need to take a good deep look at how I feel so I am not surprised again. Tristan... his comments... I found myself feeling protective... and jealous," he whispered the last of his sentence, as if saying the words too loud would cause the earth to crumble beneath him.

"While the power and God were there, pushing at me, I made a lot of those decisions and it confused me. I became angry at my lack of control and understanding. I am sorry I took that out on you."

They stayed silent, not looking at each other, taking in the words that hung in the silence between them.

Finally, Persephone reached out and grasped his hand. He jolted a bit at her touch and, when he looked at her next, their faces were closer together.

"I also found myself jealous when you spoke with Minthe. At least, I believe that is how I felt. I have no real experience with this. I just knew I didn't want you to stop that kiss. I wanted you to ignore her and, well, I needed you to kiss me."

She found herself unable to look him in the eyes as she truly felt embarrassment for the first time.

At least as far as she could remember.

Such human emotions, yet they were not exclusive to humans. Silly for her to think she was ever untouchable by human failings.

Since she had met Devon, she felt like her body had come to life after a state of just existing. Perhaps these feelings she thought of as human flaws were not at all flaws, but a state of being alive. That her heart beat did not mean she was truly alive if she could not use that same heart to love.

He pulled his hand out from under hers and moved it to her jaw as he turned her face to his.

"This is something we need to discuss," she whispered again at the look in his eyes.

Her heart raced in both excitement and trepidation about where this all would lead. The damage it might cause between two immortals who were stuck together for the rest of eternity.

At the fierce look in his eyes, she knew he had no intention of discussing any of this further. The look in his eyes only held one meaning, and it was one she could understand completely.

Words be damned.

***

Her eyes lit with Godfire at the same moment he felt another presence enter their space.

Closing his eyes in irritation at the coming interruption, he leaned away from her. When he opened them again, one of the guards stood at attention in front of them.

"My Queen, we have found Tristan and are holding him in the throne room as ordered."

Devon did not miss the furrow of Persephone's brows as she clenched her jaw.

Before he could ask what was going on, Persephone stood and turned to him.

"My guards have retrieved Tristan for questioning on some matters and as a God of this domain you are within your rights to be a part of the interrogation."

"Tristan?" he asked as the aggravation built back up under his skin, thankfully not nearly as strong as at the gala. Persephone only nodded to him in confirmation as Devon stood to move beside her.

"Yes, my initial intent on visiting the riverbank earlier was that I felt something was off in that part of the Underworld. Hecate confirmed my suspicions moments ago when she notified me that at the gala there was an amplifier that had targeted you specifically."

"An amplifier? I understand what the word means, but how does that relate to my power?" he asked as a feeling of aggravation strengthened its hold on him at someone pulling his strings like a puppet.

The doors opened by the same Reevka that always welcomed Devon to the palace. As they walked, she filled him in on her conversation with Hecate. The guard trailed them before he took back up his post at the throne room doors.

"Some Oracles with rare abilities in the past were bestowed powers of amplification through amulets. The amulets helped to push someone's power to the surface because the Titans wanted accurate revelations of the future. Unfortunately, the women given these amulets could rarely handle the power, and it ruined their minds. The power to foresee the future can be overwhelming without something unnaturally pushing them into a vision."

The guards opened the doors, and she took Devon's arm to guide him inside.

"It is illegal to use these powers without consent and overview of the Senate in Halcyon," she continued. "As of the last Senate meeting, we have no registered oracles in the region. How they were able to amplify your power without putting the amulet on you, or touching you, is a concern. The only way to focus on you in that way was if an oracle of your blood was wielding it."

With that loaded statement, she dropped his arm and strode into the throne room. He watched as her aura moved to cover her, black and red, like an angry entity all its own.

Directly ahead of them, Tristan knelt in the center of the floor, his hands shackled behind his back. He was in only jeans, which were dripping with water.

Devon followed Persephone around the prisoner to the front of the room where the throne resided. He noticed that Tristan's skin was tinted green, some scales flashing along his arms, and gills opening and closing on his neck.

Persephone took a seat on her throne. It was not the same chair he had thought of as a throne on his first night here, but one made of sharply pointed obsidian stone that looked like black horns on either side of her head. Skulls were carved into the arm rests, a black and blue cloth draped over one corner. Behind the throne hung a coat of arms, which boasted snake-covered scythes crossed under a skull, where an owl perched. He wondered at the owl for a moment before a Reevka brought the court to attention.

Flames burst over Persephone's head before calming to create a crown of blue fire. Her eyes bled black as black crept up her arms, her veins darkening beneath her pale skin. The guards took their places at the bottom of the dais on either side of her.

Persephone motioned for Devon to come up, and as he moved to stand next to her, he caught Tristan's eyes narrowing at him. Devon met

183

his gaze directly as he leaned against the throne. It was tall enough for him to do so without being punctured by the jutting horns from the top.

He kept his focus on the man in question in front of them.

Tristan's blue power rippled out like water. So unlike Persephone's power, which always looked like smoke.

"Stand," she demanded in an even and authoritative tone.

Tristan stood, holding his head high and his shoulders straight.

Devon had to give him some credit — he wasn't wavering under intense scrutiny.

Out of the corner of his eye, he caught sight of Thanatos and Hecate as they silently appeared at the other side of the dais. Thanatos winked at Devon before turning a serious look to Tristan.

"Do you know why you have been summoned to my court?" she asked. Everyone in the room—immortals and souls alike — waited with bated breath on this response.

The river deity did not fold under the pressure.

"I have some ideas, though I had assumed our Goddess was above petty transgressions," he stated, staring down Devon with each word.

Devon internally snorted at the man's attempted jab at Persephone.

"Aside from whatever you consider petty transgressions, there have been some concerns brought to my attention. One that I was privy to before anyone spoke of it to me. What exactly is happening at Cocytus?"

Tristan's face took on a look of confusion before he wiped his face clean of any expression. It was fast, but Devon caught it and he was sure Persephone and everyone in the room had, too.

"Everything has been going as it should be, my Goddess," he asserted, yet his eyes darted around the room.

"Both myself and Hecate felt a disturbance in your part of the river. You were near Devon when he was triggered by an amplifier." At this, Tristan's eyes moved to Devon's, a flash of shock there before it returned to the blank expression.

"I do not know what disturbance you felt at the river," he said coolly. "I had some of my guards patrolling and nothing was brought to my attention. As for an amplifier, where would someone who hardly leaves their river find someone with that power? Would that person not have been found out long before this?" He continued with his eyebrows

184

raised. "Oracles with amplifiers are not well known for being stealthy or great at hiding their talents, in that a majority of the time they mentally break."

As Tristan spoke, Devon caught Thanatos blinking in and out of existence, and back again, from the corner of his eye. Persephone must have caught that as well because she held out her hand to stop Tristan from speaking further as Thanatos retook his place at Hecate's side.

"What is it?" Persephone asked.

Devon readied himself for whatever Death had found out. Something in Thanatos' demeanor told that this was no small situation. That something big had happened in just the small amount of time they had been in the throne room.

Thanatos moved to Persephone with the reverence one would their beloved ruler, kneeling briefly before rising again. When she nodded for him to approach, he stepped up to the throne and whispered in her ear.

She pulled back abruptly at his words as he nodded and moved with the grace of a well-trained soldier back to Hecate's side.

"My apologies, Tristan. I know this is important, but we have a problem at the gates. You understand, of course." Persephone did not wait for a response and she motioned Devon to follow her.

Without pause, her guards became moving shadows, swirling around Tristan as the river deity disappeared in the blink of an eye.

"What happened?" Persephone asked as she moved to her feet, readying herself to jump as the shadows flowed around her.

"The gates. We've got gorgons, harpies, centaurs, giants — you name it — not letting the souls through. Charon has stopped moving them down the river since they have the left cave entrance and the gates are overrun. There is a buildup of souls starting, not to mention another increase in the incoming soul population. It's small right now, but will become catastrophic quickly," he explained. He held himself like a soldier relaying information to his commander, absolute stillness to emphasize the seriousness of the situation.

"That has never happened before. They always stayed at the cave entrance, and never in large numbers. How? Never mind." She shook her head and turned to the remaining guards that awaited her orders. "Hold Tristan until I figure out what is going on."

Before anyone could respond, she was gone in a cloud of smoke and shadows.

CHAPTER 25

The gate was completely overrun with all the beasts that normally lingered at the cave entrance to the Underworld. Had her loyal hound, Cerberus, not been guarding the gates, the Underworld itself would have been overrun.

She watched as Cerberus picked off the beasts with each of its giant maws, flinging them away from the gates.

A centaur ended up in the River Styx, the souls there pulling it down as it fought to free itself. She knew it was futile as she watched the centaur submerge completely, never to return.

The forgotten souls in the river were trying to reach the gates, thankfully being pulled back by the other forgotten souls who were attempting to find a way out themselves.

A cycle that allowed none of them to prevail.

Persephone released her Goddess form, her eyes bleeding black, horns of smoke, fire crown, and long black nails that resembled claws. Black wings similar to Thanatos' own stretched from her back.

She sensed Devon and Thanatos as they appeared behind her and felt a moment of concern at what Devon may think of her in this form. Before she could think too much on it, a Gorgon cried out and charged her.

Persephone released a huge wave of power that knocked the beasts back as she created a line of blue fire between them and the gates. Some of the beasts had not moved fast enough and ended up scorched. She could breathe a little easier with her fire holding the line of beasts at bay.

She looked at her loyal hound who was in his true form: three heads, eyes of fire, and *huge*. She moved to her beloved beast and ran her hand along his side to check for any hidden injuries buried in his fur. She felt a broken rib and noticed a deep gouge in his hind leg, though both were already healing. Still, the fact he felt any pain angered her.

"Go rest behind the gates," she ordered as she rubbed his flank. "I'll handle it from here."

Cerberus let out a snort from each head.

At that moment, a beast attempted to cross the fire. It bodily pushed through the blue flames, throwing itself with staggering determination. It flung its limbs out, landing a swipe at Cerberus.

Persephone gasped as Cerberus stumbled back, keening in pain. Furious, she whirled toward the beast that had harmed Cerberus before her eyes. It had fallen back through the fire to the other side after it landed its hit. Still, it jumped at the fire's edge with its hackles raised, out of its mind with aggression.

She slowly stepped forward through her flames and the beast backed up. Something finally penetrated its haze of anger as she caught the look of fear in its eyes at her approach.

"Return," she ordered. Her voice vibrated with energy and power, booming with authority throughout the cave. The beasts started to rile again as if to try to make it past the blue flames.

"Now!" she ordered again, and the line of beasts buckled. The power of her voice physically pushed at the beasts in the front to step back. She took another menacing step forward, her fire coming up around her but not touching her. She knew she was the vision everyone feared. The Goddess of the Underworld.

Wrath personified.

The beasts were nothing like the ones who roamed the cave entrance benignly. Something was happening here, but she had to get the souls moving before she could ponder what had caused this calamity.

She caught movement from the corner of her eye. The souls waiting in the distance to enter the gates. They must be terrified of the beasts. She could do nothing about them roaming right outside the entrance to the Underworld — but they had crossed into her domain and so they played by her rules now.

A rumble of footsteps and she sensed her soldiers flooding the cavern behind her, taking the flank formation. Her guards moved in brutal harmony with her as she marched forward into the monstrous horde.

Some beasts tripped over themselves to recede, while most snapped their jaws at her. Their eyes were wild with fire and malice, spittle flying as they roared at her and her guards.

Her guards, standing at the ready with their shields and swords, awaited her command as she crackled with power. Her flames a living thing that moved with her. She lifted a hand towards the beasts as she pulled her wraiths from the shadows.

The shadow demons that they were, the wraiths moved like liquid through the lines of guards as they focused in on the beasts.

The wraiths were hungry and desperate for souls to consume.

The beasts attempted to fight the wraiths, only to watch as one by one the wraiths devoured their fellow creatures. Their screams were eerie as each wraith burrowed into a beast to feed on their souls, the skin and eyes of the beasts turning to black as they became death themselves.

Before a beast could become mindless and turn on the innocent souls behind them, Persephone order the guards to take them to the river.

They would spend eternity at the bottom of the Styx beneath the unpaid souls.

The beasts who had moved back to avoid the fighting scurried away in fear of the mindless creatures being driven into the river. Perhaps for some of the creatures, part of them had become aware that they had crossed a line as they stared in horror at the display of wrath.

Without a word from her, they began to move as if a herd of cattle back to the entrances of the Underworld, stumbling and looking over their shoulders.

Clarity slowly returned to their eyes.

The wraiths not currently enjoying a snack followed at their heels the whole way back to the entrance, trailing behind like herding dogs.

In the crush, Thanatos released his wings and launched himself into the air to follow. She trusted he would assure the beasts stayed put and get everything back to rights.

She pulled her wraiths back in, a tedious job since none of them wanted to return to the Underworld. After the last wraith was returned to the depths of Tartarus and her guards moved the last soulless beast to the river, they too returned to shadows at her command.

She turned to the souls that cowered in a corner and let her fire die out, her eyes and skin returning to normal.

Once she looked human, she crept carefully to the souls shaking in fear. In their group was one still, strong form.

Devon had already gone to them while she had rid the area of beasts.

She watched as he calmed them. Watched as some of his power cocooned them and soothed their souls in a way she envied.

Where she used her power as an authoritarian, he had an almost nurturing element to his.

There were souls of all ages among the group of a dozen or so, the young ones hiding behind the older souls.

Persephone stepped forward but paused when she caught the winces across the group as they saw her approach. Devon noticed and joined her side in a show of unity, of trust.

She could have kissed him when she saw the souls marginally relax at his action. Such a simple demonstration and he proved she was not a threat to them. She clasped her hands in front of her as she felt Devon's power continue calming the souls.

Did he realize he had done that?

When she looked at him, he just shrugged and together they approached the souls. In all her years, she'd never accepted souls at the gates, never tasted their fear in this dank, unknown place. The chaos of the battle still simmered in the air and she could only imagine how terrifying this must have been for them.

She could let Devon handle this or call Thanatos back, but something deep inside of her needed to do this. She needed to be the one to help them through the gates.

Her domain had been violated, and she needed that power back. Needed to know she could make it safe again.

"It is safe now," she whispered, and their attention shifted from Devon to her. "I understand that you are probably confused and scared, but it is my job to protect you, and I swear on the Styx that is what I will do. My name is Persephone and I guard the souls of the Underworld."

She waved her hand to the gates where Cerberus still waited, shuffling around in his demon form before he calmed enough to shift to a Labrador-like dog.

"I will escort you through the gates myself and keep you safe from any beasts. We will shut the gates behind us and, as you saw, my hound is incredible at guarding it."

She looked back at Cerberus, who gave a cheerful bark and a tail wag. His centuries around the newly dead must have told him it was not the time to be intimidating, because he started bouncing playfully, his ears flopping around.

His little display made a small girl giggle and Persephone felt the palpable fear in the air begin to lessen.

She spotted the young girl, who flinched at being singled out by the Goddess. Persephone slowly crouched down to the girl's level.

"Hello, darling," she greeted as she read the girl's soul. She knew they would send her to Elysium. There was no way this child would go anywhere else.

"I can tell you've been such a good girl in life. Would you like to see a peacock? My sister leaves them here for me all the time, so I bet you can find one." Persephone didn't mention Hera only did it to aggravate her. When she saw the interested shine in the girl's eyes, she knew she was on the right course to help these people.

Begrudgingly, she mentally accepted her sister's attempt at being a pain had turned out to be the saving grace in a dark moment. .

Persephone thought maybe that was something even mortal siblings dealt with, and the thought made her smile. Maybe she was more like humans than she had thought all these years. Perhaps even more capable of emotional intelligence than she had let herself believe.

The little girl moved forward, hesitant. After a moment, she looked up at an older grandmotherly woman who nodded to her in permission to move toward Persephone. The girl gave a slow nod and then slowly, a grin.

Persephone was shocked when the young girl put her small hand in Persephone's larger one. She smiled as not to scare the girl and wrapped her fingers around the tiny hand in return.

She looked to the other souls as they nodded, one by one to each other, and stepped forward to follow her.

Devon took up the rear as Thanatos flew back and landed near him. She glanced at Thanatos and Devon, who conversed in whispers as the souls followed her. Thanatos had his arms folded and was obviously having a serious talk with Devon who had his hands in his pockets and his head down as he listened. She knew they would make sure the gates closed behind her when she guided the new souls through.

As they passed by the still playful Cerberus, the young girl put her other hand out to rub his head, which earned her a lick in return. Cerberus stood back after that to make sure all the souls were inside before he followed them in.

Thanatos and Devon remained on the other side, but she knew she would have to find out what they were discussing later.

As she watched the gates close, Devon looked up and gave her a heartwarming smile. She returned it the best she was able as she lost sight of him and the mortal realm.

It was time to get to work. She had souls to protect.

***

Devon remained silent next to Death as they watched the souls move through the gates after Persephone, Cerberus trailing behind them.

"Funny how this happened when Tristan was being detained and questioned," Devon mentioned as he walked alongside Thanatos, who checked to make sure the stragglers were gone from the gates.

He also checked for any malfunctioning or broken parts of the gate that could make escaping the Underworld easier for the souls. Cerberus was large when in his guardian form, so if he were thrown against the gates, he could do some damage regardless of how sturdy they were.

"All of them here at once? Their behavior... I haven't been here long, but even I could tell that was not normal," Devon stated as he watched Thanatos stand back like a master crafter, or a mechanic, hands on hips and eyes narrowed.

Finding nothing, he turned to Devon.

"No," Thanatos agreed as he folded his skeletal arms across his chest, blinking between his Reaper form and human form as if so wound up he couldn't control the change. "That wasn't. They keep to the entrance and have never strayed further than the banks. Never have I seen them come to the gates. I'll speak to Hecate about warding the gates against an attack like this again. Getting past the veil is not an issue with it being tied to Persephone's power, but incoming souls…" He let that thought trail off.

"A distraction. They were herded down here to create a chaotic situation. Take the heat off something going down somewhere else." Devon ventured to guess, his instincts telling him something else had happened somewhere in the Underworld.

"Shit," Thanatos sighed, his head falling back in frustration. The gesture was so human that Devon let out a snort.

It was bizarre to watch the skeletal form behave in such a normal way. He somehow managed to keep his composure while Thanatos continued his thought process, but as usual, Thanatos picked up on Devon's mood and looked at him.

For a flicker of a second, he saw annoyance on Death's face, which made it even more absurd. Devon was exhausted and everything was a tad more humorous when a person was beyond fatigued.

"We've never had an issue like this before," Thanatos said.

When Devon snorted in amusement again, he gave Devon a withering look.

"And…" Thanatos checked to see if he could continue, and Devon waved his hand to indicate he was done. "A distraction of this size worries me. I'll take some turns around the realm and see if anything is out of place before I speak with Hecate." As Thanatos finished, what looked to be ten guards came through the gates and started lining up along the wall.

"Well, Cerberus will have some company guarding the gates tonight. Can't imagine he will like that too much," Thanatos said, walking to the guard in charge.

As he listened to the two discuss technicalities for what felt like hours, Devon looked over his shoulder at the river. Charon came into view as his boat drifted down the Styx again to deliver another soul.

"I'll just head to the castle," Devon announced and received a distracted wave from Thanatos in return.

Devon shoved his hands in his pockets as he began the walk toward the gates. Before he moved through the veil, he heard Thanatos say his name, halting him.

He turned back to Death to see what else needed to be said.

"She cares for you. I have never seen her like that before. I have no

193

idea the extent of her feelings, but before it goes too far..." Thanatos paused, and Devon readied himself for his next words.

"She takes a lot of shit from people, thinking the fact she is the Goddess of the Underworld renders her without emotions, but you know that's not true." Thanatos extended his wings, stretching the black feathers. "If you are not a hundred percent sure you want forever with her, don't move forward with anything more. Just accept the role as another God of the Underworld and remain friendly. If you do want her, regardless of her title and power, tell her that and treasure her. I would hate to have to torture you for all eternity when I was just starting to like you," Thanatos finished and launched himself into the darkness, his wings carrying him away before Devon could so much as let out a breath.

CHAPTER 26

Devon rubbed his hands over his face. Thanatos was completely right, and they both knew it.

With Thanatos gone, Devon lingered just before the gate's reformed veil. Hands on his hips, he took a deep breath, and watched Charon float closer to the banks of the shore. The boat scratched as it hit the rocks and scraped over the beach's small pebbles. Charon eyed Devon with confusion and waved his skeletal hand in dismissal.

"Go on. No need of you anymore," Charon's gravelly voice stated sternly, but not unkindly.

He waved a goodbye to the guide as Devon decided he did not have enough energy to deal with anyone else today. He did what Persephone called a shadow jump to the castle, disappearing in a flash of green light and swirling wind.

When he entered the castle foyer, he saw shadows moving across the walls. If he was still his mortal self, the sight of ghostly, dark forms flying around the castle would have terrified him. But now, he understood the sight as the Reevkas' true, pure nature. Nothing frightening or menacing, just thoughtful servants fully comfortable moving about in his presence. He watched as one shifted into physical form to greet him.

Devon waved the Reevka off. "No need but thank you. I'll just be heading to my room."

"Of course, sir," the Reevka responded, and it took its shadowy form once more, darting along the walls to exit the room.

Devon took the stairs two at a time until he hit the landing where their rooms were. He glanced down the hall and noted the light was off in

Persephone's room.

He doubted she had returned from taking the souls to the judges, but he really wanted to see her. He needed to talk to her about the chaos at the gates, and to be honest with himself, where they went from here now that emotions were out in the open. He knew she wouldn't be back anytime soon. He'd get a shower in and a drink before he looked for her.

Or, perhaps tomorrow, he thought as he realized his entire body and soul felt drained. As if walking through the door had stripped him of the last remaining strength he had, he struggled to make it to his bedroom.

He had never had such an emotionally exhausting evening as this one.

As he moved through his room, he thought about how nice it would be if he could just summon his clothes away. The sudden chill he felt had him looking down to see he was standing completely naked in the doorway of the bathroom. He quickly moved to the mirror.

"I am really glad I figured this out when I was without an audience," he muttered to himself in disbelief, a laugh bubbling up from his chest.

He had thought his clothes away.

What else could he do?

He went to the shower and thought of the warm water. He stared hard at the knobs and waited, stepping forward just as the water came on full blast. Faltering and almost falling backwards to the ground, he stared at the water before he lost himself to laughter and stuck his hand out to feel the warm shower water run through his fingers.

"I don't suppose I could just will myself clean?" he asked himself aloud, half-afraid someone would answer. He knew this was his power, but a seed of disbelief kept him from fully accepting it.

He stepped under the warm spray and let the water relax his muscles as another wave of exhaustion rolled over him. He tried not to think as his brain had become taxed, but it was no use. His thoughts were all over the place with everything that had happened in the past few hours.

Thanatos' and Minthe's words were going around and around in his brain. He thought of how he could corner West and where he stood with Persephone.

Groaning, he let his head fall forward gently against the shower tile. The spray ran down his back as he tried to quiet his mind. He was far too tired to make any sound decisions.

He finally accepted he needed to just get in bed and hope his errant thoughts would wear him down enough to let him get the sleep he knew he desperately needed.

As he was dried off, he thought again about checking in on Persephone but figured with everything she had to deal with today, she might want some space to think.

If she needed him, she knew where to find him, he justified in his head.

He slipped in between the soft sheets as he rested his arms behind his head. He tried to meditate to keep his head clear of any errant thoughts. He knew nights when he was fatigued it was more of an effort to keep the nightmares at bay. Something he learned long ago after too many nights waking up in panic, sweating, and near tears.

Sadly, this was not how it was going to work for him tonight. He was too wound up, which was prime territory for the nightmares to take hold.

He sat up with a growl. He didn't want to drink tonight, something he had done in the past to numb the pain. A way to bring himself to the point of dreamless oblivion. It never helped really, just a quick band aid that leant itself to a horrible morning.

He threw himself back on the bed as he punched his pillow under his head and shut his eyes.

Any stray thought that slipped into his brain was kicked out. His only focus was clearing his mind. Only clouds. Pure, white clouds. Nothing else around him.

He felt his mind slipping, a calm and peaceful feeling overtaking him. Devon didn't notice what looked like pillars beginning to form before his eyelids became heavy. His mind was finally done processing for the night.

***

Devon opened his eyes again and found himself not in bed, but on a rooftop. The rooftop of a building in the middle of a battle zone.

He recognized this place, this feeling. He was reliving a memory.

As he looked through his scope, he saw his target was nothing more than a blood stain on the sidewalk.

A young child stood over the body. One he didn't remember being there when the event actually took place, but he somehow knew she was the man's daughter. The girl, no more than three years old, had watched her father fall to the ground. His blood and brains splattering all over the door to the store they had just exited.

She began screaming for her father in their native language as she fell to her knees, begging him to wake up. Pleading with him.

He knew the local militia would be on their way as he quickly took his rifle apart and packed up.

Even though he was out of there in less than a minute, it had felt like an eternity.

He heard yelling and the pops of gunfire as he made his way down the stone stairs into the stifling heat. Though it was almost nightfall, the heat was always relentless here.

Devon made it to the door of the building he was in and stashed his rifle knowing one of his team would be by later for it. He made sure it was secured, then pulled a pack of cigarettes from the pocket of his worn leather jacket and a lighter from his cargo pants. As he lit his cigarette, he began the trek down the street where people stood observing the scene, looking at the gore.

Vultures, he thought snidely, as he worked his way around an older woman, taking a drag of his cigarette.

He did not want to look over at the scene, but he did, and immediately regretted it.

His dream altered, the memory going from the gray hue his memories were normally cast in to bright and vibrant coloring.

The man who had just been dead, stood up, a black inky color coming from him. The little girl next to him took her father's hand as they walked towards Devon.

The man halted a few steps in front of Devon, his eyes an unnaturally bright purple, his hair now long and black.

"It is not over, little God. Not by a long shot." The man's face grew into a sinister smile, and he turned towards his daughter, a knife dripping with green liquid suddenly in his hand.

Her face showing absolute horror as she begged her father not to hurt her, her eyes now bright blue.

Devon shoved the man out of the way as he felt the knife slice along his arm, and he threw himself on top of the little girl to save her. When he looked down, blood ran from her mouth and her eyes were lifeless.

He was too late.

***

He bolted upright in bed as he heard a quiet, almost hesitant knock at his door.

Glad for the distraction, he slowly rolled out of bed to pull on some sweatpants before he opened the door.

His heart picked up its beat when he saw Persephone on the other side, her eyes coming to his as he opened the door fully.

"Sorry, I just..." she trailed off as he moved forward and pulled her against him into a hug without thinking. She relaxed into his embrace, and he could feel her relief.

"Need a cuddle buddy?" he teased. His voice was rough with sleep.

Please, he thought, *please let her stay.* He needed to release the tension of the dream.

Needed comfort as much as he knew she did. He was tired of them both shutting down on each other and running away when it grew uncomfortable.

Thanatos was right. It was time for him to step up and acknowledge this was his life. He was no longer a mortal man and something deep inside him had feelings for the immortal in his arms. He could fight and fight, but he would only wear himself down. He needed to work on understanding it.

He pulled back and watched as a smile tugged the corners of her mouth.

"A cuddle buddy?" Her thin, aristocratic nose scrunched up. Devon found her look of confusion unnervingly cute.

Without another word, he turned and moved his arm out to indicate the couch in his room.

She looked hesitant, as if reevaluating her idea to come to him to talk. He watched as some human emotion took hold and left her unsteady in her choices. He was getting better at reading her, and yes, she had emotions same as anyone else. She just hadn't practiced using them. Acknowledging them.

"I just thought we could talk a little, but if you're too tired..." She took a step back to the door just as he caught her hand and pulled her back to where she was.

"We can talk. I think we have both been through hell today and need to be with more than our own thoughts." He gave her a little pull, and this time she moved easily along with him.

As they had a seat and she pulled her legs underneath her, he realized she was still in the same gown she'd worn to the gala.

"Finishing up with Tristan and the souls?" he asked, his arm on the back of the couch, close enough to touch the ends of her hair.

Not yet saying anything, she rubbed her hands over her face. The tension was so obvious he felt the urge to pull her into another hug but refrained.

Instead, he waited.

"The souls have gone through judgement and were moved to Elysium without their memories. Tristan was not at all helpful. He knows something but is capable of dodging and lying better than I thought."

"I could talk to him…" he offered, knowing his form of interrogation would probably not be as polite as hers, but it might be more effective. "I have to hold my own down here as well, do I not?" he asked, genuinely wondering what his place was exactly.

Where did she expect him to stand in the Underworld hierarchy?

She closed her eyes tightly and sighed, and before she said a word, he already knew what she was about to divulge.

"He is gone," she whispered, animosity and self-reproach in her tone. "He was gone by the time I got back to the castle, after the guards had finished questioning him. The room we held him in was warded by Hecate's magic against any types of portals and guards were stationed outside. No sign of him getting out through any other means. He just… disappeared."

She laid her head back on the couch and he started to rub her scalp. She only gave him a look from the corner of her eye but said nothing and let her lids fall shut.

"The gates were a distraction. He does have something to do with this. It gave him a chance to escape. But also shows he is not working alone."

"I knew it," Devon muttered, earning a questioning look from Persephone.

In a show of utter exhaustion and irritation, Persephone let down her guard. Her hands balled into fists at her sides and her face pinched in anger.

200

"There is something happening in my realm that I didn't figure out sooner. I have had my gates breached, souls terrified, something amiss at Cocytus, and no governing deity to hold accountable," she whispered, and he could hear something in her voice he knew no one else had heard from her: vulnerability. She was coming to him and laying herself bare.

He moved his hand to her shoulder and squeezed before he massaged it a bit, her shoulder so tense it might as well have been stone.

"We will figure it all out, but not tonight. You obviously need rest, and even as a Goddess, I'd think you'd require some self-care such as food and sleep."

She only gave a small nod in response as she stared at the ceiling.

"I suppose I do need some rest. I have my entire army patrolling and Hecate checking wards, but it doesn't seem like enough. I feel like I need to get back out there…" She yawned at this, obviously in no shape to do anything.

Her eyes opened suddenly, like she just remembered something of great importance.

She turned her head towards him, her face full of something close to concern and maybe a little fear. She waited a beat, biting her lower lip, her face full of hesitation. A question that he knew she was fearful to ask on her tongue.

"When I was in my Goddess form, were you scared?" she asked and he could see how much this mattered to her.

"Persephone," he murmured, his face going into her hair as he pulled her into a hug. The scent of her vanilla and pomegranate shampoo tugged at memories he couldn't reach. The scent matching her power as it encompassed his whole self and sang to his soul.

After a moment, she returned the hug and placed her head on his chest.

"Not even a little bit. You were…" he was about to say beautiful but thought she might find that weird.

"Amazing," he finally whispered.

They remained silent for a moment, both listening to each other's breathing and allowing themselves this temporary peace before going out to face the world again.

"Thank you. I needed this… cuddle buddy," she whispered, snuggling deeper into him. "I've never had a cuddle buddy before."

"Glad I'm your first," he joked as he moved them into a comfortable position, her head on his chest as he leaned back a bit more.

Devon was pulled tighter against her.

He knew he was going down a rabbit hole, but hell if he wanted to stop himself.

"Can I stay a while longer?" she whispered into the dark.

"Always," he whispered back as he tightened his hold around her.

He did not remember falling into a deep, dreamless sleep as they held each other. The nightmares held at bay for one more night.

***

Devon woke up on the couch covered in a blanket with no Goddess to be found. He shouldn't have been surprised. She was probably walking out the door to check on the realm before the sleep was out of her eyes each morning.

He ran his hands over his face as he stood, the blanket falling to the floor. His jaw was already covered in stubble and his hair stuck up on the right side where his head had been crammed against the arm of the couch. He threw on a shirt as he left his room and padded down the stairs to the dining hall.

No one was there, but breakfast was already out, as it was every morning. Plenty of everything, from eggs benedict to pastries from around the human world.

He caught sight of Hecate as she walked past the door. He grabbed a croissant from the table as he jogged to catch up to her. Coming up beside her, a Reevka appeared and handed him his coffee.

He nodded a thanks as he stuck the croissant in his mouth and grabbed the coffee with one hand, and the other hand grabbed Hecate's arm to stop her.

"What's going on?" he asked after releasing her to grab hold of his pastry.

She had been moving through the hallway with her eyes pure silver, obviously doing something to help with regard to last night.

"Checking wards," she stated as her eyes twirled with the silver mercury.

After a moment, she shook her head, her eyes returning to normal —

as normal as silver irises could be.

"Sorry, sometimes I get caught up in the magic flow and I lose myself. The wards are all up and sturdy around the castle, so there should be no issues here. The gates were down though, large tears through the veil which concerns me as they were not near where the beasts had been."

"Persephone knows?" he asked as he swallowed a bite of the pastry he had taken while she spoke.

Hecate sighed and nodded.

"Yes, and she will run herself into the ground because of this. She will allow no one but herself to take responsibility for what happens here. That is how she has always been."

"Where is she?" Devon asked as he polished off his croissant in one bite and put his coffee down on a side table in the hallway.

"Cocytus," she answered but received a fading thanks as he did his version of a shadow jump.

***

Devon landed on the muddy banks, his bare feet squelching in the mud. He sneered in disgust as he lifted his feet out of the slippery mud and moved along the riverbed.

She was standing at the edge of the shore, staring out at Tartarus. Her hands fisted at her sides and her mouth in a grim line.

She had shadows under her eyes, and he wondered if she slept at all as he held her or just slipped out after he fell asleep. Most likely the latter.

"Hey." He walked to stand beside her, not sure what to say. Her body language made it quite obvious how unsettled she was, and he did not feel like he knew her well enough to have the right words to help her mood.

She said nothing, her gaze intense as she watched two of her Reevka guards move along the edge of the boneyard. Their shadowy eyes taking in all the details; monsters and bones.

"They look like they have it in hand," he whispered, standing shoulder to shoulder with her. His hands in his pockets as they watched the guards march back to another point where several other guards were standing sentry.

"Yes. They are the best in my army. I can hardly imagine anyone getting past them, which is why they will be posted here going forward." Her words were ones that told that the situation was handled, the enemy's capture a foregone conclusion, but her tone told a whole different story.

She wasn't sure who her enemy was right now, and that was eating away at her, making her second guess herself. She folded her arms across her chest as her eyes stared out towards the guards, but he wondered if she even really saw them.

"Can you sense anything that seems out of place? I feel as if I am missing something," she told him, her voice faltering on the last word.

She wasn't looking at him and that bothered him. He wanted to look in her eyes and tell her what she needed to hear, anything to help her. Her loss of control was eating at her and he felt the urge to protect her. Mentally, physically, it didn't matter.

He cared and when he cared, he protected. There were so few people in his existence that mattered, and every day, she became more and more important to him.

Damn it. Guess his emotional wall was dust and rubble now.

He looked out over the terrain as she asked, unsure of what he could do to help, having only known the Underworld had existed for such a short time.

"Just the color of people's power," he answered.

Persephone's head whipped around to look at him and her jaw dropped.

He tilted his head and turned to respond when he caught sight of a glowing greenish string and began to follow it without thinking.

He was being called to it, he realized, and the closer he got to it, the more he felt a small vibration in his bones. His nervous system felt jolted, like he had over imbibed in caffeine or some other stimulant.

"Finally," he heard a whisper. Not outside of himself, but in his mind as he stepped closer to the string and realized it wasn't actually a string at all, but a cord.

One that was moving on its own, full of life. Reaching out his hand, he touched it and his body immediately went rigid as jolts of power flickered through him.

"Devon?" he heard a voice far away. Almost like he had entered a tunnel, the voice faded off into the distance, and he realized he was still holding the cord. The cord that looked like it was covered in scales like a snake.

He took deep breaths to center himself, surprised the powerful jolts were not at all hurting.

"Slept so long…" he heard in his mind again. The voice sounded old, ancient. "You've kept me waiting far too long."

"Who…" his voice broke, and he paused for a moment as he tried to rally his thoughts together again. "Who are you?"

"I am you. You are me. I am the much older and far more powerful version of you. The one you forced to sleep for far too long, little God. *Far too long.*"

"I… how? I don't remember hearing your voice before…" He was sure his brain was melting at this point.

He heard an irritated sigh and wondered what this ancient being had to be frustrated about. Devon wasn't aware he made him sleep. He didn't know who or what this thing was.

"I. Am. You," it said again, the aggravation palpable. "The sooner you accept this, the sooner we can merge, and you can fully ascend. You are wasting my time and those of Chaos with your ridiculous need to stay human when you are clearly not, nor have ever been, fully human."

Devon wasn't sure if he was having a breakdown or not, but this seemed like some sort of episode. Perhaps this was what people who thought they had multiple personality disorders dealt with.

"I will give you more time and do you the favor of not flooding your fragile mortal mind with power," the being said, more than a little derisively. "But you will ascend soon. Be ready, little God. We will be one."

He felt a jolt as if he was being slammed back into his body. His eyes opened, and he knew they were glowing, casting a green haze over the riverside.

Persephone was in front of him, her eyes concerned, her hands gripping his shoulders.

His attention moved over her shoulder and he watched as lights flickered and danced around the beings in the Underworld. As they moved along, they left behind trails of color, the same as the lights around themselves.

"There are trails of color leading away from Tartarus. Ones that match the colors of the people currently in it," he mindlessly told her as his eyes focused in on the trails that seemed to be following no one. Power left behind. An almost sickly greenish orange.

"You can see people's power," she whispered, looking back over her shoulder. "The color indicates their type of power and the health of it. No one has been able to see the color of power since the Primordial Gods."

"There is one that is different... A sickly green in the orange undertones," he told her as he sat up.

"None of us can read power signatures, except now you. Whoever was here was banking on the fact we couldn't trace them. The orange is a Titan color if I remember my mother correctly. The green, I am not sure." Her voice was lost in the past as she dispensed with her knowledge.

"Why would a Titan come into the Underworld only to turn around and leave?" she continued to muse, almost like he wasn't there.

She stood up quickly and looked towards Tartarus again.

"Why break in past the veil and just leave?"

"Scouting," he replied without thought. "They were scouting it out. Planning something along this river."

He could see her thinking, her fists clenching and unclenching.

"So, they know a way in and found what they needed. The question is, what did they find and how do we keep them from coming back? They cannot open Tartarus if that is their plan."

He placed his hand on her elbow as he turned her to him.

"We plan. We scout ourselves and set up a trap, but we need to call on your sisters and your friends. You need to let us help. If there was any reason for me to be here, I am pretty sure this is at least one reason why."

Her eyes searched his before she raised her hand to his cheek.

"Thank you, Devon," she whispered, her voice low and vulnerability colored her words. He put his hand over hers as he let himself smile. A real, genuine smile.

"You lead and I will follow," he whispered back.

CHAPTER 27

Persephone heard it first. Her soldiers scrambling back to the rocky gate that held her father. She turned away from Devon to walk to the edge of the river.

She saw four of the soldiers as they moved close to Tartarus, the souls in the boneyard still mindlessly looking for whatever it was they always did, unaware of what was happening around them.

"Wait here," she told Devon before she used her earrings to turn herself invisible.

She doubted the Titan would appear with her and Devon nearby, but something had moved her soldiers to act. She shadow jumped to the gate of Tartarus first. She had seen the gate this morning and wished she had been able to see the power signature like Devon could.

Nothing looked different to her eyes. Everything else was in its place as it should be. She knelt down and looked over the wards and runes that held the gate in place. As she ran her palms over them, she felt the power pulse and push back at her. Something else besides the wards pushed at her.

Someone had been tampering with the runes, as if they had tried to find a way for themselves to open it, not knowing that only her blood could do so. She could feel the taint of the power and knew that had to be the sickly greenish color Devon described.

Someone who routinely used their power to manipulate, kill, and maim was the only way to taint true power.

She looked and noticed the guards had checked over the area around the gates and were returning to their watch.

Devon was too far away and hidden for her to see him.

She stood and dusted herself off before she shadow jumped back to Devon. Landing behind him, she put her hand on his shoulder which caused him to spin around, his eyes darting around nervously.

"Oh, right," she murmured before tapping her earrings to undo the invisibility spell.

"Did not know you could turn invisible." His eyes focused on her as his demeanor returned to a relaxed state.

"Surprise," she whispered, tapping her left earring that was a blue sapphire in the shape of a helmet. "Gift from the Cyclops for saving their bacon from Tartarus".

A small smile was there one second and gone the next on his face, and she realized she wanted more of those smiles.

"What did you find out?" he asked as his head tilted down. He must know someone might be listening and intended for her to whisper.

She followed his lead and moved closer to him to whisper in his ear. The smell of evergreen and sandalwood teased her nose, and she had to remember what she was talking about.

"I felt their power signature on the runes, as if someone was attempting to unlock it. It was not one I recognize though. I think the greenish hue you described would indicate this entity has been using their power for nefarious means."

Before she finished her sentence, he disappeared in a gust of wind and leaves then reappeared at the gate to Tartarus. She shadow jumped as well, landing near him, checking to see if they were noticed before walking up to him as he crouched by the ruins.

"I was invisible for a reason," she whispered but he ignored her as she moved to kneel beside him. He moved his fingers to the runes, and flew back as soon as he touched it, a small spark jumped from the ruins to his finger. He landed in a squat and she was impressed at his agility.

The Godfire lit brightly in his eyes.

"Amplifier," he choked out, green light running up his arms, "I recognize it from the gala. More blue color here with the orange and green. It is mixed with an amplifier."

She watched for only a moment as he started to lose control before she moved at a clipped pace to him. She wrapped her arms around him before jumping them back to the castle. Her momentum caused them to land on his bed.

He was a young God and wasn't used to having his powers triggered, especially not as often as they had been.

She had to do something. Vines already grew through the walls of his room and he was almost completely consumed by his power, the green light enveloping him. The waves of light coming off of him were overflowing into the surrounding room.

Before she could think on how to calm him, a winged serpent made of green light burst into existence and wrapped itself around him. She watched as it created a shield with its body, and became armor, scales flattening and slithering over Devon's form. The head of the serpent on Devon's shoulder like a pauldron.

Her jaw dropped, the shock of what she was seeing causing her mind to reel. The eerie eyes of the serpent took her in, its snake-like tongue moving out to taste the air. The wings trembling a bit, almost as if it meant to take flight, Devon in tow.

She pulled herself together and carefully walked up to him, her movements slow and her attention split between Devon and the winged serpent. She was unsure how the creature would react, especially since Devon was awake but not conscious. Completely inundated with his own power.

His eyes were pure green and there was no flicker of acknowledgment, any evidence that he was aware of the dragon-like creature currently wrapped around his body.

She raised her hands to show she was not a threat, and the serpent let out a hiss, but did nothing to stop her. Its nostrils flared almost as if scenting her before it laid its head back down on Devon's shoulder.

She moved beside where Devon lay on the bed and put her hand out to pull him from the vortex of power. With her hand almost to his face, she stopped and fell to the ground as a giant tree erupted through his bedroom wall. Its branches reaching out to grasp hold of wooden timbers as it leafed its way through the logs, dislodging them.

Before the tree could tear the room apart, she moved quickly and placed her hands on his jaw, ignoring the hiss from the guardian serpent.

She tried to bring his face to hers, get his eyes to see and acknowledge her.

Devon was not there, only the God. She knew she had seconds

before Devon was lost for good.

No one could withstand this sort of power and remain. If he did come back, if it went for too long, he would hardly come back sane. Just as the oracles went mad, he would, too.

"Devon..." she whispered as she hoped to see some recognition in his eyes. "Please," she begged as she ran her thumbs along the sides of his jaw.

After a moment, she caught a small narrowing of his eyes, almost like he could hear her call out to him and was trying to come back to her. She jumped when the serpent on his shoulder nuzzled her hand. She opened her fingers as the serpent lifted its chin to be rubbed, the scales felt so real for something made only of light.

The God controlling him looked at her through Devon's eyes.

"It's been too long," the deep baritone voice of an ancient whispered from Devon's lips. "He is strong, but no match for an ancient power."

"Do not let him perish," she demanded, unsure of how much power she held against the ancient.

A deep, rumbling laugh that was not at all like Devon's left his lips.

"You think to give me orders, young Goddess? A youth born of traitorous loins?"

She let her eyes bleed to black, smoky tendrils coming from the hands still holding his face. Her blue flames engulfed her fingertips as it fought back his green Godfire.

"I think I give you orders as the Goddess of the Underworld. Ruler. One who will damn your soul and drag it to depths of the darkest place in the Underworld should you refuse to release him."

Devon's face slid into a crooked smile.

"Good. I've been waiting far too long for you. I had hoped time had not diminished the fire in my lovely Goddess," the ancient whispered. Suddenly, the face in her hands contorted into pain and Devon's body bowed. She moved her hands to his arms to try and keep him from falling.

The winged serpent let out a loud screech of pain before it pushed her away and moved over Devon. The two of them in parallel states before it seemed to be drawn into Devon, moving along his body before a flash of light brighter than anything she had seen, even Hera's light, engulfed the room.

She moved her hair out of her face and took in the scene from where she had fallen against the wall after a surge of power had thrown her back.

He was no longer glowing with Godfire and the serpent was gone. She jumped up and moved to look at him as his pupils slowly returned to normal, the green light in them fading. He blinked a few times before he could focus on her.

"Welcome back," she whispered as she looked him over for any sign of distress. Her relief palpable.

He only stared at her with furrowed brows. The silence heavy in the room, only a slight breeze from outside caused the leaves to flutter from the tree that had overtaken his bedroom. He continued staring at her, his expression giving nothing away. She became uncomfortable and moved to stand up.

Fast as lightening, he grabbed her and pulled her against him, his mouth was on hers with the intensity of a starving man getting a taste of food for the first time.

Caught off guard, she allowed the kiss a moment longer than she meant to, but her hands found his chest and pushed away. His hand at her back held firm, as did the one cupping the back of her head. Not letting her go, he leaned his forehead against hers.

"Don't worry, it's me kissing you this time, Goddess," he whispered against her lips before placing an affectionate kiss there. She closed her eyes and allowed herself the embrace.

"You're back. Completely?" she asked, unsure how in control Devon was of the situation. She moved to look up at him.

His eyes held hers and a genuine smile came to his lips.

"Yes. I am," he stated with confidence. "But not just me. I..." he trailed off a moment, as if gathering his thoughts. "I am more now and I don't know how to describe it."

She knew then what he was speaking of, as she remembered when she finally released the Goddess inside of her. The moment she stopped fighting and the power that had been deemed hers by the Fates merged to become one with her. She knew how overwhelmed he must feel, and she didn't want to add to the burden, but she needed to know.

"You..." She licked her lips. "Do you remember?"

The smile reached his eyes in acknowledgement of her question.

He remembered. He should now remember every time throughout history that his soul had seen hers. Devon had the cumulative knowledge of his soul's entire history.

She hadn't noticed her hand was shaking until it covered her mouth. Her eyes burned a little as they started to water. Emotions. She was feeling such joy and relief.

He rolled over her and his hands came to the sides of her face. Memories rushed through her mind of each time she had stood before him.

"My soul," he started, "has recognized you long before my mind did, but it knew you, and now I do as well. Hundreds of years, our souls waited to join and now they can. Though my soul has been yours for so long, the Devon you know, fell in love with you before he knew what you meant to him. Finally, every part of me is all on the same page."

This must be what humans felt when they fell in love. This feeling of fluttering in the stomach and zaps of pleasure along the spine at such simple words that held heavy with meaning.

A tear slipped free, running down the side of her face before Devon's thumb caught it. Something she hadn't even known she had been waiting for had been handed to her, and the relief was so overwhelming she wasn't in complete control of herself.

He leaned forward, gently kissing the tears from her cheeks and she closed her eyes, a small sob escaping her lips.

"I took the seeds before I really knew you," he whispered against her ear, causing the hairs along her neck to stand up. "I will never regret that, and even without being bound to the Underworld, I would always return. For you. Forever and ever, just for you."

He pulled away to look at her, his eyes lit by Godfire, as if he was making a vow.

Leaning forward, he pressed his lips to hers, and on a half sob, she threw her arms around him to pull him closer.

The kiss moved into an uncontrolled passion she was sure would ignite the castle and burn itall to the ground.

She found she hardly cared at all.

CHAPTER 28

Devon watched as the people moved along the streets from where he sat with Persephone at the little seaside café in Halcyon. They found a place with outdoor dining and were seated at a quaint little table.

A very date like place, he thought, his mind running through the kiss they had shared.

Their only moment of solace they had up until now.

He had enough of watching Persephone drag herself through every possible scenario, and punishing herself almost non stop over her perceived failures at keeping the Underworld secure.

Refusing to watch her beat herself up any longer, he pulled her from her circle of shame when they returned to the mortal world for work at Cerberus Financial. He had walked into a meeting and demanded she take a lunch break.

She had been using her position there to investigate the deities of the Underworld without their knowledge. No one had heard from Tristan. None of the people the sisters used to monitor Halcyon had heard even a whisper of what could have happened to him. The river deity was now just a lost soul. Another mark against Persephone in her own head.

They had kept guards on Tartarus and were using a spy network that Hera had created long ago to keep an eye on the city.

No matter what they did, Persephone told him she couldn't shake the feeling that whoever was working against them was two steps ahead. Their goal focused solely on her father's release.

Something both of them knew they could not let happen.

He watched her as she looked out over the Thalassian sea and the ships making their way to dock. He felt a tiny bit of pride in himself that he was able to pull her from her stress and bring her a moment of peace.

He took in the city of Halcyon, with the mountains in the background on one side and the sea on the other. The temperature always seemed to be comfortable, the weather fair.

He watched as people walked leisurely to and from their destinations. Content in their strides and that they would get to where they needed to be when they got there. The opposite of what he would think the epicenter of the world's trade and business would be like.

This felt more like an island village sans tourist during the off season. Not that there were many tourist areas anymore. Not like in the history books, when half the world was not a wasteland with sinkholes pulling down everything natural and alive. Something the sisters, being the ones to watch over the sky, sea, and death realm, were still trying to remedy. To bring the world back to what it had been.

He shook the thoughts from his head. He did not need to dwell on that right now. Not on his outing, and hopefully date, with Persephone.

"I would have thought there would be more people visiting a place like this. I know there is no financial need for tourism, but this seems like a place that would call to people with money to burn," he stated as he turned his focus back to where she sat across from him at their little café table.

Persephone took a sip of the wine she ordered and nodded to the server as he poured more into her glass.

"We have tourists," she explained once the server was no longer in range to hear their discussion. "It is usually just a steady flow, not a large influx, since our weather stays mostly the same year-round."

Devon nodded as his eyes took in their immediate surroundings subconsciously. As if he might have to worry about a threat or need an exit strategy last minute.

Old habits die hard, he thought.

He caught sight of an older man walking with what he assumed was his son as they looked into shop windows. He could almost hear the boy, who couldn't have been more than six, begging for a treat he had seen in one of the windows. The father laughed, grabbed the boy's hand, and shook his head. The boy's little shoulders slumped.

The man stopped and crouched to whisper something in the boy's ear, the child perking up at the words his father spoke to him. The child danced in excitement before he took off running down to another shop that had a picture of an ice cream cone on the front.

One blink later and Devon was in a whole different place. He was no longer sitting across from Persephone at a little café in Halcyon, he was standing among miles of trees. Not his forest. Not the one he called home. A forest from a different time and a different memory. A memory kept in the darkest corner of his mind.

His father had been called out to an area where the trees were in various states of illness, all from different diseases, and no one in the area could figure out why.

Devon was only six or seven himself, but he watched as his father walked to tree after tree, touching the bark.

Looked.

Examined.

His father would close his eyes as if the tree could somehow tell him the why of its ailing health.

Feeling bored with standing beside his father for hours of the day, Devon wandered off, but not too far. He knew better, he always knew he had to stay in his father's sight, and he never went against his father's wishes.

At least not as a youth. His rebellion would come much later and at a greater cost.

He was able to make out some water, a brook, through the trees and found a spot where he could look without being outside of where his father could reach him.

He pulled his small body up onto a stone that jutted out over the brook a bit, keeping him dry, but still among the flow. He watched as all the creatures of the brook moved about in front of him, not concerned at all that a human boy with the power to hurt them could be nearby. It always seemed animals knew his intentions were never mean. Most of the time the animals went about their business, not perceiving a threat.

The children at school thought it was weird and teased him for it. The boy without a human soul. He thought that the animals allowing him among them meant he had more soul than anybody. He received a black eye from Ruben, the local bully, when he made that argument.

The water was clear as it moved smoothly over the pebbles and rocks in the bottom. He could see little fish of some kind moving through, a frog not too far down the bank of the brook.

As he looked down at his reflection, he put his small hand into the water and let the cool flow relax him as it changed path and course to move through his fingers. It never deterred from its destination. No matter the obstacle in front of it, it found a way to where it needed to be. He could understand and appreciate that even as a small child, though in a more elementary way than an adult would.

"You should be weary of water, child," a voice whispered. Devon looked up as he pulled his hand out of the water. He tried to find the owner of the voice, but no one was around.

A chill ran up his spine. His instinct to call for his father was muted somehow, as if the words couldn't find the strength to pull themselves from his tiny body.

He continued to not say a word, knowing deep down if there was a stranger here, he should not engage the person.

Instead, he stood up and began walking back to his father at a clipped pace. His father moved out from behind a tree, startling Devon, and pushed him behind his legs.

"Leave him alone, Cybil," his father said. Devon tried to look around his father and through his legs to this Cybil person but saw no one. Just the disembodied voice that had warned him of the water only moments ago.

"Demetri, he needs to know what could happen if he follows the wrong path. There are consequences," the disembodied voice hissed at his father.

"That's enough, Cybil. You want him to believe all that nonsense, you should have stuck around to teach it to him." His father had never spoken like that to anyone. His entire life he wondered if his father even knew how to get angry.

Even when Devon made mistakes that were more costly than not, his father simply took him by the shoulder and said the cost was the lesson. He had learned from the error. Repayment was not making the error again. Life would find balance and so would he.

Devon heard a laugh, but it did not sound happy. Instead, it sounded incredulous.

"Really? If I remember correctly, you told me you didn't feel like he

216

was safe in my care. You all but ran me out."

"That is not how it happened and you know it."

Devon watched as a woman appeared in front of his father.

She was beautiful, her hair long and blonde, the light making it glow like a halo around her. Her eyes were a hazel color, and she seemed to be as interested in seeing Devon as he was her, though her eyes held something unforgiving.

Something about her drove a spike of fear through his young mind that he could not understand, and made him move a little closer to his father.

"Hello, Devon. I am your mother." She smiled, but all he could see in his mind was a monster that was going to devour him. He imagined her with sharp teeth and reptilian eyes.

Scared, he closed his eyes and made a sobbing noise into the fabric of his father's pants as he wrapped his tiny arms around his father's leg.

A moment later, he found the courage to look at her again, but she looked as she did before, with human teeth and human eyes. His childlike mind imaging the monster he had thought was in front of him.

"Enough, Cybil, please leave. You've obviously stopped taking your medication and you need to go home. Don't scare the boy." His father's words were a plea, but his tone was demanding, allowing no argument.

"Mama?" Devon asked as he moved around his father and felt his father's hand clamp down on his shoulder. He gathered all his courage to address the woman, his tiny body trembling.

"Devon." His dad got down to eye level with him as he spoke in their native tongue to explain it to him. "Yes, that is your mother, but she is sick. Not everything she says is true, and you need to be careful when you listen to her words. Never speak with her alone. Promise?" His dad looked so worried that Devon became even more concerned.

He finally nodded and watched a tiny fraction of relief come across his father's face, which was immediately removed by the woman claiming to be his mother.

She was quick, one second several feet away, the next up in his face shoving his father back from him after catching them both off guard.

"Boy, you need to listen to me. No one is as they seem! Monsters look like us, I have seen them! As I carried you in my belly, I could see them all!"

She shook him as he tried to scramble away. Her eyes looked glassy, like she wasn't even really there in front of him.

"He is lying to you! You cannot allow him to hurt you. He is not done and though you may try, he will win. He will! When he does, you must choose! Choose the dark and not the water! The water flows. You may stand there, but it will go around you. Fate is not to be stopped. Life and water will continue to flow, but death is forever, and it is your only chance to keep him from his power. Promise!"

"Cybil!" His father tried to grab Devon from her, but she dug her nails into his skin, making him bleed and terrifying him. Unable to control it, Devon felt the warm liquid in his pants and cried from fear and embarrassment. The confusion overwhelmed him.

He was too scared to move but too scared to stay.

"Don't become a monster, too! I felt your power in my belly! Your father wants to believe it is not real, but you need to pick a path, death or life! You must kill the other monsters. If you die, you cannot join them!" she yelled, her voice caused a flurry of birds to take to the sky.

His father finally got a good hold, and he ripped Devon from his mother's hands. Her fingers tore at his shoulders as she shouted '*demon*' over and over again at him.

Demon. Devon. Demon. Devon.

Devon blinked and was back in the present.

He was no longer sitting quietly at the table and people watching anymore. In fact, everyone was watching him as he stood in the middle of the patio, breathing heavily, his heart pounding so loud he could hear it perfectly as if someone were playing a drum right next to his head.

He looked down and noticed that he had shadows wrapped around his wrists as if he were being shackled.

The table was overturned, glasses broken, and food strewn across the ground.

He looked around and noticed shredded pieces of plants and vines turning black all around them. Flowers in the pots next to the patio looked overgrown and dangerous, thorns jutting out of even the most harmless type of flower.

He immediately looked up to where Persephone was, worried that he had done something unforgivable, knowing he had.

It was all confirmed when he noticed the cuts on her shoulders and throat closing up. Her dress had tiny rips throughout the fabric with blood running down her arms. Her eyes were black, her fingers clawed.

They both looked at each other for several long moments, his heart working overtime as it moved into his throat.

Finally, more out of shame than curiosity, he broke her stare. He noticed the people around him were not at all staring but were suspended as if someone had pressed a pause button on the world.

He stumbled a bit, his entire body drained. A slight breeze would be enough to knock him over.

How had he become so exhausted?

He felt like he had lost a piece of his day, of himself. Lost in an illusion while his body acted out. He was confused and mortified at what had been done, at his mindless actions. His eyes roamed over the still crowd, but only one person moved aside from him and Persephone.

A man that held the demeanor of a soldier with a large muscular build and radiated a power that rivaled Persephone herself. His chin length dark hair was blowing around his face, his hands in his jacket pockets, and a smirk on his face.

An unknown amongst the crowd of strangers, but his soul knew an enemy when he saw one. The man simply did a small salute, mouthing the word, "*Soon*" before disappearing into thin air, an orange light fading from where he had been.

Devon looked at Persephone.

"What happened?" he whispered. He meant it to be louder, but he was in too much shock to put effort behind his words.

The only response he received from her was a flash of blue light all around them before the world went completely dark.

CHAPTER 29

Devon woke up feeling groggy and stiff, as if he had been on a drinking binge while doing one hell of a physical workout.

It took him a minute to realize where he was, and once he did, his anxiety increased in his worn and tired mind.

The clean, sophisticated blue and black room that was Persephone's bed chambers. He was prostrate in her giant bed by himself feeling half drugged. He moved to get up when he realized he was not alone by the *tap, tap, tap* he heard from the chair in the corner of the room.

"You said you were not a threat to my sister," the voice that could only belong to Hera said in such a low and menacing tone that Devon resisted a tremble of terror.

The shadows covered Hera, her golden eyes all he could see as they were alight with Godfire. Had he not known her, he would have drawn a weapon or run from the room for his life.

"Yet, you almost killed her right on main street. Tell me, Devon, how is that not a threat?" She growled. The tapping ceased, and the atmosphere started to feel like it was trying to pull him apart at the seams. The tension growing thicker, choking him.

"What happened?" He finally managed to ground out. His brain was too foggy to deal with this, much less understand or even try to reason it out.

He could feel himself becoming increasingly defensive the longer she stared without answering.

Finally realizing Hera could go all day, he closed his eyes to stave off the burn he felt building in his eyes and temples. A headache like none he had felt before, and he knew if it grew, he would be lost to the pain and in no way able to defend himself against an angry Goddess.

"Hera, I need a minute," he mumbled. He tried to stand up again but felt her power push him back down on the bed. Hera stood up instead and moved to prowl over to him like a lion ready for the kill. Her slow, steady predatory gait punctuated by the click of her heels on the marble floor.

As she stopped next to him he realized he was completely at her mercy. Leaning down, she used one finger, her nail cutting into his chin, to tilt his head up at her.

Her eyes were tinged with his green glow as his temper rose to the surface. The tension built up in his muscles, his body going still and readying itself for battle by sending surges of adrenaline to his extremities.

"No, what you need to do is leave. You need to go far away from here. From my sister. A remote village in some town on the edge of the wastelands where there is no way you can harm my sister mentally or physically." Her eyes flashed with gold fire. "And I will happily escort you there myself."

Devon closed his eyes, not wanting her to see him bending to her will.

She was right. He was a threat, always had been, and now they had proof of it. When he tried to rid the world of his evil, he messed it all up and brought the darkness to those he cared about. What was the point in even trying anymore when it was obvious that he could not redeem himself? The temporary euphoria of finding Persephone and allowing himself to feel something for the first time? That was a lie to himself and everyone around him. He knew he did not deserve her.

It is so easy to manipulate one's own mind when the facts were not staring them in the face. So easy to pretend it could all be okay if the ghosts are silent for a while, but they come back. They never stop pressing at the gate of the subconscious. Never.

Black smoke and shadows rose in the room as Persephone manifested, her eyes full of anger.

"Get out, Hera. I warned you not to bother him." Persephone's voice was somehow scarier than Hera's. An authority that told everyone in the room they were in her domain and would bow to her

221

wishes. Whether of their own accord or forced to their knees.

Persephone was power. She was fire that met the shadows and made them her own. She created weapons from things that cannot be touched, created love from something as dark as himself. A contrast within herself, but one he would gladly burn for.

Hera turned on her sister as Persephone took her full corporal form. "I warned you, sister. He is not well and with all the trauma, he is a danger to you. Devon has power, no longer a mere mortal, and he will only become stronger. That is when he could do something to you that I cannot undo."

He heard a note of defeat in Hera's voice and suddenly she no longer held his full ire. He wondered how much of this situation she carried on her shoulders, as if anything to do with her sisters was her burden to bear.

He thought he knew Hera, the sarcastic and vexing animal that she was, but there was much more to her than he realized. Much more.

Persephone walked up to her sister, and he noted Hera's power lessening around him.

"I understand your concern, but you need to stay out of this." Hera opened her mouth to speak, but Persephone wrapped Hera up in her shadows and removed her from the room. Her bedroom moved into a quiet stillness that allowed Devon to release his breath, as if Hera had held her hands around his throat.

"Thanatos?" Persephone called once she finished sending her sister away, her eyes on Devon.

Thanatos flew onto the balcony as if he had merely been standing by awaiting her orders.

"Please make sure my sisters take leave of this realm."

Thanatos simply nodded before giving Devon a look of concern and censure. Thanatos stepped off the ledge and was gone just as quickly as he came. The sounds of his wings opening up and catching the air before the beating of them faded off into the distance.

Persephone moved to Devon and held her hand out.

"Please, come with me," she asked softly.

"Why?" he couldn't understand why she would want to be near him after he lost his mind and almost killed her.

They all knew he was a danger as he had shown on several occasions.

222

At the end of the day, he was sure they could all agree he was broken inside. Far too damaged to be fixed, and she needed to let him go.

"Because I want to show you something. After I show you this, then you can decide if you want to stay here or leave." Devon continued to stare down at his hands as she moved to kneel in front of him.

"Please," she whispered, and he looked into her pleading eyes. Something there broke his resolve. As if there was still some piece, some fragment, held together after everything and her concern shattered it.

He owed her this. She gave him a chance to start over, and though he was unable to find the goodness in himself she had thought there, he still owed her this before he left. He gave a slight nod in acquiescence before he stood up and took her hand. She placed her other hand over his and pulled them into a shadow jump.

They landed in a sickly forest. The trees held no leaves, the roots rotting above the surface as if they were searching for nutrients and water anywhere they could. The bark of the trunks dried out and looked like they needed to be made into firewood rather than left sitting in the soil.

"This is my forest, or at least I wish it were. You see, I wanted to have something down here other than just death, some way to feel the life that is the mortal world." Keeping his hand in hers, she began walking him through the wraith like trees until she stopped in the middle of a clearing.

"When I made your room and created that window to a forest in the mortal realm, I wished I could actually make it all real for you. Create such beauty down here that you felt the happiness you felt in the forest of your homeland. You have a strong connection in your soul to nature."

He listened but took in the brown sticks that should be trees at the same time. No green to be found, if anything, it looked like some haunted forest from a children's book. The ground was sand and dust, not even close to looking like a healthy forest floor.

She turned to him and took his other hand so that she was holding both, pulling his full attention to her.

"You went through tremendous pain and trauma, and if I knew more about the human psyche, I would have known you had not forgiven yourself completely. That you were not starting on the path to healing your heart."

His face snapped up to look at hers, unsure of what she was saying.

"Devon, I want you to give me every ounce of pain, anger, fear, resentment, and self-loathing you feel and have ever felt. Do not hold back. Give me everything. I am strong enough to help you, so I am asking you to let me help. Let me share your burden. Let me hold you up when you are at your weakest. I am here now."

He shook his head and tried to pull his hands back, but she held firm as she looked at him, her eyes begging him to give her this.

She had no idea what she was asking for, as his mind was so much more than just a nightmare. It was an indescribable horror, and he wanted her safe from it. From him. He did not want his past to stain her as it had him. He wanted none of it to touch her.

Everything about her was pristine in his eyes and he was nothing but an inky black stain that should any of it touch her soul would take over like a parasite. She deserved more than that.

More than him.

"No," he whispered and tried again to pull back, but he could see she would not give in easily. She was using her power to hold him there just as much as her hands were.

"You have no idea what you are asking of me."

"I do..." she started.

"No, you don't. Leave it alone, Persephone. Don't open this door because it will never shut again. Leave me alone and let me go before I cause any more problems. I doubt what happened in Halcyon is the last of it, or even the worst. Just. Let. Me. Go." His voice grew in panic, as his body screamed its agitation. He was a wounded animal, cornered and terrified.

"No. Not until you give me this. Then you can go anywhere you want. You don't have to see me ever again, but please, give me this. "

"Let me drink from the Lethe River," he pleaded. "Then I can forget! Then it won't be a problem any longer. None of it!"

"It doesn't work that way! You don't get to pick and choose memories to forget! You lose everything!" she yelled, her eyes begging him to understand. "Just tell me! I already know a little from when I took your soul but..."

"No, you don't get it," his voice hoarse, his hands finally pulled free from her, but just as fast she grabbed them back. He knew she called on more power as he watched it flow over them, the blue light and shadows covering them.

"Then tell me!" she demanded resolutely, looking straight into his eyes.

He watched her as he finally gave in.

She wanted this?

Then she could have it.

Once she saw his dark side, she would have no issues letting him walk back through those gates and far away from here.

All his emotional turmoil being pulled from him into her, he let down the wall and felt it flood from him. Her body jolted, but he kept pushing the memories and the emotions to the surface.

A tear leaked from her left eye, but it was too late. No putting it all back in now.

"I fucking hated myself. I *still* hate myself! My thoughts were scattered on a good day. I could not focus or concentrate. It was a deep, burning pain that was always there, but you just had to numb yourself. Not knowing what a relief it would be to not live with the pain because that was just how it was. You dealt. You moved on. You just tried to *survive.*

"That is what I did, I survived. I survived the new jobs I had to do, the ones that made my skin crawl. The ones that kept me up at night and had me crying in the shower like a newborn after. The ones that made me mentally blink out, my mind going blank in an effort to not feel, because if I did, it was over for me and everyone around me. I was a ticking time bomb.

"I could not look in the mirror for weeks after an assignment, because all I saw was a monster. I wanted to rip my own fucking heart out and rid the world of the dark stain that was me. I just wanted the pain, the nightmares, everything to end, but nothing numbed the pain anymore. *Nothing.* Not alcohol or drugs or sex. I was a haunted shell of a human being who killed people and abandoned the ones who cared about me.

"My father died thinking I was a hero when I was just a monster, and I couldn't go home to tell him because I was an enemy to my people.

An enemy for the one good choice I made in my career. The one time I helped people and my reward was exile. Can you imagine? Of course not. I could not look him in the eyes to tell him and his punishment for me being his child was he died alone, without me, and I get to carry that guilt forever!" He yelled, hitting his chest with his fist, "I have to carry that guilt. You look at me and see someone screaming for help. Sad and damaged, and you want to help me. *Why do you not realize there is no fucking help for me?*"

He pulled at his hair, walking away then back again towards her. Her eyes were blue and glowed bright as she grabbed his shoulders to halt him in his pacing. He felt the rage increasing with every second, the fury at his vulnerability, and started to scream it all again at her, his spittle flying.

"I was meant to be this way! Those cards were dealt the day my mother brought me into this world. Maybe that was why she left, she saw me for what I was, and would be, well before I took my first breath. I don't blame her one bit if that is why. Not one bit. I deserve this, Persephone, so let me have this. Let me own this pain, because if I learned anything from being Devon, it was that there is no help for me. I was born for pain and punishment. I can bleed and bleed, but never will my soul be clean. Never. I am a monster. A demon. A blight on everything I touch." His voice ended on a ragged breath, his eyes full of tears, and his body worn from the emotional turmoil.

His entire body shook, and as his knees gave out, Persephone pulled him into her arms, him far too weak to struggle or pull away.

He needed this. He didn't deserve it but needed it, nonetheless.

"You have no idea what you are." Her voice left no leeway for him to argue as she held him in her arms. "You didn't choose to be a mercenary. I know enough from your soul for that. Yes, you've always been a soldier, a warrior, but mercenary was the hand you were dealt because of your situation.

"You wonder why it bothered you that you were unable to deny the emotions taking a life held. It is because you were more than what you thought. Most mercenaries are not human." His eyes widened, but she did not allow him to interrupt.

"They are people who've been killed, soldiers who die on the battlefield, and somehow their souls do not completely detach, or Death does not come for them. They hold half of their soul, and it is no longer part of them as it was you. They know nothing, feel nothing, more than the urge to hunt. They are physical shades, hunters, and they are dangerous if left to their own devices.

He closed his eyes and leaned his head against her shoulder while she rocked them in her arms.

"Some, very few, are strong enough to control the urge, to find work like a mercenary, or to hunt for something more than bloodlust. For those I can find, I help them cross over and they usually end up choosing to work in the Underworld army.

"You are not a soulless hunter, you were a human and one that deals in life, not death. Your soul bled with this life path, and I will let you bleed out this pain, but I will not let you bleed out your life. You need to heal yourself and will not do it alone. I will walk beside you this entire journey, and if you do not need me, then fine. But know this; I am here. As your partner, your friend, or whatever you have need of me for, I will never ever let you battle demons without me by your side. Ever."

He sagged, the sobs tearing from him as she held him against her. Both of them curled into each other on the forest floor.

The pain was so strong it was a wonder he wasn't broken to pieces on the ground like a shattered mirror. It was overwhelming, but now he didn't have to be alone in this. With that, a calmness started to spread along the surface of his skin.

It was so difficult to admit a person needed help sometimes, but so wonderful when they did. When they allowed themselves to be wrapped in someone else's strength and carried, their feet too tired from the journey.

Smoke and darkness wrapped around them, cocooning them. He felt her release all the pain he had sent into her, the smoke clearing after a long moment to show blue fire all around them.

Devon watched the trees burn, the ground turn to ash. He felt her watching him as the world burned down around them. As if he were the most important thing in her eyes.

"What did you do?" he asked, his voice weak from the turmoil and yelling.

"The woods were sick, so I burned them down using everything you just gave me," she whispered as she stroked his back, still holding him. "Put your hand in the ash, Devon."

He looked at her for a moment with his red and swollen eyes before he finally did as she had asked. Her body seemed to sag slightly in relief, as if some grand plan was in the works, and she worried he might argue.

"Close your eyes and think of moments in your life that brought you such joy. Time with your father, the place you grew up…"

"You," he whispered, his hand clenching as it moved deeper in the surrounding ash.

"If that is what brings you joy." He heard the emotion in her words. "Keep thinking of everything you have to be grateful for. Send those feelings of love and contentment down your hand and into the ash."

His eyes opened to the sight of his veins glowing like beautiful, neon green vines.

He looked from his hand to the ground around them. Grass spread from him like water, trees of the most beautiful greens sprouted up where only moments ago the sickly looking trees had sat. It was absolutely beautiful.

"I'm… this is all from my power?" he asked in awe, staring as the forest sprang to life around them.

"Yes," she responded, her eyes watery and a smile on her face that was so wide he was sure her cheeks would hurt tomorrow.

"How… How did you know I was capable of this? That I could use my power this way?"

"I thought using my pathetic attempt at gardening might help you learn to control your powers and find a way to help you in regard to what you've been through." She ran a finger over the green vein of his hand. "You can come back from this. You can take the pieces of you that are dark, burned, and ashy to grow something new and wonderful. Everybody deserves to have a chance to make themselves anew and you are no different. This forest is yours, Devon. Use this to heal your heart."

After a quiet moment, she stood and dusted off her pants. He saw in her face that she was giving him time. That she knew it was a lot for him and while it would take a while to heal, it was an important first step.

"Stay here and let yourself grieve the loss of who you were and celebrate the rebirth of who you are. I am your friend, Devon, and I always will be, but when you give me your heart, if you choose to," she corrected, obviously hoping not to overstep. "I want it whole."

She turned and began to walk away when he jumped up and grabbed her arm, pulling her into a hug.

"Thank you," he told her as tears fell down his cheeks. She smiled and placed her hands on his jaw, using her thumb to wipe a tear away.

She leaned in and kissed his cheek, her shadows slowly encircling her.

"Always, Devon. Always," she whispered.

CHAPTER 30

Persephone was not at all surprised to be accosted by her sisters when she returned to the castle.

"I see Thanatos was unable to escort you out." She slanted a look at the man in question and received only a shrug in return.

"It wasn't without effort, believe me," Thanatos mumbled, glaring at Hera.

"You'll live without it," Hera returned, a devilish smile.

"Not a life I want to contemplate living if I am being honest." He eyed Hera warily as he moved himself further away from her and behind Persephone.

"Keep crazy away from me," he whispered as Hera snapped her teeth at him.

"Fates! She is your problem now," he muttered before he moved to sit down in the chair furthest from her and her sisters.

Hera's eyes moved from him to Persephone and she watched them blaze with an onslaught of questions. Ones that she was feeling less than stable enough to deal with answering, especially with her sister's oncoming mood swing polluting the air.

She signaled to a Reevka in the corner as sat down. She knew she would need a drink to get through this inquisition. Her sisters followed and sat across from her in a way that made her feel like they were trapping her in the room.

"Explain," was all Amphitrite said.

It surprised Persephone that it was her and not Hera making demands.

She sighed as a glass tumbler was placed in her hand with amber liquid. She swirled her glass a moment before she went into what she saw in Devon's eyes during the flashback.

The flashback that had his powers lashing out at everything within a mile radius. As if he was playing the puppet without any idea on who held his strings.

"Could his mother have been an oracle?" Amphitrite asked as she looked at Hera.

Hera simply bit her lower lip as she mulled it over.

"She must have had many visions that caused her to become so overwrought that she abandoned her baby. Oracles lose touch with reality fairly quickly after coming into their abilities. Either his mother was a late bloomer or something triggered her powers. Pregnancy is a strong enough force to do such a thing." Hera's voice held a serious tone as everyone knew Hera held no love for anyone who dismantled the family structure, contrary to what people believed of her male alter ego, Zeus. "Could she have foreseen what all we are dealing with?"

They looked to Persephone, and she saw the question in their eyes that she pondered herself. The one that would not leave them unscathed.

"Can we ask his father? He has crossed into this realm, has he not?" Hera asked, oblivious to the debt that would be owed at such a request.

Persephone simply nodded, sighed, and then gulped down the rest of her drink.

"I'll work on setting that up. In the meantime, I need to focus on securing my realm. If it is a Titan and they somehow manage to free Cronus..." She was cut off before she could finish.

"No. We will not allow him free. We worked too hard to put him in there to let some of his little loyalists do anything to jeopardize that. I will send a few of my men to help secure the gate."

Hera stood and disappeared in a flash of light, leaving no argument about what she planned to do.

Amphitrite stood and moved to kneel next to Persephone.

"You do not get to deal with this alone. Hera and I have always been here and always will be. Rest, dear sister, and we will return with reinforcements." Amphitrite ran her hand along Persephone's shoulder as she too disappeared into her beautiful aquamarine light.

As her sister's lights faded, she turned to look at Thanatos who sat smugly in his chair and watched her with a raised eyebrow.

"You could have easily gotten rid of my sisters," she stated with a voice full of irritation.

"Yes, I could have, but you need them. You have to learn to work with your allies. You do not need to shoulder this burden alone."

"Does it ever tire you to play such clashing personalities?" she muttered under her breath.

Thanatos stood up and walked over to her, placing his hands on the armrests of her chair as he leaned forward to look into her eyes.

"It only tires me when you do not heed my infinite wisdom and advice. It can be exhausting to be right all the time. One day you will listen to me and know this as I know it. I am smarter than all of you, most especially Hecate."

He winked at her before placing a kiss on her forehead, fading away into the shadows before she could reply.

***

Devon stood in the middle of the forest he had created, turning to take in the lush green foliage and strong sturdy trees. What his power had both destroyed and given life to, which told him he was more than capable of healing himself.

He shoved his hands in his pockets as he walked through the trees, touching the bark and leaves, taking in and accepting what he was capable of. It was not darkness that came from him, but new life. New beginnings. Just as Persephone had told him not very long ago when he only saw the end.

After hours of wandering, he stopped below a tree and looked up to find it full of perfectly ripe apples. He smiled, grabbing one of the low hanging fruits and sat down at the base of the trunk to enjoy it, remembering times in his youth when he would sit under a tree just like this with his father, perfectly content to enjoy nature in all its beauty. He looked out over the land while enjoying his snack and noticed a small opening in the trees similar to the one his father had chosen to build their cabin on.

He stared at the spot as he finished his apple, placing the core of the apple to the earth and watching the ground absorb it, the grass growing greener where the core had been. Standing, he dusted his hands off before he moved to the open field and stood in the middle. As he turned to look at the trees surrounding it, he thought of when this was all over.

The battle that was on the horizon and the cabin he would build them once they had a moment of calm. One just like he grew up in, right in this clearing. A place of respite for him to find his way back to himself.

He would bring Persephone here and show her the one place he knew he could always find peace. A place he would use to heal his damaged soul.

The soul that knew the pain of centuries, but also knew the joy of having loved and been loved. Not by the fading faces of his lifetimes, but by the twin soul calling to him from the realm of the dead.

The beautiful Goddess who stood on the battlefield with him when he fell to his knees in loss and anger, and her the fallen angel that gave him hope. The woman who held the souls of his soldiers in her embrace and cared for them.

Her smile that told him that all would be well as the wind blew her beautiful black hair, the setting sun creating a glow around her porcelain skin.

She had stood beside him so many times, and yet he could only remember her. Never the lives of the men he had been.

He was, and had been for so very long, completely in love with her. A love that felt so much like hurt sometimes in its depth. In the way it could overwhelm and just as quickly bring the most beautiful peace.

After waiting for so long, he could finally physically hold her and be with her the way his past selves had only dreamed of.

The small moments of pure joy when he joined her for a mere moment in time as he took his last breath. When they looked upon her face as they moved into her world.

Everything was not perfect by any means, but he knew he had the power to make his world better. Maybe not in the way he needed yet, but he knew he was capable of getting there, and that in and of itself was a miracle to behold.

Piece by piece, he would get there.

He had let the darkness have him for too many years, ignoring the light that flickered in the void of his depression. He would run towards that light and bask in it, no matter how long of a run it was.

He was determined and refused to give up on himself any longer.

***

Persephone returned to her rooms after going out to check the gate of Tartarus and speaking with all the new guards her sisters had sequestered to the Underworld.

She knew she was trying to keep herself busy so she wouldn't be tempted to bother Devon. He needed time to be alone with his thoughts, but it had been hours and she worried. She was actually surprised to find herself happy to handle the Furies and their unique methods of keeping themselves occupied. They could cause some extreme reactions if they chose not to stay in their part of the Underworld, as sometimes they became a bit overly enthusiastic in their work.

As she moved out of her business attire, she released her hair from her chignon and let the strands fall around her shoulders and back. She was in desperate need of some time spent relaxing in a warm bath, her muscles tight from the stress of the day, and her worry over Devon and his final decision.

She had received a report that members of the Senate had been asking around about the happenings in the mortal world in regard to the attempts on her domain.

Still no answers and no clues on the why and who of the attack.

The Moirai had all but disappeared, no longer taking calls from her or her sisters. They rarely left their domain in the sky. Not since the Great War of the humans and she knew their absence would soon turn into a war between them and Hera. Her sister was not the most patient on the best of days and as Archon, she had the power to detain the Moirai. Something none of them wanted to do, but just might have to.

Sitting on the edge of the tub, she filled it with water having decided on a blazing hot bath as opposed to a warm one. She ran her hand under the water and once it was almost too high for her to get in, she turned the knob and slipped in letting her muscles relax for the first time in days.

As she skimmed a hand along the top of the water, she smiled at the thought that Devon might actually be able to understand how important he is, how important he was becoming to her.

Her thoughts moved to him frequently these days and soon she started to have lustful fantasies of the man. It was obviously time to get out of the tub before she took her imaginings any further.

As she pulled the plug in the drain and grabbed her towel, she looked at herself in the foggy mirror. For the first time she wondered what a man saw when he looked at her.

Running a hand through her long black locks, she wondered if Devon found her beautiful. She knew what she looked like, lean, pale, dark hair, and blue eyes. At times, she found herself comparing her looks to some of the ghostlier souls, wondering if she came across that way.

She shook the thoughts away. This was something she did not have the time and energy to dwell on. She needed to be happy with what she saw and not allow that happiness to hinge on another person's perception of her. It was none of her business what they thought when they looked at her.

Walking past the balcony, she saw that all seemed to be well in the Underworld as everyone was winding down for the day.

That was a relief after putting out one too many fires in the Asphodel Fields this past week. The souls were anxious and there was no explanation as to why, which she was sure had more to do with the gate attack than anything.

She put on her most comfortable night gown, one that brought her back to her days when the Greeks still worshipped Gods. The straps came down into a low-cut neckline that only covered her breasts and an open back with the waist cinched in below her chest.

It made her feel like the Goddess she was and that brought her a small bit of comfort in these most recent nights.

Grabbing her brush, she went out to the balcony that overlooked Elysium. Brushing through her hair, she watched people dancing and lovers running off for a tryst. It brought a small bit of happiness to her soul on occasions in the past to see this, but now she just felt a sense of jealously. She would love to just run off with Devon. To give herself to him; body and soul.

A knock on her door pulled her away from her thoughts.

As she shook her head at her ridiculous desires, she walked back inside, putting her brush down as she crossed the room to open the door.

Something was amiss. She assumed it was a servant since that was normally who would knock this late at night. However, Thanatos had seen how drained she was and offered to handle any issues in her absence. Perhaps it was something more than he could handle.

She sighed. She knew she was too tired to think, but she had duties to attend to no matter her state of mind.

As the door opened, she found it was not a Reevka but Devon on the other side. Her nerves lit up when she took him in. His eyes seemed so much clearer than they had been since he had first entered her realm. The shadows in his eyes were not as prominent. It was almost as if his will to fight for himself was back.

He looked at her in a way that made her hands catch fire and she stepped back as Devon stepped forward, catching her hands in his. She swallowed as she watched the flames dance over their skin, not harming him one bit.

"I've waited for you for so long. I walked in the forest until I knew for a fact that no matter where I went in this world, my soul belongs here. With you. You are my always and I never plan to leave your side, so I hope you are prepared for a whole lot of Devon." He smiled, squeezing her hands.

She felt like she was spinning, and then it all too abruptly stopped, taking her off balance. As her brain tried to reason out what Devon had just said, Devon moved forward to grab her face and kissed her.

Her brain was random impulses and fire. She allowed him this, opening her lips to him as the kiss became hotter than any Godfire.

"I feel desperate for you. I've held back for far too long and I need you like my next breath," he whispered, nuzzling her neck.

"I feel the same," she replied on a shaky breath as she ran her hands up and down the planes of his back, feeling the muscles moving under her palms. He looked down into her eyes, the glowing green penetrating her soul.

"What you did for me was more than anyone has ever done." He moved his hands to her jaw, covering her hands with his.

"The fact that you did that, knowing that I might walk away, was completely selfless. How did I ever do anything to deserve you?" He stared right into her eyes with so much emotion, that it scared Persephone to breathe.

"I want you to be happy, Devon. That's it. With me or without me, but I had hoped with me," she whispered, not looking away. Her fingers moved along his hands that still held her jaw.

"That's the thing, Goddess, there was no choice. I knew it as soon as I got here that this is where I belong. I didn't realize why until I met you, got to know you." He leaned his forehead against hers as he whispered, "You tell me the Moirai say 'balance' every other word, implying my powers, but you balance my soul. My soul was a dark room, one I was stuck in, terrified of what was in there. You came in shining a light so bright that all the monsters in there with me left. You saved me, Persephone. You took me, a broken man, and made me whole. Made me yours."

She could feel the hot tears as they ran down her cheeks. His thumbs wiped them away as she had done his in the forest.

"I did nothing but stand by you when you needed someone. Something I will always do." She felt emotions far bigger than herself fill her chest. Devon leaned forward and kissed the tears from her cheeks.

"We make each other whole... stronger," he whispered against her cheek. He was quiet a moment before he continued.

"Persephone?" He smiled the most gorgeous and sincere smile she had ever seen on this man. He pulled back to look her in the eyes.

"I've never said this to anyone in my life, well the one I can remember at least, and I need you to know that," he told her.

She grew concerned, but he held her face still.

"Persephone, I love you. My heart is absolutely yours. It was before I ever even laid eyes on you as Devon."

Her eyes closed as the tears fell freely now. He leaned forward and kissed her forehead, her cheeks, and finally her lips. She threw her arms around him in a hug, as he pulled her closer in return.

"I love you, my warrior," she whispered as she tried to regain her composure.

He put his hand to the back of her neck and pulled her into a kiss that was heated with more than just the words they confessed.

"Please tell me this is okay," he whispered against her lips, and they both knew what he meant, what they had been leading up to. For days. Weeks.

She simply nodded as Devon moved the strap of her gown to the side, his lips trailing kisses along her shoulder. She felt a purr leave her lips as his hands removed the other strap, letting her gown fall to the floor in a puddle at her feet.

He stood back, taking her in. Her nudity not affecting her, but his look of pure desire caused her to take a deep inhalation.

"Gorgeous…" he murmured before moving back in for a kiss that ravaged.

Her hands slipped to the bottom of his shirt, pulling it up, aggravated she had to stop kissing him for the small moment it took to pull his shirt over his head and toss it away.

Their passion engulfed them in Godfire, their kisses unceasing as she pushed his pants and underwear down, leaving him bare to her. Both of their movements impatient and full of the desire they had held back for so long.

Before she could take in the visual of the man she loved fully nude, he lifted her, her legs wrapping around his waist as he moved them to the bed.

She could feel his hardness pressed against her and felt a thrill of excitement run up her spine.

"This will not be the slow love making I had hoped for our first time," he whispered as he laid her down, his mouth moving to her breast, gently licking and sucking at her nipple, lavishing it before he spoke again. His deep voice a chill against her naked flesh. "I don't have the patience for it. That will be next time, I promise."

He moved up to kiss her again, and in a suddenness she was both unprepared for but in desperate need of, he plunged inside of her, her gasp caught by his lips.

Her nails dug into his back as he rocked against her, her head rolling to the side as he kissed her neck, whispering every desire he had and all his declarations of love. His body took hers in the carnal way she had only dreamt of until now.

It didn't take long before a white light burst across her vision, her body going stiff as she found a release that cleared every thought but him from her mind. She heard a far away voice call out his name, one that sounded like her own. As the white light receded, she caught his smirk full of male pride before he kissed her long and hard, finding his own powerful release.

No words were spoken between them as Devon continued to kiss her, not leaving her body.

"I meant to take my time, but I have needed you for so long..." he murmured as he pressed another kiss to her swollen lips.

"No," she whispered against his lips, his head pulling back to look at her. "It was perfect. Just perfect."

A smile she had never seen before moved across his face, brightening his eyes, and not with Godfire, but true happiness.

Contentment.

Devon made good on his promise to make love to her slowly after that. They explored every inch of each other, memorizing each other after having been held apart for so long. Neither of them sure if this was real or the most spectacular dream.

Two broken pieces of a whole, separated for lifetimes, had fused back together. Though it still bore the scar of being separated, the tissue of that scar had only made it that much stronger.

Their bodies and souls finally together as one.

CHAPTER 31

Devon pulled her down on to his chest as he kissed her hair and told her to rest.

He ran his hands over her back as he felt her move to get comfortable, her head right over his heart that was beating way too fast. Her hand moved over his chest, following the paths of his scars that had once run across his torso in his previous life.

In the past he was careful not to let anyone see his scars, much less allow them to touch them. He released a breath as he felt a weight lifting from his soul at finally letting someone in, having someone to love him as he was.

With his mind at peace, it took hardly anytime at all for him to fall into a peaceful sleep.

As if he had only blinked his eyes closed, he opened them and was no longer in bed holding Persephone but standing in what look liked a large field, clouds moved along the ground as they would in the sky. He turned a full circle but could recognize nothing of his surroundings.

He caught sight of something, or someone, moving towards him through the clouds. He watched until he could clearly see it was Persephone walking towards him.

Her hair was bound back with flowers, a golden crown on her head, a long white dress that look like a second skin on her body with a golden belt. She was barefoot he noticed, and his throat bobbed with some unnamed emotion at seeing her like this.

A Goddess of the Ancient Greek myths.

"Devon," she whispered as she stood before him. She looked around herself as he moved to take her hand.

As soon as her hand was in his, he noticed he was in long white robes himself. He felt the heavy golden crown on his head, too, and looked back at Persephone for some clarification.

"Is this a dream?" he asked as he moved closer to her.

"I don't think so," she admitted, as lost as him in that moment.

Why was anything able to surprise him anymore?

As soon as he finished that thought, the ground began to shake, disturbing the clouds around them. He grabbed Persephone and pulled her to him, unsure of what was happening.

Pillar after pillar shot up out of the ground, dust flying off them as they grew up toward the sky, encircling him and Persephone. He stared at the columns before sharing a lost look with her.

A stone, smaller than the gigantic pillars, but large enough to reach their midsection, came between them, forcing them apart. Words and symbols carved into the stone glowed, written in a language he did not understand.

Persephone's eyes widened before narrowing. Almost as if she could remember the words, the symbols, written on them.

"Persephone?" he asked as he moved to stand next to her, his hand coming to the small of her back to try to gain her attention. When she finally turned to him, her eyes were full of confusion.

"I've never seen anything like this, and I hardly remember the symbols on there and their meanings... only life... and stone..." She tried to move forward but his hand halted her.

Nodding, she assured him that everything would be alright before she moved closer to inspect the glowing carvings.

"It feels like..." she whispered before she ran her hand over the symbols on the stone. "I've never seen anything like this before, but... Ow!"

She pulled her hand away, blue flames running over where drops of her blood had fallen against the stone. The angle of the stone pulling her blood lit in blue to the symbols.

"That was in no way something from a dream. This is more than our subconscious." She stared at the already healing wound on her hand before looking to the symbols, the flames there moving as if they were alive and beckoning.

He felt a pull on his power then, as if the stone were alive and

241

begging for him to place his hand upon it as Persephone had.

"I can hear it in my head, telling me to move forward," as he spoke, the pull became strong enough to move him to the stone, his body jolting as he placed his hand where Persephone had hers, something sharp piercing his skin.

His green flames mingled with hers and his eyebrows shot up, his mind racing as a zap of electricity ran along his nerves and across his body.

Words repeated through his mind obsessively, ones in an old and foreign language he had never heard spoken.

"What is happening?" he asked, watching the dancing flames.

As he spoke, the lights and flames were then sucked into the stone as if a vacuum. Their conversation halting as everything became eerily quiet.

The stone suddenly lit up again, blindingly bright, for a mere moment before everything went back to its previous state, the light fading.

Someone stood in front of them, not a human, not a God, but a being made of pure light.

Persephone gasped, blindly reaching out for his hand as she bowed her head, him doing the same after a moment of hesitation.

"I've heard of the Gods before the Titans, I descended from your kind, but I've never seen one," she whispered, looking up to the being.

"Persephone, child of the Titans, you have reigned well, as have your sisters. You've all done far more than the Titans, child of Cronus and Rhea, but there is a war coming and no generations to follow. As Eros, I am here to bind life and death, so you may be stronger and wiser, rule fair and just, and keep the earth from escalating into war and carnage yet again. I will not do this unwillingly, so you must choose. A choice I hope you make wisely. Do you plan to work as equals, stand strong in the face of your soulmate's fragility and allow them to carry you when you find yourself at your weakest?"

"There is no breaking something like this. If it even truly works or if any of this is real," she stated more to herself than him or the being called Eros.

"What do you mean if it works?" he replied and cautiously eyed the man made of light.

She looked at him as Eros stepped closer to them and spoke, "A soul bond only works if the two souls are meant to be bound. If both souls are not committed, it will reject the bond. It is a deeper, more meaningful connection. A more permanent one than a human marriage. This stone knows your intent, and if you are found worthy and willing to be faithful to only each other, you would be bound to each other for eternity."

"This… um… this is more than I anticipated," she murmured, "We only just found ourselves in…" She seemed at a loss for the right words.

"We only had sex for the first time, so this is almost like marriage on a first date," he stepped in, Persephone's eyes going wide with horror at him telling Eros this.

"You were born mortal, but your soul has longed for hers, regardless of your physical passions," the being stated and Devon could almost feel the irritation Eros felt having to explain this to him. "Some things are much bigger than you, child. Your power will need her power, and her power yours, to survive. Your bond could change the tides."

Devon almost laughed at this ancient being calling him a child, but he knew what the point was of this. He was more than happy to let the stone be the judge of him, and his fate, in regard to her since he knew the truth deep in his soul.

He held out his hand as he watched a look of surprise cross Persephone's face. Her eyes moved from his hand to his eyes.

"Devon?" Confusion and something else warred in her eyes as she watched him move into place near the stone with his proffered hand.

"Let's do it. I cannot imagine loving anyone else in this lifetime or the next. I know you are the one I've waited for. So, let's do it. Let's bind our souls. Husband and Wife, God and Goddess style." He smirked.

She only stared at him like she was expecting him to be kidding.

"You're giving a guy a complex, Goddess," he joked, but had started to feel a little weird holding his hand out, with his heart bleeding in it, as he waited for her to take it.

After what felt like an eternity, she took his hand, her eyes still showing some concern as she placed their clasped hands over the stone.

He felt the sense of relief coming from Eros in that moment. The fact that their bond was so important to this being was baffling.

She looked him in the eyes, words that had halted at Eros' appearance were again flooding his mind. Persephone squeezed his hand to let him know it was okay, it was normal.

The words repeated until he realized he needed to say them aloud. He nodded at Persephone as they put a voice to them. The words being carved into the stone as if by an invisible hand as they spoke.

"We bind ourselves, mind, body, and soul. We let the mountain of Olympus take our bound selves upon this stone for it to remain for all of eternity, never to break, as our bond will never break. As long as Olympus stands, so will our bond."

They looked from the stone to each other.

"I know your soul and I bind mine with yours," they both finished the vow.

As the last words left their lips, Eros placed his hands of light upon theirs and a bright white glow moved over their entwined hands then up and over their wrists.

Devon watched the light as it danced over their skin before he felt a strange warmth move over his left hand.

With their fingers entwined like a lover's embrace, the light encircled their hands and wrists, growing brighter and warmer as it moved up their arms. It flowed in between them, almost making a figure eight around and through their hands. As it settled against their skin, it seemed to absorb into them, creating a tattoo along their left wrist and circling up and around their left forearms, only to move like an infinity sign back to their ring fingers.

A skeletal serpent with narcissus and poppy flowers growing around the skeleton had been tattooed there. They both looked at each other as the illumination and fire faded, only the light of their eyes still glowing bright.

"You are the first to be bound with soulbond marks since the ancients. The first. This will change the tide when the war finds you both. This will only make your power that much stronger; Olympus stronger. Chaos bless you," Eros' voice, full of joy, whispered on the wind as he disappeared.

"I believe, my Goddess, our bond was accepted."

***

They both woke up from the dream at the same time, right where they had fallen asleep in her bed wrapped in each other's arms.

His arms tightened around her as they came fully back into awareness. Neither of them said anything for a moment, just breathing in and out as their heartbeats moved in sync. The rhythm a peaceful sound in the quiet night.

His mouth finally found the words to break the quiet of the room, yet his head still spun, as he found himself stumbling through his words, unsure of himself.

"Was that real?" he whispered as if speaking too loudly might break the joyous feeling in the room. As if it would bring them back to a reality that did not include being bonded to each other. He was surprised at how much he needed what happened to be real, that he was forever hers and she forever his.

She pulled his left arm out and stretched hers next to it, the soulbond mark there just as it had been in the dream.

Yes, it was real, they were bound. All the anxiety left him in a rush, his heart feeling a wholeness he could never even fathom was possible.

"It was. It is," she whispered in just as much awe.

He felt a sudden wave of self-consciousness about how she might be feeling now that it was real life and not some dream. He had jumped at the chance when he knew what was laid in front of them, yet she had hesitated and that made him feel like maybe he had rushed her.

Maybe that was why she was so ready to do it, the fact that they thought they were dreaming. His heartbeat picked up, and he swallowed to ask the question on his tongue, having to lick his dry lips.

Why was he so nervous? They were already bound to each other, but yet, if this was something she did not want, what would he do?

If it read her intention in the dream, but here... he wasn't sure he was strong enough to handle her rejection, especially after everything he had come to terms with since he first came to the Underworld.

Perhaps he had jumped the gun in his excitement to find himself again, a happier and less depressed version of himself at least. He had a tendency in the past to push a little too quickly into things. To jump without thinking.

245

"Persephone," he breathed, and she turned her head to look up at him, her fingers tightening around his.

"I know what you're thinking, and you are wrong. I meant it there just as I do here. I am as happy to be yours as you are mine." She leaned in and pressed a kiss to his soulbond mark.

This woman still loved him even though he wore his wrong decisions on his darkened soul. The memories of his sins preserved as scars on his soul but no longer his body, memories he did not care to see, but was finally beginning to accept.

He had made mistakes, but those choices led him to this woman. A woman he could not imagine living without.

The pain was worth the reward.

They left the world to its own reveries as they spent the last hours of the night in bed. They laid in each other's arms while they talked between kisses and love making. Laughing and enjoying each other's company before the world knocked at the door and demanded to be let in.

By early morning, they knew they had to face the day, much as they wished they could just remain in bed. The afterglow of their bond gave them the feeling of floating on air. Something they knew would run its natural course as they would eventually find a love that was less chaotic, steadier, but just as strong, if not strengthened by time.

They were starving, but it was still early enough that the Reevkas were not yet moving about. They dressed themselves to preserve some modesty in case some shadows lingered about, and she grabbed his hand to take him to fill their stomachs. After their night of bonding and lovemaking, they were finally ravenous for something besides just each other.

They walked into the large kitchen, knowing the cooks always left plenty of food from their daily meals and preparation in case Persephone came home late from the office. Settling on cheese and crackers, she grabbed his hand and pulled him into a shadow jump to her office at Cerberus Financial. The large windows of her office looking outover the city center of Halcyon. The glowing lights twinkling like stars.

She smiled at him as they found themselves seated on the couch in her office, enjoying their snacks while the rest of the world slept.

"I have a ton of questions," Devon started, putting some cheese on a cracker, and feeding it to Persephone. "One is how has no one ever done that ritual before?"

It seemed surreal that they were bonded. That he was forever her mate.

"My mother told me it was possible, but no, no one had ever been chosen for it," she responded after swallowing her bite of food. "Many years ago, Hecate wanted to try doing an earthbound version of it. We had a couple here who fell in love working the palace grounds. The souls who work in the Underworld have their own city and live right outside the palace walls, which I will have to take you to sometime.

"Anyway, this couple was in love, but it is not like marriages are well known in the Underworld, and the souls did not remember their human cultures. Hecate created this spell, using words similar to human vows but not quite, to bind their souls. It did not work, because as it turned out, the man was not sure of their union. Days before they performed the spell, he met the blacksmith and was unable to get him out of his head. After the spell failed, he knew he wasn't for her," she finished.

Devon raised his eyebrows. "So, you never actually saw it work?"

"No," she smiled softly. "Mother was sure if the souls were truly meant to be bonded, it would work. None did though. We just assumed that it had to be the chosen work of the universe." Persephone shrugged, "I guess she was right."

Devon reached over to take her hand in his and ran his thumb across the marking on her skin.

"Rebirth and faithfulness," she whispered as she watched where his thumb trailed over the tattoo. He looked up, her eyes following to his. "The mark, they symbolize rebirth and faithfulness."

Devon gave her the most gentle and loving smile. "Perfect," he whispered. "Absolutely perfect."

CHAPTER 32

Devon woke with a start and realized he must have fallen back asleep when they'd returned from their early morning snack. He rolled over to find Persephone gone and groaned knowing that meant it was time to get back to reality.

Not bothering to get up, he used his powers to portal to his room. He assumed since he didn't use the shadows to move through portals, his would be called a light jump, like Persephone's sisters. He'd save that observation to speak with Persephone about later, he needed to focus on dressing and calming his nerves before seeing his wife.

His wife.

Descending the stairs, a smile started to cross his face before he heard the voices coming from the study. Persephone was here, and unfortunately for his plans to relax this morning, so were her sisters.

He really wanted a moment with Persephone alone, but it was best he got this over with. Now that he was bound to Persephone, he really needed Hera to not want to skin him alive everytime she saw him.

Moving past the Reevkas with a nod as they opened the door, he froze as the room went eerily silent at his entrance.

"Demeter," Hera whispered, her hand coming to her mouth, shaking. "The forest outside… that was you?"

Devon stared right at her, caught off guard by whatever was happening in this room.

"Your father's name, what was it?" Hera asked Devon as she stood up, then turned to Persephone before he could answer. "What was it?"

Persephone looked to him as her eyebrows furrowed before answering.

248

"Demetri," she responded, then watched Hera's face transform with clarity while he felt like he had fallen down a rabbit hole.

"A family name?" Amphitrite asked as she moved closer to examine Devon like he might hold the answers they had been looking for.

Devon simply nodded, not really looking any of the sisters in the eyes. Persephone stood as if she knew this was becoming all too much for him, and grabbed his hand, interlacing their fingers.

"My father chose not to continue the name with me. Told me I would be a fresh start, but I never really understood what he meant."

"It worked…" Amphitrite whispered and Devon watched as her eyes filled with tears. "It really worked. She would be so proud of us."

Amphitrite's hand reached out to take Hera's and Persephone's. Persephone kept Devon's hand in her other one, refusing to release him.

"What did?" Devon said in a slow and impassive tone.

Surprising them all, Hera put her hand to Devon's shoulder and moved him to sit down in one of the winged back chairs. The Goddesses all moving to sit around him, Persephone closest to him. She continued to hold his hand, stroking over the veins along the back.

Hera and Amphitrite took seats on the floor in front of them. Not seated as Goddesses, but as family and friends.

"We were not the only children of Rhea," Hera explained, the name of their mother bringing a sadness to her eyes he had never seen before. "We are just the three who survived." Hera stopped and let that settle in for a moment.

Devon moved his eyes up to hers, his green eyes glowing fiercely as they lit up her face. He reined in his power, his emotions, as his eyes returned to normal.

This was important. This would answer the questions he had held in since he first set foot on the shore of the Styx.

"We had a sister, Demeter. She was the Goddess of agriculture, rebirth, and law," Hera continued, and he started to put the pieces together in his mind. Everything that he was, in every lifetime, all coming full circle.

"Stop," Devon put his hand up, halting Hera before she could start her next sentence, "I am not sure I can handle finding out I am related to Persephone. That is going to be way too much for me to handle."

Amphitrite let out a loud, very un-Goddess like snort at this and she covered her mouth. She looked embarrassed. This caused Hera to let out an equally unladylike cackle in return.

"No," Hera told him as she tried to reign herself in. "You are not having relations with a sister, niece, or cousin."

Persephone cleared her throat for Hera to continue the story.

"Though if you asked some of those Ancient Greeks, that was the preferred method of marriage and sex. If you were not directly related, why bother? Not to mention for hundreds of years I was a promiscuous God that was blamed for every transgression a wife committed that caused an illegitimate child. Oh look! I have another kid! Such a phallic loving society."

"Hera, you went down and stoked the fires of those rumors on many occasions yourself." Amphitrite scolded Hera.

"Oh, come on! I just wanted a little fun. Who knew I would be such a stud!"

"What a fun era that was," Amphitrite mumbled taking a drink of the refreshments the Reevkas had brought in as she spoke. "It is quite obvious what all the lead in the water did for them to fall over you like that."

"Really, Amphitrite? Was that necessary?" Hera stared at her sister.

"Oh, I am sorry, did I offend you Queen Goddess? Will we have an over dramatic show here in a moment to entertain us." Amphitrite laughed as Persephone put her face in her hand.

"Sisters..." Persephone warned only earning an eye roll from Hera and a smirk from Amphitrite.

"Moving on," Hera started as she relaxed from the near confrontation with her sister. "Some of our sisters did not come into their power upon death. Their souls were stuck here, their Goddess power would not release them even though their bodies had long gone back to the earth. We thought banishing Cronus would help, but still they stayed, and the longer they stayed, the more they became a shade."

At his questioning look, she explained. "Once a soul has stayed too long on the mortal realm, they become a shade. It happens a lot to bodies that were not buried, since Charon cannot let them cross if they have not had a proper burial. Anyway," Hera waved the words away. "A shade loses all sense of their human self and becomes more animal like. I believe some cultures call these poltergeists.

"Well, our sisters were becoming less of themselves and more of a feral otherworldly being. Shades hold no memories of their lives; they just mindlessly roam, terrorize, and are very difficult to handle, but we try to keep them from causing too much carnage."

Persephone took over when Hera nodded at her to finish. "I brought in Hecate and Thanatos, and together we knew we had to separate the power and the soul. It was difficult, and Hecate slept for two weeks after. Thanatos disappeared for a whole month, but we managed, and after an exceptionally long, drawn-out conversation-"

"Basically, ending up with us drawing sticks." Hera laughed, and Devon wasn't totally sure she was kidding.

"It," Persephone shot Hera a look, "was decided I would watch over souls and guide our sisters to the Underworld. Unfortunately, the power trailed them and tried to reattach. The only thing at that point we could do was find someone new to hold the power."

"Like a host for a parasite?" Devon interrupted, mildly disturbed by that idea. He felt his eyebrows wrinkle in disgust at the thought.

"Well, aren't you a little ray of sunshine," Hera muttered as she rolled her eyes. "I bet you're all the rage at parties."

"No, not at all," Amphitrite chimed, cutting Hera off before she could agitate the situation further. "We went around the world, found women who were carrying female children and had a need of that power. We knew the power would not fully manifest since they were mortal, but as with Demeter's power, we found a pregnant woman living in an area ravaged by famine. Her child was able to bring fertility to the land again. She thanked us by naming her daughter Demeter. Obviously, it was honored through the generations."

"So, there are latent Gods walking around?" he asked skeptically. "Then how come my dad didn't get the chance to live as a God?" Persephone could feel his rising anger. "How come he had to die? I would think he would be a hell of a lot worthier of being a God than I am."

Amphitrite moved onto her knees and sat back on her heels. "Because he simply was not fated to be. It is obvious the Moirai chose you since your soul, not any of your ancestors, was already calling to Persephone. You were meant to rise as the God of rebirth and law when the soul found the power of your ancestral line. When they merged, you became

251

who you are. They were separate before you."

"And fertility! Don't forget he is the God of fertility," Hera all but yelled as she gave them a lascivious wink. "Fortify your loins, dear sister."

Hera jumped up from her seat.

"Does anyone in this house of horrors work? I need wine," she muttered as she stood up with the obvious intention to rummage through the kitchen and cellars.

"And yet she was the one mother saved," Amphitrite muttered as she stood to go watch her sister, making sure she did not over imbibe and sleep her way through the city.

"How are you?" Persephone asked once her sisters had disappeared, her eyes holding concern as she rubbed his hand between both of hers, her fingers moving over the soulbond mark as she traced the lines.

Devon let out a little laugh. "I am not sure. Confused, sad, relieved? I am happy that I am finally where I was meant to be but am working out how my whole soul was waiting to be born into this familial line. It is so much bigger than me and it feels odd that my fate was determined so long ago, but I am extremely relieved that this means I can be with you. A little weirded out that part of your sister is in me, but as long as our kids..." he stopped himself.

She grabbed his chin in her fingers and moved him to face her, and he hoped he hadn't said too much. The fact that he brought up children caused his heart to thunder. He had enough to think about in the present and not the long-term future.

"You have been gifted this power, and it is yours, not Demeter's. It's been yours since the first mortal ancestor sowed the first seed full of power."

She leaned forward to kiss him.

"Always saving me, my Goddess, even from myself." He whispered against her lips.

"Alright!" Hera returned as she clutched an open bottle of wine in her hands and waved it around.

"Time to figure out what fresh hell our dear father has planned."

Hera let herself fall into a seat as she swung her legs over the side of one arm and took a hefty drink.

"To the newlyweds!" Hera held the bottle up in mock cheer.

Amphitrite grabbed it from her sister and took an equally impressive swig.

"Sorry we have to plan a battle instead of a party," Amphitrite smiled as she offered the bottle to Devon and Persephone, both of them shaking their heads.

"Are we discussing Cronus or getting drunk?" Persephone asked after sharing a smile with her sisters in thanks.

Amphitrite handed the bottle back to Hera, who took another healthy swig and finished the bottle off before she let it drop from her hands.

As it fell, she clapped her hands together, the sound reverberating through his mind and flashes of light sparked out from her hands like lightening.

The room spun around them as if they were in the center of a tornado, completely untouched as everything blurred together.

He realized he never even saw the bottle hit the floor before the study they had just been in disappeared. As if they had been pulled into another dimension, he now stood in a room that looked almost exactly like the place Eros had bound him and Persephone in their dream.

Olympus.

Hera turned to them and smiled.

"Welcome to the war room, my lovelies."

CHAPTER 33

Just as the sisters started toward their thrones, the earth began to quake.

Hera held her hands up to hold back her sisters and Devon as cracks moved across the floor towards the thrones.

Not cracks, Persephone realized, *vines*.

They moved to the empty area next to her throne and dug deep down into the marble floors before bursting back out, building on top of each other.

Something was wrapped within the vines. Something made of stone.

The vines flowered then fell away as if going through the four seasons all in the space of a few moments in time. The remaining vines pulled back and retreated into the earth.

There, next to Persephone's throne, was another throne fit for the God of rebirth. At the top, where all their symbols were carved to indicate whose it belonged to, was the winged serpent.

Devon moved to it and ran his hands over the marbled serpent. He looked to Persephone, the memory of their soulbond glittering in his eyes.

"A winged serpent. How fitting. A tattoo and now a throne." Hera waved her hand with a mocking bow. "After you, God of things that hump in the night."

Persephone watched Devon give Hera the side eye before he moved to the marbled seat of power.

Golden velvet cushions appeared as he sat, and the throne lit a bright, brilliant green before the light slowly faded away, leaving only a crown of green fire above his head.

He was no longer in just sweatpants and a shirt, but a forest green button down and slacks.

Devon looked down at himself then up at Persephone with a lopsided grin. His eyes shone in amazement as he took in everything around him.

The crown of fire subsided, leaving a laurel crown much like the ones her and her sisters wore. He reached up as he pulled it from his head to look at it.

"Holy..." he started to speak before Hera cut him off.

"None of that here, brother. This is sacred ground." Hera gave him a serious look as he sat up a bit straighter.

"Ignore her. Hera has said words that could raise the dead when in a temper. Even here." Amphitrite muttered.

Amphitrite shot Persephone a look of exasperation and Persephone rolled her eyes in response.

Hera clapped her hands together. "Good, good. A fourth God has been installed at Olympus, let us proceed."

The three Goddesses moved to their thrones and as they sat down, their appearances all changed.

For Hera, her crown of white fire glowed above her head before it turned to a crown such as the one Devon wore, only hers was a brighter gold with a diamond inlay set into the leaves. A long white dress formed down her body, one shoulder bare. There were golden flecks around the bodice and a golden belt. Her throne sat in the middle of the others, and as she was the Queen of the Goddesses, hers was elevated slightly higher with her signature thunderbolt carved into the headrest.

Amphitrite was beside her, in a long stunning aqua dress that looked like water running down her body. Her hair fell in long auburn waves to her waist. The aqua crown of fire turning to a crown of sea glass, and her throne was engraved with the trident.

Persephone was seated between Hera and Devon. Her robe morphed into a long black silk dress with a silver belt, long slits up the sides where her long legs were on view. A pomegranate necklace was on display along with her exposed shoulders, the straps draped in the style of the ancient Greeks. Smoke came up around her, making a crown above her head that ignited into blue fire when she sat on her throne, a crown made of sapphire replacing it. Her throne was carved with a

255

pomegranate surrounded by Narcissus flowers.

All the symbols engraved on the thrones were encircled with laurel wreaths, and even though everything was made of marble, the thrones were not uncomfortable as one would think due to the golden velvet cushions.

For each throne there was a sash across the back of it in the color that represented their realm, same as their dresses. No one was allowed to sit in the throne but the Goddess, or God, themselves.

To do so would mean the sash would restrain that person until the throne's owner came to dispose of them.

Torches of fire were on every pillar, though light was hardly needed with how bright it was here, being so high up on Olympus. High enough up, clouds moved around their feet as they walked, throwing up plumes like smoke.

Persephone watched Devon take in the pristine white columns encircling them. The thrones surrounded a marble floor where other deities brought forth issues or concerns for the Goddesses to hold court. On very extreme occasions, a human might be allowed to come before them, but they needed some power within their blood to withstand the level of energy here on Olympus.

"A Titan has decided to pick a side and made attempts on the Underworld," Hera started. "Sadly, it is the wrong side in my opinion, but nonetheless, the only logical conclusion we can come to is the goal of getting Cronus out of Tartarus. Do we know of any others who've decided to throw rationale and sane thought to the wind and join him or her?" She turned to look at Devon.

"Nature boy, did you see any other power signatures down there? I've been made aware you can see such things," she finished regally.

"Nature boy?" He arched an eyebrow but shook his head at her question.

Amphitrite's eyes became completely aqua, the pupils and whites gone. "I do not feel any unnatural presence near the mortal seas, but something feels off at the gates, near the river Styx," Amphitrite stated. She blinked and her eyes returned to normal.

Standing, Amphitrite made a large circle with her hands, and the center of the floor opened up, revealing a large rotating globe rising up from the darkness beneath. Lights flickered on it in areas of dense population.

"Is this our actual earth as it might look from space?" Devon asked in awe as he stared at it.

"Yes," Persephone replied, "We can see anything happening anywhere in the world from here."

As if to prove her point, Hera stood up and walked to the globe. As she put her hand up, the globe responded to an unspoken demand and moved to Halcyon. An image came out from it engulfing the room to where one might think they were walking among the crowds. People were moving through Hera as she stood before the globe, lost in thought.

A projection

"Would they not come to where the majority of the deities reside, the seat of our power, if they wanted to know our movement and spy on Olympus?" Amphitrite asked.

"Yes." Hera stood in the middle of the live image and looked around. "I can promise that demon of a Titan has people here," she stated, referring to Cronus.

Hera turned to Persephone. "How would someone bypass the gates? Obviously, if they went through Cerberus, they would have been a very stringy dog chow. How else could a Titan get down there without a link?"

Persephone shook her head. "They couldn't. They would have had to gain entrance through someone at the gates or me. Not to mention, they were able to get all the way to Tartarus. It would have to be someone that could move freely through, but even so, how could they do so without me knowing? The moment their foot touched the ground in the Underworld I would've known, regardless of who approved their entrance."

Hera stared at Persephone a moment longer.

"Who has access to the Underworld unhindered?"

The quiet was unpleasant as Persephone's power rose and chilled the air around them.

"Calm down, Persephone. I am not blaming anyone... directly." Hera's eyes moved over to Devon, the temperature dropping further at Hera's focus on him.

"Devon, tell us of your mother?" Hera asked. The abrupt and off topic subject change had Devon do a double take.

"My mother? What would she have to do with this?" he asked with disbelief in his voice.

"Persephone got a vision from you of your mother having... well, visions. Could she have been an oracle?"

"Hera, enough..." Persephone started, but Devon only shook his head.

"I have no idea what was going on with her. She left when I was a baby, but in the memory I had the other day, she said she saw things..." he drifted off in thought.

"Perhaps your father would know?" Hera asked, earning a glare from Persephone, the temperature around them frigid now.

Persephone turned to Devon, sighing she told him what had been discussed, and Persephone had hoped, put to bed. No such luck.

"I have found a way to return your father's memories for a moment of time. It will not be long and will be completely up to you on whether or not we do this."

Hera made a small sound of disagreement but held her tongue at Persephone's withering glare.

"I have never personally restored memories to a soul, and it is not without consequences. Should you choose to, it may be difficult to ask about your mother, but it would help us if she did in fact see something of use to us."

Everyone waited as Persephone gave a quelling look to her sisters. Devon needed to work through this without their input.

He finally looked up at her and she saw hesitation and fear in his eyes, but he simply nodded his head.

"I'll do it."

***

Devon felt like his heart was going to beat out of his chest as Persephone took his hand and shadow jumped him to Elysium.

They were right outside a little cottage, something he could imagine being his father's paradise as it fit the man so well.

People were wandering through a garden near them as they worked to pick fruits and vegetables, placing them in the baskets at their feet.

258

He felt nature all around him and it left a euphoric feeling in his soul.

He froze as he caught sight of his father walking towards the cottage with a large spade in his hands. He wore one of his old flannel work shirts, the same he wore in life, and his dingy, dirt-stained pants from working out in nature all day.

Without saying anything to him, Persephone started towards his father as Devon tried to hold his bleeding heart in his chest with his bare hands. He followed her and before he knew it, or even felt ready, he was standing in front of his father for the first time in years.

His father's eyes looked them over.

It was obvious he recognized Persephone, since everyone here knew the Goddess, but it hurt to see that he didn't recognize him, his own son. Devon knew he wouldn't, but he'd hoped some seed of remembrance would have been triggered at seeing him again. Just as he was sure every other soul had the same wish when they came to the Underworld.

"Hello," she greeted, bringing his father's attention to her. "May we have a seat and chat a bit with you?"

His father simply nodded, not saying a word, and turned to enter the little cottage that they had been standing in front of.

Devon watched as his father placed the spade next to the door, just as he did in life. He pulled off the dusty boots and rubbed his hands together before washing them and preparing to make tea.

Persephone followed him into the kitchen, but Devon could only stare.

"Please, let me," she asked as his father began to fill the kettle.

"Oh, I cannot let the Goddess do…"

The breath left his body as he heard his father's voice for the first time in forever. His father was a quiet man, but he remembered all the times growing up when that rough baritone calmed his childish temper.

"I insist." She smiled as she held out her hand for the kettle, and his father hesitated a moment before handing it to her. She motioned for him to have a seat with Devon.

Devon felt a weird tinge in his chest at how domestic this all felt. He imagined Persephone as a mortal woman and them sitting down for a family meal with his father. The tinge in his chest quickly became an ache.

259

His father sat down in one of the blue chairs at the small wooden table in the middle of the kitchen, as Devon caught sight of Persephone pouring water from a flask into a teacup. He said nothing as she heated the cups with her hands, the kettle untouched, and put tea bags in each before distributing the cups.

Devon quickly grabbed his to have something to do with his hands and tested the heat. He was so nervous he worried they could hear his heartbeat in the quiet room.

"I want you to meet Devon," she started. "I've put some water in your tea that will help your memories to return," her eyes darting to Devon quickly then away as she spoke.

He realized she was nervous, too, as if unsure if she made the right call here. He gave her a small smile of reassurance, a promise that they would get through this.

"My memories, my queen?" his father asked as he slowly wrapped his aged hands around the teacup.

"Yes, I want you to remember who Devon is. I would like for you to speak with him about your life before you came here. Is that alright?" she asked as she placed a hand on his father's gnarled fingers that held the teacup so delicately.

"Yes, my queen," he whispered as he stared into the cup.

"Demetri, you may call me Persephone." She smiled as his father looked up at her, his eyes wide and glistening at her request. Right then Devon saw the love she held for all the souls here shining through her eyes.

Persephone patted his and his father's hands, then stood.

"It will only last for half a day at most, so please," she glanced at Devon, "make the best of it."

Devon just stared at his father as the man who raised him took a sip without saying a word after her speech.

Persephone moved to Devon and grasped his hands, her eyes full of fear and apology. "I am sorry this was sprung on you, but I had to make a deal to move forward with this and I didn't have time to warn you before it was retracted, or before my sisters called for it."

His hand went over hers as he looked deep in her eyes and whispered, "Thank you."

She nodded and disappeared into the shadows of the room.

CHAPTER 34

Devon waited, not sure if he was breathing as his father finished the cup.

When he set the empty cup down, he clasped his hands on the table, looking at Devon with the calm countenance he had known growing up. He watched closely and saw the moment recognition flooded his father's hazel eyes. Before Devon could make a move, his father had already stood up and pulled him into a hug.

"Dad!" he whispered as sobs built up in his throat. He grabbed his father just as tightly. The man he hadn't seen since he was a young eighteen-year-old leaving on an old and dirty military truck.

"My boy," his father whispered through his own tears. "I've missed you." He felt his dad kiss his hair before he pulled back, holding him by the shoulders to look him over.

"My dear boy, you've been through hell." His father's eyes held pain and sadness as he moved his hands to take Devon's face.

"I am so sorry I never came home, Dad," Devon cried, not even trying to rein in his emotions, but his father never expected him to. He always claimed one couldn't fix something broken if it was hidden away.

"My son, when I passed the gates, I asked of you. The judges allowed me one request, and that was to see you. All of you. I know what happened, and I did not once blame you for the decision you made. There was no choice there but evil and the destruction of evil. You did something that man may have seen as wrong, but in the morality of the universe, you set things right. You went above human law, such a law that has flaws, and I am proud of you. I watched children that would have died without your choices grow into amazing people. They did not know what you did, but I do." He told him with glassy eyes. Devon could barely see through his own tears.

"How did you die?" his father asked with sadness creasing the corners of his eyes as his hands cupped his son's face. He knew his father had hoped he would have lived out his days with children and grandchildren of his own.

"Mission gone wrong," was all Devon said and his father simply nodded sadly at the news.

"And you were here in Elysium with me all this time?"

"Uh, kind of. Maybe we should sit?" Devon motioned to the chairs and his father took the one closest to him, grabbing Devon's hand between his own.

"Well, Dad, it turns out there is something quite off about me." He watched as his father's eyes narrowed. "When I died, I was brought to the Underworld, but not as a soul for eternity. My soul and an ancient power merged, which was released when I left my mortal body, and I don't really know how to explain this all without sounding crazy, but I am immortal. I have Godly powers over nature and I work alongside Persephone, the Goddess." His words came out in a rush before he calmed enough to finish. "We are bound. Married, so to speak."

He watched his father's jaw go slack.

"You are a God?" his father asked as his eyes pierced through Devon. The fingers of his father's other hand pulled into a fist on the table.

"Yes, as weird as that is to say, I am. The Goddess Demeter... well, it turns out I have her power."

Instead of seeing confusion on his face, his father gave him a warm smile as he patted Devon's hand in the loving way he remembered him doing when he was a boy.

"You are married to the Goddess?" his father asked.

"Yes." Devon wasn't sure if the heat in his cheeks was a blush or not. His dad was not one to miss a detail or let a subject drop.

"I was so sure you would marry that girl, Greta. Do you remember? Her father had the best crops at the markets. I was sure her adoration would win you over. When you left for the military, she asked for your information to write you."

Devon let out a little laugh. "Yeah, I remember. She said she would wait for me. I told her to move on. Took her about two months to announce she was getting married to the Stuart guy down the road." He looked at his father. "You know I never felt for her that way."

"Oh, I did. I worried you never showed any interest in anyone, then I thought that perhaps women were not what you desired. At least until I found you with Maria that one time…"

"Okay, yeah, let's not rehash that. I didn't want to die a virgin, but I definitely did not want my dad to walk in on it." Devon was very sure he blushed now and cleared his throat. He grabbed his tea and hoped the embarrassment would go down with it.

"Yes, we both could have lived without that moment in the loft, but you never seemed to look at anyone with the spark in your eyes. I just wanted happiness for you, my son. I wanted you to know that."

"I have that," he told his father and a warm smile cross his father's lips. Devon hated that he had to segue to the next subject, but he needed to discuss this while he could.

"You didn't have that. Mom was-"

"I thought she was ill. I was wrong." Devon's head snapped up at his father's words. "She was very much a lovely woman when I married her, but something changed in her over time, something I didn't understand.

"She had something in her blood that gave her dreams that seemed to be more. The blood of someone who had visions of things to come, and not knowing what they were, they drove her mad.

"I should've believed her, but no one truly believed in religion anymore after the Great War and pandemic. I tried to take her to one of the older churches that still had inhabitants, but what I thought might be older clergy was no one but refugees. Doctors wanted her to be medicated, which I chose to push.

"Do not take this as your fault, for it was not, but I know now she saw you becoming more than just a human boy, that was why she behaved as such after we conceived you. She saw this." He motioned his hand over Devon, as if his mother saw him as he was now. "She was cursed with a gift that I wish I had known how to help with."

It shocked Devon to hear his father speak of it this way.

"Her gift… what kind of things did she see?" he finally found the courage to ask.

Sighing, his father sat back and clasped his hands over his abdomen.

"When we found out we were having you, she started to have the dreams. Ones where you were covered in blood not your own," Devon flinched at this, but kept silent. "Then the dreams started to become more… abstract and she would space out during the day with them, to the point where I worried about her even taking a bath or walking to the market alone."

His father reached up to scratch his eyebrow in thought before he ran his hand down his face.

"She would see large trees or vines pulling headstones and graves down underneath the earth. Wraiths walking beside her, vines wrapping around her ankles and pulling her down. She would see what she thought was Hell and someone crawling from the ground, the person was pure starlight, if that makes any sense at all. Your mother feared that person greatly."

Devon remained quiet as he watched his father process everything and try to remember things from so long ago.

"The water. She was so fearful of water before she left us. It never made any sense to me, but she said, 'The water could change the course of our fate. It would betray and take from us, yet we worshiped it as if it brought life.'

"That was about when I thought her mad. She refused to go to the river by herself, sure that a river demon would kill her. It just became more bizarre until I was fearful she would hurt you. It wasn't long before we woke up one morning after a fight where I told her as much and she was gone."

He stared down at his son's hand in his. Devon's hands must look so much larger now. His father's hands were as he remembered, but more wrinkled and spotted. The same worn marks from hard work adorned his skin.

"I had that for a time before she started with the dreams; the spark. It is important. It is more than lust. I see you finally have it, my boy." He looked at Devon as he patted the top of his hand. "This Persephone, our queen, you care for her. She must for you, for to take the waters of memory always requires a sacrifice. She gave something for our time together. I am happy you have that but I worry what it means that you are attached to such a powerful person. Don't lose yourself in her shadows. Stand beside her and not behind her, that way you do not allow the potential of what you could be with her fall through your fingers. You should find balance with her if she is your true soulmate."

The soulbond mark on Devon's wrist lit with his father's words as if in agreement.

***

Devon told Persephone all that his father had conveyed to him of the visions. She seemed to know immediately who the river demon was and how a Titan had found a way into the Underworld.

"Tristan!" she shouted, bolting up from a couch in the study.

"Tristan," he growled in agreement.

"Wait. Tristan was not ruling then, but his father was. She most likely saw Tristan in the future, and with his behavior the other day and his escape, he has to be the one bringing the Titan in through the river system. I had thought it a few times, thinking the attack at the gates had something to do with it, but never enough evidence to prove it. You were right — that was a diversion for them to make their attempt on Tartarus. Perhaps the orange coloring was the Titan giving power to Tristan in an attempt to trigger the gate..." she mused as she paced back and forth.

She stopped suddenly and held her hand out to him.

"Come with me?" she asked, and he nodded in response, relieved to feel the pieces finally starting to come together. He felt her pull him into a jump and they were suddenly inside a familiar office building overlooking the city through floor-to-ceiling windows. He stayed quiet as Persephone guided him to sit across from three empty seats.

In a flash of light, three women, the Moirai in their separate forms, were in the seats before them. He managed not to jump at their sudden appearance or how unnerving it was that they started to giggle as one.

The Moirai were extremely creepy creatures.

He glanced at Persephone as she laid a comforting hand on his arm with a little eye roll that helped to relieve his discomfort.

Before he could gather his thoughts, he watched Persephone pull her cold demeanor forward. The Goddess and C.E.O. merged into one as she turned her focus on the creatures in front of her.

She held a powerful grace that reminded him of a lioness.

A Queen.

"You know a Titan is attempting to open Tartarus." Persephone's voice was cold. Her hands on the armrests of her chair and an expectant look on her face.

"Explain what you know now. I am done with your trickery. You are putting my realm in a position of vulnerability and I'll not have it any longer." She let out a growl on the last syllable that would have had mortals stepping away in fear.

The Moirai hardly flinched.

"Percy! Devon! So good to see you both again!"

"Not now, Clothos." Persephone snarled. He reached out to put his hand over hers, the Moirai letting out a collective purr at his gesture.

Feeling embarrassed, he started to withdraw. Persephone reached over before he could, squeezing his hand with her other one before she let him go and leaned forward. Her elbows to her knees and hands clasped in front of her.

"Give me something other than one-word nonsense." Her voice low, but impactful. The threat clear for anyone within hearing distance to pick up.

"Balance!" the middle one sang as she swayed a bit in her chair to music no one but her could hear.

These ladies were definitely missing some marbles.

"Yes, *balance*. Great. Give me more, like a name or what to look for. I doubt they will make the same attempt twice. Do you know where Tristan is?" Persephone growled, her lips making a flat line of anger as her power built up and flowed through the air thick as smoke.

"No light escapes, but light is needed to see." The one on the far right explained. "Nothing can grow without light."

Out of the corner of his eye, he watched Persephone put her shaking head into her hand. He wasn't sure he had blinked since they had shadow jumped from the Underworld.

For such a mundane looking room, the creepy factor was maxed out.

"Do you know where I can find Tristan?" Persephone asked again in exasperation as she dropped her hand. The Moirai simply started the swaying thing again and Devon looked for an exit. If they started chanting, he would have to jump out the window. His nerves were shot, and they just kept upping the ante.

"Trust your instincts!" They all said in chiming tones at once. "Devon will bring balance in your death! He will balance everything and make it as it should so the war can be won!"

Devon felt his heart stop.

Her death.

His head swung to Persephone as he watched the Moirai disappear into thin air from his peripheral vision. He didn't care at all about the crazy women, chanting and dancing in chairs like he had walked into fun Friday at the insane asylum.

She would die?

Both Devon and Persephone sat there for a moment longer. He watched her and wondered how she could find herself injured bad enough to die while she stared vacantly where the Moirai once sat.

"Your death?" Devon whispered not moving his gaze from her face. She was so caught up in her own thoughts she hadn't realized he had been staring a hole through her.

"Obviously not my actual death, I am a Goddess," she reassured him, but even then, he saw in her face that she was not fully sure of that statement herself.

"Once again, the Moirai have managed to make everything substantially more confusing somehow. Thank you so much for more of nothing!" Her voice rose in anger as she spoke until she was screaming the last of it into the empty space in front of them. He wanted to step forward and wrap her in his arms, but he wasn't sure that was the right thing to do at that moment.

She took a deep breath and pulled her calm demeanor back over herself before she stood up. Turning to Devon, she straightened her shirt and regarded him with a coolness that sent shivers down his spine. He felt like some missed opportunity had fled right past him, and he would never get that chance with her again.

"We need to work on finding Tristan. He is the one holding the key to all of this."

He moved to stand up, unsure if to comfort or stand his ground. Everything in his mind was a jumbled mess that just kept returning to the words, 'her death' over and over again.

His fists were clenched, and he had to calm himself before he acted

267

out in a fit of anxiety.

"We need to do whatever it takes to get up to muster for what is coming. I am not taking the chance of anything happening to you." He moved closer to her but stopped before he reached out, unsure if any comforting gestures would be welcomed.

Something was happening inside her and he could tell she was feeling unsteady, her normal cool, calm, and controlled attitude was beginning to shatter before his eyes. He knew how it felt when the world spun out from underneath him, and he knew she needed time to process.

He could give her that.

"I might hang out a bit here, if you are cool with that?" He hoped she would take the only thing he could offer her. Time alone.

"What if..." she started. He watched as she grew even more agitated and hoped he wasn't misreading the situation and about to make a colossal mistake.

The last thing he needed was for her to start resenting him because she never had a moment alone to process and think.

"Alright, but..." she stopped as she looked at him and saw he was planning to dig his heels in on this one.

Nodding, she released a breath and some tension left her shoulders. He relaxed at seeing the change in her posture and knew he had made the right move.

"I'll see you soon," she stated as she stepped back. He could still see some hesitation, so he walked backwards towards the door and gave her a small wave before she could talk herself out of it.

She simply nodded once again before she turned and shadow jumped mid-stride.

CHAPTER 35

He waited a moment in the empty room, unsure if the Moirai would pop back into existence so he could ask a few questions of his own. Nothing to that effect happened, so after a few awkward minutes of standing in an empty room, he decided to take a walk around the city. He knew Persephone would find him no matter where he went if she needed him.

As he made his way out of the Fates Consulting, he found the rest of the building completely empty. No one in the hallways, at the front desk, or even security at the door when he walked outside. He guessed they really enjoyed making everything as creepy as possible, but most likely these people were just parts of the Moirai themselves, since all the power trails that moved like rivers through the building were the same color.

Stepping outside, he felt the heat of the sun and a light breeze touch his skin. Perfect Weather. If ever there was a time to check out the city of Halcyon, it was now.

He started his little jaunt as a tourist by making his way down the main street. He took in the coffee shop, bookstore, metal works shop, and transportation services building.

All the vehicles there plugged into a large central station since vehicles no longer ran on ancient remains from the earth. The humans had exhausted those resources long ago, burning through them as if some eternal supply was hidden beneath the soil.

He always found the concept super weird.

As he walked into the city center, he spotted an engraved plaque on a nearby building declaring it the International Relations building. It stood proudly as if it were a welcome beacon to the city, or a sentry at the metaphorical gate of Halcyon.

As he moved past the exquisite building, he noticed a large statue of a woman looking out over the city with a blindfold on, a sword in one hand, scales of measurement in the other, and a lion resting at her feet. The sun caught the marble tone of her skin and lit her from behind. It made her look like a Goddess come down from the heavens to protect her city and not simply an immovable slab of stone.

Deciding not to enter the main part of Halcyon, he turned down the road away from the International Relations building, catching sight of the sun glinting off the Thalassian Sea.

Large ships drifted in and out of the port, full of exports and imports from other places on the continent. He always wondered how far the ships could go before they entered the dangerous waters he had heard rumors about.

No one he knew ever ventured from Zephyr. The areas beyond their continent had been destroyed to the point that no one could safely navigate the land or water. These different places fascinated him as a child, or what they once were.

All of that was gone.

He knew of only Zephyr.

He tried to find books on the world before the Great War, what had happened, but could never find anything current or even relevant. As if all the information regarding anything but Zephyr was burned in the wars

Catching sight of a large ship with Oceanus Industries written in tall, proud letters on the side, he thought of West. His closest friend as a human. The man whose entire back story had been a lie, crumbling the foundation of their entire friendship to dust.

Weston Murphy was the heir of Oceanus industries.

How many lies can one human be dealt and still believe in anything or anyone ever again? He watched the ship pass by him with his hand in his pockets, the wind blowing his dark blonde hair into his eyes, his thoughts melancholy.

"Dev," he heard from behind him.

He froze for a moment before he turned to take in his longtime friend.

Gone was the man who drank next to him, talked about the jobs they did or had coming up, and how their career choice had stained their souls.

Gone was the man who wore the same tactical gear and was amazing at getaway plans, mostly by water, which made sense now.

Before him stood a different man in an expensive pea coat and jeans that probably cost more than Devon had made in a month. Hair slicked back from his face, he looked how the well-dressed heir of an empire should.

"Weston Murphy, heir apparent." He laughed without humor. "Who knew?"

"Dev, I wasn't him for a reason. Actually, a lot of reasons, but holy hell, man! You were dead. I saw you die!" West looked like he might actually get physically sick from the memory of it. "I went to your funeral. I gave the fucking eulogy!"

West rubbed his hand over his face and Devon noticed it looked like his friend had aged a few years since he saw him last.

"I did die." Devon asserted, but found it only came out as a whisper.

West looked at him, squinting his eyes, and Devon could see him processing his words.

He knew what he was about to tell his old friend would most likely make him think Devon had lost his mind. There was no way to explain what had happened without sounding like a lunatic.

"Yet here you stand before me, very much alive." West moved closer to Devon, his face torn in a misery Devon could understand all too well. "I checked your pulse and stayed with your body while it cooled," West explained, his voice distant though his focus was completely on Devon.

This was not the West that he had known. The West from before was always the funny one to Devon's more serious nature. Unable to stand when someone was down, he always tried to cheer them up and break the tension.

"I think we need a drink and a lengthy talk," Devon replied as he nodded to a bar near the docks. "You are never going to believe any of this, especially not without alcohol in your blood."

He caught West looking at him from the corner of his eye and saw his old friend, the West from before, shine through for a moment.

"Try me," West smirked before he bowed with a flourish that was all

West.

***

Once seated at the closest bar with a few beers, West rapped his
knuckles on the table.

"Alright, tell me of your resurrection."

"First, why didn't you tell me who you were? Why would you work
as a mercenary for five years when you had everything you could ever
want? Tell me that and I'll tell you everything that happened from the
moment I died until now," Devon compromised as he watched West
with a weary look.

Both men stared at each other for several moments before West
finally broke eye contact. He shook his head and took a large gulp of
beer like he needed liquid courage to tell his story.

"Ah, yes. Why did the golden child go rogue?" West moved his
elbows onto the table and folded his hands together, his head falling
forward a moment before he finally looked up at Devon.

"Daddy dearest had plans for me to take over at the young age of
twenty-one. I was way too busy being a spoiled brat, enjoying my
women and my drinks. Obviously, being the heir of the world's largest
shipping company put a huge target on my back with my father's less
savory competition, and I was unaware that some of my father's
enemies had some pretty appalling ways of dealing with those they
found to be a threat." West took another long pull of beer before he
slammed his drink down on the table, having drained it, and made a
motion for another.

Devon assumed this was going to be a story that required a lot of
booze and finished off his own beer.

"Anyway, one night I went home with a lady I met at a club. We went
upstairs to her apartment and I was enjoying a relaxing evening up until
a group of men broke in. Or, so I thought. Turns out she lured me so
her and her buddies could get some cash from dear old dad.

"They beat me within an inch of my life, dragging my unconscious
body across town and kept me chained to a chair in a warehouse. Since
I was known to go on benders, no one looked for me, and so they got
the joy of my unending pain for days while trying to contact daddy

dearest for apayout.

"However, that wasn't the worst part." West looked away, his jaw clenched. "The worst part is the lady working with them thought she would actually get a cut. They decided they didn't have to share anything with her if she wasn't around. She was the lure and nothing more, yet she never picked up on their plan. I was barely aware of their argument one night while I sat in that gods-forsaken chair, crumpled and bleeding. Finally, the main guy had enough arguing and offered to compensate her for her time. The way he said it told me everything I needed to know about how he planned to pay."

Now West did look at him.

"Every man in that room took turns with her before the last one put a bullet in her skull. I was held down, getting punched, kicked, even stabbed trying to stop them."

West took a moment, mindlessly wiping condensation off the glass with his thumb. "I couldn't go back to my life after that. When my dad's people finally found me and took me home, it only took a week after healing before I snuck out for the last time. I swore to find every asshole in the world who thought they could treat another human being in that way and end them. I pulled all the money I had set aside for me to drink and whore away my life and used it to fund most of our jobs."

Devon sat back and ran his hand along his jaw. He looked at West. Really looked at him.

"Did anyone else ever know this?"

"No," West said simply. "No one did and no one ever would have. I still won't tell them. Even if they showed up here, Oceanus lit up behind me with arrows screaming my real identity, I still wouldn't tell them."

"I get it," was all Devon said, but the words seemed to mean a lot to West. He watched the relief on West's face at Devon's acceptance and confidence on the matter. No more words were needed on the subject.

After a long moment of silence, West looked over at Devon.

It was story time.

"I was very dead. I saw my body…" Devon started as West's eyes went wide at the confession, and he leaned forward as if this were an interesting fairytale and not the story of Devon's death.

"As I stood over my body, I couldn't move, like my feet were

273

planted to the floor and it completely freaked me out. I was confused and unable to think, my mind was completely fogged over. Next thing I know, the woman you saw that night at the gala with me walked in, and she was like a lighthouse showing me the way. My mind just... cleared.

"I just felt this deep sense of trust in my gut when I looked into her bright blue eyes. Like she was what I had been waiting for. I was unsure what everything meant, what was happening, so I started pacing." He watched West nod. He knew how Devon was when he was frustrated or confused, how he would pace and run his hand through his hair. It was something that both amused and annoyed his friend.

"She was holding this string that went into my chest, so of course that only freaked me out more. Finally, she spoke, and it was like that was all I could hear, just her. She gave me these seeds to eat and it turns out those seeds bound me to the Underworld." He paused and looked at West before he continued.

"She is the Goddess of the Underworld." He shrugged as West's jaw dropped open in shock.

"Yeah. My thoughts exactly. Now I am bound to the Underworld with powers and a throne at Olympus."

Devon sat back and crossed his arms. He felt more than a little uncomfortable waiting on West to say something.

"I know, unbelievable, huh?" Devon asked, trying to elicit a response.

"Understatement," West whispered before breaking eye contact and looking down at his hands on the table, his face scrunched up in confusion. "I never saw your body in the casket; they kept it closed. Did she bind you back to your body?"

Devon shook his head. "Nope, my mortal body had bound my power, not sure how all this works, but I am basically my soul made flesh. I don't have the scars of my death and from before."

Devon waited, not wanting to say more until he knew West processed what he had already told him. Waiting to see if West was going to be able to take this all in and accept it.

Finally, West looked up at him, "Man, I don't care if you're the devil himself, I am just so damn glad you're alive," he stated with a smile as he slapped his friend on the shoulder and laughed an almost manic laugh. Devon allowed himself a small chuckle, relief at his friend's response.

"So, you rule the Underworld?"

"I am not the ruler of the Underworld, Persephone is. The one you met at the gala with me that evening."

"So, your girlfriend is the ruler?"

"Not my girlfriend." This part he felt more anxiety explaining than he had about becoming a God. "My wife."

West spit his beer all over the table and a guy walking by to the bathroom.

"What?" West sputtered as the man stopped in his tracks, beer splattered across his white shirt.

"What the hell, man!" The guy moved toward West, but something in Devon made him stand up between his friend and the very angry male covered in beer.

The man halted before stumbling back, staring at Devon with panic in his eyes, and turning to move at a clipped pace to bathrooms. Turning back to West, he caught a flash of awe in his friend's eyes.

"Whoa..." West was staring at him, a dumbfounded look on his face. "Your eyes just flashed green."

West moved closer as he sat back down, waving his hand in Devon's face as if he could trigger his eyes to light up again. Devon laughed, pushing West back, and was rewarded with a grunt from his friend.

"Wife?" he repeated back to Devon, both of them staying quiet for a moment after that revelation.

"Yes." Devon spent the next part of an hour explaining everything from the moment he came to the Underworld until now. West watched him, absorbing this new information.

Once Devon got to the moment that they had run into each other outside of the docks, both men stayed quiet for a while.

"You and your wife are in charge of Hell." West stared off into space as he stated this.

"Not Hell. It's like here on Earth. There are whole cities and villages that operate from people working jobs like they did as mortals. Yes, there are hellish parts, like Tartarus-"

"Tartarus is fucking real?" West loudly whispered as he leaned over the table. His eyes were wide like a child seeing proof that his favorite fictional character was in fact real.

"Yes, it is. And so are the Fields of Punishment, but then there is Elysium, which is paradise, and now I know my dad went to his version of heaven. I... I spoke with him."

"Holy shit, Devon!" West sputtered. "You saw your old man? What did he say when he saw you?"

Devon shook his head. "That is an entire discussion for another time. I am not sure I am emotionally capable right now of discussing that particular subject."

"Just answer me this. Did you finally get closure?" West asked, his face completely serious. He knew how Devon had reacted to the news of his father's death. He was there to take him drinking, to sit with him on the roof in a run-down city among the sand and just listen to the desert animals scurry about without a word between them.

Devon looked out the window where people were milling about, dock workers loading ships, and kids playing along the boardwalk. He looked back at his friend and nodded.

"He was happy to see me, and it killed me that I didn't get to say goodbye in person, but yes, I have some closure. I asked him if he was happy and he claimed more than he could ever remember. A total dad joke since he knew his memories of the human realm were gone. I wonder if I even really deserve it though. After all, I left. Would he have been so happy to see me in life before he died? Would I be worth that happiness?"

"One day Devon, you are going to see your worth, and I hope to all the Gods, Goddesses, whoever is listening, that I am there to see it."

CHAPTER 36

Persephone was losing herself to panic.

She had never lost herself to such emotional turmoil this way. Anxiety seemed like such a foreign concept to her, but the racing heart and tight chest seemed to follow along the lines of what the humans claimed to be an episode of panic.

It made sense she would feel so lost and out of control, not knowing who her enemies were, how they managed to get past her, and what they had planned. She had a clue at their end game, but not the method of which they would use to get there.

Pacing her bedroom, she fought the urge to scream and throw things. Such an odd urge it was to bring attention to oneself and damage their own things through anger. She felt it strongly though, as her hands itched to break something.

Her mind was not a stable place anymore. It was fraught with worry, shame, and fear.

Sitting at the foot of her bed, she found herself exhausted, her pulse slowing as her adrenaline filled episode ran out of steam. Placing her face in her hands, she heaved a heavy sigh, completely unsure of the next step.

Looking up at the window to the Underworld, a sight that used to bring her peace but now only brought anxiety, her hands covered her mouth and her elbows moved to her knees as she tried to think. She needed a plan, one that would help her gain the control she required to obliterate this horrible feeling.

Feeling a pulse of power through the Underworld that announced Devon was back from the mortal realm, she closed her eyes and pushed her hands into her hair as she felt panic rise up again.

She needed to keep this place, and him, *safe*.

At her wits end with all these thoughts, feelings, and emotional turmoil, she stood back up, pacing again. The feeling of the adrenaline flooding back into her veins, her fists clenching and unclenching in both anger at herself for feeling so out of control, and frustration at not having any answers.

Turning abruptly and without a plan in place, she made for the door to her room. Anxiety the main force driving her in her current state.

How was she feeling all this? Was it solely because of him that now she could feel such raw emotions? Had he somehow made her more human?

It was time to stop thinking and act, she thought.

No more wallowing. She would go to the river and find someone with answers, even if that someone was Minthe.

Minthe. The one person who would gladly stand in between her and Devon. This thought caused another, more powerful emotion to rise to the surface of her psyche. She had never felt it before, but she knew what it was.

Jealousy.

Shaking her head, she chided herself. There was not time for such nonsense.

She turned the knob and flung it open as she walked right into Devon. He caught her as she pitched forward into his arms.

Graceful, Persephone scolded herself.

"Oh, hey…" he greeted, but before he could say anything more, she grabbed him by the shirt and pulled him into her room. Her mouth was on his before the door slammed shut, by whom, she wasn't sure. The moment their lips connected, she was lost.

His immediate reception to her kiss emboldened her to take it deeper. His hands moved into her hair and he held her head in place while he shared in her enthusiasm.

He must have turned her without her being aware, her back hitting the wall as his hand hitched her leg up and around his hips.

Her eyes shot open, her lips stilling caused his eyes to open as well.

Both of their eyes were lit with Godfire, their colors reflecting on each other's faces.

"You enjoyed that?" she asked as she tilted her head in question.

His eyes went wide in disbelief.

"Did you not?" he asked, his grip loosening on her, her hands tightened on his shoulders telling him she wouldn't let him pull away just yet.

"I did. However, I thought perhaps the feeling of anger and irritation would leave after I kissed you, but now I am even more upset."

Devon looked at her incredulously as he held up his hands and took a step back from her.

"Let's unpack that a little. You were mad, so you kissed me to not be mad anymore, but now you are even madder?" He ticked the statements off on his fingers before he dropped his hands to his sides, his entire body on edge.

She rubbed her eyes with the heels of her hands, sighing before looking back up at him.

"I apologize. That is confusing..."

"You think? Also, a little damning to my ego to be honest."

"I will explain." She waved him to sit down on the couch, but he stood in the same spot, only crossing his arms across his chest with his eyebrows up as he waited.

She sighed. She had mangled this far worse than she thought.

Emotions were such pesky, confusing things that caused all sorts of trouble.

"I was thinking of how to solve this puzzle of what the Underworld threat might be. Tristan is missing, so I thought of asking you to see if Minthe could find him." She observed him, though she did not know what she was even looking for in his face. "Then I felt this... anger at the thought of you talking to her, and it was confusing, so I thought maybe if we just kissed and got it over with..."

He moved forward and cupped her face in his hands before lightly kissing her lips, a grin on his face.

"Why are you smiling? Does this make sense?" she asked, baffled.

"Yes, and my ego is well inflated. The damage completely reversed."

"I've never felt jealous before. It is odd, but I can see how it would lead to wars," she whispered as she stared into his smiling eyes with confusion.

"No need to go to war on my behalf. I am pretty taken with you as well."

His eyes, beautiful green, focused on her as she basked in his attention.

"Should I decide to start a war, we both know who the victor would be," she smirked, feeling her body relaxing into his embrace. Such a turnaround from her emotional upheaval moments ago.

He closed his eyes as he pulled her against him, his face in her neck as he chuckled.

"You'll get used to all these silly emotions soon enough. Annoying as they can be, they make life a lot more interesting." He whispered against her skin before pulling away to look at her. "So, we can go interrogate Minthe and you can breathe easy knowing that you will be the only one kissing me out of anger after. Side note, perhaps we can kiss without the anger sometime?" he asked as he leaned back further with a cheeky grin and waggled his eyebrows.

Rolling her eyes, she opened a portal to Cocytus, hearing his deep laugh as they were wrapped in shadows.

***

They had not been there long before Minthe approached them from the river, water dripping off her body, her gills and scales turning back to human flesh

Averting his eyes, he realized she was planning to converse with them nude as she made no attempt to cover herself.

"Hello, Devon," she purred his name. He closed his eyes and shook his head at her obvious disrespect to both Persephone and him.

Opening his eyes, he kept his gaze on her face, catching the lustful look she held on him for seconds too long. She did nothing to hide the almost frantic and desperate need in them.

How had he missed these warning signs?

He thought back over their time together and realized he had never been around another woman in her presence. She always had him all to herself. After his rebuke of her offer at the gala, he was surprised she was still trying to rekindle their very short-term arrangement.

Shaking his head at her, he hoped she understood the silent message he was sending her.

Nope. Never going to happen.

280

Her jaw clenched and her eyes narrowed, but she looked away from him to Persephone.

"My Queen," her voice almost mocking in its tone. It held no reverence for the Queen of theUnderworld.

Persephone straightened and held Minthe's eyes in warning before she spoke.

"Minthe, your brother was detained in my castle and escaped during an event at the gates. Any information you have on him, his plan, and his whereabouts are needed in order to help me keep the realm safe from threats."

"I do not know," Minthe shook her head, her eyes cutting to Devon for a split second before looking back at Persephone. Her eyes unable to hold his gaze in that moment.

Devon knew then she was hiding something. He was not sure if it was in regard to her brother's whereabouts, or something else, but whatever it was, she wasn't going to tell them. Not willingly.

"Where is Tristan? That he would abandon his people and river..."

Minthe stiffened, her eyes narrowing at Persephone.

"I cannot believe that my brother would abandon us. Are you sure he wasn't taken?" She angled her head in mock innocence. Devon started forward, tired of Minthe's display of misplaced jealousy, when Persephone held up her hand in warning to stay back.

"You think someone walked into my realm, into my castle, and stole away someone out from under me?" She walked towards Minthe as she spoke, her gait predatory.

"My brother does not abandon what he loves!" Minthe yelled, the dam breaking that had held back her emotions.

"You forget yourself, Nymph," Persephone growled.

Devon watched as Minthe's skin took on a pearlescent sheen.

"My apologies, Goddess. I found I've lost more than one man I loved recently and am a tad defensive." Minthe's glassy eyes looked to Devon as she said this.

"Minthe, enough," he growled quietly. "It's over. Has been over for a long, long time."

He moved to stand at Persephone's side when Minthe's eyes flashed, her focus on his wrist; his soulbond mark.

"No. No. *NO!*" Minthe screamed, her voice like that of a banshee calling for someone's death. Her body becoming liquid and dropping to the ground before disappearing into the wet sand of the river shore.

"A trait of cowardly siblings," Persephone murmured.

"I didn't realize she had felt so strongly," he replied, moving to wrap his arm around Persephone's waist.

Persephone looked from the river to him.

"Minthe had an obsessive personality long before she left for the mortal world. If Minthe thinks you are hers, then she will stop at nothing to make that a reality."

CHAPTER 37

Devon walked into the study where Persephone sat watching the fire, lost in her thoughts.

He took the seat next to her, staying silent for a moment before he broached the subject that had weighed heavily on his mind since speaking with his father.

"What did you sacrifice for my father to remember me?" he asked. He finally had his closure, thanks to her, but at what cost?

Her eyes moved to his after several long and drawn-out seconds of silence.

"To have his memory long term would mean his choices of being reincarnated were gone, and I didn't want choices to be made without your knowledge or his blessing. So, I had to work with Mnemosyne, the Titan who guards the pool of memory, for a short-term solution."

"And that was?" he prompted. "What did you offer her?"

"A champion for the restless souls. The ones that wander the shore of Styx, having not been given funeral rites. A champion who will bring nightmares to the mortals who choose the wrong paths but are not so far gone they cannot redeem themselves. To haunt these individuals in the hopes of turning the souls back from the darkness."

"You're going to start haunting people? Do you even have the time to do that?" he halfheartedly joked, concerned she had taken on even more responsibility to help him.

Her eyes flashed up to his, an eyebrow raised.

"Not me. A part of me," she whispered.

His eyebrows drew in with obvious confusion at this statement.

She sighed at this and his pride stung a bit that he wasn't catching on.

"My child. I will have a daughter who holds power over ghosts and nightmares," she finally explained, watching him for some sort of response.

His mind froze as the words tumbled around his head, lacking meaning as he tried to understand the heavy sacrifice she had made.

She sacrificed her child to this fate for him to spend a few hours speaking with his father.

Folding her arms across her chest, she watched him as he remained quiet. A flash of annoyance crossing her face before she looked back at the fire.

"Stop looking at me like that. Any child I have will be powerful in their own right, so it is no hardship to know beforehand what their powers are. And I hardly think it is wrong for those souls to have someone to fight for them, do you?" she asked.

He finally nodded as he realized the truth of that statement.

"Knowing I would have gone down a path similar to some of those souls, it would have been nice to get a heads up that I needed to change course to avoid eternal damnation," he agreed.

It was a nice reassurance that there would be someone out there, Persephone's daughter, to help guide souls along the right path before death came for them.

Those words halted his train of thought.

Persephone's daughter. She would have a child. That could only mean that he would also have a child, and that she would carry a heavy burden.

"I…" he had to clear his throat. "I am assuming I would be the father of this child?"

Her eyebrows shot up in shock at his question before she laughed.

"Who else? Certainly not Thanatos," she pretended to shutter.

Looking back over at him, her brow furrowed in concern.

"Are you well?" she asked as she watched him intently.

His mind was running through a myriad of emotions.

Would he have a child, a family, after he died? How did he feel about all this? Could he be a good father being that he wasn't quite human after all?

Then again, neither was Persephone.

A family was something he denied himself as a mortal, but if he had the opportunity to do so now? He would jump at the chance. He would happily make a family, a future, with her.

She laughed a little.

"You are thinking too much on this."

He smirked, his mind moving from the idea of having a child to the process of making one.

***

Persephone felt the moment someone stepped from the Cocytus River onto her domain.

"Trespasser," she whispered at the same moment that Devon's eyes lit up with Godfire. He'd felt it too. Their bond had strengthened his tether to the Underworld and its needs.

She grabbed his hand and pulled them into a shadow jump.

When they landed near the entrance of the boneyard, she turned to Devon, only to step back in awe. He had taken on his full God form.

Green light bled from every pore of his body, his eyes lit with Godfire, vines writhing at his feet, and grass the Underworld had never seen before was overgrowing and tangling around his legs. He hardly seemed to notice as he took slow predatory steps towards the boneyard.

Her eyes watched as the winged serpent emerged from his light and moved along his skin, like a tattoo come to life. Devon lifted his arm, and the serpent darted out from him, becoming its own entity of green light as it had once before.

She watched in fascination as the winged serpent slithered alongside Devon as they hunted their prey.

"Devon," she whispered as she moved to walk next to him on the opposite side of the serpent, who let out a hiss but made no move towards her, instead focused on the unnamed threat in their proximity.

A laugh pulled her attention from Devon, her concern diverted to the Titan that had just manifested far too close to the gate of Tartarus.

"Crius…" she whispered, as she remembered the uncle who had helped her father overthrow her grandfather so long ago.

His long blonde hair was plaited in the braids associated with the Vikings of old. Tan skin, hard brown eyes, thick corded muscle that made him look more youthful than the eras he actually was in age. He wore jeans and a shirt, the casual apparel of the humans, but it made him no less intimidating.

Crius only sneered at her before his gaze moved to Devon and the serpent made of light.

"Boy, who are you?" He called out to Devon, his voice a loud boom in the quiet terrain.

Devon said nothing, only assessed Crius as he did him.

She felt a gust of wind behind her, her shadows moving along the ground after she quietly put out a call of power.

"Ah, niece," Crius finally acknowledged her, his eyes filled with malice. "Do tell me why this man is in your domain, standing here as if he could withstand even the slightest bit of power from me? Are we bringing strays home?"

She locked her cold demeanor into place knowing he would capitalize on any perceived weakness without mercy.

"How did you get into the Underworld, Crius?" Persephone demanded, her voice that of a Goddess ready to smite this man down, family or not.

Devon still had not unlocked his body, his muscles coiled in preparation to strike, to tear apart this man who dared to enter their territory. The serpent grew larger in size until he towered over Devon, hissing with rage.

"His eyes..." Crius was staring at Devon with interest as Persephone moved in between the two men. "So much like his dear mother. How is she, child?" he asked as he looked at Devon with a vicious smile.

Persephone could feel the strong emotions coming from Devon at Crius' words through the bond. The bond she now always left open.

Confusion. Anger.

Alongside the emotions, she could feel waves of his power rolling and building up around both him and her. Stronger than when the amplifier triggered his powers causing them to surge, yet he was still in control of himself.

Amazing, she thought. It had taken her so much longer to come into her powers, much less handle them.

Persephone was brought out of her thoughts when she heard an almost feral growl come from Devon, her eyes darting over to see that Crius had taken a small step toward them.

"Ah, what a well-trained dog," Crius said with a sneer, halting where he was.

"You created the amplifier and used it on him. You've known this whole time Devon was of the Demeter line," she seethed as a malicious smirk crossed Crius' face.

"Ah yes. I see my little helpers have been playing with my toys," Crius laughed. "Yes, that is right. This is the whelp of my chosen oracle."

Persephone froze.

"You did that to his mother?" she murmured.

Devon moved next to her, his hands curled into fists at his sides and Godfire engulfing him in his anger.

"It is hardly my fault she felt the need to open her legs for a man who wasn't strong enough to handle his powerful offspring. Especially one with the power of a God. However," Crius crossed his arms and tapped his chin with his pointer finger in mock concentration. "It is interesting that he can wield such immense power when he is so new to this life. Perhaps Atlas had the right of it all along."

Atlas, Persephone thought, her father's general from when Cronus had reigned the world and heavens as king. A Titan with the force to change the tide of the oncoming battle. They could not fight Atlas alone, much less if he had amassed an army.

Crius took another step towards Devon but wasn't quick enough to dodge as the serpent of light struck out with its tail. A line of burnt skin ran across Crius' cheek from where the serpent's tail had met flesh. The air stunk of burned skin.

Crius' eyes glinted with anger for a moment before the skin healed, unblemished, and he started laughing.

"Interesting, indeed." His dark eyes held little amusement when he turned to look at her, his eyes full of hatred.

"I've come because you've done enough damage, little Goddess, you and your sisters. We've waited too long for you to release him, so we will be taking it into our own hands now."

"He has been imprisoned for reasons of his own doing. I will not release him, nor will you access the gates..." A loud boom cut Persephone off.

Crius had clapped his hands together causing the ground to vibrate,

287

knocking down stones that had covered the gate. One large stone headed their way, and without thinking, Persephone grabbed Devon and shadow jumped them out of the way.

Her eyes moved from the gate to behind it as a herd of ghostly rams crested a ridge to the north of the plains, running straight at them.

Crius had moved up the hill and started to physically pull the rocks down while they were distracted.

"Enough!" Devon boomed, throwing his hands out. Black vines with razor sharp thorns shot up from the ground. Some moved at an incredible speed towards Crius, while the others moved to the herd, tripping and curling around the rams, turning them back to the dust they had been created from.

She could feel Devon pulling power from the Underworld, and the Underworld happily allowed it through his bond with Persephone.

A smile crossed her lips as she let her eyes bleed to black and released the Goddess within her.

The vines made it to Crius before he had a chance to jump down from the pile of stones. They grew around his hands and yanked him down flat on his back in the boneyard surrounding the gates.

Thorns cut into his flesh, meat and white bone showing where he struggled, his ability to heal no help against the onslaught. The vines squeezed him tighter as he tried to escape, his blood dripping down on to the ground where the Underworld absorbed it and took his power to funnel it into her and Devon.

She called her wraiths up from the ground, watching as they moved in and out of the Titan, blood flowing freely from his mouth.

Devon's vines tore Crius' outside to shreds while Persephone's wraiths tore through his insides.

"We are not done here," Crius yelled as he choked on the blood coming up from his internal injuries. "You've already lost, little Goddess."

A loud pop echoed around them, the Titan disappearing, leaving only the dead husks of vines falling to the ground, the breeze carrying the dust of the vines away on the wind.

Persephone looked over to where Devon stood, his eyes aflame watching his vines disintegrate while his dragon returned to his skin, a new tattoo peeking out from under Devon's shirt. His hands shook a little as he turned to her, his eyes returning to the beautiful green she loved.

"No one should be able to leave the Underworld without my say so." Her voice cut like glass as anger colored her tone. "We have a lot to discuss."

CHAPTER 38

By the time they strolled into the castle, dirty and exhausted, they hadn't spoken a word.

Devon could feel her anger pulsing outwards, rage visible in Persephone's demeanor, and was not about to trigger her further with questions over what the Titan had said.

The discussion he knew was coming could wait, she needed time to decompress. Everything in her world was changing after being the same for centuries, and though everything was lining up, answers finally finding their way to the light, all of it had to be grossly overwhelming.

She stopped at the foot of the stairs with her hand on the newel post as she turned to him.

"We should clean up before we call a meeting." Her words were clipped, but he knew it was nothing personal. He simply nodded, knowing that like him, she just needed to get out of her own head for a moment.

A feeling he knew all too well.

Shadows erupted around her and she was gone. It was a cold and abrupt departure, even for her, but they both had a huge feat ahead of them. His knowledge on the Titans was lacking, but even he could smell the war brewing.

"Sir?" a Reevka appeared next to him having taken his lack of movement as a summons.

Shaking his head almost absentmindedly, Devon turned to walk up the stairs, the Reevka disappearing back into the shadows without a word.

Without conscious thought, he found himself standing in front of

Persephone's door, his hand raised to knock, unsure of why and what his intentions were.

She needed space, yes, but he was concerned. He knew she could handle herself, but he was her partner, and as such he had promised to share the burdens of life with her.

Slowly lowering his hand, he took a step back. He also needed to know when to let her have time to think. To have a moment of peace without having to worry about him or what he thought. He should go ready himself for the meeting like she was most likely doing behind that door.

Turning away with every intention of doing just that, he froze when he heard a large crash from inside her room and found himself shoving her door open before his mind even processed that he was moving.

He looked around for a threat, only to see a splintered chair strewn across the floor.

Persephone's back was to the door, taking deep breaths with her fists clenched at her sides.

"Not the best time to have a discussion, Devon," she growled, her voice rough with emotion.

Noticing the veins of black trying to claw up her arms, the thick smoke clouding the room, he slowly shut the door behind him and leaned against it. This was her breaking point and he would not leave her to navigate it alone.

"Leave," she ordered. Her power saturated the surrounding air, and he felt a physical push from it as he crossed his arms and held his ground. He could feel her control slipping through their bond and the fear that she was losing command of her domain, and self, for the first time in her very long life was palpable.

"You didn't let me fall apart alone, so I will not let you go this alone either."

He felt wind pass over him, and in a split second, the Goddess of the Underworld was in his face. Horns a shiny onyx jutting from her head, her skin pearlescent, eyes completely black, a crown of Godfire, and wings of pure black feathers.

He simply looked her over before meeting her eyes.

"You're beautiful," he whispered, and she froze, her black eyes widening in shock.

He knew people most likely ran in fear from her in this form, but he found all her forms beautiful and unique in their beauty. This form radiated a power that called to his, strengthened it.

Fueled it.

She stumbled back from him, only to have him follow as his own God form took over. The crown of golden leaves; the vines that moved over his body like tattoos come to life; his serpent tattoo moving from across his neck to his back before going dormant again at the lack of threat; his entire body engulfed in green fire.

Nature and rebirth standing before death and darkness. Two opposites but balanced all the same.

"You put this all on yourself when it is bigger than just one being. You see that someone crossed into your home, and that as the guardian here, you've failed. I get it. I've carried my own guilt for far too long. I carried it until you made me release it into a field of dying and dead trees, only to have my power create a new forest and a new hope. So, if you think for one second you will scare me into walking away so you can dwell and destroy yourself, you are incredibly naïve."

Her head tilted as her eyes lost the black, becoming the blue he loved just as much. He watched the horns disappear, and before she could do anything further, his hand was touching the feathers at her back.

"A fallen angel," he whispered with a tiny smirk. "I get where the legends come from."

His hand moved along the ridge of her silky wing as he took in the stunningly iridescent quality of her feathers.

"Beautiful," he whispered again, then met her eyes. "Just so damn beautiful."

Before he knew what he was doing, his hands moved from her wings to her jaw. He cupped her face as he took her mouth.

This was not the slow passion he had felt the other times when they had lost themselves in each other. While he was reverent in his touch, she was punishing.

Her mouth crashed against his, teeth clashing as she took from him what she needed. While he gave her all that he had to give.

She ripped his shirt, the buttons scattering across the floor as she discarded the fabric without a care. Pushing his pants down, she turned them towards the bed and gave Devon a shove. He landed on his back, pants around his ankles as she climbed atop him, joining their bodies, her wings flaring out behind her.

The sight she made was unbelievable. His angel. His Goddess. She was the most gorgeous creature he had ever seen.

It was almost more than he could take, and had he been mortal, he would have surely died from such a vision. Such bliss.

"Persephone," he murmured, his hand moving up to cup her cheek. Her eyes opened and the bright blue Godfire lit the surrounding room.

He was not with Persephone right now, but the Goddess of the Underworld. The same person, yet not. Deep inside he knew this was the real her in that moment. One she was scared to show anyone yet trusted him enough to love him in this form.

He felt honored.

He felt...

"Fuck," he felt his climax hit in a rush and roll through him. He lost himself, felt her pull his body against hers as she arched into him, chest heaving while she found her release before giving him another punishing kiss.

Behind his eyelids he could see the green Godfire as it lit the room up, his power flooding and bending around hers.

Pulling her lips away, she gasped.

"Devon..." Her eyes wide, her pupils dilated, but her beautiful wings remained. He touched his forehead to hers before she could escape.

"I think my actions have spoken well for how I feel, but in case you are still confused, I love you. In all ways. In all forms. Whether you walk the earth as a mortal or as a goddess who could bring me happily to my knees."

Before the last syllable left his lips, hers were on his again, gentle this time.

Her hands ran through his hair as she looked down into his eyes, their bodies still connected.

I'm finally free, he thought as he pulled her down onto the bed next to him. No words were spoken between them as he ran his hand up and down her arms, thankful when she relaxed against his chest and fell asleep.

Their light faded from the room as they rested their tired bodies and wary minds.

He would hold the world at bay for her. The problems could wait until tomorrow. Tonight, she would be watched over.

For the first time, but not the last, he would carry her when she needed it.

***

Persephone sat in a chair near the bed, reading a book one of the humans had written over two hundred years ago as Devon slept.

Poetry. Something she never understood until now.

Smiling, her eyes flitted over the page, but her thoughts were on her husband asleep in their bed.

This man who would not allow her to stand alone in the face of an oncoming war. Who gave her peace and renewed her soul.

"Interesting choice of reading material…" The voice gruff with sleep pulled her attention away from the book.

She looked up to find him on his side, his head propped up on his arm, looking at her.

"What?" she asked, surprised.

"Never thought of you as a fan of poetry. Now, gothic horror…" he grinned at her.

Grabbing one of the throw pillows from the window bench, she threw it at him, him catching it and letting out a loud, boisterous laugh that brought a smile to her face.

Devon placed the throw pillow under his head as he laid back and looked at the ceiling, the sheet moving down to expose his navel and causing a shiver of lust to move through her.

"It is still weird you are what I always knew to be Hades. That… is still a lot to take in."

Persephone let out a small laugh of derision.

"I was mostly here in the Underworld, so Hades was more elusive than his 'brothers'. Not surehow she managed, but Hera had fun playing Zeus. The rumors and gossip she created, then showing up as Hera, the wronged wife. Oh, she really enjoyed the thrill of having these people fall over themselves to get back at the God of the sky for whatever reason, never knowing it was her all along."

"That sounds exactly like Hera," he laughed before a scowl crossed his face as they felt Hera's
power enter the room.

"Yes, well out of all my sisters, I did always enjoy a good lark." Devon sat up to watch Hera and Amphitrite walk into the room without an invitation.

Hera raised an eyebrow at him before she turned to Persephone.

"Now, why do I smell the stink of a Titan?"

CHAPTER 39

"Crius was here," Devon responded as Persephone watched Hera's eyes glisten with gold. Her power unfurling.

"Hera, how did you know we had a trespasser? I have not sent messengers." Persephone stood and moved between her sisters so Devon could put on the sweatpants she had handed him.

"We felt a power shift," Amphitrite responded as she took the lead from Hera.

This was the second time she had done so and Persephone felt unease creep into her veins. Hera only became blasé like this when she felt out of control, which did not bode well for what was to come. They needed Hera in her fierce, almost feral manner, for this battle.

"It was on the ocean floor," Amphitrite continued, "so I went to check it out and found Tristan." Amphitrite stopped a moment before she moved to stand in front of Persephone and take her hands in her own. "He is dead, Persephone."

Persephone felt shock wash over her body and wrapped her arms around herself as a chill that had nothing to do with the temperature moved down her spine.

"How?" she heard herself demand, but her voice sounded like it came from somewhere far away.

"He was killed with a blade covered in hydra poison and left for the sea to take back. He had... been left there a while." She winced as she delivered the news.

"It seems there have been secrets kept from us, my dear sister," Hera responded, glaring at Persephone.

"As I said, I haven't yet had time to call you down, so no true

secrets, but yes. A Titan, Crius, was here attempting to open Tartarus."
She omitted her breakdown was actually the reason she had waited.
That, and she needed the time with Devon to refresh her body and
mind.

"Oh, bloody fantastic!" Hera threw her hands up as Amphitrite took
a step back, her face shocked. "Now we have to worry about the
remaining Titans staging a coup to get that old bag of shit out of
Tartarus."

Amphitrite shot Hera a scathing look.

"What? Why are you giving me that look? You want that wreck of a
man out running around, rutting, and destroying everything? We only
barely got him in there the first time, and it was not an easy task if you
remember. He has other Titans working with him?" She turned to
Persephone. "Anyone we know?"

"Only Crius, but he mentioned Atlas," she whispered. The name like a
sonic boom in the room, the silence deafening.

Suddenly Hera laughed, the sound not at all humorous.

"Atlas. If that swine is around, where are the rest of them, hmm?"
she demanded, though it seemed she was not speaking to anyone in
particular. "Him and his heathen army work for daddy dearest, then
disappear and show up again so many millennia later?"

She turned back to look at them, her eyes completely gold now as
energy crackled around her hands and up her arms.

"How are they getting into your domain, sister?" Hera looked
right at Persephone as she demanded the information, her power
pushing the limits of the room.

Persephone curled her fist as her own power surged with her anger,
Devon moving quickly to stand beside her and sending calming magic
through their bond.

"The river. He was working with what I assumed was Tristan, but
obviously that was incorrect as he has been dead this whole time!"

"And you've done what? How are you keeping Cronus contained?"
Hera's voice took on a rasp, the power amplifying her authority, in turn
causing the coldness to seep back into Persephone and allow her
methodical self to take back over.

"You dare speak to me here in such a way? What have you done to
watch above ground? Have you kept tabs on the Titans before they

came here?"

Power crackled in the room, the air saturated with it as wraiths began to dance along the wall, avoiding the sparks of electricity that came off Hera.

"Perhaps we could avoid a confrontation that would lead to the need to rebuild the castle?" Amphitrite murmured, moving out of the way of Hera's sparks.

Hera moved into Persephone's face, her eyes alight with power and rage before something wrapped around her stomach and pulled her away from Persephone.

Persephone turned to see Devon covered in green light, his vines retracting from where they had grabbed Hera and threw her across the room.

"Enough," he growled, his voice that of a God. "We are on the same side in this fight, so quit throwing power around at each other like toddlers and let's get a plan together to stop the Titans."

Persephone looked over to where Hera narrowed her eyes as she regained control, standing up and dusting herself off.

"Well, seems the baby God has found his teeth. Kudos. Next time you wrap one of those vines around me, I'll fry you to a crisp and sauté you in them."

He looked at the sky Goddess and caught the tilt of her lips. The sardonic smirk she wore like a uniform.

"Whatever helps bolster your ego, Goddess, but for now I think the focus should be on the threat to our realm."

Smoke formed in the room before Thanatos stepped from the shadows.

"Looks like part of the problem came to us. We found Minthe at the gate of Tartarus," Thanatos explained. staring directly at Persephone as he spoke, the room cooling dramatically as shadows began to writhe again in the corners of the room.

Devon moved to her as her entire body became smoke with wisps of blue fire moving in and out of her hazy presence.

"Do calm down, sister," Amphitrite requested, but Devon watched the smoke that was his wife disappear in an instant.

"Shit," Thanatos muttered as he looked to Devon. Both of them disappeared to find themselves outside of Tartarus at the same time, near the rocks that covered the gate where they had felt Persephone's power land.

Devon walked past Thanatos to where the Furies were moving along the riverbank where the River Phlegethon met the River Cocytus. Before he made it out of the boneyard, Thanatos caught up to him and grabbed his arm, stopping him.

"Wait, can you feel that?" Thanatos said right as he pulled Devon out of the path of a rolling cloud of shadows and fire. Persephone stepped out of the haze in all her Underworld glory with Cerberus trailing behind her, looking three times his regular size with his hackles up.

"Where is..." Devon pulled away from Thanatos, making his way towards the shadows where Persephone had emerged.

From the shadows, Persephone's wraiths glided along the ground towards the riverbed, swirling around the riled Furies and delving into the water. Seeing this, the Furies began to chitter and bounce on the balls of their feet in anticipation.

Breaking the surface, the wraiths pulled the form of a woman from the water and dumped her unceremoniously at the Furies feet.

Persephone moved to the woman, a very weak Minthe, as the Furies restrained and toyed with her, snapping their sharp teeth near her face.

Looking past Persephone, her wings spread out and obscuring his view, he caught sight of the wandering souls of the boneyard as they moved closer and closer to them with every heartbeat. Before Devon could warn Persephone, wraiths diverted from where they swarmed near the Furies to stop the interlopers.

"Tell me, Minthe, how Crius got through my world without being detected..." Persephone was nonplussed, her voice silky and deceiving as she stood over the nymph, shadows moving in tighter around them.

"... didn't..." Minthe gasped, her voice raspy with disuse and her eyes wide with fear.

Devon tried to feel pity for the woman he had called a friend, sometimes lover, as he watched her gills open and close as if gasping, but the thought that her actions had brought a Titan to the Underworld boiled his blood.

"He tried to trick me!" Minthe yelled, her voice almost a sob. "Crius! He promised that no harm would come to us if he went through the river system. That he would bring my brother back alive."

The shadows and Furies slowly adjusted Minthe until she was face to face with Persephone, keeping their hold on the nymph tight. He realized Persephone was not allowing Minthe her mortal form, keeping her in as much discomfort as possible in order to get answers from her.

"You have been part of the Underworld and trusted. Given important responsibilities and freedom few others have been bestowed. Yet, it seems I made quite the error in trusting you after your father conferred the mantle of river God upon your brother... and for your greed, you will have nothing." Persephone's voice sounded like a hiss as the power thrummed through the air.

"Goddess, no! Please! I did nothing but give him access to the river! This can easily be undone," she pleaded as she tried to escape, the wraiths only curling tighter around her body.

A Fury pulled Minthe on to her lap, scraping her face with their sharp teeth and lapping up a tiny rivulet of blood.

"You will remain in the dungeon under constant guard until Crius is dealt with." Persephone's voice sounded low and threatening.

Devon moved to stand beside her, Minthe not missing what his body language was saying or the presence he presented; a united front. Even in her obsessed mind, he did not know how she could miss the significance of his movement.

His power felt the intruder well before the physical body manifested near them on the banks of the river.

"Let her go, my dear little Goddess," Crius demanded as he appeared in a burst of starlight. "She is innocent of everything except lack of intelligence."

"You dare enter my realm again, Crius!" Persephone shouted as Thanatos appeared from the shadows on the other side of her, his skeletal form and wings out, with his hands deceivingly loose at his sides. Devon knew when a person was coiled to strike and the power emanating from Thanatos confirmed that. He was ready to tear Crius apart to keep Persephone safe, and for once, Devon was thankful for the Reaper's sudden appearance.

Persephone turned to the Furies, and with a wave of her hand, the Furies disappeared to another part of the Underworld with Minthe.

Moving to Persephone's other side, Devon covered her right as

Thanatos covered her left. The aura of an impending battle swallowing them up as they faced Crius. Cerberus let out a low, threatening growl from behind them.

"You think to enter my realm as you please and attempt to release Cronus from his punishment." Persephone's voice filled with power as she took step after slow step towards Crius.

Be wary of the water... he heard in his mind. His mother's voice was in his head all of the sudden, her words repeating over and over.

Choose your path, dark or light.

Devon felt his power roll over him as if the amplifier was near, but unlike in the street when he lost himself to it, he could handle the flow of it. He had finally accepted his power and in return it allowed him control, melding and becoming one with him; an extension of himself.

He pulled the God to the forefront, keeping himself on equal footing as his eyes and veins started to glow green and his vines grew around him, crawling and knotting into a shield in front of him.

The green light moved over his skin until every inch of him glowed and the winged serpent tattoo moved and writhed before it left his body and became a tangible thing.

Devon caught sight of a figure in his periphery but when he turned, they had disappeared.

Trap, the serpent whispered into Devon's mind and before he could even take a defensive stance, Crius flung his hands out, wind and light swirling around them and the churning dirt becoming rams.

"How? How did you block my sisters from my realm?" Persephone demanded as the fire bled from her onto the ground around her, catching as if the soil were covered in accelerant. Her wings were spread out behind her and he could see the feathers twitching in anger.

He hadn't noticed, but she was right, Hera and Amphitrite were nowhere to be found. He knew they could sense their sister was in danger, yet they were not here. If there was one thing he could respect of her sisters, it was that they would never let Persephone stand alone against an enemy. Something had to of happened.

Crius laughed, his head thrown back and arms out. "I created chaos on earth. Your sisters are working hard to save those pesky insects you call humans. Then, it was easy to spell this place so they are all but locked out. That left the gates open, and thankfully since I was not bound during your little rebellion against your father, I'm here to free my king," he growled.

"Now, I can undo everything that his demon spawn daughters and waste of a wife did to send my baby brother to this place. All because of a falling out," he spat, his face warped in a menacing smile that made Devon feel sick. It was a culmination of every sinister and evil smile he had ever seen as a mortal. This man embodied all the evil he'd fought so hard to rid the world of as a human.

"Only you would call Cronus murdering me and my sisters a 'falling out'," Persephone seethed.

Crius simply ignored her and continued with his monologue.

"Oh, niece, you have no idea how the fate that your father dealt you will compare to what Atlas has planned. A drop in the ocean compared to the torture you will receive at our hands," Crius smirked.

Atlas. He had said he was working with him, so did that mean Atlas had access to the Underworld, too? He knew deep down a loss here meant Persephone would be stripped of power. Losing her power could mean the death the Moirai foretold.

Him, too, but he knew he could survive without it. He had only just begun to wield his power so it was not as strong as hers yet. She'd spent eons with hers and it was as much a part of her as her soul.

He was brought back to the fight when the ground began to shake violently. He saw Thanatos brace himself, his wings flaring out to the sides of him to balance. Persephone seemed wholly unaffected as she stared down Crius, her teeth gritted, and fists clenched.

Devon felt the vines move deeper into the ground before shooting back up and wrapping around his legs to anchor him.

Crius fell to his knees, pushing his hands into the ground as impacted earth expanded from him and released more of the rams made of the earth. The animals moved as a herd, circling them as their hooves kicked up dirt and bits of bone.

"Devon!" Persephone yelled over the booming noise of the earth coming undone. Her hair slapping her face from the wind coming off the stampeding rams.

Crius threw his arms out wide as he stood atop the gate of Tartarus and the rams stamped all at once on the ground and created a fissure that grew between him and Persephone from the impact. He missed a step, the ground giving out beneath him as the fissure continued to grow before his vines wrapped around him and pulled him back to solid ground.

As he found his footing, he realized he was on the opposite side of her and Crius, split from them by vegetation and open ravines.

Use the earth, the serpent growled with a small huff of annoyance.

Falling to his hands and knees, he felt the ground respond to him as the soil moved under his power, pulling away from Crius.

Before he could do anything more, he was hit with a flash of light that knocked him back several feet, his head hitting the ground hard. The hit sent electricity through his entire body, making him shake violently as he tried to hold on to consciousness.

His vision wavered before he could focus again and attempt to stand up, still dizzy from his fall. Putting his hand to the back of his head, he was not surprised to see blood after taking such a hard hit to the head.

Not good. Get up. Get up!

A grunt from in front of him had him raising his aching head. The pain a fading concern as he came face to face with an angry ram staring him down with blood-red eyes.

"Shit," he muttered, calling to his vines as he scrambled to get up.

The ram screamed in panic as Devon's vines moved around it, crushing its body until the dust it had been created from scattered to the wind.

As the dust cleared, his heart stopped at seeing Crius and Persephone alone in their confrontation. Behind her, Thanatos and Cerberus were fighting back rams in a seemingly never-ending battle to keep them from her as she fought. One ram would fall to dust as two more rose from the ground.

He attempted a light jump, but something was holding him back from opening a portal. Most likely the same something keeping her sisters away.

He moved quickly, his mind giving way to adrenaline, as he looked for a way across the ravine. He pulled in as much power and strength as he could, calling his vines forward. The large, green vines moved, crossing over each other to make a bridge to the other side. To Persephone.

As he ran across, hoping the vines would hold him since he hadn't taken the time to check, another bolt of blinding light flashed in his periphery, heading straight for him. Panic fueled him as he was halfway across a bridge of vines only held together by his power and concentration. If he took the hit, he may plunge into the deep ravine below him.

Throwing his hands up to protect himself last minute, he was surprised when nothing hit him. The light had hit something else. He looked up to see a shield made of green light.

No, not a shield, his winged serpent had taken the light and absorbed it.

A shield was in front of him. No, not a shield, his winged serpent had taken the light and absorbed it.

Stop trying to die, mortal, the serpent hissed into his mind.

That is part of my goal here. Not to die, he thought back. The serpent rumbled as it flew around him.

Could have fooled me. Do Better.

Devon growled as the serpent cut their link, getting the last word in.

Crius moved in for an attack, using Devon's discarded vines to create more rams, but Persephone's blue fire easily took them down. The roots burned up midair as the wind spread the ash before it could make it to the ground.

"Who else is working with you? Who else have you pulled into this pointless battle?" Persephone screamed at Crius. He could see the blue of her power pushing, trying to find a weakpoint in the shield Crius had constructed to protect him.

"Oh child, I cannot disclose all my secrets! I will tell you I was helped by a friend who will find themselves in a mutually beneficial situation when I kill you." Crius snapped a handout toward Devon, throwing a bolt of power that looked like silver starlight at him as he made it to the other side of his vine bridge.

Devon rolled out of the way once he hit the soil, landing in a crouch as Persephone used her power to call up a dense black smoke he had never seen before, growing to the size of a bus before it split into four distinct forms.

Crius moved back in confusion as the smoky forms took on the shape of four *giant* horses with bodies of smoke, eyes of onyx, and manes of fire. They pawed at the ground, nickering, waiting as if for a command.

Devon caught flashes of sharp teeth through the smoky snouts before Persephone threw her hands out. The horses took off into a run, aiming straight at Crius. He blinked in and out of existence in an attempt to avoid the horses, but the horses moved in the same manner as the smoke they came from. They were able to diffuse, rolling towards Crius before forming into the giant, angry beasts again.

Devon moved to Persephone's side as she put her hand to the ground, whispering a chant he had never heard before, as black began to creep up her arms

One horse hit Crius, his skin immediately reddening at the area of impact. The affected flesh began to weep from pustules that burst open on the pestilent skin.

Another horse hit him from the opposite side while his attention was on repairing his skin. He grew thin, as if starving.

Persephone had called up *The Horses.*

Pestilence. War. Famine. Death.

Crius attempted to throw another bolt of starlight, but one of the horses stood in the path, catching the bolt before charging Crius like a horse made for battle.

That, Devon thought, *must be the horse of war.*

Crius twisted away and shot another bolt, but the bolt hit a shield Devon had erected, green light dispersing from the impact point. He kept his hands up just in case dropping them meant dropping the shield.

One of the four horses had not made a move on Crius, just slowly walking around him as the other horses charged and attacked. The horse stopped, Crius still fending off the others, but Devon watched as the last horses' eyes began to weep blood.

Ghostly hands came up from the ground, wrapping around Crius' ankles, pulling at him.

A single wraith materialized in Persephone's palm, darting forward as the ghastly hands kept Crius from escaping.

It ran through Crius as he let out a mix between a laugh and a sob, blood spilling from wounds being created by the wraith as it moved in and out of him.

Devon watched as the other three horses moved back, letting the one weeping blood move up next to Crius. The Titan started to scream as his cheeks began to sink in, his ribs showing through his shirt. He was starving to death in front of their eyes.

Crius' eyes began to hollow.

An explosive blast of starlight blinded him, everything disappearing into the light.

As the smoke and debris cleared, he saw the ground where Crius had just been scorched, the Titan no longer there. He had escaped.

Again.

Devon released his shield, his arms heavy with the sudden exhaustion that hit him.

Persephone let her immortal form recede, her horns and wings disappearing, and her eyes once again blue.

"He cannot have escaped again. Not again!" Persephone yelled, her voice ragged with exhaustion and emotion as they took in the boneyard. The horses and ghostly hands gone with everything else they had summoned in this battle.

As suddenly as he disappeared, Crius was in front of him. His eyes enraged to the point of no longer understanding reason and logic.

Crius' eyes were not what halted Devon in his tracks though. It was the frail woman he pulled in front of him like a shield, her back pressed to his blood-soaked front.

Devon faltered at seeing his mother after so many years. Of what Crius had done to her.

Her hair was white and her eyes milky. She was as emaciated as Crius had been just moments ago.

"She warned me you would not be easy to beat, but how she left out so many details," Crius seethed.

"All that time I had her leashed, but she still kept so many secrets!" he yelled, as he shook Cybil. A small squeak left her dry lips before she was shoved to the ground, her frail, bony wrists barely catching her.

His knees nearly buckled at the sight, but he pushed himself to stand between the Titan and her.

The suddenly eerie smile on Crius' face told him he had just fallen into a trap. The laugh that followed confirmed it.

"It is always difficult for a man to choose between his mother and his wife. Which family will he fail to keep safe now!" With a bow, Crius stepped aside and Devon caught sight of Persephone.

Her face marred in shock, his name on her lips as she looked down at the sword protruding from her chest.

CHAPTER 40

"Persephone!" Her name tore from his throat as he ran and caught her as she fell, her blood making her slippery in his hands.

His knees hit the ground hard, but he didn't feel it.

"I am so sorry, but you wouldn't leave her. I had no choice," he heard a woman's soft voice from above him. Minthe.

She stood over them still holding the sword she had used to impale his wife, her eyes glassy.

He snarled up at Minthe before looking down at Persephone, his Persephone, her beautiful face growing more and more pale. He pressed his forehead to hers, their tears mingling as they ran down her face. The war at a standstill around them.

With bleary eyes, he looked up to see Thanatos attempting to stop Crius from moving toward the gate. Minthe stood over him, but he couldn't bear to look at her when just behind her, their entire battle was lost. Something happened to Thanatos, him disappearing in Crius' starlight as Crius knelt down beside Tartarus with the bloody sword. He hadn't noticed Minthe had moved next to Crius until that moment, but he couldn't bring himself to care with his wife bleeding in his arms. To him, the worst had already happened.

And then the world exploded into light.

Souls screamed across the realm and Cerberus let out an unearthly howl.

Devon covered Persephone with his body and pleaded.

To the Fates. To Chaos. To anyone who could fix this.

"Stay with me, Persephone, please..." he begged. His anguish felt like it was alive and choking him, the light so bright around them that he couldn't see.

"I…" she whispered, unable to speak with the blood filling her mouth.

The world quieted as something covered them, protecting them.

Run, the serpent said as it wrapped itself around him and Persephone. *They come.*

The gate of Tartarus had been opened.

Crius stood back up from where he had just used Persephone's blood to create the symbols on the exposed gate of Tartarus.

No, this can't be happening.

"You can either get her help or stop Crius, but you cannot do both," a nearby voice called out, muffled by the serpent.

Devon could see his mother's milky eyes staring at him through the light of his serpent companion.

"Take her to your forest, my child," she ordered before she turned to face Crius.

"Mother…" he breathed as he held Persephone tighter to his chest, his face streaked with blood and tears.

She looked back over her shoulder at her son, a warm smile crossing her face. One that brought back a memory that wasn't his own.

Her having just given birth. Her face lit with so much love as she looked down at her baby boy.

At Devon.

The memory slipped away as his mother moved into the line of sight between Crius and Devon.

"Go!" she yelled at him as Crius raised the blade to cut down his mother.

She told you to go, as have I. Do not remain here to die, the serpent growled into his mind.

Before he could respond, or do anything, he watched Crius thrust the sword through his mother's stomach. She'd sacrificed herself to buy him time enough to escape.

Devon felt something break inside his mind, like the chains that had trapped some part of him shattered as power flared to life.

As everything around them went white with an explosive power.

His mother had used her last breath, the last of herself to amplify his powers.

One last time.

Devon used the surge to take Persephone to the safety of his forest.

***

He heard the crackle of dry leaves as his knees hit the forest floor.

"Thanatos! Hecate!" he screamed, his voice piercing the quiet of the night. "Help me! Fates, please!"

He looked back down at Persephone. Her eyes closed. Her chest still.

"Persephone, no! Please, please hold on," he pleaded, his voice breaking as his sobs grew louder and more desperate.

Someone dropped to their knees beside them, attempting to take Persephone. Devon let out an inhuman growl before pulling her closer. Looking up, his vision too blurry to see through the tears, he finally saw an injured Thanatos, and a terrified Hecate.

"I need you to let me help, Devon." Thanatos stated, Devon finally realizing he was still clutching her against his chest, refusing to let her go.

He placed her on the ground but kept a hold of her hand. Thanatos placed his own near her wound before letting out a loud curse.

"Hydra poison," was all Thanatos said as he grabbed Persephone and jumped all of them to the castle.

Hecate shoved maps and papers off a table in the study before Thanatos laid Persephone down.

"Persephone!" Devon heard Amphitrite run into the room as he focused on the pallid face of his wife.

"Calm down," Hera ordered from somewhere else in the room. "Find someone to fix this. Now."

Moving to take Persephone's face in his hands, Devon felt his power, stronger from being amplified with his mother's last breath, as it moved over them both.

Ignoring the sounds of glass breaking and people gasping, he focused solely on Persephone, the world around them a dull hum in the back of his mind.

He felt something move along his bond with Persephone.

Life. He felt life.

310

The ebb and flow of it.

The push and pull.

An almost transparent string came into view, one that was connected to her from him, tethering and binding their souls together.

He pushed his life force down into her through the string, not worrying about the consequences.

A torrent of shadows and leaves swirled around them, trapping them in a vortex of their own making, and keeping the others from stopping him should they try.

He suddenly understood why Eros was so determined that they bond. He could feel the state of her soul in the mark on his wrist as it responded to his magic. The mark warming as he fed his power and life force into her. Their bond keeping her tethered to this world. To him.

He gave all of himself. Pushed everything he had inside him into her. Giving her back life at the cost of his own.

Refusing to stop, he continued to fight for the woman he loved. If she died, then he was going to follow.

Whispering those words against her neck, he felt his entire body go lax beside her.

As his soul reached out and moved from him to join hers.

As everything around him went black.

***

Persephone gasped for air as she regained consciousness.

Blinking against the bright light, her eyes focused on a sunny sky filled with clouds.

The mortal realm?

That couldn't be right. Hadn't she been run through?

Persephone looked down at her unblemished chest. No blood nor open wounds.

"Welcome to my domain, friend."

Turning her head in the direction the voice came from, she slowly made out the blurred image that became Hecate in her true form.

Her silver hair floated in the wind, eyes pure mercury, skin shimmering like moonlight. A dark purple dress that opened to her navel, slits up the side to her hips, and a belt with moons on it holding the dress in place.

Hecate's doubles stood behind her, not real twins of hers, but ones created from her power. One for each road and each choice, so they could guide the soul to their final destination. The three roads veering off into different directions.

"Crossroads," Persephone whispered, finding herself weak as Hecate bent to help Persephone up into a sitting position.

"The one and only. I had hoped you would come here, but I still worried."

As she pushed herself up into a standing position, Persephone felt a bolt of power rush through her.

It was painful, causing her to double over and try inhale a deep breath

"Devon is pushing himself to the brink of death to bring you back. You need to make your choice soon," Hecate stated, grabbing Persephone's hands.

"I thought I couldn't die," Persephone whispered, gritting her teeth as she pushed through the pain.

"Yet here you are. Anyway, you are not dead. All immortals seriously injured are given this option." Hecate stated. "Your choice to return to him or return to Chaos. Only you can make this decision, but if you don't make it soon, Devon will be joining us."

Persephone felt the mark on her arm burn as the skeletal form of the serpent became something almost alive, writhing and curling itself tightly around her wrist.

Devon. She felt Devon through the serpent.

As she looked up into Hecate's moonlight eyes, she whispered her choice.

She had promised Devon she would never leave, and she hated to lie.

***

West stood in the doorway of the fish market, gripping the frame with white knuckles after the first aftershock. He had hoped that was the whole of the earthquake.

The street he had just been walking on was destroyed. Cracks and fissures everywhere, buildings reduced to piles of bricks and rubble.

A sudden wave of people, panicked and terrified, ran past the door of the shop he was standing in. They attempted to avoid the cracks in the asphalt, but their fear made them mindless, causing many to stumble and be trampled by those behind them.

Running out into the street, he pushed against the tide of panicking people to see for himself what was happening. It took him a moment to realize they were running from the sea. Far longer to accept what he was seeing with his own eyes.

The water line was receding rapidly away from the docks. Fish flopped on the empty seabed, the water having moved too fast for the fish to find safety. Ships along the dock hit the ocean floor, the water gone and building up further out.

A tsunami was imminent and there was nothing anyone could do about it. Halcyon was going to be under water in a matter of minutes.

He felt his heart rate pick up from a fear he had never felt before.

"Get to a high point!" he yelled, shaking a few people frozen in shock. "Go! Get higher! Tsunami!"

He started running, banging on store doors, yelling for people to evacuate.

A woman came out of her store at his insistent knocking and looked past him right before letting out an inhuman scream of terror, causing him to turn in time to see the large wall of water heading towards them.

Debris flew as the water crushed the docks as it made its way to shore, tearing the wooden platforms apart.

A large ship had been picked up by the wave and thrown into a shopping center, the water flooding the building in its wake.

It was too late.

He was going to die.

West dropped his hands to his sides, his body in shock, but his mind screaming at him to run.

This was it for him. He couldn't escape in time. Everything he had hoped to change, do in his life, would not happen.

Before he could completely fall apart, he felt an anger rise within him at both the situation and his lack of self-preservation.

Something inside him, something he had always felt deep down trying to claw its way out but he never let come to the surface, began to tear its way through him like a wild animal.

313

It forced him to face this fate head on.

To not cower in fear.

To stand tall in the face of death.

Throwing up his hands and closing his eyes, he released years of pent-up rage and fear.

"Fuck you!" he yelled and everything around him went silent.

The roar of the water had stopped, causing him to open his eyes, and he almost fell backwards at the sight.

The water had paused, frozen in the air as if something held it in place. As if it had hit a wall.

Yet, that was not the most terrifying part. What both scared and confused him in that moment was that West could *feel* the water. Could feel it pushing, *wanting and pleading,* to get past him.

The shock of it made West lose his grip for a moment and the water pushed forward a foot.

Using his very unnerving connection to it, he mentally pushed at the wall and watched as thewater rippled out from him.

Gathering all his reserves, he gave a huge mental shove at it. The water lost its height as it started to flow backwards, finally receding back to the sea, leaving a bewildered and terrified West in its wake.

He could still feel the water as it moved over buildings, roads, and the docks before it was finally back safely in the Thalassian sea.

A contentment washing over him that wasn't his.

"How…?" he heard from behind him.

He spun around to face the person who put a voice to his thoughts.

A woman with long auburn hair and aqua eyes stood in shock, looking between him and thereceding water.

West dropped his hands in exhaustion as a headache began to form behind his eyes.

"I have no fucking idea."

***

Devon woke up to the smell of smoke permeating the air as he tried to open his swollen eyes. His body so incredibly sore that it made him think he had been in an accident.

"I'm so sorry, Devon. I wish I were whole enough to stop this," a

314

voice whispered as he felt a hand lightly touch his hair.

Ow. Even his hair hurt.

"Who are you?" Devon asked without moving, his words sluggish, still fighting to open his eyes.

"Sadly, I am a good reason you are in this mess, and for that I am sincerely sorry. However, I am not so sorry that I would change it. My sister has a great need of you. Though she is strong, she is not infallible."

Devon finally peeled his eyes open and pushed up onto his elbows as he looked up at the woman who sat next to him. A torch that had been lit, with the pointed end of it pushed into the earth near him, illuminated her face.

The woman was petite, light brown eyes, and auburn hair. Though she did not share in the coloring of her sisters, her features told him all he needed to know about her identity.

He had a pretty strong suspicion he knew who she was.

"Demeter?" his voice weak, barely above a whisper. Demeter gave him a warm and loving smile.

"How?" he asked, using what little strength he had to push himself up into a seated position as Demeter let out a little laugh, her eyes holding only kindness.

"You hold my power and though I no longer wield it, it still calls to me. Alas, what you see is my soul. Mortal as it is." Demeter tilted her head to him as if silently contemplating something.

He could only raise his eyebrows in response.

"This world never made sense to me," Demeter continued, looking out at the trees of his forest. "A father who was supposed to care and protect his children kills them. Innocents are killed while evil walks away unscathed. People are left behind to grieve those who've died. I've seen all this from life and behind the gates, but only one thing rang true, when the souls made it to her, my sister balanced it all out. The innocents were given a freedom mortality never held and evil was punished. I watched her make sure the souls had what they needed or received the justice that the universe cried out for. Along the way, I watched my sister losing her own sense of balance, only finding it in the small moments she was near you."

He listened as Demeter explain something he already knew, but from a different perspective.

She took Devon's hand and moved a finger over his soulbond mark.

"She was losing her humanity, Devon. She needed someone to bring her back to herself as much as you needed to be saved, and I am thankful my power was given to you to do so."

Something in her words brought everything that had happened to the forefront of his mind. As if he had been in a stasis while she spoke.

"Why am I here? Persephone!" He scrambled to stand up, dizziness hitting him as he fell to his knees.

"They brought you here so the forest could heal you, Devon." Demeter chided as she caught his arm before he fell again in yet another attempt to stand up.

"Demeter, I have to get to Persephone..." he whispered, his eyes begging her to help.

Demeter's face held a sadness before her eyes moved to something over his shoulder, her eyes flaring with anger.

"How did you get here?" She asked, her voice full of disbelief.

Devon attempted to turn his head, which was so heavy on his neck that it took all of his remaining strength.

The man from the café in Halcyon stood at the tree line. His hair bound back and his body covered in ancient armor as if he were preparing to lead an army to war.

The man walked slowly and methodically from the trees towards them.

"Run, if you can, I will try to hold him off," Demeter whispered, pushing Devon behind her as the man walked slowly and methodically from the trees toward them.

"Atlas, you have no cause or right to be here!"

Atlas. This was Atlas. This huge man made of pure muscle was who they were fighting against? Devon almost gave up and laid on the ground right there in defeat. Even if he had all his strength, and an army, there was no way he could battle this man and win. He was built for war in a way Devon had never seen.

Atlas simply ran his hand across Demeter, her form disappearing from view as he stepped in front of Devon.

"I told you, little God, I would see you soon," the Titan smiled before putting his huge hand on Devon's head and everything went dark.

***

Hera stared down the Moirai after blasting into Fates Consulting, ordering them to fix the mess they had made that led to her sister being stabbed through the chest.

"There is not a string for us to follow," they said all at once as Hera dug her nails into her palms.

Cowardly old witches, she thought to herself.

"That is not going to work here, ladies. You pushed my sister into a situation that took her from this world, so if you enjoy living, you will find a way to bring her back. That is not a request." Hera's eyes glowed gold as sparks ignited in her palms.

"Hera, our sweet..."

"*Don't*," Hera growled. "Do not use your nonsense garble to try and give me a fucking piece to a broken puzzle. I've listened to your rambling for centuries and put up with it. Now, know this, I tolerate a lot, but anything regarding my sisters is *not* fair game. I will make anyone who harms them pay, even you three. Consider this your warning. *Fix. This.*" She pointed her finger at each of the Moirai as her eyes glowed.

"The story has not met its completion," Lachesis replied as the other Moirai continued to be unnaturally quiet.

"And what the fuck does that mean, Lachesis?"

Hera's skin and eyes glowed brighter, like a star about to explode.

A warning from the universe the Moirai knew they would be wise to heed.

"It means there is more story to be told. Nothing has been balanced yet. Give it time before you act as we do not have all the players on the board yet." Clothos replied, keeping an eye on Hera.

If Hera were to attack, it would be fast, and they knew this. She would not give them time to defend themselves before she had them on their knees, pleading for mercy.

"One day I am going to burn this building to the fucking ground. How all of this plays out will determine if you burn with it," Hera seethed before she disappeared in a bright flash of light.

***

Devon felt himself come back to consciousness, the heaviness in his limbs telling him he was no longer in the Underworld.

His mind was spinning. The fight, Crius... someone stabbing Persephone and the look in her eyes...the pain and fear. Demeter... Atlas.

Atlas.

Rolling over, Devon pushed himself up to a kneeling position as he tried to work out where exactly he was. Darkness and rock surrounded him.

A cave?

He finally made out Atlas, who watched the flames of a fire from a few feet away.

"My brother brought you humans fire. Ridiculous creature, thinking to help such weak, pathetic beings. You have the lifespan of fruit flies compared to us, yet he thought you were worth it. They say Zeus banished him to Tartarus to have his liver eaten by Zeus' pet." Atlas threw a log in the fire as the flames grew higher and shadows danced along the ceiling. "Lies."

"Must suck to know that your brother got all the goodness and soul in utero." Devon murmured. He tested his strength and found he had a bit more than he did before Atlas abducted him.

Atlas looked towards Devon, the fire reflecting ominously in the giant Titan's eyes before he stood and sauntered over to where Devon sat.

Devon tried not to let out an audible gulp as he used the last of his reserves to stand, hoping he could muscle up enough of his power to fight if Atlas attacked.

"I have been the general of the great army of our King of Gods, Cronus, long before your ancestral line was walking up right. You dare speak to me as if I am nothing but some fledgling human?"

Atlas shoved Devon, and he found himself no longer in the cave but looking out over the coast of some unfamiliar island with Atlas still beside him.

"Before Cronus was banished, this land around you thrived."

All the trees were dead along the coastline, the sand gray, and the water inky with who knew what beneath.

"Half this globe looks like this. Had Cronus been in power, this would not have happened. His pathetic offspring did not know how to put true fear in the hearts of the humans and this is whatwe have. Death and destruction."

"Humans did this to themselves," Devon replied as he watched a whirlpool opened in the ocean, moving closer to the coastline and taking everything down in its path. The trees trembled before they were pulled down into the abyss as it moved along the shore.

"Yes, because the Goddesses were too weak to stop them." Atlas turned to look at Devon. "There is a war. We, the Titans, intend to take back what was ours before the betrayal of our king's progeny. You were a soldier and are capable of great power. We had every intention of you joining our team, as that was the plan from the beginning. I waited for you and watched you grow, but you were not fit to fight past your prime, so we took action when you were at your most capable."

Devon felt as everything clicked into place at Atlas' words.

He felt the earth tremble around him as the land disappeared into the sea, but he was lost.

Lost in the memory of his death.

The moment when he was killed by something he could not see. He closed his eyes, now with the ability to see what a mortal could not.

He watched as Atlas, shielded in shadows, pulled the trigger of the gun he had focused on Devon at point-blank range.

The bullets as they tore through Devon's human flesh.

As Atlas lowered the gun and disappeared deeper into the darkness. As Devon fell to the floor, his life blood leaving his body.

He watched it all happen in front of him like a movie playing out.

"You killed me so I would fight for your side," Devon muttered, his mind piecing all the events that had transpired since his death almost faster than his brain could handle.

"As you still can. You've ascended and are a God in your own right. Maybe you do not carry the blood of a Titan, but you carry the power of one." Atlas explained.

"You... killed me. I couldn't see my attacker, but that was because I was still mortal and unable to see through your wards, to see your power signature. Had I been a God..."

"You would've known me from the start. I even managed a spell from some witches to hold off the reaper, but the damned Fates tied your string to the weak progeny of the great Cronus!" Atlas sneered and his bulky shoulders tightened even more.

"Why would I ever work against the Goddesses after you killed me?" he asked incredulously as his eyes met Atlas'. He was baffled that this man admitted to both killing and attempting to recruit him in a matter of minutes.

"We had leverage, albeit I did not know how weak it was," Atlas growled. His eyes fierce as a warrior and mad as a lunatic.

"My mother," Devon stated. The thought of the torture she went through at the hands of this Titan burned his blood.

"Yes, we used her blood and power to create an amplifier that worked perfectly at forcing your powers to surge. It was all planned out. Though, I hadn't intended for your little love to die. That was just a nice surprise."

"Didn't stay quite dead though, did she?" he heard the soft, yet firm voice from behind him.

Persephone was here.

He almost cried out in relief as his arm warmed where the soulbond mark was. Green magic lit along the serpent in the mark as it came to life, no longer skeletal, light pulsing from it as if in sync with his heart.

The pulses strengthened as if someone was feeding life into them.

Persephone stepped beside him and grabbed his hand, both of them shaking from weakness and relief.

She looked at him for a moment and gave him a slight nod.

She was alive!

He wanted to grab her and take her far away from here.

"Hello, Atlas. I see you've been running around like an unattended toddler. I believe it would be best if you took a time out to think about what you've done." Another voice stated from behind him, the words full of jest yet the tone completely serious.

Thanatos.

In a flash of light, Crius and Minthe appeared next to Atlas.

"Were you able to take care of any of them or were you just letting your rams stretch their legs while pretending to follow the actual plan?" Atlas asked Crius, eyeing the blood staining his clothes from the already healed wounds from their previous battle.

"I killed you," Minthe sneered at Persephone, hatred in her eyes.

"Did a terrible job of it, too," Thanatos shot back.

"Thanatos, this is not the time," Persephone warned.

"Why," Devon interrupted, "would I be a soldier for you after you killed me? It doesn't make sense!"

"Because," Atlas seethed, "you wouldn't have known we were the ones who killed you. You think we haven't kept tabs on the lines holding the power of Cronus' offspring? That we wouldn't know how to play our cards when the time came? Of course we did! Now that all the lines are in Halcyon, we have the chance to end the reign of the Goddesses. Once and for all."

"They are all here?" Persephone asked with a shocked voice. "Hestia?"

Atlas ignored her.

"Now that the gate is open, Cronus can raise the army once again for me to lead to victory." A sword appeared in Atlas' hand. "And if you will not join me, Devon Aideonous, I will consider *you* my enemy. You have this chance to join the stronger side. We will prevail."

"Cronus is not coming. The gate is closed. I closed it." Persephone held herself as tall as she could, trying not to allow the weakness from her injuries to show.

She wasn't fully healed and he could feel her strength receding like the tides.

"And anymore damage to the land at your hand will be part of your unending punishment in Tartarus. Your choice to stop will only help to lessen the severity."

Atlas' eyes became fire once again.

"You lie, little Goddess…"

"No," she stood firm, "The gate remains shut. You may have cracked it open, but I sealed it back. Your attempt at a coup failed. Surrender and go willingly or…"

As if timed, the sky lit with a flash of lightning and an angry sea with large waves rolled towards them.

"They come." Persephone said as she turned back to Atlas, the wind picking up from the impending storm that was her sisters. "If you will not willingly submit yourself to Tartarus, my sisters will happily help me escort you there."

Atlas turned to Persephone with a sneer.

"Ah, yes. The other little Goddesses throwing their weight around. Cute."

Persephone stepped forward, a cue to Devon she was done talking.

Before Atlas could say another word, Devon fell to his knees and thorny vines shot up from the ground as they moved rapidly towards their three enemies.

Crius attempted to release his ram, but wraiths came from the Underworld and wrapped themselves around the creature, pulling it apart with an ear-piercing scream that would haunt Devon's dreams.

Atlas threw his power into escaping the vines as they struggled to hold the Titan. His brute strength tore through several vines before Devon called up more, only to have those shredded, too.

In a moment of panic, Devon turned the ground beneath Atlas into quicksand. The more Atlas struggled, the faster he went beneath it.

"Brilliant," Thanatos said as his skeletal form walked past Devon to Atlas.

Crius started to charge Persephone but blue fire engulfed him, his screams almost as piercing as the ram's.

Persephone's shadows swirled about Minthe, as she fell back on a scream at the sight of the Furies emerging from the ground. Their eyes sunken and wings ripped to shreds as they crawled on all fours towards Minthe.

"Traitor," they hissed as their bones popped into odd angles and their sharp teeth snapped at her. Before Minthe could muster a scream, the Furies descended onto her.

Hundreds of wraiths materialized from the ground and circled Atlas, Crius, and Minthe as Persephone and Devon watched on.

The wraiths flew fast enough to create a tornadic effect, their dark forms blurring into solid black. Devon ordered the ground to pull their enemies down through the earth and veil.

His vines took the three people, who had caused nothing but heartache, stress, and trouble, to the Underworld.

Persephone grabbed his hand and shadow jumped them to the gate of Tartarus.

They landed in the boneyard, and Devon felt a renewed strength run

322

through his veins as the Underworld replenished him. A tenderness ran across him for the place he now called home. It knew what he needed. That he had to stay strong for Persephone.

They moved to the gate, and he watched Hecate's powerful bands of silver light restrain the Titans.

Guards stood silent beside the trapped Titans as they awaited a command.

Persephone stepped up to one of the high-ranking officers of her army as he handed her a dagger. Cutting her palm, she walked to the gate of Tartarus to write in her own blood to open it.

Thanatos moved to hold the gate open as the soldiers marched Atlas and Crius into Tartarus. Leaving them there for what hopefully was the rest of eternity.

Her guards returned with a salute to indicate the job was completed and Thanatos closed the gate. Persephone dipped into her blood again to seal it. Her Godfire illuminating the runes as the gate sealed shut, the light fading away as it left only the runes behind.

Hecate released the spell of the manacles on the Titans and nodded to Persephone.

A sense of relief passed through all of them as Persephone turned to Devon and passed out into his arms.

CHAPTER 41

Thanatos walked into the bedroom where Persephone lay motionless, but very much alive, thank the Fates. Her body was weak from the hydra poisoning and the energy she expended to rid the world of the Titans.

The Underworld was healing her and Devon was told she would return to consciousness soon, but soon was taking far too long.

"She is crossing the banks. I'll wait at the gate for you." Thanatos blinked out of existence without another word.

Devon put down the book he had been reading while waiting for Persephone to wake.

He stood at the side of her bed, running a hand over her hair, before leaning into kiss her forehead.

"Got to run and do something really quick. I'll be right back," he whispered against her skin.

Pushing his hands into his pockets, he light jumped to the gates, catching sight of Thanatos and Hecate standing near the ghostly form of Cybil.

His mother. The woman who abandoned him and yet with her last breath, protected him.

Moving slowly towards them, he found himself unsure of how to act as he stopped in front of his mother.

Her eyes widened in surprise, and he saw that they were clear, and her hair once again a dark blonde. It was like she had gone back in time to the day he first saw her in the forest as a child.

Nodding to Thanatos and Hecate, they left him and his mother in a swirl of silver moonlight and shadows.

Devon felt like his tongue was too large for his mouth. His throat too tight to allow any words through, much less the air in which to vocalize them.

A moment passed before she threw her arms around him, shocking him out of his moment of hesitation and his arms slowly pulled her into a tighter hug.

"I am so glad you are okay, my darling," she whispered words he had always longed to hear. "I worried for you even when they tried to pull my mind from me."

He swallowed down the emotional turmoil as he stood back, his hands on her shoulders. He knew he only had a small amount of time to deliver her to the judges, who would then go about erasing her memory, and he needed to know what happened.

"So, when did Crius get a hold of you?"

She ran her hand through her hair as she shook off some emotion.

A trait from her, he mused.

"Two years before your birth. He worked on your father's family farm. All my life I had visions, though I said nothing as that would have put a target on my back, but the visions of darkness always had Crius in them.

"I was engaged to your father and had told him how Crius always seemed to be watching us. Your father moved us away, but Crius would still show up here and there, as if to taunt me and drive me mad. When I realized I was pregnant with you, it was too late. Crius had known Demetri held power inside of him that he would pass on to you. That I would be the perfect weapon to use against you. He attacked me one day near the forest where your father worked and took blood from me to put in a necklace. My blood was able to amplify your power when he wore it near you."

"How would he know all of that when even the Goddess knew nothing about me?" he asked, irritated that someone out there might be sitting around with all the answers.

"Because they have watched the sisters since the beginning. Watched them struggle to rebuild society and humanity. They watched what happened with the sisters who did not survive the manifestation of their powers and they watch now, because they want Cronus out. He holds the key to them taking back everything, but only if all five of the sisters' power stay dormant. If they ascend, the Titans have no chance."

He felt anger and fear over what she was saying. The Titans taking back over humanity, laughing as they sat upon their mountain, and watched their greed spread through the land like a plague.

Humans would be nothing more than cannon fodder for the Titans.

"Thank you for telling me," he whispered, taking her hands in his.

"I stayed away because I feared they would use me against you, but I should have been stronger for you and your father. I should have worked to control my visions, to not let that be the reason I was unable to raise my son, and to not have left myself vulnerable to Crius and his minions. I regret so much, but I am so very proud of you. I've followed you the best I could, seeing you in my visions. Fighting the darkness. When you fought, you fought for life, and the heroes in the story always stand against the darkness to light the way for others. You, my son, are the hero."

She put her hands on his cheeks to bring him down for a kiss to his forehead.

"The only thing I've ever done right was creating you." Her smile when she stepped back pulled the breath from his lungs. It was a smile he had dreamed of as a child. Full of love and pride.

With eyes full of tears, he pulled his mother into a hug for the last time.

"May the Fates shine kindly upon you, my darling," she whispered in his ear.

***

Persephone woke in her room long after the red sun had left the sky to the purple moon.

"You're finally awake," Devon whispered from the chair next to her bed as he moved forward to put his forehead against hers.

She reached out her hand to run it along his jaw. He obviously hadn't shaved in a good while.

"Are you," she started, her throat dry. "Are you okay?"

Devon reached for some water and handed it to her as she sat up to drink it.

"I am perfectly fine." He smiled as he took the water from her and set it back on the nightstand.

Scooting closer, Devon wrapped his arms around her. She snuggled into him and breathed in the scent of her mate, letting the calm she always felt at his presence wash over her before reality hit her with the force of Hera's lightning.

"It won't be over. There are others," she whispered. "Hestia, my other sister, the descendant of the line that holds her power, is here in Halcyon."

"A problem for another day when we have both recovered our strength," he murmured into her hair as he pulled her closer.

"I thought I had lost you." His voice was full of vulnerability.

"I told you that I am a Goddess and cannot truly die if I choose not to," she mumbled against his shirt.

"In that moment, I was sure that wasn't true. You were not breathing... no heartbeat," his hand trembled. "I went unconscious and disappeared before... Atlas."

Silence blanketed them before Devon spoke again.

"I was so relieved when I found out you lived, but so angry you didn't stay in the Underworld where you were safe," he admitted.

"As if you would sit back if I were in trouble. No, we are to stand together." She pushed away so she could look up at him. "I will not let you go charging into battle without me by your side. I never have and I never will. I will always be there when you have need of me. In the light and the darkness, I am here, my warrior. This I vow."

"You and your oaths," he replied with a smile.

Grabbing her hand, he put their wrists next to each other where the soulbond mark was tattooed on their skin.

"When you came back to me, our marks took on a less skeletal look."

"Rebirth," she whispered, noticing the word brought a pensive look to Devon's face.

"So much of the world has died," he replied. "I have the power to bring parts of it back."

She saw the resolve in his eyes when she looked at him. The need to use his powers for something greater.

"You can help the land, and you should."

He pulled her closer to him as he kissed the top of her head.

327

"Before I throw on my superhero outfit," he whispered into her hair, "We have to speak with the Senate."

He smiled at her as she groaned and fell back, putting a pillow over her face.

Her mood plummeted even more when she realized there was still one more loose end that couldn't wait.

***

As Devon finished readying himself to leave, Persephone ordered the shadows to take her to Cocytus.

She walked along the shoreline to where Minthe was bound. Far enough away to not be able to reach the water, but close enough to see and smell it. Her body was dried out. Her skin and lips cracking. Minthe was using the last of her energy in a desperate attempt to crawl to the life-sustaining current.

Persephone moved to stand next to the traitor and look out over the river.

"Looks refreshing, doesn't it?" Persephone asked as she stepped between Minthe and the water, squatting down so she could see Minthe's face. "You've been working with Crius a long time, helping him into the Underworld through the river system. You were scouting for Crius that night at the gala and you agreed to work with him because you thought it was your only way to get Devon back."

When Minthe said nothing, she continued.

"A knife with hydra blood on it to make sure I couldn't come back because Crius told you that was how Cronus killed me the first time. Should have done more research on whether that would actually kill me now that I am no longer mortal."

Minthe's eyes took on a deep, murky green hue.

"You betrayed me and killed your own brother all because Crius made you false promises. Because he promised you Devon."

"Fuck you!" Minthe rasped, "That is not how it went! We were lovers and I could have ruled the Underworld alongside him far better than you. I could have protected him far better than you ever could or did," she trailed off weakly. "If Tristan had stepped aside from his own desires to rule the Underworld, I wouldn't have had to kill him. He wouldn't... wouldn't help me," Minthe let out a sob, "So, I killed him."

Persephone watched the pitiful creature stew in the consequences of her decisions.

"Devon didn't return your feelings, so like a petulant child, you decided to take care of anyone he chose to love. What did you think would happen when I died? That he would fall into your arms again?"

Persephone waited for some evil scheme she'd hatched to come from her dried and bloody lips, and though no words were said, Persephone saw the answer in her eyes. Minthe didn't care about the power like she thought, she was just consumed with owning Devon. Her obsession stronger than her conscience.

"You most likely thought Devon would make you his Queen and you would rule together," Persephone mused as she looked back to the river and took a deep breath of the brimstone smell emanating from Tartarus. "But you failed and now you are at my mercy. This is my realm." She looked back at Minthe. "I run things here and if I chose to send you to the Fields of Punishment or the pits of Tartarus, there is not a damn thing anyone could do about it."

She looked into the woman's eyes. "Are you paying attention now?"

Minthe whimpered but held Persephone's gaze.

"I thought of an eternity in the Fields for you, but that seemed to be what is expected of me. The Furies would love another shot at you after you escaped them.

"However, people might associate that with me not thinking rationally, and who knows what scheme you might concoct with all that time on your hands. That might give you hope that I can be reasoned with, and after your betrayal, I do not believe I can be."

"I highly doubt I can find it in myself to care if you will not allow me to stay in my human form. Either kill me or let me die in peace." Minthe tried to put power in her words, but she was far too weak.

Persephone stood and smiled down at her.

"I think I like the idea of you always seeing the river, but never touching it. Never feeling the water move between your fingers or over your skin again."

Minthe let out a huff.

"Need me weaker so you can kill me? Scared of me? Or is it that Devon took me to bed long before you, kept me around, and you know if I get to full strength, he might just take me back to his bed? He almost did the night of the gala. He definitely thought about it. I bet I could work and weaken his resolve enough to bring him back to me."

"Make it easy for me, nymph, please," Persephone growled as her eyes lit up and her foot stepped down onto Minthe's neck.

Minthe's eyes went wide as she felt Persephone pulling the power from her weakened body.

Minthe struggled to hold on to her magic, panic flooding her system, but Persephone was markedly stronger than her.

A loud, piercing scream left Minthe as her power was finally released, completely drained from her, and rising into the air around them.

Choking on tearless sobs, Minthe went slack as the last piece of her power left her body.

Persephone put her hand out, and the magic swirled into a white ball just above her open palm. As she closed her fist around the ball of magic, Minthe let out a pained noise.

Staring Minthe in the eyes, she crushed the magic in her fist, it slipping through her fingers like grains of sand before fading out and disappearing completely.

All the river nymph's power went back into the Underworld.

Persephone opened her hand and Minthe cried out at the sight of her empty palm, her missing magic. No tears would stream down her face at the lack of hydration in the water deity's body, though Minthe did try to cry.

"Oh no, you do not get to cry," Persephone growled as she leaned down over Minthe to lay the same hand that had just crushed her magic onto Minthe's forehead.

As Minthe looked up into the bright glowing eyes of an angry Goddess, she saw no mercy. She closed her eyes one last time as she felt Persephone's power blast into her.

Minthe was engulfed in a sudden burst of flame, but the fire dissipated just as quickly as it had appeared.

Persephone stepped back from where Minthe had been. Through her bond with Devon, she had finally created something.

Bending, she tugged a leaf from the plant that was once the traitorous nymph.

As she rolled the leaf between her fingers, a minty and fresh smell rose up, briefly covering the stench of brimstone.

Persephone let the mint leaf fall from her hand as she stood.

"Finally, you are of use to me, Minthe." Persephone let the shadows take her back to the forest her mate had grown.

She needed to speak with her sister.

***

A freezing wind blew past her as she caught sight of flickering torchlight. Her sister was nearby. Her heartbeat sped up, but she calmed herself down before Devon felt it.

They found they could feel each other in times of emotional stress, and pleasure, through their bond. Two halves of a whole in an almost literal sense.

Her sister moved out from behind one of the trees, holding her torch as if searching for someone.

Persephone swallowed down the emotion of seeing her beloved Demeter again.

"I was looking for you." Demeter smiled as she moved forward to embrace Persephone.

She found she suddenly lacked the ability to speak, couldn't do anything more than stare at her long-lost sister. Her heart hammered in her chest, and she had to hold herself back from barreling into Demeter.

To stand before a loved one lost to death, to know you have a second chance to speak but that the chance was limited to a short window of time, was terrifying.

"Always the quietest of the sisters," Demeter laughed as she pulled Persephone into a hug.

"Sorry, I just… it is a shock to see you again. I feel like perhaps I made you up in my delirium, looking for something to help me through…" she whispered but couldn't finish. She was feeling her emotional state spiral as she hugged Demeter tightly. Something she never thought she could do again.

She stepped back to take in Demeter's appearance. Her sister had not changed one iota since Persephone had first walked her past the gates.

"Oh, my sweet sister." Demeter smiled as she shook her head, pushing a strand of Persephone's hair behind her ear. "Always stoic on the surface but so full of love and emotions inside. I worried about you as a child, that the world would make you cold. Make you refuse to feel what you needed to be truly human."

"I have missed you." Persephone's words came out on a sob.

"As I have with you, too. I couldn't remember anything until my powers were bound to another immortal, then... I just remembered." Demeter shrugged before her face took on a serious expression. "I remembered you pushing me into a dark room each time father was angry. How that last time you told me to stay put with our sisters and not to come out. I remember..." Demeter stopped, a tear slipping down her cheek. "Him stabbing you. You were killed saving us, yet you hold on to that as a punishment when in fact you deserve none of the sort. Why do you not forgive yourself?"

Persephone started to shake her head, but Demeter held her gaze.

"You always protected us... me. Always. I know you've carried that with you as Devon carried his grief before. You helped him heal, but I need you to heal yourself. You didn't let me die, you kept me alive. Father killed me. You saved me. My soul is saved... you took on the burden of the Underworld to walk me in the gates yourself. My dear sister, I beg of you to please allow grace for yourself. You have been torturing your own mind for long enough. Release the worries and the grief into the ether and be happy. Live a life that all of us wish for you."

Demeter ended her sentence with a kiss on Persephone's cheek.

Persephone blinked back tears, but when Demeter pulled back, she nodded to her. Yes, she would do as her sister asked and push as much grief and burden that she could into the ether.

She knew it wouldn't completely leave, but she would work on it. She owed that to them and to Devon. They deserved her happy and whole as she deserved from them in return.

"I don't think my memories returned just for this talk, though I do appreciate the opportunity." She took Persephone's hands into hers, holding her sister's gaze. "There are whispers floating throughout the Underworld. That there are Titans looking to release Cronus."

"I know," Persephone stopped her. "Crius and Atlas are there with him after trying to break him out."

"There is more," Demeter interrupted, quickening her words as if something or someone might steal them away before she could finish.

"Before Atlas was banished, he had Titans raising an army outside of Halcyon. You need to find whoever holds Hestia's power. That is when everything will truly be balanced."

"He said Hestia's power was in the city now."

"Then you must find them," Demeter begged Persephone.

"I only found Devon when his soul merged with his latent powers, and that was only after he was killed. How could I know who holds that power if they haven't yet ascended?" Persephone asked in disbelief.

"Atlas gave you the location. You need to move to find them before another Titan does. Should that person side with them, we would have no hope."

Only after the promise that she would do just that left her lips did the tension lift from Demeter's shoulders.

Demeter leaned against Persephone, her head on her shoulder.

"I need you, and our family, to stay safe. I need you to win so that I know everything will be okay for you and our sisters."

Persephone could only nod, her mind reeling at what her sister was telling her.

She felt a lightness where Demeter's head had just been and turned to see her sister's soul fading.

"No! Wait!" Persephone pleaded, trying to pull Demeter into a hug, her arms moving through Demeter.

Demeter stood back with a smile.

"I assume my memories will wane as I return to Elysium. Remember your promise, Persephone, and that I love you always."

"I love you, too. So much, Demeter." Persephone's eyes glowed as she watched her sister fade away. "I will keep our sister's safe. Rest, my darling sister."

Demeter covered her heart with her hands before the Underworld returned her soul home.

CHAPTER 42

Persephone and Devon intertwined their hands as they strolled through the main street of Halcyon. Market stalls lined both sides of the road and young men moved about to light the gas lanterns just as dusk hit.

She was thankful no one had been lost in the attack on the city. All reports to the Archon had shown structural damage and some injuries, but no lives lost.

That was a reason to celebrate and she was glad to see her city taking time from the repairs to do so.

Devon ground to a stop and pulled Persephone in front of a booth full of jewelry. A young lady not much older than twenty and an older woman stopped unpacking boxes at the sight of them. Devon moved to touch a ring placed in the center of a small silk pillow.

"Our local stone artisan, my husband, makes these. Symbolism in all of them, and especially strong during the solstice." The older woman walked to where Devon stood eyeing the ring.

His hand moved over the sapphire stone encircled in little leaves of silver. It reminded her of the sapphires she wore for invisibility compliments of the Cyclops.

"Ah," the older woman smiled as she took the ring and held it out for Devon to touch. "Wisdom and devotion. A good one for a marriage as you'll need both." Without asking, she pulled a matching men's ring from behind the counter. It held smaller sapphires in between silver vines that wrapped around the ring. A wedding set.

"How much?" he asked as he pulled out his wallet from his back pocket, Persephone's hand moving to stop him.

"What are you doing?" she whispered.

The woman waved them away and pointed to the soulbond mark on his wrist.

"A gift from the son of Arges to the newly mated rulers of the Underworld." She smiled as she placed the rings in Devon's free hand. Persephone pulled in a loud breath and rushed to take the woman's hand as it drifted from Devon's.

"He is alive?" Persephone asked the woman in wonder.

The woman smiled and nodded. "Yes, him and his brothers are doing well and have so many wonderful things to say of you and your sister Goddesses. Our family owes you a debt of gratitude for saving them from an unearned sentence in Tartarus."

"Please, can you ask that he comes to visit me at Cerberus Financial? I would like to speak with him. There are some things we may need help with in the coming days," she pleaded as Devon looked on.

The woman patted Persephone's hand, smiling, and nodding in assurance.

"Now then, take those rings and wear them with the thanks of all the descendants of the mighty cyclops."

"Thank you," Persephone whispered.

Devon put the sapphire ring on her left ring finger and she did the same.

"I've heard they wear rings like that in the older western cultures," the woman said, beaming at the sight of the rulers wearing rings made by her family.

Persephone smiled back at the woman before turning to Devon. "Now we really are married in all ways".

"I'm a sucker for tradition, wife," he murmured as he leaned forward to give her a quick peck on the lips.

Winking at the merchant, he thanked both the women and pulled Persephone back out into the market air.

***

335

They caught sight of Hera and Amphitrite outside of the Senate building, a reminder of their actual reason for being in Halcyon.

"Guess it's time to face the music," he sighed and Persephone squeezed his bicep consolingly.

Hera turned as they walked up, sticking a very phallic looking cookie in her mouth to take a bite as she stared them down.

"What is she doing?" Devon mumbled as Hera continued to stare straight into his eyes with every bite of her cookie.

"Being Hera," Amphitrite muttered.

"You're not the giant asshole I thought you were," Hera stated as she shook the phallic monstrosity of a cookie at him before taking another bite. "Congrats on not being a huge disappointment to us all."

"Wait... are those...?" Devon laughed as he realized the sexual nature of it.

"He gets it," Hera winked before pointing what was left of it at Persephone and Amphitrite. "The beauty of the fertility part of the Solstice is wasted on you all."

Devon snorted as Amphitrite rolled her eyes.

"Enough of this, we need to discuss what happened and what we need to do next," Hera stated as she bared her teeth in a semblance of a smile.

Ah, there's the Hera I know and tolerate, he thought as Hera did a light jump, leaving them on the front steps of the senate building.

"Ridiculous woman," Amphitrite muttered as the large wooden double doors opened, a guard standing aside allowing them to enter.

"The Archon and Senate awaits you," the man informed them.

Devon leaned over to whisper in Persephone's ear as they entered the building with Amphitrite trailing behind. "What kind of circus are we about to walk into? I am having a hard time imagining Hera as a serious leader."

"I'll let that be a surprise," she replied with a wink as they walked into a large oval room filled with curved benches for spectators of the court. Columns much like he remembered from Olympus surrounded them, and at the front of the room, at a large-curved table sat Hera and the Senators of Halcyon.

"Goddess and God of the Underworld, you bring before us information on a Titan uprising," Hera stated in an official tone from the center of the table.

Devon arched an eyebrow at Persephone, but she just smiled with a slight shake of her head.

"Yes, Archon," Persephone stated with just as much authority. "Crius and Atlas were banished to Tartarus for their attempt to release Cronus from his punishment. There has been a rumor that General Atlas was amassing an army nearby prior to his banishment."

A Senator with golden hair that was to his chin and strange golden eyes sat forward, "The Titan general has already created an army?" he asked, his voice gruff and disbelieving. "He has not been heard from in centuries and now he returns?"

"Hence the uprising. Something usually done in secret," said a woman with long dark hair that fell to her shoulders. It was apparent that her ancestors descended from Goryeo, with her piercing almond-shaped brown eyes.

He knew these were all mortals with small amounts of power passed down through demi-god ancestors. They lived lifespans just slightly longer than a mortal and could earn their immortality through trials that only Chaos was capable of dishing out.

The golden-haired Senator shot a look at the woman from Goryeo.

"Have you spoken to the Moirai, or an oracle, in regard to this?" said a male Senator with slicked back dark hair and a strong familial resemblance to the woman from Goryeo.

"We have not," Persephone stated. "I am unsure of where we stand as far as allies."

"Yet you brought it before our senate?" he asked. "How can you be sure you can trust us?"

"She damn well better be able to," Hera seethed.

"Fates, you are a piece of work, Kiran. Maybe take that nonsense back to your hovel," a woman chastised. "What is the next step?" she asked as she shot a salacious wink of her honey-colored eyes at Devon.

Persephone let out a little laugh at his discomfort from being the center of the beautiful female's attention.

"Gods of the Underworld, that blush is adorable!" The woman laughed a little, her curls shaking.

Persephone cleared her throat to answer, earning a playful wink from the flirty woman

"The next step is finding the person who holds my sister Hestia's power. We have it on good authority that they are in Halcyon." Whispers erupted in the room, before Hera smacked her hand down demanding quiet.

"Whose?" Kiran asked.

"Mine."

Kiran met Persephone's eyes before sitting back, as if withdrawing the question. Though Devon didn't miss the longing looks Kiran sent his wife's way, nor the angry looks towards Devon. It was suddenly apparent there was some unrequited lust on Kiran's end.

Devon smirked at Persephone this time.

"We need to find them then. Can you start the search for us, Finley?" Hera asked the woman with similar features to Kiran.

"I can," Finley responded, quiet but powerful.

"Then we will meet again when we find the person who holds the last of our lost sister's power and reevaluate our situation." Hera formally closed the session and everyone filed out of the chambers.

Devon noted all five of them for future reference as they passed by him: the male Senator with the golden hair, the male and female siblings with Goryeon ancestry; Kiran and Finley, the flirty female senator with honey-colored eyes, and the one who stayed silent, her stature that of a soldier.

These were their allies, and he knew they would be part of what stood between Halcyon and the Titans.

They would rewrite what the humans knew of the Gods and Goddesses.

They would create their own army.

They would create the Olympians.

EPILOGUE

It took several days for West to gather the courage to walk into his father's office.

His mind kept him up at night with the how and the why of what had happened along the docks.

After far too many sleepless nights, he was finally ready to confront father, who he knew instinctually was at the center of this.

Not bothering to stop at his father's receptionist's desk, worried he might lose his nerve, he could hear the woman begging him to wait as he barged through the doors to his father's office.

West didn't want to wait until his father could think of some excuse.

Why this was this and that was that, creating some false narrative of what happened as a fluke. He wanted direct answers, and he would only get those if he caught his old man off guard.

Standing before his father now, he was shocked to not see the man who was always well put together with a salesman smile on his face. Instead, his father was as he had never seen him.

His head in his hands, looking defeated.

The man who seemed totally at ease holding the weight of the world on his shoulders looked like he was falling apart.

"Dad..." he mumbled as he felt his anger dissipate, making way for confusion and concern.

His father looked up at him as a sorrowful smile crossed his face, making him look so much older. The man who he teased about never truly aging looked like he had aged ten years in the past week.

"I should have told you sooner. Done something sooner. I am so sorry, son." The dejected tone in those words knocked the wind out of West's sails.

What the hell did that mean?

West went to sit in the chair facing his father's desk as his father excused the receptionist. His sad eyes moving from the closed door to West.

West was validated in his theory that his father was aware of what was going on, but it didn't help him feel any better about it.

"You knew I could do that with water?" West asked, terrified to know the answer, but needing the truth more.

He expected his father to deny it, maybe joke that West must have been seeing things… anything but acknowledging it as the truth.

He thought he came for answers, but what he really wanted was his father to tell him none of this was real.

His father looked down at his hands folded on top of his desk.

"You can do more than that."

His father waved his hand and water in a cup on his desk rose. He watched as it glided through the air in some sort of dance.

West sat back, not even sure what to say, as numbness crept over his consciousness.

His father could control water?

Words were lost in the air between them at the fact that he had kept this secret from West his entire life.

"I lived many lives before this one. Had many mortal children." West felt his eyes pop open in surprise as his heart rate increased at his father's declaration.

"What are you saying?" West asked.

His dad released a sorrowful laugh.

"I was in a dark place when I met your mother. That's the problem with immortality, my son, you watch the people you love go back to the earth from which they came. It wears on a person after a while."

His father looked at a framed photo of their family on his desk. They were at a beach somewhere when West was just a toddler. A small West with a mop of dark hair laughed while he sat on his father's shoulder, his mother looking up at her son with her hands wrapped around her husband's waist.

340

"I became infatuated with your mother when she was a nurse at Halcyon Memorial Hospital. I worried about marrying another mortal and producing offspring that I would watch return to Chaos, so I did something that could have me banned to Tartarus."

His father wouldn't look at him, his shame written on his face.

"What?" West asked as his heart thundered in his ears, his father looking at him with an expression of apology in his eyes.

"She died, West. I was driving to meet with a family that had invited me to dinner and the roads were unseasonably icy. As I drove along the edge of the mountain, I saw what looked like brake lights flickering from the side of the cliff. I went to check it out, and saw a car there, crushed against the ledge.

"I saw your mother as she lay broken, her soul not yet lost to the Underworld, but I knew death would come soon. She held some naiad blood, not truly human, but not a God or Titan. I pulled your mother from the car..."

His father stopped and rubbed his hands over his face.

"I gave her my power. I flooded her with it and bound her life to mine. If I die, she dies, and vice versa. I stopped death's call, which is something that could cost me my immortality."

He pushed his hand through his hair and looked out the window.

"Her naiad blood took over and she came back as that. Not mortal. Not anymore. When she opened her eyes, they glowed and lit up our surroundings before going to her human color of brown. Her injuries immediately healed, and I told her she hadn't been injured. She never knew she died."

Standing, he walked around his desk and leaned against it to face West.

"I kept my distance, worried about what I had done. Then I found out she was pregnant with my child when she died and came back. At that point, I couldn't stay away any longer. I worried what my power and her power could have done to you. I had planned to only stay until you were born, just to see what happened with our powers going into you. I had planned to keep my distance emotionally," he stared at West as he continued.

"But, when you were born, I couldn't help but love you. Once you grew and I watched your power emerge, I had no choice but to bind them. I couldn't let anyone know about you. Something when that Tsunami hit released your power. I am not sure how, but I felt it."

West stood from his seat, feeling completely numb, unable to respond, but his father didn't need a response.

"Then you left us to go work with that mercenary group." West's eyes snapped wide open again. The surprises just kept coming.

"Yes, I know. I kept an eye on you while you were gone. Not because you are the heir, but because I love you. I did everything I could to keep you safe, to never have to lose you as I've lostothers."

His father hung his head, looking completely lost as West ran through a myriad of emotions.

When his father looked up with glowing sea-green eyes, West fell back a step.

"Son, I have stayed out of this war as long as I could, and yes, there is a war brewing that is being brought to our doorstep. The name I was known by before you and your mother was Oceanus. I am a Titan, one that is older than the Goddesses. I have stayed neutral through everything, not throwing my hat in, but seeing what Crius and Atlas had in store... what they did... I cannot let Cronus walk this earth ever again." His father's face looked torn yet West saw the resolve there.

"I am very sorry for keeping this from you for so long." His father, not Zale Murphy but Oceanus, put his hands on West's shoulders as he looked into his eyes. "I bequeathed you with my power before you took your first breath and I will care for you until my last. This I swear as Oceanus, Titan of the seas, to you, Weston Murphy, son of my blood and my heart. This will be along battle that, had I not sworn neutrality, I would stand beside you and fight if I could." His father's hands lit up on his shoulders and he felt a shock as power moved through his body like electricity.

The power flooded through him, as if it had been leaking through a crack in the door and someone finally opened it wide.

He looked into the eyes of his father, blue with flecks of golden brown, just as they had been his whole life. But for the first time, West saw a stranger.

He saw a Titan.

THE END

ACKNOWLEDGMENTS

Thank you to my editor, Rain Brennan, for helping me through this whole process. You have no idea how much all the work you put into this manuscript meant to me. You helped me figure out this whole confusing process and I cannot wait to work with you on the rest of the series!

To my Beta Readers: Meg, Bettina, Luna, Rain, and Emily. Thank you for giving me honest feedback and working with me on a deadline.

To Nismeta and Kate, thank you for getting this book ready by editing and helping me keep my vision in focus.

Thank you to GermanCreative for such an amazing book cover and helping to bring my vision to life! You are a truly gifted artist.

To my friends, thank you for listening to my crazy ideas and supporting me through this. I'm sure I was annoying, but I brought wine and all was forgiven. Right? Right??

Alyssa, you had a wedding to plan and a move across the country to handle, and yet you stayed invested in this book. Thank you for being such an amazing friend and cheerleader. Scotland, here we come!

Mom, you bought me all the mythology books I pleaded for and dealt with my dramatic personality. If that doesn't qualify you for sainthood, I don't know what would.

To my children, thank you for understanding why mommy was a little crazy while writing this book and not judging me too harshly. I love you both!

To my husband. The man who has supported me, pushed me, made sure I was eating and sleeping so I wouldn't die, cooked, and cleaned when I was in my writing cave. For some insane reason, you still love me after all this. You are my soulmate and best friend. Thank you for not killing me and making it look like an accident. I know it was tempting at times.

Finally, dear readers, thank you for giving me a chance to make a dream of mine come true by reading this book! I hope you will reach out and converse with me. I would love to hear your thoughts!

ABOUT THE AUTHOR

C.D. Britt began her writing journey when her husband told her she needed to use her excessive imagination to write stories as opposed to creating a daily narrative for him. Ever since she penned her first words, life has been a lot more peaceful for him.

She currently resides in Texas where she has yet to adapt to the heat. Her husband thrives in it, so unfortunately they will not be relocating to colder climates anytime soon.

Their two young children would honestly complain either way.

When she is not in her writing cave (hiding from the sun), she enjoys ignoring the world as much as her children will allow with a good book, music, and vast amounts of coffee (until it's time for wine).

C.D. Britt is the author of Shadows and Vines and the upcoming book, Sirens and Leviathans.
Both books are part of the Reign of Goddesses series.

STAY CONNECTED!

www. authorcdbritt.com

Instagram @authorcdbritt

Facebook.com/authorcdbritt

Join C.D. Britt's Street Team on Facebook for new release information and giveaways